NOWHERE YET

A NOVEL

EDWARD COZZA

Pinot Dog

Pinot Dog
Encinitas, California

Pinot Dog™

Published in the United States by Pinot Dog, Encintas, California.

http://edwardcozzawriter.com/

ISBN: 978-0-9881906-2-7

PRINTED IN THE UNITED STATES OF AMERICA

For Mary Elizabeth
None of my dreams would have ever been possible without you.

NOWHERE YET

A NOVEL

PROLOGUE

The phone in Grant Pettitte's living room rang. It startled him, because the phone never rang. In the stillness of the mostly empty room, amidst the furniture that he had made, the ringing phone sounded like a gun going off. Grant wondered why he hadn't had the thing disconnected before now. Its presence added nothing to the nearly bare environment of his living quarters. One less cord to trip over would be fine. The loud intrusion into the quiet confines made him flinch in his worn leather chair before he answered it.

"Hello."

"I knew you'd be there."

It was his friend Rex Schmidt. It took Grant a few seconds to gather his words, as Rex had been missing for a couple of years. But he easily recognized his voice, his East Coast accent.

"How did you know I'd be here?"

"You never go anywhere."

"How would you know? You're not here."

"I just know. Glad to hear from me, aren't you?" Rex laughed.

"You don't know shit these days. I'm indifferent to hearing from you."

"That's mighty fancy talk from a cowboy. I know you used to go lots of places when I was around to get your sorry ass moving, but that's been quite a while ago. Why the indifference?"

"What do you want?" Grant asked.

"The usual, money, food, booze, women. I'm a little bored, but bored is good right now."

"The only one of those you were ever any good at was food. Bored? Read a goddamn book. Get a dog."

"You're the one that really should get a dog. You are such a fucking hermit, and even fucking hermits have dogs, but back to me. I still am good at food." Rex sounded like he was opening some sort of cellophane bag, followed by crunching noises.

"That's great to know that you still know how to eat, and thanks for providing the audible proof. I'll sleep much better tonight." There was an awkward pause.

"Right, I've been meaning to call you—"

"That so?" Grant injected bitterly. "I left you a message—sorry, no, make that six or eight messages. I forget what the messages were about, since it's been a few years."

"It's pretty complicated, Grant." Rex was still crunching food on the other end.

"It always is with you."

"No, really, that's one of the reasons I'm calling, but both are good reasons."

"Ah."

"Listen, I understand you being a little pissed, but things have been, well … they have been, eh, there has been some kind of serious shit at work. I didn't want that to spill over onto you."

"Hmm, always looking out for others," Grant said.

"Without going into all the shitty details, the firm I was working for got into some trouble. Some of the people at the top might end up doing some jail time. It has been a pretty shitty couple of years, pretty harsh all the way around, and I didn't want anyone to know, or seem connected to me for their own good."

"You do anything illegal?"

"No."

"That's hard to believe."

"The law firm did some wacky shit, but I wasn't involved. They got in with some rather shady characters, and that's what got the Fed boys' attention. I'm sorry I didn't get back with you, but I think radio silence was actually a good thing for you, as well as for anyone who knows me. It has been pretty miserable. Hell, I don't know. All I can think about is if I make it without getting popped, I'll throw one ginormous party, you know, to make-up for lost time. All kinds of things went through my head, I don't expect you to understand, and I actually would prefer to talk about it in person, just in case someone is listening to our conversation, if you know what I mean. Anyway, I kind of wanted—wanted to get together with you, with you and Annie. Talk about all the crazy shit that we did, which I know Annie didn't like, but maybe she can laugh about it now. Hell, I'm just rambling," Rex said, sounding out of breath.

"You are always just rambling, and somebody listening to our conversation? I think you may have finally and completely lost your fucking mind. What might be good would be for you to tell me something I don't know … like what does Annie have to do with this?"

"The point is, it came to me that with all the things that have been going down at work, it was boiling down to those bastards telling me they might take away everything, and everyone I ever cared about, and maybe end up in…."

"End up in Texas?" Grant asked, laughing.

"No, jail, or worse. Texas. Always the cowboy."

"You could survive jail, I'm pretty sure you wouldn't survive Texas. What do you mean worse?" Grant paused. "And why are you bringing Annie into this conversation?"

"Yeah, that's one thing we agree on. We never had good luck in Texas. By worse, I mean the Fed boys, some shady characters might be after me, because I wasn't—look, I'd rather tell you in person, not on the phone. They got ways of, aw shit, just let me tell you when I see you, it would be safer. As for your other question, you were going to marry her, weren't you?" Rex asked.

Grant said nothing.

"Hey, it's not my fault she married someone else."

"She didn't marry someone else!" Grant was instantly upset. It was never beyond Rex to say things to get him excited, and he was mostly certain that Annie had not married. Still, though, this was not something he wanted to joke about.

"I know she didn't, I'm just fucking with you, but you are pissed that she didn't marry you."

"I don't know for sure that she didn't, but I don't think she did." Grant paused. He was unsure of himself, and did not want it to be a reality that Annie was married. Rex was always difficult to keep up with, and this was no exception. Those two things made the conversation difficult.

"Look, I know you were in love with her, may still be. You two were going to get married, and you may still. Anyway, I just have sort of been thinking and, well … looking at things differently."

"I'm not sure I understand, but that's normal for the things that you always seem to get yourself involved in. If you are thinking at all, that is a big upswing for you. How 'bout we leave Annie out of the conversation? I am still skeptical about you looking at things differently, considering the part of your anatomy your head is used to residing in..." Grant looked around his living room.

"Hey, it's not too late. You could see Annie and we could probably have a pretty good time. I haven't forgotten how to have a good time, but I can't speak for you. Unless you have a better offer, but I'm guessing you have no offers."

"I thought I said to leave Annie out of the conversation. It's been a couple, probably three, maybe four years since I even knew where she was. I ... she wouldn't see me, I'm sure. Hell, I haven't talked to you in a couple of years, and her for a couple before that. In your case, it probably hasn't been fucking long enough."

"You seeing a trend here in the behavior you bring out in people? I mean the 'haven't heard from in a while' part? After people get out of school, the time really hauls ass. I think it's because there aren't any breaks any more. No spring break, no summer break. The only break, is break your ass to make money. Anyway, I talked to her," Rex said.

"Just because I haven't talked to you in a while doesn't mean I now accept bullshit as legal tender."

"It's not bullshit. I have talked to her, quite a bit actually. That seems to be more than you can say," Rex said, sounding more proud of himself than usual.

"I stand by my previous analysis, that you are completely full of shit."

"I have talked to Annie several times. You will be pleased to hear that, well, for one, she is not married, and two, though she made me jump through some hoops, she agreed to meet us in Palm Springs for a weekend. She was always the good soul, pretty smart and such—well, certainly smarter than you, but that's not saying much. She cares about everybody. I don't know how she does it, never did. Hey, she's a full on doctor now, unless you messed her head up by being around her and she quit entirely since I talked to her last. Maybe she lost faith in humans; could have become a veterinarian possibly. Animals are much better than people. Animals care, people don't. We need more vets, for that reason alone. Still, maybe she can fix us—err, fix you., I'm fine, mostly," Rex said. "I still think you should get a dog."

"There's nothing wrong with me. You, on the other hand, that's different.

But where did you, how did you—now what?"

"The Ritz, Palm Springs."

"I know where Palm Springs is, dim bulb." Grant paused. "Annie and I went there once. I think it was our first trip to California together. Stayed at a small place, built in the thirties, I think. Annie told you she would...."

"She told me she would meet us there. She said she still didn't trust me, so she was bringing or meeting some friends there, I forget which. Said if I flaked-out, she still was going to go out there and have a good time. Annie did mention something, about some little shitbox motel where you two stayed. Well, we ain't staying at some little stick-it-inn on my watch. We're going to the Ritz. You two get there, you can wax nostalgic with each other about some deadbeat place where you saw stars in each other's eyes. It might actually give you one last chance with her. Plus, give me a chance to buy drinks and shit, and make—" Rex stopped.

"She didn't say shitbox. Give you a chance to make what?"

"I forget. Plus, I haven't seen any nice girls in quite a while either, so this ain't all about you, you know. Nice girls might do me some good. A not-so-nice girl might do me even more good."

"I get that part, I just—Annie said—she knows I'll be there, and that you'll be there, and she still agreed to show? She hates you," Grant said.

"We both know Annie, unlike us, is not capable of hate, which I never understood. Besides, even though I have been in the middle of the worst ordeal of my life, I can still be quite charming. Let's just say I charmed Annie into showing. Besides, I just want to get my life back. To do that, I have to put some air in your flat fucking tires, in which case, Annie is the air."

"You are thinking of someone else with the charming stuff. I don't know whether to pound the hell out of you before I see her, or after. Both might be better. But Palm Springs, you sure that's the place to go?" Grant said.

"Why do people always think that they need to go to Nepal, or the top of some fucking mountain somewhere to get insight? Me, I just like to go different places once in a while. It doesn't need to be all woo-woo and shit, just someplace fun. If a person goes someplace fun once in a while, they are bound to find some sort of, I don't know ... direction, so I'm pretty sure it will come to you. You have two weeks to determine the sequence. If you don't show up, I'm going to be so fucking pissed. Goodbye," Rex said, then hung-up.

Grant sat there in the silence of his empty house. This kind of banter with Rex had been a constant with the two of them. They had known each other since high school, and this was always how they spoke with each other. He looked around the room, holding the phone as it began to beep at him. He was having a hard time believing he was going to see his best friend Rex. If Rex were telling the truth, and Grant doubted that he was, he was going to see Annie Sims, the woman he almost married, the woman he still thought about, even after all the time that had passed since they had been together. The vision of the small motel he and Annie had stayed at the last time they were together in Palm Springs came into his mind. He wasn't even sure how long ago it was. He remembered how great it had been when he was with her, and worries were few when they were together. He knew if he thought about it more, he could remember exactly how long it had been, but it also would remind him how much it pained him to not have Annie in his life.

Grant noticed how quiet his living room was, how confining the room suddenly seemed, despite the conspicuous lack of furniture. He was here all the time, but he was suddenly pained by the absence of conversation, the absence of anyone ever in the room but him. What he would have given to be back at that little motel with Annie, and their life together ahead of them. He would have done things differently this time around, so he could be having the conversation with Annie right now, instead of thinking about this mysterious trip to Palm Springs that his newly-resurrected friend had concocted, and what would Annie say when she saw him, and how long had it really been since she walked away from him that night in the dark? He thought about pulling the telephone out of the wall, but that would serve no immediate purpose, save for a quick release of his now overwhelming anxiety.

As he looked around his living room, he could hear the wind blowing outside and the churning of the nearby ocean. So many things and so much time had all come and gone so quickly. There had always been goals. Go to school, get out of school, go to more school. Get a job, get a better job, get an even better job. He wondered what the goal was now. Along with pursuing and achieving these goals, there was no mention of the good things that came and went and that might never return. No mention that there would, or would not be, better times ahead. Grant was haunted by the absence of his friends, wondering if the best times were now past him, if this was all he would have, all he would be. He gently laid the beeping phone back in its cradle.

CHAPTER ONE

Two Weeks Later, Friday, 3:00 PM

Grant looked at the woman behind the bar—she was beautiful. Even from across the room, she was quite captivating, her hair black, her skin tanned, but naturally olive in hue, the smile highly powered, all set off by her bright white, crisply starched shirt. She appeared to be in great physical shape, looking like she did something besides mix drinks to be that way. He suspected she was of Spanish, perhaps Mediterranean heritage, maybe both. She was of average height, but her composure and confident aura made her seem taller. What he did know was that he really liked the looks of her. It baffled him that the impression she made came that quickly. He could not remember ever being in a Ritz before, so he was impressed with the décor. He was more impressed with the woman. Maybe it was the woman that made the bar look as fine as it did. He approached the bar, finding a seat. When she spoke, he liked her even more.

"Welcome to the Ritz."

"Hello."

"Who am I meeting today?"

"Grant, my name is Grant."

"Well Señor Grant, I am Isobelle," she reached across the bar and shook his hand.

Grant could instantly feel the energy when she touched him. This was something new for him. A strong grip, but there was something more than that. There were callouses there, but that was not what he noticed first. What he noticed was more like a vibration. The feeling gave way momentarily, but he felt the energy between them, emanating from her hands, linger in the air.

"Are you all right?" She asked.

"I never know, but why do you ask?" Grant replied. He could feel the chemistry between him and this beautiful woman.

"I can sense that something has happened to you today."

"Really?" Grant asked, surprised.

"Yes. You have had some … some upheaval in your life today, maybe there is more to come."

"And you know that how?"

Isobelle quickly changed her demeanor when she realized what she had said.

Grant was stunned by the power he was feeling from her hand, and not just because she was a beautiful woman. It was like the energy of a fast moving stream, with nearly the same calming effect. He tried to look around the room, but he could not. He could not detach his eyes from hers. He stared at her hand for a few moments, and then looked up into her brown eyes. The look in her eyes told him that not only she did she know what had happened to him, but also that she was going to make sure nothing else bad was going to happen while she was around. Her eyes saw more than just folks ordering drinks—they could see into people, and Grant could almost feel her eyes penetrating his soul. This made his ordeal thus far seem almost worth it. She was shorter than she had appeared from the other end of the bar, five-foot-four, maybe five-five, but the way she carried herself made her seem taller. He felt something stir inside him when their eyes met—something he hadn't felt in a long time.

"Forgive me." She let go of his hand, but her smile did not dim.

"Have had sort of a rough patch today, but you probably get that a lot." Grant turned his head, showing that his neck was stiff, and that it was difficult to do so. He took a seat at the bar.

"Sometimes, but I feel your difficulties are real." Her gaze was still fixed on him, and she knew he was in pain.

"Car wreck."

"Yes, I can tell."

"What?"

"Nothing. You should take it easy."

"I'm meeting someone, maybe several people today. At least one of them won't understand, no, make that won't accept 'take it easy.'" He brought his head slowly back center, focusing back on the woman behind the bar.

"Well, I understand take it easy, so please relax. I am not that busy, so you can relax here, unless you think you need to go lie down."

"Nope, this is better."

"You are meeting friends."

"You asking me, or telling me?" Grant squinted.

"Could I get you something to drink?"

"Oh, water would probably be a good start, if that is all right."

"Of course." Isobelle did not have to reach far for the pitcher, so she kept her eyes on Grant. "You are not from here, but from the looks of you, you have not come far."

"Meeting this knucklehead friend of mine that has been missing for a while. May be meeting someone else too, that I have been missing for a while." Grant put his hand up to the side of his head. "How is it you know this about me?"

"Lucky guess. Tell me more."

"Here from Encinitas, friend has been in some sort of trouble, haven't seen him in a while, a guy ran a red light and plowed into the side of my truck, that pretty much sums it up. I've been in wrecks before. This one wasn't that bad ... except for trashing my truck. Not too happy about that,"

"That is quite a bit. Anything else?" Isobelle placed a coaster on the bar, then a glass of water in front of Grant.

"No."

"Are you sure? You seem to have more on your mind."

"Oh, not that I want to talk about."

The drive and the subsequent wreck upon his arrival did remind him that he didn't know why more people didn't just fall victim to the spell of the highway and drive off the road. It was so numbing that Grant wondered why more people didn't just give in to the angst and ennui that seemed to germinate on that hard, black torrent. Maybe the guy that ran into him had done just that. Maybe he had just had enough. It had been a long time since Grant had been on a road trip, and based on the early results of this one, he was not thinking about scheduling any more anytime soon.

"Well, it is very fortunate you were not injured more severely." Isobelle continued to watch Grant very closely. "Does anyone know you are here?"

"I'm not sure how to answer that, but probably not." Grant placed his hand up to his neck, rubbing the back of it, hoping it would ease how tight he was. "You see a loud, obnoxious guy, few inches shorter than me, east coast accent, sort of sandy, dirty colored messed up hair, looks like an unmade bed? Anyone of that description been in here today?"

"I do not believe so, as I would have remembered someone like that. Is he a friend, or relative?"

"He sure as hell isn't related. Jury's still out on the friend part. How about a blonde woman, not very tall, in great shape, really good looking?"

"We get a lot matching that description, but none so far today." Isobelle's expression hardened slightly.

"Well, I would suppose you do." Grant slowly brushed back his dark brown hair.

Annie Sims was all Grant could think about. He wanted to see her brilliant smile, her glimmering blonde hair. The anguish he felt at the thought of not being with her was almost more than he could bear. Time had moved so rapidly. Law school, the jobs since he got out of school, the time alone. The thought that nothing was ever going to slow down, that everything would just keep flying past, yet the time he spent alone did not pass quickly. That time just crawled. But the years before, the really good years, the years with Annie, they were fading quickly. He wanted to believe things would be good again. When things were good, there was a feeling they always would be. Now, Annie was gone, jobs came and went, and here he was alone. The thought of seeing Annie again gave him hope that maybe the best had not come and gone for good, but might yet return again. If he could see her, there was hope.

"Are you sure I cannot get you anything else? Something to eat, perhaps?"

"No, but thanks. Is it all right if I wait here? My friend would not think to call the room, but he will think to come here. He might come here and stay here, never make it to his room."

"Of course, you may stay here as long as you like." Isobelle smiled.

"A lot worse places to be than a bar."

"I think so, as well."

"Kind of quiet in here, I'm OK with that. My friend gets here, we can kiss that goodbye."

"He does not like quiet?" Isobelle cocked her head to one side.

"Oh, I don't know if you could say that. Quiet just sort of seems to vaporize when he's around." Grant nodded his head very slowly.

"Does he talk a great deal?"

"Something like that."

"How long have you been friends?"

"Since high school."

"You are from the same place?"

"No. He's from back east, but moved west. He sort of wants everyone in the west to know he is smarter than they are."

"You do not seem like that, so how is it that you are friends, and for so long?"

"Well, believe it or not, he is really smart, and can be pretty funny. I would never tell him that." Grant made a clicking sound with his tongue. "He's been in some sort of trouble, and I haven't seen him in a while. Just have to see how bad he is."

"I am sure he cannot be that bad."

"You will probably have to tell me about his trouble, because he'll probably forget. As for how bad he is, you'll see."

Grant leaned back in his chair at the bar, feeling the tightness of his body. His thinking was slow. Lack of sleep the night before, combined with a car wreck, and precautionary pain medicine given at the hospital were not allowing him to function as he would like. He wanted to get out in the sun for a while, but knew Rex would come to the bar, and probably stay there until they hauled him out before he would come outside to look for him.

"Just relax here, I am sure your friend will come along, and that he will not be any trouble. I will be right back." Isobelle said, walking away and out of sight.

Grant laughed, watching her as she left. He looked around the room. The space was so much larger than the small motel he and Annie had stayed at on their first visit to Palm Springs together. He could not remember how long ago, four years, probably more. The décor of the hotel was so ornate, it reminded him that had he stayed with being an attorney, places like this would not seem so foreign to him. He looked down at the snaps of his western shirt, at his hands resting on the knees of his blue jeans, down to his cowboy boots, then back around at the adornment of the furnishings of the room. He leaned, looking at the arms of the chair he was sitting in, then back around the room. He was clearly out of place, dressed in his cowboy attire, surrounded by luxury. It had been a long time since he had been in any place remotely this nice, and that was back when he and Annie were together. He was having a difficult time determining which was nostalgia and which was automobile accident, thinking his life not dissimilar to the wreck. He could hear a commotion around the corner that seemed to be coming his direction, just like everything else.

"You probably just called me a sonofabitch," the commotion yelled across the hotel lobby. "What do you have to say for yourself?"

"Your ears burning?" Grant saw an unkempt figure with sandy dirty-colored messed up hair, just short of six feet tall, waddling briskly, which was Rex's way. Grant stood up, slowly, carefully.

"It's been a long time. Look at you, still dressing like a goddamn cowboy. I never thought I would say this, but it's great to see your sorry, skinny ass!" Rex said, throwing his arms around his friend.

"Been a while. Easy there."

"Still a talkative bastard. What's the matter, what happened now?"

"Some bastard ran a stop light and plowed-into me."

"Shit!"

"No, but it's a wonder I didn't." Grant tried not to laugh at his own joke.

"Damn, that sucks."

"At least I'm still above ground. And this is the first time I had ever had a police car take me somewhere I actually wanted to go."

"Still above ground, and didn't mess yourself … always the wit. What's a guy got to do to get a drink around here?" Rex asked, loudly.

"I would think the usual way, though it's a possibility that here they may they do it by telepathy."

"That's why I picked this place, 'cause you're too goddamned dumb to fucking ask for stuff, so they just do it for you. Maybe we can throw everybody but the good looking women out of the place, and close the doors 'til Sunday, what'd ya' say?"

"Might want to let somebody in later…." Grant said.

"Oh, right, food, good thinking. Man, that sucks about the wreck. How'd the other guy fare?" Rex had his arm around Grant.

"I think they hauled him in. You want to put that bag up in your room?" Grant said, motioning to Rex's bag.

"Nah, get one of the guys," Rex looked around for one of the staff passing by until he made eye contact, pointed at the bag, took money out of his pocket and waved it just above his waist. He pointed to the bar. "They'll get it, they always do."

"Still an ambitious bastard, aren't you."

"I love that western talk. You know how long it's been since I heard anybody talk like you?" Rex smiled.

"Decades?"

"Seems like it. Probably a couple years, for sure. Nobody in LA talks like that. They talk like, ah, you know, ah, like totally, really—"

"Like really not like you?" Grant said.

"Precisely! Everybody should talk like me. There would be less wasted time, more time to get on with things."

"Not to mention complete clarity."

"Exactly!"

"You look pretty good for a hermit. Let's get the ball rolling in this nice bar and see what they've got. Oh boy, and a pretty one back there to bring us the medicine!" Rex said, noticing Isobelle emerging from the back room behind the bar. "Do I know how to pick 'em, or what?"

"I might not need any medicine." Grant scratched his head.

"Good afternoon, sir." Isobelle approached them.

"She's talkin to me," Rex said, looking at Grant, then back to the woman.

"Obviously not, or she would have said 'dipshit.' "

"Better let me take this one, you've undoubtedly been through an ordeal, so would hate to see you fuck this up from the get go."

"Said Prince Charming."

"Damn straight." Rex turned to the bartender. "Hello there! You must be the owner, because someone as good looking as you are would not be working here."

"Welcome to the Ritz. If I owned the Ritz-Carlton, I would most certainly not be working behind the bar. I see you are either looking for free drinks or a job. You must be the friend."

"Every day of my life. The 'free drinks' part, anyway."

She looked at Grant, he shrugged his shoulders.

"You are so sweet," the woman said, still looking at Grant, talking to Rex. "I'm pretty sure we are not hiring, but the free drinks are up to me. I think I will give one to the quiet one here." Isobelle smiled at Grant.

"What about me?" Rex pleaded.

"Can you keep quiet?"

"Yes."

"Well then, we should run a little test and I will tell you how you do. What can I get you?"

"I'd love something with tequila, if you please, ma'am."

"Oh, shit," Grant said, putting his hand up to his head.

"I think that's a good starting point, don't you?" Rex turned to see the hotel staffer he had flagged down to get his bag. "Oh, good, here, thanks chief. Name on the room is Schmidt, Rex Schmidt." He reached in his pocket and pulled out a wad of money that looked like each bill had been wadded up individually before it was wadded up with the rest. He found a ten dollar bill and gave it to the staffer.

"Thank you, sir."

"You got it, chief. Don't be going through that, I think there's dirty clothes and my pet wolverine in there, so don't say I didn't warn you."

The staffer looked at Rex, not knowing what to say.

"I'm kidding."

"All right, sir." The staffer turned to leave.

"It's not a wolverine, it's a badger."

The staffer stopped walking, looked down at the bag he was carrying, then walked away.

"So, where were we?" Rex turned back to Grant & Isobelle. "Something about telepathy? How am I doing? I'm Rex, by the way." He held out his hand.

"You are the friend. I have heard about you." Isobelle shook his hand. "Your friend has had a difficult day, and says he needs some quiet. As for you, the troubles you have are not yet over. You still have a ways to go yet. As for right now, you are taking a test … a test to see how quiet you can be today," Isobelle said, laughing at him.

"A test? This yokel here put you up to that? How do you know about my troubles? Are you working for the government?"

"Remember, you are taking a test. It's nice to meet you, Rex," she said in a whisper, then let go of his hand. "And no, I am not working for the government."

CHAPTER 2

"How about a margarita?" Rex asked.

"No one by that name works here," Isobelle replied, looking at Grant.

"The drink, you know, with tequila and lime. Margarita."

"Does your friend want one of those as well?"

"He wants what I tell him to want," Rex pushed Grant on the shoulder.

"Is that so?" Isobelle asked Grant.

"I never want what he tells me, except for now," Grant replied. "Maybe you could tell him what he wants."

"I do not think so. I have just met him, but I could believe that it might be difficult for anyone to tell him anything. I will bring the margaritas." Isobelle turned away to prepare the drinks, quickly glancing at Grant.

The woman certainly had a confidence about her. Her movements were fluid, never deliberate. Grant had been in countless bars before, but he had never seen a woman move with the same grace or sense of purpose before, though the more he thought about it, her composure did remind him somewhat of Annie. Her comment about his trauma, along with the feeling that he had seen her face somewhere before perplexed him. He wondered how she had known about his accident.

"See, I told you it was a good idea to come here. Man, am I beat, and hungry too. You suppose they got some good food around here? 'Cause I'm fucking hungry!" Rex said, intervening in Grant's thoughts.

"Always thinking of the others, aren't you? You are always fucking hungry."

"Sorry, forgot you got in a wreck today. What the hell, man? How long before your—and you can't drive for a while, either?"

"That's what they said," his eyes still fixed on Isobelle.

"Well, that sucks."

"I may have to hang here for an extra couple of days. They probably still won't get my truck fixed by then," Grant said.

"Lucky to be alive, I guess," Rex said, sincerely.

"Just like always. What about you?"

"Well, like I told you, I have been under the gun, and am not sure when that's going to clear. I didn't do anything, but those fuckers sometimes just pop you because they can. I didn't want to talk about it on the phone."

"Because you are three of the most paranoid bastards I've ever met."

"Funny, but really. These shit heels do that kind of thing just to fuck with you." Rex lowered his voice, looked around the room, then back to Grant.

"What shit heels are you referring to?"

"The fed boys, I don't know which fucking branch. The branch that fucks with you."

"That doesn't narrow it down much."

"Justice department, US Marshalls. I didn't make this shit up. Even I'm not that fucked up. Anyway, this law firm I was working for did some work for some guys that were into some illegal shit. The government found out about it, about the, let's say bad guys, came after the bad guys that were doing the illegal shit, and then came after the firm for not being, fuck, I don't know, not being more something."

"Not being more something, that is a high crime."

"Look, cowboy Sam, this has been tortuous shit. In case you forgot, I have been out of touch for a while."

"I didn't forget."

"Now, I don't know if I'm in the clear or not. One of the guys in the firm said not to be surprised if the bad guys tried to fuck with us also."

"Where does a person have to go to join a club that can attain the level of paranoia that you seem to prescribe to?" Grant shook his head slowly back and forth.

"That bartender, what was her name?" Rex asked.

"Isobelle."

"Right, I don't know why I thought it was Margarita. She's something, huh?"

"That's the drink, margarita, and she is really something," Grant said. He finally took his eyes off of her figure and looked at Rex.

"What do you think about Annie coming? Have you figured out how to thank me yet?"

"Maybe if you pass Isobelle's test."

"I knew you put her up to that. Who says that to someone you just met?"

"I just told her … never mind. Let's get more on the preliminaries about you first, and try not to take me clear back to when laws were first codified. Then we'll talk about Annie."

"Worst years of my life … not sure about what they are going to do, which could suck big time. She's really attractive," Rex said, watching Isobelle make the drinks "and I think she likes you. She was watching you the whole time." Isobelle looked back at them. Rex waved. "She didn't even look at me."

"Can't blame her there, not sure I want to look at you either. So that's it? You don't know what's going to happen?" Grant asked.

"No, but she seems to think I'm not done," he said, nodding his head at Isobelle. "What the hell is up with that? Telling me I still have a ways to go. Maybe she's a gypsy or some sort of … she does kind of have that look about her. Anyway, what can I tell you, Grant? It's been shitty every hour of every day. I didn't want to reach out to anyone, for fear they would get on anybody I reached out to. I'm surprised they didn't call you anyway. Hell, it wouldn't surprise me if they showed up here at this hotel to watch me. They know we're friends, they know everything. First they stick a microscope up your ass and then down your tonsils, they got everything on you."

"In that order? Do they clean it first?" Grant smiled.

They both started laughing. Isobelle returned with the drinks, and a small bowl of olives.

"There you are, gentlemen: two of my best margaritas, and some locally-grown olives. Judging from your smiles, you are happier already."

"You didn't ask us how we liked them made. The drinks, I mean," Rex chimed in.

"You are men, no?"

"I am, at least. Can't speak for this one here," Rex said, elbowing Grant.

"Men would not want these blended. They would want them gently shaken, with the finest tequila, lime, and curacao. We come to the finale with just a kiss of Grand Marnier, to remind them of a sunset they once viewed with a beautiful woman somewhere, and of course, salt, because these men work hard," Isobelle said, placing the drinks in-front of them.

There was a pause, as Rex and Grant sat in mildly stunned silence.

"I knew that," Grant said first.

"Me too," Rex added.

"Good. Will you be staying long?" Isobelle said, looking at Grant.

"Longer now, I bet," Rex said.

"Yep," Grant said.

"Excellent. What brings you here?" Isobelle asked.

"A little reunion. Just us and a few beautiful women, just like you said," Rex said.

"Is that so? I can believe that." Isobelle gave a quick glance at Grant.

"Yep, the two of us, Grant's old girlfriend, probably four or five other fantastic women. You fall in that category too, so you can come too, if you want."

"Thank you for the compliment, but I thought we were testing you to see how quiet you could be," she said, changing her gaze from Grant to Rex, her eyes narrowing slightly.

"She's great, Dad! Can we keep her?" Rex asked, looking at Grant.

Isobelle looked back to Grant, waiting his answer, she and Rex now both looking at him.

"Sure, if it's alright with her," Grant said.

"You heard the man, you're in, and I think it's great. Could we please have two more of these drinks?"

"You haven't even started those drinks yet."

"By the time you get back, there'll be tumbleweeds blowing through here. Here's to you, and you," Rex said, nodding at both Grant and Isobelle.

"Sure," Grant said, reciprocating the gesture, with both men taking a drink, and Isobelle watching, waiting for their reaction.

"Man, that's the kind of sugar papa likes," Grant said with a sigh of contentment. He looked across the bar, as if at some vision only he could see.

"You are pretty good at this. You knew just how we liked them. This is going to work out just fine. What about that other stuff you knew about us?" Rex asked.

"I am glad you like the drinks. I was just projecting, which I should not do, and you have my apologies. I will get you two a couple more drinks. Now, I am not going to have any trouble from you, am I?" Isobelle asked, wanting to change the subject.

"Sort of depends on your definition of trouble. If you don't hold us completely to the rules, things should work out in everyone's favor," Grant said, surprising both Rex and Isobelle.

"Wow, what was in those drinks?" Rex blurted out.

"Nothing unusual," Isobelle said, smiling. "I do not think I will be too strict today, after all, you are guests of the hotel. I will let you, how do you say, sodbusters, enjoy your fun. Just do not go shooting up the bar, and getting the management all upset, or I will have to run you out of here," Isobelle said, before turning back to her liquors to go satisfy Rex's request for additional cocktails.

"Hey, hey, hey, she's a keeper for you, Grant boy! Annie is going to love her!"

Grant watched Isobelle as she walked away. He suddenly felt light and warm, as though the harsh hotel air conditioning had been shut off abruptly. He tipped up the drink and was sucked in by the clarity of thought that washed over him. Clarity of thought, after such a brutal car wreck, was rather surprising, so he was reticent to trust the feeling. He couldn't deny, however, how good it felt to sit in such a nice bar, speaking with this beautiful, enchanting woman. He had not felt that ease since Annie had been around, and that was a long time ago. Isobelle looked nothing like Annie, but she was beguiling and she had the same confidence.

"I still can't believe you got Annie to say she would come here. Pretty tough believing she would talk to you at all."

"Hey, can't help my boyish charm," Rex smiled, enjoying his drink.

"Bullshit, you ain't got any boyish charm. She's just a good soul and felt sorry for your pathetic ass, which I didn't think was possible."

"She is a good soul. I'm still not sure why she didn't like me in the first place."

"Maybe because you're an asshole, you were always stirring up crazy shit that got me in trouble!" Grant said.

"Yeah, Angel Grant … wouldn't say shit if he had a mouthful. Always a gun to your head to make you do things you didn't want to do. Hey, I got a gun. How bout I hold it to your head and we do some crazy shit this weekend?"

"Guns, yeah, that's exactly what you need. I really am trying to rule out any behavior that even remotely resembles anything that you would do," Grant said.

"Yeah, like it was never you."

"People change. I've been in a car wreck already, what do you want?"

"Maybe that qualifies. If we were keeping tabs in the fucked-up sweepstakes, you are in the lead. The bartender seems to like you, though, so there might be hope," Rex said.

"I'm not here for the—the bartender. I'm here for Annie ... and you, sort of."

"Thanks for the afterthought."

"I haven't seen Annie in years. It's been longer since I saw her than it has since I last saw you. And I know for a fact she is still better looking than you."

"It'll be great to see her, won't it?"

"She's really coming?" Grant asked, still perplexed by the fact that this might be a real possibility.

"You are such a fucking putz! Yes, she's coming! Just relax, try not to be your usual dumbass self, and enjoy the ride. Wonder if she's bringing a bunch of hot friends, what do you think?"

"I'm sure I don't know."

"Hey, don't get pissy. I had to do a bunch of shit I didn't want to do to get Annie to say she would come here. So in return, you should just keep the bartender happy, so she can keep the drinks coming, which, in turn, will make me happy. That, and if Annie brings some hot friends along with her. Maybe the bartender, what's her name, has some babe friends, too. I bet she does. A woman that good looking doesn't hang with ugly people," Rex said.

"I don't see Annie here yet, and listen to you. Did your ordeal make you regress to high school? What do you mean doesn't hang around with ugly people? I let you hang around me, and look how goddamn ugly you are," Grant retorted, as bitterly as he could. Already he could tell he was getting too defensive of Isobelle.

"Almost to high school," Rex said, setting his now-empty glass down on the bar. "Look, and maybe it can be like old times. Well, okay—maybe not completely like the times you and Annie had when you were together, but maybe it can just be some of the fun that the three of us had back then. She doesn't like it, she can leave. And if that's not good enough for you, I bet that woman behind the bar would be more than happy to hear you tell her some stories. Any of that compare with your exciting life back in Encinitas?"

"I thought you were going to be quiet," Isobelle said, returning with round two.

"That's really not a fair test for him," Grant said, smiling slyly at her.

"This, I can believe," Isobelle smiled back.

"I can be quiet. I just have a lot to say. Most people,"—Rex gave Grant a fiendish look—"find what I have to say to be interesting," Rex said.

"Are any of those people who find you interesting here in this bar today?" Isobelle asked, deadly serious, playing him word for word.

Grant started laughing.

"Well, it looks like the bar is empty, except for us," Rex said.

"I know, that is why I asked the question," Isobelle said.

"You know it is not a given that I will leave you a tip," Rex said, a smile creeping onto his face.

"No, but you probably will because I will see to it that you are well taken care of, whether anyone is listening to you, or not," Isobelle smiled back. "But we should still complete the test, just to be certain."

"That's for sure," Grant added.

"I stay quiet, you are going to have to pass notes to this one if you want to get a response, I'm just tellin' ya. If you are waiting for him to make conversation, we will probably go through several shift changes before Sunday," Rex said, looking towards the service access part of the bar.

"You stay quiet, even a little while, I will make sure your friend here is comfortable speaking with me," Isobelle said.

"I don't think we can take that chance. His vocal cords might grow shut, which, now that I think about it, isn't a bad thing. On the other hand, it might impact his drinking, which would certainly impact your tip," Rex replied.

Even with this beautiful woman standing in front of him, flirting with him and teasing Rex, the only thing that occupied Grant's thoughts was the hope of seeing Annie again.

CHAPTER 3

As long as Grant had known Rex, Rex had never been one to talk much with or about his emotions. It wasn't that he didn't have any, it was more that his family dynamic had never been warm and welcoming. They were all well-educated, but not prone to discuss emotions, good or bad. Theirs was always a methodical discussion of why people did, or did not do certain things, with only the most logical and reasonable motives being considered. Rex had always tried to compensate for that by being reckless, and always including his friends in whatever happenings he was generating. He might not tell his friends how much they meant to him, but he always had something going on that would enable him to show, in his own way, how much they meant to him. He was always more outgoing than Grant, and having Grant share in his escapades forced Grant to be more outgoing than he would have been without Rex. This interaction brought out a rapid-fire banter between the two that spilled over onto anyone else that managed to get in the swirl they always created. Some flowed along with it, and some were swept away.

"I had to beg Annie to get her to come here," Rex said.

"I'll bet you did."

"That's not all I had to do. You want to hear what else I had to do?"

"Do I have a choice?" Grant said, blowing air out of his mouth.

"I had to write her a formal letter of apology, can you believe that? Me, write an apology letter. I don't write letters to anyone. That was a tough one. The whole list of things I had to do was crazy, even by my standards, which we know are, well, out there. I had to send her flowers for two weeks, send her a huge box of Teuscher's truffles, the biggest box of some almond toffee I could find, and some other stuff too. Wine, Pinot Noir, I think maybe, not cheap."

"She always liked the truffles and the toffee. I used to buy them both for her. She never gained an ounce … I still don't believe you."

"You keep listening, you will."

"What else?"

"She said I had to go to church for a month, get a note from the padre each time and send it to her. She wanted a box of cigars, and I had to send a picture of me sitting on a pony," Rex said.

"A picture of you smoking the cigars on the pony?"

"No, just sitting on the pony."

"What else?"

"A Slip-n-Slide, a Wrist Rocket, and a Yahtzee game."

Grant could not believe he was having this conversation. He half-wondered if it wasn't a hallucination, an after effect of the events of earlier in the day, combined with medication.

"Anything else?"

"A bottle of Roederer Cristal, or Clicquot Grande Dame, I forget which, and some caviar. That shit's expensive."

Grant was starting to laugh out loud now. "What else?"

"Ice cream. Blue Bell, and Graeter's. Goat cheese from somewhere, I forget where."

"That's all?"

Grant was doubled over and having trouble breathing at this point, he was laughing so hard. He was having trouble speaking, as well.

"A Kentucky ham, some really good bourbon … do I have to go on?" Rex pleaded.

"Yes…." Grant barely able to get the word out.

"I couldn't find the case of Fizzies she asked for. I don't think they make them anymore. Pop Rocks, or Chocodiles, I don't think they make those either."

"She asked you to get Pop Rocks and Chocodiles?" Grant asked, speaking louder than before.

"No, not those. I just always liked them, and since I was already on a shopping spree, I tried to find them for myself. You liked those too, as I remember."

"Just get on with it."

"Anyway, I think you get the overview here that there were some hurdles that needed to be cleared before she would acquiesce and even talk to me. She made me send her a goddamn hula hoop, and something called Wine Gums, which sounds more like a disease. You ever try to package a hula hoop for shipping? Do you think I deserved all that? Do you think it was really necessary for me to go through all that to get her to talk to me?" Rex asked.

"She let you off easier than I would. I'm surprised she didn't ask you to shave your head and paint it blue."

"It was mentioned…."

Grant was still laughing and barely able to talk. He was still not convinced that this was on the up-and-up, but for right now, at least it was starting to sound pretty funny.

"I can't imagine why she asked for some of that stuff. It doesn't really sound like her. She doesn't smoke cigars, or drink, really. I do see some of it, but she—"

"Maybe all those years you two were together finally took its toll on her. She's finally chain-smoking cigars and cannon balling the booze. She just couldn't take it anymore." Rex was laughing now.

"Still strange. Damn funny, but strange," Grant was still laughing.

"The shit I do for you, and you're still giving me grief about going silent for a few years? You are such a douche. It ain't my fault you two broke up, so don't keep giving me that shit."

"You didn't help out though, that's for sure. Back then, I mean. Maybe this punch list now helps a little bit, but…."

"But nothing! Look, it ain't my fault either that you gave up on law after you got out of law school and went the way you did. You had stuff on your mind and it didn't work out, get over it, get on with it. Get over her, get on with her …. You got yourself into this mess." Rex took a deep breath before he launched into the second part of his tirade. "Look, with all this shit, I decided to start my own thing, my own business, so I don't have to worry about crap that somebody else is doing that could get me in trouble. Now, I get in trouble, it's my own fault."

"It usually is your fault," Grant added.

"You know what I mean. Look, you seem to like working with computers, so...."

"Computers don't intentionally screw you over."

"Right, so that's ok, there's nothing wrong with that."

"I didn't say there was."

"No, but you have this 'things-didn't-work-out-like I planned' thing about you. Hell, nobody's stuff works out as planned. Shit happens, and you shouldn't worry about it. When were you the happiest?'

"I don't know."

"Bullshit, you know the answer to that question."

"Computers are easier to deal with than people. I did the law thing ... I don't know. I was with a firm, like you, and found the thought of just being another number was not ... not—not something. I don't know what it was, but I know what it wasn't, and it sure wasn't right for me. Computer work is steady. I work for some high profile companies. Only problem is, I keep thinking about getting out of the contractor racket and getting somewhere permanent, but every time someone wants me on staff permanently, it doesn't work out for some reason or another. Things are always good, just don't last as long as I would like," Grant said, looking out towards the exit to the bar.

"Sort of like all the meaningful events in your life, eh, chief? Look, I want you to at least think a little more about still doing your own thing, but maybe doing it with me and...."

"And what?"

"Just think about it, that's all I'm asking. Think about getting off the corporate teat, strike out on your own. You could do it with me." Rex said.

"Strike out?"

"Poor word choice. Go off on your own. Not have to put up with a bunch of douche bags around the water cooler talking about how busy they are."

"I'll think about it."

"Promise?"

"Yes, and don't make me swear, unless by swear, you mean to say fuck you."

Rex laughed. "I miss those days, chief. Those days when you used to say shit like that all the time."

Grant seemed to drift away in thought and paused. "You know what I've been thinking about? I've been wondering if this is it. The best times were then, and now they're done, is that it? Years, gone, just like that, flying by. Are there more coming? I don't have a clue."

"Well, you got the last part right," Rex said.

"How's that?"

"You don't have a fucking clue."

Isobelle tried not to look too interested in what the men were saying, but she was having a hard time keeping her eyes off of Grant. She had gone back down to the other end of the bar, busying herself cleaning the bar, arranging the liquors, and polishing glasses.

"So just have some fun with me and take the pressure off. You can still do the things you want to do, only now you've got somebody who cares about you to look after you. 'Cause boy, you sure as hell need someone looking after you. Look around, enjoy your life, enjoy Southern California, and pay attention to the good looking women around you. You could also do worse than meeting an attractive bartender. What's her name? Isarita? I mean, you've only been with me for a few minutes and look how things are perking up already!," Rex said with a grin, waving at Isobelle. She began heading back their way.

"Her name is Isobelle, you mor...." Grant's voice trailed off, his head turning as he noticed two very beautiful women walking into the bar. They were about the same build, not tall, and they looked like they could be sisters. He didn't recognize one of them, the shorter of the two, but he certainly knew the other one. They were both blonde, very tan, both extremely fit. He recognized the taller one instantly by the confident glow she carried with her everywhere she went. She could peer into his soul, even from across the room, and every time he saw her, she made him feel like he had just won the lottery. There was a certain composure about her that made her seem like she was on a higher plane, but was always willing to step down onto the same one he was on, which always baffled him. It was not conceit, it was not ego. She was still the enchanting woman he remembered, maybe not drop-dead gorgeous to anyone but him, but Grant, after all this time, still thought that Annie was just that. The tennis she played in college, and probably still played, had given her a bronzing, a sculpting that would probably never go away. About five-foot-six, her sparkling blonde hair tied back, just like always.. Grant barely noticed the other woman. He was watching Annie, the woman he had been waiting to see for five and a half years. His insides started to turn.

The two women approached the bar where he and Rex were waiting. Though he was sitting down, Grant's legs suddenly felt extremely weak, to go with his uneasy stomach, and the desert outside seemed to have abruptly moved into his mouth. He was having trouble breathing. He hoped it was the pain medicine. Both men rose to their feet, though Rex jumped up eagerly, not experiencing the same flood of emotion, nor car wreck fallout, that Grant was currently feeling.

"Well, look at this! Must have been the Yahtzee game that was the kicker to get you here!" Rex said, beaming.

"That was my idea," said the shorter of the two women. "I'm Kat," she said, extending her hand.

"Hello Kat, I'm Rex, and this—"

Kat cut him off. "This must be Grant. I've heard a lot about you. Hello, Grant," Kat said. She stuck her arm out to shake Grant's hand as well.

"Hello," Grant said, briefly shifting his gaze from Annie to Kat.

"Talkative sonofagun, isn't he? Have you heard a lot about me, Kat? Annie, how are you?"

Both men wanted to hug Annie, for different reasons, but they both thought privately that was probably not a good idea.

"Good, I'm good," Annie said.

"Of course I've heard of you," Kat's eyes, now narrow, turning back to Rex.

"What is it with that look? Second time today I've gotten that."

"Probably only two because it's still early in the day," Kat said with a charming smile.

"Hello, Grant," Annie said.

"Hello, Annie. Good … good to see you. You look great," Grant replied. It was even more of a struggle for him to get words out of his mouth than usual.

"It's good to see you. You look great."

"Skinny. I say he is skinnnnn-eeee! Too skinny. Makes me look bad."

"Is that a difficult thing to do?" Kat cocked her head to one side.

"So, you have heard of me! Well, I don't know what you heard, but I'm a changed man."

"What did you change into?" Kat turned her head to the other side.

"Hey, I like her!" Rex backhanded Grant on the shoulder.

"Oh, what luck for me," she rolled her eyes.

CHAPTER 4

Isobelle came over to deliver the second round of drinks Rex had commanded. She was trying to determine the overall relationship of the newly expanded group. Even though she had just met him, she knew Grant was struggling, and that his accident did not help his condition, but she needed more time to tell much more than that. She was really attracted to him, and she was hoping no one else was picking up on that. She did not think the newcomers could, but she figured if anyone was going to pick up on it, it would be the shorter woman. She could sense the nostalgic air about the party, the feelings between Grant and the taller blonde woman. This just intrigued her more.

"Here are your drinks, gentlemen, though it seems your party has expanded to include a few ladies, as well."

"Just like I said was going to happen … umm…." Rex stuttered, fumbling for her name.

"Isobelle."

"Right, Isobelle. These are our friends Annie and Kat."

"It is nice to meet you," Isobelle said.

"Nice to meet you, too." Annie smiled.

"Have you known these two fellows for a long time?" Kat asked.

"No, I have not, so you will have to tell me all about them." Isobelle smiled back. "What may I bring for you?"

"It looks like they're having margaritas, and that sounds good on a hot day." Kat said.

"See, I told you I liked her," Rex said smiling, and looking around at the growing group. He was enjoying having people around him. "Isobelle here, she can read minds, too, or something like that."

"Just water for me, thanks," Annie said. "Read minds?"

"Water? Come on, Annie. I'm more fun after a few drinks," Rex added.

Annie just smiled, laughing to herself. She looked as if she wanted to say something, but contented herself with just a smile. She looked at Grant, and he smiled back nervously.

"I think the gentleman may have given me too much credit about the mind reading part. I'll be right back. Please make yourself comfortable and let me know if there is anything else I can get for you," Isobelle said, turning to make the drinks for the new additions.

"How have you been, Grant?" Annie turned to fully face him.

"Ok," he was still standing, his legs feeling more weak, his insides churning, even more.

Rex turned to Kat, motioning to the chair. "Have a seat. As you can see, this conversation might take forever … though you'll probably only get about twenty words an hour from him. Let's hear about you."

"No, no, we chose names on the way here, and I get to go last. Besides, I would rather hear about you all first. There seems to be quite a long history you three have together." Kat patted Rex gently on the shoulder.

"I know you want to hear about me, everybody does," Rex paused, waiting for someone to laugh at his joke. When no one did, he continued: "So, you and Annie have been friends a long time, or did she just hire you to make sure she doesn't kill me?"

"I'm the backup plan," Kat smiled.

"Her idea, or yours?"

"Mine."

Rex started laughing.

"Have a seat," Grant said, looking at Annie. He needed to sit more than anyone. Isobelle was down the bar a ways, and she could tell when a customer needed to get off their feet.

Grant was rattled. The combination of Annie's physical presence next to him, the reminiscences their impending meeting had inspired, and being in a car wreck earlier was getting to him. He still loved her, though he had been working on denial for a long time. He was hoping she might show some sign of tenderness or affection towards him, but so far, Annie's behavior seemed to say that for her, this was just a meeting of old friends. Grant was hoping there was more, hoping there was something left for him. He couldn't take his eyes off of her. Clearly, his mouth was not getting the proper electronic impulses from his brain, because he was currently incapable of speech.

Grant did not want to leave Annie even for a second, but he was concerned that he would be contributing nothing to the meeting. He figured the women were now contemplating the possibility that he had suffered a head wound—which, ironically, was true, though the doctor who examined him after the car accident had assured him that there was nothing to be concerned about. Grant was so glad to be with his friends that he was not even paying attention to what was being said. The only thing he knew was that whatever words were being spoken were definitively not coming out of his mouth. He couldn't get over how great Annie looked, though he wasn't surprised that she had maintained her perfect fitness and striking facial features. As usual, he was completely taken aback by her presence. Over the last few years he had made a determined effort to get over his deep physical and emotional attachment to her, but now, after only five minutes, he was back where he had started. Maybe, he thought, if he intentionally ignored his feelings for Annie and went after Isobelle instead, he could put his life on the right path again. "Emotions and car wrecks … great combo," he grumbled to himself.

He made eye contact with Isobelle, in between his constant focus on Annie. He looked back to Annie and pulled one of the bar stools out for her. He couldn't get any words out, but he gestured vaguely at the stool, indicating that she should sit.

"Thanks," Annie smiled, taking the offered seat.

Annie sat down, feeling a little shaky herself. She was trying to be cordial to Rex, someone she deemed obnoxious, and she was skeptical that he was an entirely new person after his brush with the law. She thought perhaps even a brigand deserved some compassion, but that was her nature. He did seem a bit different, in all the times he called her, so she thought maybe that was why she had given him a second chance. She was glad to see Grant, more than she thought she would be. She didn't think it ran much deeper than putting the past behind and being friends, but that couldn't stop her from reminiscing about all the sweet moments and good times they had shared together. She hoped she wasn't showing these feelings, as she still hadn't resolved them all herself. She never liked lack of resolve.

"We have a couple of hours before we have to meet some other folks. I mean, while we're here in Rancho Mirage." Annie said. It came out abruptly and hesitantly. Grant was startled; Annie never did things awkwardly.

"Hey, you just got here, but the more, the merrier!" Rex said.

"They probably aren't ready for you yet," Kat responded.

Isobelle began to move back to the group. She found all this to be fascinating. . She wasn't in the habit of hitting on customers, but she was now more than considering it. She thought it a daunting task, given the strange dynamics of the group that she had yet to completely figure out.

"A margarita and a water," Isobelle said, presenting them with their drinks.

"Thank you, it is hot outside," Annie reached for the glass, giving her hands something to do.

"There is always a great thirst here in the desert, and too much thirst can be a dangerous thing," Isobelle said, looking first at Annie, and then at Grant.

Annie paused before taking a sip of the water, watching the way Isobelle looked at Grant. Rex broke her focus.

"I know I'm going to need a lot of this while I'm here," Rex added, pointing to his drink.

"We will try to make sure everyone gets everything they want, and more," Isobelle smiled.

"I think she likes me," Rex said quietly to the group.

"We all do, as far as you know," Kat added.

"You do, for sure. Annie probably has to work up to it," Rex said turning to Kat.

"Water isn't going to get that done," Grant said.

"Hey, get him another one of these, they make him talk, so maybe, what, sixteen of them, you think?" Rex said, looking at all the women.

"You think you're funny?" Grant looked at Rex.

"It's not braggin', if you can do it."

Kat laughed. "I have known Annie quite a while and it is nice to get away to the desert like this. I know Annie and I both needed a break for a bit, even if you're here," she said, looking at Rex.

"This is too good. You got some bohemian in you, I can tell. Maybe we should do shots of ouzo next."

"No!" Annie said quickly, still not recovered from Isobelle's comments about thirst.

"You're right. We should keep our drinks in the same country. That only leaves Kahlua, or mezcal. I don't think they have pulque."

"No! Please?" Annie smiled.

"Tempting, but I'll pass," Kat said.

Kat was fairly pragmatic, like Annie, but Rex seemed right for once: She was certainly a free spirit, so none of this repartee bothered her. She noticed Isobelle's more than passing fascination with Grant, and she also now could see why Rex annoyed Annie so much.

"Well, it is pretty warm here, but I like the desert, always have," Grant said, not knowing what to say, and figuring the climate was safe to talk about without messing up.

"Yep, that's my boy. Hasn't seen us in years and years and he wants to talk about the weather. You know, maybe we should get you up to Hollywood, get you your own talk show. If they paid you by the word … you would starve to death," Rex said.

Grant just fidgeted. The three women saw that he was uncomfortable.

"Yeah, Hollywood, that's what I need," Grant said, continuing to look like the seat had been brought in out of the desert sun. If he didn't have to talk, he would have been content to just sit there, looking, listening to Annie, maybe for weeks. He really needed time to gain his composure, if he were going to get more than eleven words out.

Well, if he's waiting for a break in the conversation, he could be here awhile. We all could. You take up a lot of talking space," Kat said, smiling.

"Don't go feeling sorry for him. Tall, cowboy-looking guy like him? He doesn't need anyone making excuses for him. He can talk, I've heard him. He can cuss better than anyone I know."

"Such a definite distinction," Kat said.

"Well, he can. Come on hillbilly, cuss for the nice girls," Rex said.

Grant thoughts were quickly turning towards the brilliant idea of punching Rex. He could see that Kat was trying to make things easier for him, which he appreciated. This helped his disposition, unfortunately not his diction. He was going to have to get away for a few minutes to regroup.

"I forgot something … in my room. I'll be right back," Grant said.

"Now look what you've done," Rex said, glaring at Kat with mock-anger. "You're scaring him off."

"Me? I'm on his side!" Kat protested.

"How come you're not on my side?" Rex asked.

"Is anyone ever on your side?" Kat replied.

"No!" Annie said, surprising herself by the vehemence of her exclamation.

"It would seem not," Kat said, looking at Annie, then at Rex.

"Is everything all right?" Annie asked, looking at Grant.

"I, uh, yes. I just need to go check … you know, I just forgot something … be right back." Grant nodded, fussed with his things and got up to leave.

Behind the bar, Isobelle hurried to where her few customers were sitting. She wanted to ask if Grant was all right, but she thought that might be too obvious. She wanted to make sure he was coming back—if not now, then later.

"Is everything…."

"I think he's all right, he just forgot something in his room, I think. He said he would be right back," Annie said, reassuring herself more than Isobelle.

"He just felt a little ill. His friend here probably made him sick," Kat said, looking at Rex.

"He's fine, probably still a little shook up from the car wreck," Rex chuckled.

CHAPTER 5

"Car wreck?" Annie said.

The women on both sides of the bar watched as Grant walked out. Kat looked at both Annie and Isobelle, judging their responses. It looked like Isobelle was trying her best not to look disappointed, but surprisingly, so was Annie. Kat knew none of this would affect her one way or the other, but it was interesting for her to watch these relationships develop.

Kat thought this opportunity might give her a chance to learn more about Grant. Rex was watching everything in the bar except Grant, wholly unconcerned about the probability of his return.

"He'll be back," Rex said nonchalantly.

"Are you sure?" Isobelle asked.

Annie and Kat seemed surprised at the comment and looked at her.

"I—I mean, we want our guests to enjoy themselves at our hotel, and he seemed out of sorts" Isobelle said.

"He's fine, he just went to get something, you know how he is. Well, Annie knows how he is, at any rate."

"Let's get back to the car wreck thing, what are you talking about?" Annie asked.

"He's fine. Just a bit beat up. Some guy ran a stoplight and plowed into him on his way here."

"Well, is he all right?" Annie asked.

"Says he is," Rex replied calmly, not responding to the urgency in Annie's voice.

"Did he see a doctor?" Annie persisted.

"At the hospital, yeah." Rex said.

"At the hospital?" Annie and Kat said, almost in unison.

"Yeah, the hospital. They looked him over, let him go, said he's OK. They wouldn't let him go if he weren't OK. You docs don't do that, do you? You're not a veterinarian, are you?" Rex asked

"Aren't you worried?" Annie asked, paying no attention to the veterinarian question.

"No, not really. Believe me, if he weren't all right, he'd say so," Rex played with his bar napkin, but the others were unconvinced.

"Nice try, Rex. Grant doesn't say anything, ever," Annie responded, bitingly. It was apparent she was concerned, and frustrated with Rex's apparent thoughtlessness.

"Look, Grant has been doing very well, he's busy as hell and we were talking about the two of us working together. I mean look at the guy. He's in perfect shape."

"Really? He's thinking about working with you? He must have hurt his head in the accident," Annie said.

"Yep, we were just talking about that before you ladies came in."

"Has he lost his mind?" Kat asked. "Maybe a second opinion on his condition is in order."

"Maybe a long time ago, but why do you ask?" Rex asked.

"I don't know, but it would seem that working with you would help him develop, what, his annoyance skills maybe?" Kat asked.

"Hey, you are a live one!" Rex said.

"Is he really thinking about working with you? You aren't still in trouble, are you? And are you avoiding telling us more about this car wreck?" Annie demanded.

There was now a great deal of concern in Annie's voice.

"Somebody ran a stoplight and plowed into him, like I said. It was just down the street from here."

"I wish he would have said something, I could have examined him," Annie said.

"You think he wants to bother you with anything like that?" Rex asked.

"It's not a bother. If he's hurt, that's important," Annie said.

"You try telling him that, and see if he opens up about it," Rex said, swirling the ice in his empty glass. "If someone needs to examine someone, I'll start with examining Kat and go from there." Rex put the glass back up to his mouth, finishing the sentence with his nose in the glass.

Annie was trying to give Rex the benefit of the doubt in her head. She had been hoping that maybe he had really changed; however, she never did have much to say to him before, and now she was feeling exactly the same animosity. The thought that Grant might be injured was worrying her, and she found Rex's complete lack of concern for his friend's welfare incomprehensible. That Grant might get involved with Rex in a business venture didn't offer her any comfort. He was talking a lot, and he always talked more than anyone in any room. He seemed almost giddy, for some reason. Maybe he was happy that he had finally gotten something to work out properly; or maybe he was just happy to have his old friends back together. Or both. Whatever the reason, he still irritated her—that hadn't changed over the years—and his lack of complete openness on the subject of Grant's accident didn't help matters.

Kat seemed to love the verbal joust. She had heard stories about Rex, and saw no reason to cut him any slack. She saw no risk in offending him, being pretty sure no one was capable of that.

Two women entered the bar, and moved to the end opposite from where Annie, Kat and Rex were seated. Their dresses seemed to be composed more of air and wind than of fabric, and the prints appeared to have been spray painted onto their bodies. Rex took notice immediately.

"Well, ladies, I guess word's out that Rex is in town."

"Police blotter, probably," Kat said.

"Maybe. If so, those are two pretty good looking cops, so maybe they could take me somewhere … you know, for questioning," Rex said, still looking at the newcomers.

Annie shook her head, looking down at her hands. Isobelle had been hovering nearby, and as soon as she noticed the two women, her demeanor changed.

"Moll and Mag, but I have some other names for them," she said bitingly.

"Are they friends of yours?" Annie asked.

"Doesn't sound like it," Kat added.

"Hang onto your wallet," Isobelle said, looking at Rex.

"Oh, so they're on the wrong side of the law, not just a great looking appendage of the law. Now I really want to know them." Rex was watching them out of the corner of his eye, though he did not stop talking. "I think I should be the one to listen, and to take down their stories."

Annie looked at Rex, relieved her disdain for him was not without merit. He was still a blow hard in her mind, and she didn't think she needed to hide her feelings. She really wanted Grant to return. If she hadn't been waiting for him, she would have left immediately.

Kat just laughed.

Isobelle was clearly not happy that the other women had entered the bar. It was not obvious that she wanted Grant to return, but Kat seemed to sense it. The women at the other end just added a little more tension.

"I had better tend to them, or they will complain to the front desk," Isobelle said with a sigh.

"They would do that?" Annie asked.

"They have done it before," Isobelle responded.

"Gosh, why would ...?" Annie started.

"I could tell you, but that would be inappropriate. I'll be right back," Isobelle said, turning to go tend to the new arrivals.

"So, Annie, how's the doctor business? I don't think you told me what your specialty was." Rex was trying to be on good behavior.

"Small practice, general medicine. I like knowing my patients, not having it be an assembly line, with not enough attention to detail."

"De-sembly line, you mean." Good behavior for Rex was a nebulous thing.

"How about you? What part of the saw bones trade you in?" Rex looked at Kat.

"I'm a psychiatrist."

"Holy shit!"

"Yeah, I don't get that much."

Rex wanted the talk turned back to Grant. Rex wanted to plant all the good seeds he could while Grant was away, as he knew Grant would not say much anyway, but he definitely wouldn't talk about himself. As selfish and conceited as he might have appeared to the women, Rex really was trying to look out for his friend.

"It's been a long time, Annie. Used to be nonstop-wacky-madcap-fun, you have to admit that much," Rex said.

"There were some really good times," Annie said, smiling, a glimmer of reminiscence in her eyes.

"Damn right there were. There could be again, too," Rex replied.

"That was a while ago. A long time ago, Rex," Annie said.

"Not that long ago! Not like grade school era," Rex said, his eyes opening wide.

"Did you go to grade school?" Kat asked.

"No. Actually I went straight into college," Rex said.

"I thought as much," Kat said, rolling her eyes.

"Seriously though, it wasn't that long ago," Rex said quickly. "Ok, what, you haven't seen Grant in four or five years, grad school was … undergrad was … why are you making me do math? It's under a decade, how about that. It's not like old people thinking back on shit, we're not that old."

"I have a new li—a … err, a different life now. Working a practice takes a lot of time and I can't be worrying about … about…." Annie started to look around the bar, casting around for the most diplomatic way to make her point.

"About what?" Rex asked.

"About whether the two of you are going to go streaking, or get arrested for some … some stupid thing," Annie said, closing her eyes, tilting her head down.

"We never got caught streaking," Rex said, very slowly.

"You never got *caught* streaking," Annie said. She was having a hard time not laughing.

"That's right, we never got *caught* streaking," Rex said, sticking his chest out. "So what's it matter?"

"There were other indiscretions. Sometimes, you guys were so, so … in…." Annie said, now trying to find the right word.

"In…?" Rex asked, before she could finish.

Annie paused, looking at Rex. "Insensitive."

"Ah, insensitive," Rex said.

"What is Grant doing now?" Kat asked.

"Right now? Taking a leak, probably," Rex said, his eyes trained on the women at the other end of the bar.

Annie was embarrassed. "Not right this minute! Gosh, Rex, you just…."

"Sorry. He is working, and he has been … you still say gosh! I always loved that. Anyway, he's been doing this computer gig for himself. He does some pretty high powered tech support stuff. I'm not a tech head, so I'm not exactly sure how it goes, but he is in the high level of the support food chain. It needs to be a pretty bad screw up to get to him. He's the guy the companies need to fix their big problems. Was doing that for the phone company, for some healthcare company, all big groups. Some of them lay him off, then bring him back as a private contractor. That's how fucked ... excuse me, how messed up companies are. They tell you that you are a piece of ..."

"It's Ok, say it," Annie said.

"Shit, they tell you that you are a piece of shit, and that they don't need you. Then, they hire you back, without benefits, and have you do the same stuff. You try to leave, they tell you they really need you now. It sucks, big time. So, I told him, screw that corporate bullshit, and we are talking about the two of us working together."

"So he's doing well, aside from the car wreck? That didn't come out right," Annie said, showing her frustration.

"He's tough. Yes, he's doing great, just wrapped up in his work, he needs a break."

"Who doesn't need a break?" Kat said. She was content to listen, but she was here to support Annie and didn't want Rex to just roll over everyone.

"So, are you sure you are not a lawyer?" Rex asked.

"Yes, quite sure. I'm a doctor. Maybe I should explain it to you. You see, doctors make people better," Kat said slowly.

"Is that how it works?" Rex asked

"Just think the opposite of how people feel after they deal with you," Kat said, tilting her head.

"There any more like you at home?" Rex leaned closer.

"What?"

"Nothing. You married?" Rex backed away.

"No I am not, are you?" Kat leaned closer to Rex.

"Nope," Rex answered.

"Previously?"

"Nope."

"Because...?"

"Because I had better things to do. You thinking about you and me sneaking off to Vegas?" Rex smiled.

"I was thinking about what I'm going to have for dinner tonight, or what I'm going to do tomorrow, or what I'm going to do when I get back to La Jolla, or ...do you want me to go on?" Kat asked, still tilting her head, not smiling.

"That's ok, I get the picture. I—hey, La Jolla, wow! Pretty nice living. You could take me back there with you, surprise the relatives."

"I didn't say I had relatives there."

"Friends maybe."

"I could just tell them about you, which would probably be better. I know just what to say."

Isobelle returned from serving the two women who had caught Rex's attention at the other end of the bar. She really wanted to hear more about Grant, but the other women were making things difficult. She looked around, hoping that he had returned, but was disappointed when she saw that he had not.

"How is everyone doing down here?"

"Get my friends here another drink. Watch this one, she's on her second water," Rex pointed at Annie.

"And how about you?" Isobelle asked.

"I was hoping you would ask. Yes, I think another drink would be lovely," Rex bowed.

"How about your friend, the one that left. Is he coming back?" Isobelle looked somewhat concerned.

"We never know, but we think so, so bring him another drink also. He doesn't show, I get it," Rex said, looking around Isobelle to the other end of the bar.

"Rex!" Annie said.

"You're right, where are my manners? Annie, he doesn't show, you drink it."

"I'm fine right now," Annie replied.

"Ok, I just want to be hospitable." Rex said, matter-of-factly.

"You know, I thought that hula hoop I sent you was a stretch. Now after meeting Sigmund Freud here, I think I get it." Rex looked away from the other end of the bar, and back to Kat.

Kat just grinned, not showing her teeth in her smile.

"Thought so," Rex said.

"Good, drinks for most, water for one," Isobelle said.

"Maybe you could spike the—" Rex began, but Annie cut him off.

"Don't even think about it."

A man and a woman entered the bar, getting a table off to the side. They were dressed very conservatively, rather like they did not belong here. They both had sunglasses on, which they left on when they came in. Rex noticed them immediately.

"Are those people looking over here at me?" Rex got a serious look on his face.

CHAPTER 6

As Grant walked back to his room, he noticed the interior surroundings more than when he had walked through to the bar earlier. Maybe the pain medicine was wearing off. He was still rather numb, and he was not sure if it was because of the accident, seeing Annie, or meeting Isobelle. Though they were in the desert, Grant thought the hotel opulent. It was certainly no normal desert motif. The wood was dark and ornate, and he liked the plush carpets cushioning his heavy gait.

He stopped to talk to some of the hotel staff on his way back to the room. Talking with the hotel staff and hearing (if not participating in) actual conversation with his friends made it brutally obvious that he had spent far too much time alone. He was lonely. He hadn't had this many people to talk to in a long time, and he somehow felt he had lost the ability to converse easily with strangers—and friends. The walk back to his room took longer than it should have. The sight of the interior of the hotel made him realize that up until now, he had been on a pretty bland social diet.

More like a prison diet, he thought.

He entered his room as quickly as possible, suddenly feeling nauseated. He ran into the bathroom, where he immediately threw up.

"Great. Should have gone fishing."

As Grant leaned on the counter in the elegant, stately bathroom, he was surprised by how much better throwing up made him feel. He went out to the sleeping area of the room, noticing the refinements there, the embellishment that seemed to decorate every square foot. The fabric on the furniture, the pillows that seemed to be everywhere and that matched everything perfectly, the lamps that looked like they had been brought in from China that morning, with fresh new shades on all of them. He didn't have that many pillows in his whole house. All the art on the walls was perfectly coordinated with every color in the entire space. went back into the bathroom, hoping for and finding items housekeeping had placed on the counter. He was in luck, as mouthwash was part of the sundry line-up. He busted open the tiny, sealed bottle, took a few swigs, and swished it around in his mouth. The minty taste refreshed him. Who would have thought that the recipe for a clear head involved vomiting and a miniature bottle of mouthwash? He turned the faucet on, letting the water run until it was as cold as it was going to get, then filled his cupped hands and splashed the water on his face.

"Pretty good start," he muttered to his reflection in the mirror. "Puking … talking to everyone but Annie. Yeah, the puking was a real nice touch."

Grant left his room and made his way back towards the bar, admiring the antique furniture that seemed to be everywhere. He stopped in front of one of the hallway pieces and looked it over. He pulled out one of the drawers part-way, and bent down to look underneath it. He pushed and pulled on the drawer until he finally pulled it completely out of the piece. He looked at the sides and muttered something about it being "good dovetail." A hotel employee startled him, asking him, if you please, sir, what are you doing to this armoire?

A brief exchange ensued, regarding the craftsmanship and quality of the work done on the piece. Grant reflected aloud on the irony of the fact that he couldn't get his life in order, but he did know about working with wood.

"Could you direct me back to the bar?" Grant said.

The man was now placing the drawer back into the hole in the piece. "I can take you there, sir," the man replied.

"No need. You can just tell me. Not quite sure how I got turned around. Well, I am, but…."

"I'm going that way anyway, sir, and it would be my pleasure."

"Thanks. Course, you might just be looking after the furniture."

"Sir?"

"Nothing. What's your name?"

"Fausto. My name is Fausto," the man answered. "What's your name, sir?"

"Grant."

"Welcome, Señor Grant."

"Thanks. This is quite a place. I don't get to places like this much. Or ever, for that matter. Guess I'm not supposed to take the furniture apart, am I?"

"I am sorry, sir. We recently had some students from the universities here and they were not the best of guests. I should not have been so disrespectful of you. Please forgive me," the man said, now embarrassed.

"Hey, no need to apologize. Did you say universities? College kids stay at the Ritz? Hell, I used to sleep in my car, or on the ground ... which is still a possibility for this weekend, actually," Grant said, looking out the window.

They made their way back to the bar, passing more pieces of wooden furniture in the lobby, and dining areas. Grant paused to look at almost every piece of furniture along the way.

"I never know so many things about the furnitures. You know so much," Fausto said, admiringly.

"Love working with wood. May be the only thing I'm good at," Grant said, scratching his head.

"Could I help you with anything else?"

"Not unless you can go in there and talk with the three ladies in there for me," Grant said.

"Tres?"

"Si, tres."

"No Señor Grant, I have trouble talking with just one. You are here to see the three women?" Fausto said, his eyes open very wide.

"Well, not really ... sort of. It is, well, I came to see an old friend, and hopefully a woman. I didn't know about the other two. That doesn't make sense, does it?"

"Not to me, but maybe to you," Fausto said, his head turned to one side.

"Well, my life doesn't make sense to me, either, so you're not alone," Grant said.

"I suppose."

"Me too, for what that's worth. Thanks for the tour, nice to meet you. Maybe I will see you around."

"Thank you, Señor Grant, and watch out for the making the women loco-mad."

"You want to tell me about your pals down at the other end of the bar?" Rex asked Isobelle, his gaze on the women a short distance away.

Annie and Kat glanced at each other.

"Are you sure he is with you?" Isobelle said, looking at Annie and Kat.

"I wouldn't even begin to know how to answer that," Annie said.

"I do," Kat said.

"No Kat, it's not necessary."

"I have time," Isobelle said.

"Annie, here, used to go with the man, Grant, who left. This one here, big mouth, is Grant's friend. Apparently, they are a package deal, and no matter how much Grant might disappoint you, this one can make you absolutely furious. Great combination, huh?"

Rex looked back to the group.

"Kat. That short for … what, Katrina?"

"Yes," Kat answered

"That's Greek. You're blonde."

"Yes. My name is Katrina Ballas, but everyone calls me Kat. There are blonde people of Greek descent."

"I'm just messing with you about the hair, but you should have said something sooner, Katrina Ballas, I would have ordered Metaxa. I would love to get a good Metaxa buzz going," Rex said, looking back and forth, between Kat, and the women at the other end.

"What does Metaxa taste like?" Annie asked.

"Can't remember, I was drunk," Rex smiled.

Annie, Kat, and Isobelle chuckled at Rex's comment.

"See what I mean?" Kat squinted.

"What's funny?" Rex held his arms up.

"You, but in a different way than you probably think," Kat patted him.

"Ok, so are you going with the good looking, quiet one now?" Isobelle asked.

"No," Annie said.

"She's seeing someone else, these two don't know about that," Kat whispered.

"I … you don't…." Annie blushed.

"You should have a drink, Annie. I mean if we are going to spend all our time with this one, it might help." Kat said.

"Yes, can I get you something?" Isobelle asked.

"No, thank you, I'm fine."

"He'll be back in a minute, so don't worry," Rex said, suddenly engaging with the group again. "Don't base your decision to drink or not on whether or not Grant is coming back. Me, I'm on vacation. I'm going to drink regardless. I am glad to see you, Annie, even though I know you never liked me much. Grant is glad to see you, too. Oh, and I like your friend here."

"I never said that I didn't—" Annie started to say, but Rex cut her off.

"Look, even though I am not as smart as your doctor comrade here—tell me what do doctors do again?—I am smart enough to know you just sort of, I don't know, maybe toler—"

"Stop it, Rex. It was all a long time ago, and the main thing is we are where we are now. Back then was … it was…."

"Was a lot of fun, and you know it," Rex said, looking straight at Annie, challenging her to disagree.

"Well, it was…."

"It was fun, don't deny it. It was a helluva lot of fun."

"It was…."

"It was fun," Rex said determinedly, emphasizing every syllable.

Annie turned back towards the entrance to the bar, where Grant was re-entering.

"Yes, it was fun," Annie said quietly.

"I knew it!" Rex said, slamming his hand down on the top of the bar.

Grant had quietly returned to the bar, but jerked back as Rex's hand hit the bar, clearly startled. He tilted his head as he approached the table, easing back into the chair.

"You starting things here in the bar?" Grant sat back in his chair.

"They started it, they are picking on me! Can you imagine that?" Rex said.

"Somehow I can imagine them doing something, but 'picking on you' probably isn't the phrasing I would use," Grant said.

"The friend, she's pretty sharp. And not that Annie's not sharp, we all know that she is smarter than us. By us, I mean me and Grant. Well, Grant for sure," Rex said.

"No explanation needed," Kat responded.

"Agreed," Isobelle said.

The group all turned to look at her.

"But what do I know?" Isobelle said, suddenly embarrassed that she had been listening in to their conversation. Trying to save face, she sputtered, "She seems very smart to me."

Annie laughed quietly to herself, seeming more relieved than before. "Everything all right, Grant? Rex told me you were in an accident," Annie said, touching him on the arm.

"Yep, could have done without that. What did I miss here?" Grant asked, trying to change the subject.

"Are you sure you are all right?" Annie looked worried.

"A little bunged up, but I'm upright."

"Well, your friend here was just charming us while you were away," Kat said.

"Really? I wasn't gone long enough for Rex to become charming. We're only here for the weekend, and that would take several millenniums."

CHAPTER 7

"Well, I suppose that in certain circumstances he could be charming, but I have yet to encounter any of those circumstances. Then again, I've only been around him a short time," Kat said.

"He is amazing. We know that," Isobelle said.

"You know that because he told you that he was amazing," Grant put his hands together.

"Exactly!" Kat did the same.

"He has that capability," Grant wiggled his fingers.

"To be amazing?" Kat trying to sound startled.

"No, to tell you he is amazing," Grant retorted.

"Well, he did."

"Ah."

"So now let's hear about you," Kat opened her hands in Grant's direction.

"About me?" Grant asked.

"Yes, about you. It sounds like you've had an eventful day."

"Well, yes. Having somebody run a red light and plow into me was not on my list of things to do."

"Well, I'm glad to hear you're okay, at least. But we all want to know what you have been doing lately. Isn't this the part of the program where we wonder how we all managed to get here together at this moment in time?" Kat asked.

"Oh, maybe," Grant moved his head slightly. He still wasn't feeling great.

"Then let's hear it," Kat turned her palms up.

"I work, I work out … you know."

"That's it?"

"Well, I guess so. I ride my bike a lot, swim," Grant looked down. He didn't have a big story to tell. "Oh, and woodworking. I make furniture. Oh, and I like to fish."

"We all exercise. Well, maybe not him," Kat said, pointing at Rex, "but the woodworking thing, and the fishing, that sounds cool. I bet you don't exercise, or do anything cool," she said to Rex.

Rex laughed, looking back down to the end of the bar where the other women were, then again to the couple with the sunglasses in the corner, then back to the group.

"I work. Satisfied? Hey, you notice anything odd about those two over in the corner?" Rex asked.

"I thought you were interested in the two at the end of the bar. This is just fascinating, both of you. Annie is probably beside herself to learn these revelations about you two." Kat tilted her head back, opening her eyes wide.

Annie again was laughing to herself, and her face seemed to show a great deal more peace than discomfort. She was happier now that Grant was back.

"What does he keep looking at?" Grant asked.

Annie and Kat looked at each other, and then both motioned with their heads towards the other end of the bar, to where the other two women were seated.

"Ah, I see," Grant said.

"Local, how do you say … gold diggers," Isobelle said, looking at Grant just a little more than she was the others. "I know nothing about the other two."

"Any chance we could get them to hit him with the shovel while they are digging?" Grant asked.

"Perhaps I could propose that."

"Grant?" Kat persisted.

"What?" Grant asked.

"Let's hear more about you. I'm sure Annie would like to know. I know I do."

Annie blushed slightly, but pushed ahead. "Yeah, how is everything? Rex tells us you are thinking about starting a business with him."

"He said that?"

"Yes. He said you were talking about it just today," Annie said, looking at Grant in a way that suggested she wanted him to say this was not the case.

"Well, uh, we were … it was mentioned, I guess."

"That would be, umm, really something, if you worked with Rex, Grant," Annie said. The hesitation in her voice made it clear that she was anything but excited at the prospect of Rex and Grant starting a business together.

"You had better tell the bartender when she gets back, because she also seems to be is quite interested in what you do," Kat added.

"What?" Grant said.

"It wouldn't be the first time someone was interested in you—" Annie stopped herself, wishing she hadn't said it.

Grant leaned forward, staring at her, as if he was trying to bore a hole into her soul.

"I never …" He started, feeling the need to defend himself.

"I know you didn't. I'm sorry I said anything." Annie paused. "So, business is good?"

"Ok. Constant. What about you?"

"The same. Nothing to talk about."

"Too modest. Always modest. I still want to know," Grant said.

"Me too," Rex chimed in.

"What about you?" Grant asked, turning to Kat, though he kept his eyes fixed on Annie until the last possible minute, when he turned to Kat, waiting for her answer. His body was still facing Annie, his hands on the bar, pointed in Annie's direction.

"Ask her to tell you the difference between a doctor and a lawyer, and then guess which one she is," Rex said.

"Annie and I have been friends a long time. I'm a psychiatrist. I work at a clinic in La Jolla, and I…." Kat said.

"You live in La Jolla?" Grant asked.

"Yes." Kat shook her head, as trying to shift from describing her work to where she lived was funny to her.

"Not far from me, I live in Encinitas," Grant said.

"I love both places," Kat said.

"She wants me to meet her relatives," Rex leaned in.

"Nobody wants you to meet their relatives," Grant glanced at him.

Annie started laughing, out loud, which she seldom did. Everyone looked at her, surprised, but she just shrugged and grinned.

Isobelle had been following the conversation as closely as she could. She was enjoying listening to Annie and Kat, but her facial expressions when she looked toward the other end of the bar, clearly showed disdain for the two women. But Rex's interest in the other women did please her, as she thought it might remove him as a possible obstacle. Isobelle didn't know whether to warn Rex about the two women, or to let him find out on his own. After a few minutes, she decided that letting him find out the hard way would probably keep him busy and out of the way longer.

"Moll and Mag," Isobelle said.

"What?" Rex asked.

"Moll and Mag, the women at the other end of the bar, those are their names. At least, that's what they call themselves. They asked me to send you a drink," Isobelle said, looking at Rex. This was not true. The women had not sent a drink to Rex.

"And you're just now getting around to doing it?" Rex exclaimed, motioning with his hands.

"Sorry. I will make it for you now," Isobelle said.

"Well ... you send them one from me," Rex said, straightening up in his chair.

"Very good," she said as she moved to prepare the drinks.

"Things are looking up. You all might have to try to do without me for awhile, while I go talk to my adoring fans down there," Rex said, beaming.

Annie was now noticing Isobelle's attention to Grant. It was almost as if she was a little jealous, and it gave her pause, as she realized this was the first time she was ever jealous of someone else and Grant. There were no flirtatious moves, just a keen sense of paying attention to all of Grant's actions. She would expect that from Kat, as she was a psychiatrist, but that would be for different reasons. She doubted Isobelle was a psychiatrist. Grant had never been a womanizer—in fact, in the past, he paid attention to no one but Annie. But now, she could tell, he was definitely noticing Isobelle.

"Well, don't you worry about us," Kat said.

"I assure you, he isn't," Grant responded.

Annie laughed again.

"This is kind of nice, seeing you laugh like this, Annie," Kat said.

"I laugh."

"Not usually this much."

Annie again blushed, still smiling.

"You know, we have to go, to meet some other people...." Annie said, her voice trailing off. She wished she had not said it.

"Oh," Grant said, looking disappointed.

"Well … when we were planning this thing, we weren't really sure…." Annie said, seeming not sure how to finish the sentence, and still be polite.

"Weren't really sure that Rex would show up at all? Or that I would be here either?"

"No! I mean, no it's not like that. Well, maybe Rex, but not you."

"You all can thank me later for making this come together," Rex said, still looking at the women at the end of the bar.

"If only we can figure out how to thank you appropriately. A parade, perhaps?" Kat said.

"I have some ideas about how you could thank me. Hadn't thought of a parade, but we could do that after," Rex replied.

"But we could meet back up, after we see our friends, couldn't we?" Annie asked. It was a struggle for her to get the words out.

"You mean your better friends?" Rex added brusquely.

"That's not fair," Annie said, her tone changing.

"Who said anything about fair?" Rex asked.

"Look, it just sort of happened …" Annie said.

"That would be great, Annie. Whatever works for you," Grant said.

"You'd better meet up with us later, or your friend, Zorba here, is going to miss me way too much. Plus, the bartender might jump Grant, so I'm just giving you fair warning," Rex said.

"I feel like I want to miss you more," Kat replied.

"See? Great, isn't she?" Rex smiled, patting Kat on the shoulder.

The group all got a laugh at the exchange. Annie looked at Grant, though Rex's comment about the bartender was not something she seemed to want to hear. Annie and Kat got up to leave.

"So we'll get together later?" Grant asked.

"Yes, I would like that," Annie said.

"So would your buddy," Rex chimed in.

"Wouldn't miss it," Kat said.

"Well, thanks for coming. At all. No, I mean it," Grant said, not quite believing he had actually phrased it right.

"I'm glad we're here, and I'm glad you're all right," Annie said.

"Of course you're glad you're here, 'cause I'm here," Rex added.

"That's the reason!" Kat said.

"Listen, we'll see you in a little while. Just take it easy. Even though you think you're all right, a car wreck is a traumatic thing, so just go slow, all right? Don't let Rex drag you into anything too crazy," Annie said.

"Just being around people is enough of a traumatic experience for him, so I can't promise he will make it through," Rex chuckled, looking down towards the other end of the bar.

"I'll be fine," Grant said.

"Of course you will. I'm counting on it," Annie said, smiling at Grant. Grant smiled back. Was she flirting with him?

"Don't go putting extra pressure on him, you're just asking for trouble," Rex added.

"Well, let's put some pressure on you, and ask you to be nice, and to be quiet. You think you can do that for us?" Kat asked, looking at Rex.

"Can I still drink?" Rex asked.

"Yes."

"Chase women?"

"Yes, just not us," Kat said.

"Then I think we're good."

"Good. We have to go. We'll see you later," Kat said.

At that, Annie and Kat turned and left the bar. Isobelle was watching from the other end, and Kat and Annie waved at her as they left. Isobelle smiled and waved back at them. Annie was relieved that the initial meeting with Grant, after all this time, had gone as well as it did, considering how close they had been and how long it had been since they had seen each other. She did not hold any bad feelings towards Grant and seeing him, even for this short time, was good for her.

Kat was happy with the meeting. She had heard a great deal about Grant and Rex from Annie. She was curious to meet Rex, to see if anyone could be quite like Annie had described him, but she was more interested in meeting Grant, and in being there for Annie. Grant and Rex did not appear to be people who would create any real problems for the weekend, and if they did, she and Annie could spend time with their other friends, away from these two.

Grant felt less nervous than he had before he had purged himself in his room, but his body was still sore from the wreck. He was glad to see Annie and watched her gentle, confident stride until she was out of sight. He still cared for her deeply, there was no denying that. He could have done without the throwing up, but maybe it steadied him. They would return, as she had said, and they could talk more and really catch up, though he knew he would have to participate a little more in the conversation to keep her interested.

Rex was happy; being with his old friends again after his several-year-long work ordeal meant a lot to him. He showed his feelings differently than the others, so the more fun he was having, the more he lined up for the verbal joust. He was also thinking about the ladies down at the other end of the bar. He didn't think a diversion like that would detract from the meeting with his old friends. The man and the woman with the sunglasses did make him feel uneasy. After all the things that had happened, though, he would not have been surprised if someone were watching him.

Isobelle was happy. She liked Grant's stature and grace, his quiet composure even in the face of a car wreck and his over-eager friend, and his gentle way of speaking to his friends. Given the quiet type of person Grant seemed to be, and the short amount of time she had to work with, she knew it wouldn't be easy, but she was determined to get to know him better. She felt that things were going to work out just fine.

CHAPTER 8

"How long we known each other?" Rex asked Grant.

"Since high school, something like that."

"When did we meet Annie?"

"In college."

"How long ago was that?"

"Oh," Grant paused, thinking.

"I'm making a point here. As much as we've tried to avoid it, we're older now. She was with some friend of hers when we met her in college. I'm not sure why I remember that."

"Yeah, and you pushed yourself on them, ruined their day, as I remember. Probably ruined Annie's life, if you were to ask her."

"Not all of her life," Rex smiled.

"Just part of it. Still a serious offense."

"Hey, she wasn't doing anything, you weren't doing anything, what did it hurt? Look, if I hadn't have intruded on Annie's life that day, you would have been doing nothing, all by yourself, all those years you were together, instead of doing things with her."

"I don't know about that," Grant said.

"I do."

"You and I raised a fair amount of hell, it's not like you were cheated," Grant said.

"That we did, but you sort of got religion after you met her."

"Religion?"

"Well, let's just say you were not wanting to risk things as much after you two got together," Rex said.

"I can't be a screw up like you my entire life."

"But you missed it, and came around eventually."

"Missed what?" Grant asked.

"All the wacky shit we used to do."

"Look where that got me. I'm here now, talking to you, and she's—with someone else."

"She's going to meet her real friends. But, I promise you, she's asking herself right now why she left, when what she really wanted was to be here," Rex said.

"You don't know that."

"Yes I do. Just because I don't want to be around the same woman as long as you do doesn't mean I don't catch a vibe now and again."

"How 'bout you catch a vibe to the jaw?" Grant said, draining his glass.

"I think you should get your new girlfriend to bring you another drink. How those drinks working with your pain meds?"

"Wonderfully. Better since I threw up, I hope," Grant said quietly.

"Look, how long has it been since you were sitting in a bar, talking with an—no, no, sorry, talking with two, no, three attractive women?"

"You'd better drink up, you're not quite drunk enough yet."

"I think two of them actually like you. The Greek girl, she's hard to read. I like her, but she's got an edge on her," Rex said.

"Like you don't? You an expert on women now, I guess? You, of the 'love-'em, use-'em, mostly abuse-'em' brigade?"

"Never said I wanted to settle down like you did.. You became right respectable there for a while when you were with Annie. Now … you're just a goddamn hermit."

"You just like raising hell."

"So do you, but you liked the girl more."

Grant leaned back in his chair, looking around the bar. He hadn't really stopped to look around this part of the hotel, as Rex had been talking when they walked in, and Isobelle caught his eye immediately when he saw her. Annie and Kat came shortly thereafter, and then he had to go upstairs and throw up. A two-hour drive, a car crash, a hospital visit, and a reunion with two very old friends made him think he had covered quite a bit of ground in a very short time. Maybe now it was catching up to him. He hoped he wasn't going to be sick again.

The bar was like the rest of the hotel. It was old looking, dark wood. Not the kind of thing you would normally see in the desert, but more like the boardroom of an old law firm somewhere in New York or Chicago. He thought again of the small motel he and Annie had stayed in the first time they were in Palm Springs. It was simple, like his life then. He could see the small pool, the lounge chairs, Annie. He shook his head to clear his mind. He needed to think about the hotel he was at now. Annie was here.

Grant was sure that the Ritz was not a new experience for Rex, but Rex wouldn't notice things like the interior, the manicured grounds outside. Usually Rex would only be looking for his next adventure. Although, perhaps his recent brush with the law had siphoned some of the swagger out of him. Grant certainly hoped so. He glanced at Isobelle, and his thoughts shifted. He admired the way the darkness of the wood perfectly framed Isobelle's olive-brown skin, with her white, starched shirt.

"Are you listening to me?" Rex asked.

"Not usually, if I can help it," Grant said without looking at Rex.

Isobelle returned from the other end of the bar, bringing a drink for Rex. "Here you are," Isobelle said.

"I wanna meet 'em," Rex said quickly.

"Is that so?"

"Yes, it is. I can't sit here and waste my time with this goober all day. If I go down there, will you introduce me?"

"Of course."

"And … "

"And what?"

"And you will keep my friend here company while I go talk to the lovely ladies at the other end? Not that you're not lovely, too."

"Of course," Isobelle smiled.

"See why I picked this hotel? They even provide baby sitters. What about those two over in the corner?" Rex asked, looking at the man and the woman in sunglasses.

"What about them?"

"Do you know them?"

"No, I do not, why do you ask?"

"They just look out of place, don't you think?"

"That is hard to say. It is a resort hotel. We get all kinds of people in here. Like you, for instance," Isobelle said, still smiling.

"Are they watching me?" Rex asked.

"They are wearing sunglasses. I cannot tell where they are looking. Why might they be looking at you?"

"Long story."

Grant watched Isobelle as she was talking with Rex. Seeing Annie again made him feel great, in spite of how his body felt from the car wreck. Before, when he had been en route, still uncertain if Annie was even going to show up at all, he hadn't been at all sure how he would feel, but he found it an energizing experience. His attempts at amity with other women had all gone badly, or had not gone anywhere at all. It always came back to their comparison with Annie, which always fell short. Trouble was, he was still in love with her, which he had hoped was not the case.

He had been all this time trying to put his feelings behind him, trying to forget what had happened, trying to get on with his life, miserable as it was. Seeing her walk into the bar today made all his aches disappear. Her tanned skin, her fit body, her smile that would make you forget where you were, what you were doing. Her shiny blonde hair invited you out in the sun, to be where she had been. Her blue eyes told you everything was going to be all right. The thought that he might be seeing her for the last time just made him lonelier. Now, he had to deal with his feelings for Annie all over again. He had to move on.

Talking with Rex again was a help. Even though Rex could be difficult at times, he still brought back a lot of memories, some of which he had been trying to suppress, or dislodge completely, but it was refreshing to have them brought to the surface of his mind. Grant kept his gaze on Isobelle.

"Listen, I'm going to have one more drink with you, and then I'm going to go see if those ladies at the other end of the bar want to fight over me."

"They probably want to fight with you. Why wait?" Isobelle said.

"Hey, are you getting any of this?" Rex said, looking at Grant.

"What?" Grant asked.

"Still not the bright one. You'd still be moping around whatever shithole you are living in now if it weren't for me. You certainly wouldn't have a shot at a couple of good looking women sitting there alone at your place, now would you?" Rex asked.

"My place isn't a shithole, you've never been there, you wouldn't know."

"That's not the point. The point is, you would be doing nothing, like always."

"You don't know what I'm doing," Grant said.

"I know what you're doing now, and you wouldn't be here at all if I hadn't put this thing together."

"You always...."

"Don't hit me with absolutes," Rex said.

"Why don't you come with me, and I will introduce you to your new friends?" Isobelle interrupted.

"Annie's parents haven't liked me since I missed that flight that time. You, you didn't get me to the airport in time to make the flight," Grant stammered.

"Where the hell did that come from? You still carrying that shit around with you after all this fucking time? You were the one who told me her parents never liked you."

"It probably was a turning point with Annie. You never showed up to take me to the airport, and with the weather ... I couldn't get another flight, and they all left on a ski vacation. They never approved of me after that," Grant said.

"Well...."

"I didn't come from money, like Annie did. She had been groomed to do what she was doing, and they didn't want someone to derail the plans they had for her, certainly not someone without the background, without the money," Grant said. Isobelle was standing behind the bar, waiting for Rex to come with her, awkwardly caught in the middle of this heated exchange. Neither Rex nor Grant seemed to take any notice of her.

"Well, it wasn't hard to fall out of favor with them, because you were never in their favor. You can't haul that missed plane thing around with you, when it wouldn't have mattered anyway. The cards were already stacked against you. She may have liked you, but they weren't going to let her be with someone like you," Rex said.

"Yeah, I suppose ... sorry I brought it up."

"Damn right, we talked about it before, but it didn't matter. It wasn't that it was you. They had somebody different in mind. Probably would have been nice if she would have told them 'piss off, it's my life, and it's none of your goddamn business,' but that's another story." Rex let out a loud breath. "You think she's perfect, but she let them get into her fucking head, and that probably did more to shit-can the relationship than any of the creative forms of self-expression you and I came up with."

Grant let out a loud breath. Rex's statement made sense. "You and me streaking at that school function that Annie and her parents were at probably didn't help much either, you think?"

"No, I think that really would have helped if you had told them it was you!" They both started to laugh. "That didn't help with Annie, maybe we should call them now and tell them," Rex laughed.

They were both really laughing now.

Isobelle stood silently behind the bar, perplexed. She was trying to follow their conversation, which seemed to go from surprise, to anger, to laughter in a matter of mere seconds.

"Yeah, always making the right decisions back then," Grant said, shaking his head.

"Think about the time you borrowed that guy's truck and we went goose hunting," Rex said.

"And drove off the road and into the lake...."

"I can take you down there now," Isobelle tried to interrupt again, but Grant and Rex seemed not to hear.

"And you bet me I couldn't hit that goose while we were sinking. Pretty easy twenty bucks I made. Bet that guy is still pissed about his truck," Rex said.

"I'm still pissed about having to pay you the twenty bucks."

"I think I still have that twenty."

"Cheap bastard," Grant said.

"No, I just always wanted to have it to rub in your face."

"How about you stealing the flower shop delivery van?"

"Or you stealing that motorcycle?" Rex asked.

"Saved your ass from the campus cops with that motorcycle."

"Yeah, that was pretty funny. Driving it through that wedding party in the park was funnier."

"Felt bad about gettin' all that mud on the dresses, tuxes and such," Grant said.

"No you didn't."

"I might have."

"Probably not."

"It's funny now."

"It was funny then," Rex crunched on the ice from his drink, looking out of the bar and into the hallway.

"I suppose."

"See, these are the things you need to think about, not that shit with Annie's parents, or what you did, or didn't do right with her. After all, Annie is still here, she didn't leave town after seeing you. And she said she'd meet with us later, which is good and … Oh, here's your new girlfriend. You play your cards right, you can spend time with your new girlfriend, then spend time with your old girlfriend. Feeling really lucky, maybe you spend time with the two at the end, though I saw 'em first! May need a wingman, I don't know," Rex said.

Grant continued to laugh. Isobelle wanted to get Rex out of the way, and down to the other end of the bar, but seeing this Grant finally find the smile that had been eluding him, she could not help but smile herself.

CHAPTER 9

Isobelle could see that Grant was now in a better frame of mind, much better than before. With Annie and Kat now gone, she could focus more of her attention on Grant. Whether he knew it or not, just by giving him someone to talk to, she was helping him be more comfortable. Now, finally, she would have a chance to talk to him. Grant's interaction with Isobelle would not have been so positive a year ago, a week ago, a day ago. Seeing Annie again gave him confidence. Badgering Rex gave him recollection of better times. These things alone had propped up his conviction and self-esteem, which had been missing for quite a while. The energy he felt from Isobelle when he shook hands with her and when he listened to her speak was thrilling. The fact that she had somehow known he had been in an accident without having been told was astounding. He wanted to know more about her, but even this surprised him: The idea that he might want to know anything about anyone other than Annie was new.

Rex began to make eye contact with Moll and Mag, who smiled back at him.

"So, would you like me to serve your drink down at the other end of the bar?" Isobelle asked.

"I think that would be a good idea. Though it took a few minutes to loosen up, I think I'm working my usual magic in making things happen, so he's all yours," Rex said.

"Well, I hope my drinks were of assistance as well, even though you certainly did all the heavy lifting. You do still seem to be talking, however, which is not what we agreed upon."

"I don't think I agreed on that no talking part, I think that was your deal," Rex added.

"I am not so sure we did not have an agreement, though if you are moving to the other end of the bar, it is of little consequence now," Isobelle said, looking at Grant.

"My work here is done for now, but someone has to keep an eye on him. You think you're up to that?"

"Yes!" Isobelle said, a little too enthusiastically.

"Wow, that was quick."

"Sorry, I am only trying to be helpful," Isobelle said.

"I'm not going to the other end of the bar with you. You can mess that up all by yourself. I'll probably go for a swim while you go strike out with those two," Grant said.

"I am having dinner with some friends later at La Casuela's. Would you care to join us?" Isobelle said, looking at Grant.

"Sure, we'd love to," Rex answered.

"I assumed you would be busy with those two, down there, so I was asking him," Isobelle said, looking at Grant

"I know. We'd love to, anyway. What time and where?" Rex said, trading glances with Isobelle, and the women at the other end of the bar.

"I think I'm meeting Annie and Kat later, but I'm not sure about you," Grant said.

"Well, perhaps another time then?" Isobelle responded.

"No, relax, tonight's good. The more the merrier, we'll be there, but I'm ready to meet your friends at the end of the bar now," Rex said, looking at Isobelle.

"I think you said that already," Isobelle answered, "but let's go."

"See ya, probably at the pool, we can talk more there," Rex said.

"Right, because it's always easier to talk when I'm under water. Should have thought of that sooner. How about if I hold you under water and see what you have to say?" Grant asked.

"You know it, chief!" Rex got up from his bar stool and moved with Isobelle towards the women at the other end. Grant was reminded that Rex's attention span had never been very long. He would not be surprised if he didn't see Rex the rest of the time they were here. He would just call and say that he had to deal with something important, and that he wouldn't be able to make it back. This had happened so many times Grant couldn't keep track any more. Rex's recent brush with the law was the only time he actually had an excuse that sounded plausible.

There was so much going on in Grant's head that he thought his skull might actually spring a leak. So much time had passed since he had seen Annie. He had thought of nothing but work, with the occasional fits of remorse about Annie, and now here it was more than just a fit. He was thinking about her even more. The unbelievable part was she was here, in this town, and presumably staying in this hotel. Even though he had stumbled a little at the beginning of the meeting, he thought maybe he was going to be all right now.

"You do not look like a golfer. Tennis, maybe, unless you can put spikes on those cowboy boots," Isobelle said, as she had returned without Grant noticing.

"What? Oh … you noticed my boots? Friend of mine made them for me," Grant raised his leg up to bring the heel to rest on the bar. "Did a damn fine job, too."

Isobelle pushed his pant leg up to expose the entire boot and looked at them closely, not offended by the casual way he put his boot up on the bar.

"Nice work. Your friend must be a fine artist. I like the silver conchos at the top, adds an older, more sophisticated look to them … not trashy like the outlet stores. I don't see many really fine boots anymore."

"You know boots," Grant said admiringly, lowering his heel and leg off the bar, not bothering to pull the pant leg back down to cover the top.

"Yes, my father is a boot maker," she said proudly raising her leg to let the heel come to rest on the bar, as Grant had done. She was standing however, so it was a bit more difficult for her. She quickly realized what she had done and looked around to see if anyone was watching. She didn't lower the boot until Grant had completed the same inspection she had performed on his footwear.

"Very nice, good work," he said.

"Great work, and thank you," she said, now bringing her leg back to the floor.

"How'd you do that without falling?"

"My mother was a flamingo."

Grant smiled and laughed. "How did you do that other thing earlier? That thing where you knew about my accident, without me having told you."

Isobelle's expression changed. "I was out of … it was not my place to say that. I am sorry."

"No need to be sorry, I thought it was pretty amazing. How do you do it?"

A group of hotel guests descended on the bar, and it suddenly got louder. Grant's trance was broken with the interruption, and Isobelle was uncomfortable answering his question. The newcomers were golfers, from the looks of them. It was not so much that they were wearing golf attire, but more like they were wearing après golf attire. If it had been a contest to see who could don the most tartan, it would have been a dead heat. If someone could produce a plaid hat, or plaid earrings, he would be declared the winner. Grant started watching the checkered ensemble and began to laugh.

"This the standard attire around here? You should have said something, I would have gone somewhere and picked out a table cloth to wear in here, or maybe some old car seats," Grant said.

"You are terrible. Keep it down, they might hear you. I am amazed that someone can be so moved by plaid, but if it inspires you to talk, I consider it a good sign."

"I don't think they could hear anything over the noise of those get ups. Must be some sort of checkered circus in town. Hell, for all I know, a place like this always has a checkered circus in town. You don't dress like that when you're not here, do you?"

"Yes, I do. I have been struggling with my addiction to plaid my entire life. It's right up there with talking to strange bar patrons in nice cowboy boots," Isobelle said.

"You should get some professional help."

"For which affliction?"

"Both afflictions," Grant was speaking to her, but watching the plaid party and laughing.

"I was kidding about the clothing part, but I definitely need to combat my addiction to talking to people like you. I see no good can come from it."

"Based on the ability you showed me earlier, I think you know otherwise, but would you feel better if I went out and got a checkered shirt or something?"

"Maybe you should have your friend make you a pair of plaid cowboy boots."

"He-yah!" Grant said loudly, and all the members of the tartan clan turned abruptly to look at him.

"You are something," Isobelle said, trying hard to hold back her own laughter.

"Don't usually try to be, just works out that way."

"I've got to go in a few minutes," Isobelle whispered, "but I would like to see you later. I do not mean to intrude, I just think it might be fun. I don't know if around seven would be all right for you. Remember, the dinner I spoke of earlier?"

"Yes, I think so. Well, no, but thank you. Actually I am hoping to meet someone later. I could use a recommendation on a good place to go around here—not that this isn't a good place."

"I understand. Well, perhaps we will run into each other."

"Maybe another night?"

"Perhaps. For now, I will leave a note for you with some places, how would that be?" Isobelle asked.

"That would be very nice of you."

"It is my pleasure. I will see you again soon," Isobelle said, touching Grant's hand.

Grant again felt the energy from her touch. He did not want to let go. If he could hold on, he thought, maybe he could determine how the energy radiated. Isobelle was more than happy to satisfy his curiosity, and made no attempt to let go.

"How do you do that, I mean that run the electricity through your hand stuff?" Grant asked.

"You should come to the restaurant later. I believe you will learn more of what you seek on this journey."

"Really?"

"Most certainly. I will leave the restaurant information for you. Thank you for coming in today."

"What about the check?"

"I have taken care of the check."

"You don't need to do that."

"It is my pleasure to take care of someone like you. It is not often, if ever, that this occurs," Isobelle said.

"I'll say."

"Good. Be there later," Isobelle said, as she released his hand and walked away.

Grant had no idea what to say. It had been quite a day already, was all he could think.

He glanced around the bar one last time after Isobelle disappeared from view. Grant felt a peacefulness that did not seem to be even remotely associated with his drink, or the pain medicine. It was clearer and lighter than that, more composed than either of those things would let him be. He felt a strange force compelling him to obey Isobelle's orders, to meet her later that night. He gathered his thoughts and decided he wouldn't be able to bring himself to go down to the other end of the bar and wade into Rex's welcome wagon routine. With both Isobelle and Annie gone, he suddenly wanted to be gone himself. He left the bar and went back to his room to prepare for the swim. He could use the swimming time to get a handle on everything that had transpired. Annie had seemed much less upset or worried about their meeting than he thought she might be, though that wasn't really the term for it. More importantly, she did not appear to be uncomfortable, which was more than he could say for himself.

"Doubt very seriously that she threw up."

Grant returned to his room to change and get out to the pool.

"The people at the hospital who checked me out after the wreck didn't tell me I couldn't swim, so it must be all right. Hell, it might actually help," he thought. He changed quickly and headed back out through the hotel, not stopping for furniture investigations this time around. He was hoping to avoid getting sucked into Rex's harem starter kit and just to get out to the pool unnoticed.

He was glad to be outside, even as warm as it was. He would be at home in the water, as he always was, and though his day had started poorly, it had continued into several drinks and strong portions of emotions, and been mixed with good company. He was glad he was not at the bar with the women Rex had decided to pester. He had enough to focus on with seeing Annie again and meeting Isobelle. It was impossible not to think about her. He wanted to find out about the current that seemed to be flowing through her, and how she knew about what had happened to him.

He made his way over to a chair by the pool and sat down to further survey the poolside layout. There was a true calm about the place. The far-away din of an occasional vehicle and the low hum of the water misters were the only sounds he could hear. No one was in the water and he was thinking about going in when a member of the staff shook him out of his reverie.

"Cold towel, sir?"

"Hah!" Grant laughed. "You're kidding me."

"No sir, the guests find them very refreshing, along with the chilled strawberries. Would you care for some of those as well?"

"You are kidding, aren't you?" Grant was amazed at the thought of this. "Don't mean to be a yokel, or anything, I just never … well, sure, what the hell, load me up," Grant said chuckling.

"Very good, sir. I see you do not have a regular towel. Let me bring you a large pool towel instead," The man said, turning to see to his task.

"Maybe some mint for the juleps later," Grant said, smiling. The man turned back towards Grant.

"I would be happy to bring you some mint, sir."

"Thank you, but I was kidding," Grant said. "You would do that?"

"Certainly."

"I'm all right for now."

"Very good, sir." The man left, leaving a small, chilled towel and a small plate of chilled strawberries.

"Cutting a fat hog," Grant muttered to himself.

He sat there by the pool, taking it all in. He thought about the small hotel again, he and Annie enjoying the simplicity. This immense pool area of the Ritz was a huge contrast. He removed his shirt, shorts and sandals, making his way over to the water. He stretched his arms skyward, palms raised, then bent forward, leaning over and grabbing the edge of the pool with both hands, hovering over the edge. He sprang forward out of a perfect Olympic-style crouch and into the water. He glided along for a few seconds and began to swim a few butterfly strokes before he realized that maybe a more slow and easy pace might be a better tonic for someone who had been in an accident that day. Just being in the water would help.

"Sure glad I had those drinks," he thought.

He switched to the back stroke, continuing to think. He was hoping to wash away the car wreck. It was going to be a hassle getting his truck fixed, but there was nothing he could do about that. He was alive, and he thought that a plus. He looked up at the desert sky from his relaxed position in the water. The joy he felt at seeing Annie again was indescribable. Even if she had run screaming from the bar, fleeing the hotel, never to return, he still loved her, difficult as that was for him to resolve.

CHAPTER 10

"That was pretty quick," Kat said.

"What do you mean?" Annie asked.

"Well, we weren't there very long."

"I know. I guess we should have stayed a little longer. I honestly didn't know what to do."

"What do you mean you didn't know what to do? You always know what to do."

"It seems like it to you. I guarantee you, I don't always know what to do."

"Well, if it felt uncomfortable for you, then you did the right thing. We talked about that before we got here," Kat said.

"That's the thing that was strange."

"I don't understand."

"It was … I don't know, comfortable, and that made it … well, uncomfortable," Annie said.

"I return to my previous statement about not understanding."

"You know, you don't see somebody for a long time, no matter how close you are to them … well, you don't know how it's going to be," Annie said.

"Right, and?"

"And, gosh, so you just think it's going to be 'hi, how have you been, let's promise to keep in touch' kind of thing and…."

"You have completely lost me."

"I felt comfortable. I felt happy. It wasn't uncomfortable or awkward at all.

I suppose, in the back of my mind, I thought it was going to be uncomfortable, even though I didn't want to admit that," Annie said.

"Still looking at a different page than you are. "

"It felt fine. It felt fine, and I didn't think it would feel fine. That's what made me uncomfortable."

"Did Rex have that good looking bartender slip something in your drink?" Kat said, looking at Annie's eyes, as if to check her condition.

"She was good looking, wasn't she?"

"Kind of mystical, too, don't you think?"

"Yes, she was. And no, she didn't slip something in my drink."

"You just felt good, which … made you feel … bad?" Kat said.

"It didn't make me feel bad. I just wasn't ready."

"For what?"

"To be so happy after so long," Annie said, quietly.

Something was plinking Grant on his chest, once, twice.

"What the hell?" He stopped swimming.

Rex had decided to take his new friends out to the pool, where they were pelting Grant with ice cubes. Grant floated for a moment, then stood, wiped the water from his face, brushing his hair back to see Rex talking with other people around the pool.

"Thought we'd better check on you," Rex yelled. "This is Moll and Mag," They were all holding drinks in one hand, ice cubes in the other, the girls dropping the ice when Grant looked their way. Moll and Mag waved.

Isobelle did not like the idea of Moll and Mag going to the pool where Grant was. She was fine with them playing Rex, but she did not want them to get Grant to join that list of participants. She had a very good feeling about him, but knew she could not control everything that went on around him. She had one of the waiters follow them out to the pool to help keep an eye on things. If things started to head down the wrong direction, she could intercede to get things back on track. Isobelle paused briefly, thinking about how long it had been since she had met a man that she really liked. Being a female bartender meant the parade of suitors never stopped. The trouble was, they were suitors in their minds, and not hers. For every Grant—and she couldn't remember one even remotely like Grant—there were thousands like Rex. Now, here was someone that was not only not on the make, but clearly was conflicted internally. She saw his conviction, and thought his apparent lack of depth might just be a result of too many failures. If he was not an honorable person, he would have been after her. It was his lack of pursuit that made her want to know him even more.

Rex was having a great time. He had only been here for few hours, and he had seen his old friends together for the first time in forever, and now he was with two beautiful women who were paying a considerable amount of attention to him. He didn't care about their motivations. They weren't going to beat him at chess, so he really didn't care. He figured if they could outsmart him, maybe they deserved his money, but he wasn't that sloppy. He didn't care. It was fun. And now someone was sending him drinks, for a change, so he wasn't shy about accepting. This was as light as his life had been in a long time. He was back where he liked to be, with his friends, and holding court with people who weren't going to do him any harm. He held up the recently delivered libations.

"Compliments of your new girlfriend! Come get yours," Rex shouted.

Grant shook his head, and went back to swimming. Rex continued to try to engage Grant in conversation while he was swimming, which only made the noise level rise. Grant knew his swim was over.

Moll and Mag wanted to know why they were not included in the libation guest list, but their concern was short lived, as Rex offered to take care of their drinks poolside. The noise level continued to rise, and Rex was clearly taking great pleasure in contributing to the volume.

Grant concluded his short swim and exited the pool to head to his room. He eyed Rex's convention, passing them on his way, not wishing to stop.

"It won't kill you to have a drink with us," Rex said.

"It might."

"No way! We're harmless," said one of the women.

"Yeah, harmless," said the other.

"I doubt that's possible, considering who you're with," Grant responded.

The two girls pleaded with Grant to stay, batting their eyes and flashing perfectly-bronzed legs at him.

"Look, I don't want to be rude, but I need to be somewhere," Grant said.

"We all have someplace to be," Rex said, pointedly.

"We got places to be, too," Moll said.

"We sure do!" Mag followed.

"That's the spirit!" Rex said.

"Ok, we all have places to be. I just need to make sure I do this right … er, that I get ready—get ready in time."

"In time for what?" Moll asked.

"Are you going somewhere?" Mag asked.

Grant turned to look at Rex. His look suggested that he badly wanted to punch Rex in the chest and throw him in the pool, but chose to say nothing.

"Rex said you were nice," Moll said, with a smile that indicated she thought he was probably a lot more than just "nice".

"Real nice," Mag added. It was obvious who was the leader in their little duo.

Grant did not turn his stare away from Rex. Rex realized his own safety was no longer a guarantee.

"You got a bad case of the jitters, chief. Get the hell out of here and go get ready to meet the love of your life," Rex said.

Grant moved slowly, still not taking his eyes off of Rex, no longer hearing the girls. He would not be deterred from getting back to get cleaned up for meeting Annie later. The intellectual gap between Rex and his two new lady friends was impossible not to notice. Rex was extremely well-educated, although that didn't have any bearing on his social manners, and the women were not at all, which somehow always seemed to be part of the formula with Rex. Not one to seem snobby, Grant relaxed, ever so slightly, thinking it funny that though they certainly never won any scholarships, they probably did win a few beauty contests.

"Give credit where it's due," he said as he left the table.

Again, the desert air felt good as he walked. It always felt good to him, and he missed the hot, arid climate. It was not unlike the feeling he had of being with Annie. It was the feeling of something he had loved once upon a time, and he wondered why he had ever let it get away from him in the first place. He again entered the hotel and the frigid air-conditioned interior knocked him upside the head. He was still wet, and now freezing, and he took a moment to wonder why the thermostat was turned down to a cool sixty-three degrees when all the hotel patrons were dressed for ninety-five.

He made it back to his room and now felt very tired. He noticed a bottle of red wine on the table. He felt pretty certain that it hadn't been there earlier, but he couldn't be completely sure about anything right now. Red wine, Santa Lucia Highlands, Pinot Noir. He scratched his head, looking around, as if someone would be watching. He started to open the bottle, now noticing flowers in the room that were also not there earlier. He went ahead and accepted the generosity, and cranked a bottle opener into the cork. The sharp "pop" as the bottle opened startled him.

He poured himself a glass and looked out the balcony door towards the mountains. He shook his head, managing a half smile. He opened the sliding glass door and walked out on the balcony, relishing the sun and the warm, dry desert air. He raised his glass in a toast, towards the mountains, towards the sun, and he stood there, contentedly thinking of nothing. He blocked pieces of his past that were trying to invade his thoughts, to replace the calm view of those peaks as they began to throw their blanketed shadows over the Coachella Valley. The heat from the sun felt good against his wet hair and skin. He set down his glass and the light refracted in violet and maroon through its contents. He looked back to the desert hills, the mountains above, and the impending setting sun beyond. He had to drink it all in now. There was too much beauty here to ignore.

Grant moved slowly back through the hotel. He would go back to the bar or to the front desk to get the names of the restaurant recommendations that Isobelle had said she would leave for him.

"What could it hurt?" he thought. He would then go tell Rex where he was going and try not to get drafted by the gypsy brigade out by the pool. He owed Rex notification, if nothing else. Grant's mind was still on the colors of the sun on the mountain, coming through the glass of wine. He turned a corner and ran right into an oncoming pedestrian.

"I'm so sorr—Grant?" It was Annie.

"Uh—"

"I should have watched where I was going. Gosh, you scared me."

"Are you ok? I should have...."

"I'm fine," her face reddening, his doing the same.

"Just like me, never paying attention. Guess I haven't changed much."

"Oh, I think you might be a little hard on yourself." Annie slowly started walking, and Grant fell into step beside her, forgetting where he had been going before.

"Well, better late than never ... except in my case it probably is worse late than earlier."

Annie gave him a gentle, sympathetic smile. She always had a way of doing that, even when things were bad. If she did think things were bad, she didn't show it to Grant. That was something else that Annie had a way of doing. She never let her pain show. She was a trooper.

"I'm sorry we didn't get to talk more, you know, earlier. You doing all right these days?" she asked.

"Seem to be. Except for vehicle-wise, otherwise everything is good. I've been working the same profession for quite a while, which is pretty good for me."

Annie laughed.

"Been keepin' out of trouble, which is also pretty good for me."

"I don't believe you."

"Which part?"

"The part about trouble," Annie said, still laughing slightly.

"Nope, it's true. Work, workout, do a little wood working, repeat, that's me. Mixed in with the occasional car wreck, of course. Maybe the wreck woke me up."

"Well, the active part sounds like you, but I don't think you needed to have an awakening."

"We all need an awakening, and by 'all', I mean everyone except you," Grant said.

"Except me?"

"You were always on the right track. Still are, near as I can tell."

"Your friend claims he had an awakening, but I'm not so sure."

"Well ... Rex and I haven't seen each other in a long time, so that might have something to do with it. Not that I want to take credit for any spiritual adjustment he might be in the middle of."

"I could hardly call those two ladies at the end of the bar 'spiritual,' so should I be expecting the usual misguided pyrotechnics from Rex this weekend?" Annie asked.

"Can't speak for him for certain, but none of that from me."

"You sure?"

"I'm never really sure of anything ever, but I'm not looking to shoot off firecrackers in the lobby and ask for free drinks 'cause of the noise, if that's what you mean."

"That doesn't sound good. I mean the, 'can't speak for him for certain' part," Annie said.

"You know me, always oozing confidence."

"I always thought you to be quite confident."

"Maybe when it came to getting into trouble, I never doubted that I could," Grant said, looking down at his feet.

"Well, you were really good … I mean, you seemed to, I don't know…."

"You don't have to say it. I know. I know Rex and I used to do some pretty crazy stuff that might have been better if we, you know … I wish … um…."

"Let it go," Annie said, putting her hand on his arm. "You were young and adventurous. No one knows how to do everything all the time."

"You're better at it than I am, which maybe isn't saying much, but you are better at just about everything than I am. I just made too many mistakes and maybe I'm still paying for them." Their strolling had led them back outside. Grant was comforted to be looking at the mountains.

"Look, sometimes, or most times, things don't go the way you'd like, but that doesn't mean that things went wrong. You may think you haven't gotten anywhere yet, but you have gotten somewhere, as you said. So cut yourself some slack. Oh, and by the way, I made mistakes too, plenty of them."

"You never make mistakes, except for maybe meeting me that day in Boulder. Good for me, not as for you."

Annie looked around the hotel, suddenly paying attention to the decor. She wasn't uncomfortable; she just didn't know how to respond. She thought about telling him she was moving closer to where he lived, to take over her father's practice, but thought that maybe that might not be a good idea right off. She just was enjoying her time with Grant, as brief as it had been.

"I wish I had not made arrangements to meet my other friends for dinner tonight. I just, you know, didn't know … well, with Rex, you just…."

"You don't have to apologize to me. Making a schedule that depends on Rex is madness, so that's understandable. I'm surprised you agreed to come here," Grant said.

"Well, maybe I shouldn't…."

"No, it's great that you did, and I am glad you did. Why don't you and your friends come to dinner with us? Unless that would be too awkward for you or for them."

"Well, gosh, I don't know."

"Well, the offer is there. If it works for you and it works for them, come on. I would really like you to, sorry. Not that my opinion counts for much."

"Well, you're right, it would be fun. I'll ask them, or I'll just come and meet you, whether they come or not."

"Good, I hope so. I can leave you a note with the name of the restaurant and what time to meet us."

"It might be nice if just the four of us had dinner. Well, the three of us, maybe. Kat is a really good friend and I think you would really like her."

"She gives Rex hell, so I like her already. Maybe if the four of us had dinner with Rex tied up and gagged we could have a great time. Course, he's with his new girlfriends at the pool, so it may not be an issue. He might be tied up for real somewhere else, which would work out much better for the rest of us."

"You want to see him, he's your friend, and he's been through a lot. I understand."

"He's never been one of your favorite people."

"Well, things change sometimes."

"You feeling all right? It is Rex we're talking about. Were you in a car wreck this morning?"

Annie laughed and paused for what seemed like a long time. Her eyes looked glassy.

"Nothing like Rex." She looked down at the floor, then around the room, then into Grant's eyes. "Yes, I'll meet you for dinner. That would be great. I can see my other friends another time. Kat will help with everything, she always does. It really is good to see you." Annie leaned forward, kissed Grant on the cheek and walked away.

CHAPTER 11

Grant went back into the bar, surprised that Isobelle was still there. There were more people in the bar now. He hadn't really noticed anyone in there before, except for the plaid patrol, who were pretty hard to miss.

"So, Señor Grant is back. Where are the troops?"

"Sort of all over, but coming together later, I think. I thought you had to leave?"

"I came back to personally give you the name of the restaurant, I think I mentioned it is La Casuela's. I also put the directions on here for you. Some very dear friends of mine own this restaurant, and they would take very good care of you here. I know I mentioned it before, just not that they are friends of mine, you would want for nothing." Isobelle made a sweeping motion with her hand.

"You know how persuasive you can be, don't you? How did you know that I would be coming back here and that I wouldn't just call the front desk?"

"Sometimes I can just feel how things are going to be. I do not know of the persuasive part."

"I'm starting to notice that. That's quite a gift, and I think you know exactly how persuasive you can be." Grant said.

"I know, and I am very thankful for the gift. Sometimes it is overwhelming, but I can usually deal with that. Did you like the wine I sent to your room?"

"What? Oh, that was … I thought … I …yes, it was great, thank you. You didn't need to do that. There appeared to be a sunset coming right out of that bottle, pretty impressive," Grant managed to stutter out, still flummoxed by the look in Annie's eyes, the kiss he had just gotten, and now Isobelle's partial acknowledgement of her unusual abilities.

"Well, it is my pleasure. You seem to have a lot on your mind. If you need help with any of that, perhaps I can assist."

"How would you assist with that?"

"As I said, I see things sometimes. It is rather difficult to explain and perhaps we will get more time. I believe that we will get some time away from here, so that we might discuss it. It is not something I usually discuss with people here on the property. I really do not discuss it much at all. Can I get you anything before I leave? It is on me," Isobelle said.

"You just sent me wine. I don't remember seeing a bill from when we were in here earlier either. You can't be giving me all this, I might not leave."

"Well, I can think of worse things. I am looking forward to seeing you again this weekend when I am not working." Isobelle said.

"That would be good. Still not sure how you know that's going to happen," Grant said.

"Sometimes it is not for us to know the how. It is only important that we recognize that certain things are possible beyond what we normally think is possible. Once you accept that, all things are possible. Does that make sense?"

"Sort of."

"Let me say something, and then I will let you be on your way."

"OK, shoot."

"Isobelle reached over and took Grant's hand, looking into his eyes, closing hers for a moment, then opening them again.

"You are tortured for things that you feel you should have done. You should not be. We all have regrets. The woman will be, or she will not be. You must not blame yourself for things that happened a long time ago. When you can see this and accept it, change will come to you. You have some difficulty ahead, but I will help you with that. The dog will also help. Now, I must go. I will see you later." Isobelle let go of Grant's hand, took a deep breath, and walked away.

Grant had no idea what to say as he watched as Isobelle walk out of sight. The past twenty minutes were hitting him harder than the vehicle through the intersection. The look in Annie's eyes, the kiss, and now this mysterious Isobelle talking to him about his future. He now felt more tired than before, and certainly more than just car-wreck-rattled. He left the bar, moving deliberately through the hotel, back out to the pool area. He could hear Rex as soon as he got outside, and Rex started yelling at him as soon as he saw him approaching.

"Just in time! I was going to send somebody in to get your bartender girlfriend to bring us another round," Rex said, almost shouting.

"Yeah, another round," Moll said.

"I agree!" said Mag.

"Aren't they great?"

"Great," Grant said.

"He thinks we're great," Moll gestured towards herself with her thumb.

"Yeah, he thinks we're great," Mag, said, right behind her.

"Well, he ought to know, he's a pro at this sort of thing," Grant said, pointing at Rex.

"Really? He's professional?" Moll asked, her thumb turning upward.

"That's amazing!" Mag said.

"You should see his credentials," Grant said.

"Oh, we wouldn't … we haven't … we just met.…" Moll said, suddenly trying to act shy.

"We're not like that," Mag chimed in.

"Glad to hear you're not out flashing your credentials at the Ritz." Grant said, starting to laugh. "Hate for us to get thrown out of here."

Rex was now laughing hard and could hardly speak. "You'd better have a drink," Rex stuttered, finally able to get the words out.

"Nope, I'm good for now. Got somebody trying to give me drinks everywhere I go, even when there's nobody there. You seem to be having fun here," Grant said.

"I always have fun! If you were more like me, you'd have more fun too."

"If I was more like you, I'd jump in front of some moving farm equipment."

"Always a damn hillbilly, even at the Ritz," Rex said.

The girls were not paying attention to Grant and Rex's conversation. They were looking around the courtyard and pool area of the hotel, pointing things out to each other, occasionally tossing something at each other, reaching over, flipping each other's hair. Grant looked over at them to verify he was seeing what he was seeing at the table.

"Maybe you could buy them a monkey … or get them a ball and a stick," Grant suggested.

"Wish I had that hula-hoop Annie made me send her, I think they would be good for the rest of the day."

"I am sure they would," Grant paused.

"You think if I threw a ball, one of them would go after it?" Rex asked.

"Most certainly."

"You got one?"

"No, or I would throw it, right the hell now. Maybe we should buy one. Hey, you're going to dinner with us, and don't even think about bringing those two for dinner with Annie. I'm a little nervous about even taking you," Grant said.

"You wouldn't be here if it weren't for me, so just knock that shit off. All right, Annie's coming! Good going, chief. You have to give her anything to get her to say she would do it?"

"No. She only does that with people she doesn't like."

"She likes everybody," Rex said.

"Everybody except you. Can't say I blame her there."

"Hah! Everybody loves me. Just ask my two blonde bookends there," Rex said, pointing at the two women. "Bottle blondes, but who gives a shit," he said quietly. "Besides, if Annie hates me so much, how come she kept in touch with me after I reached out to her? She could have just ignored me. The scavenger hunt was a pain in the ass, but she could have just done nothing."

"You do make a point, which is rare, but I really don't want to spend all my time thinking about you. Those two … maybe you get a dodge ball game going with some of the other kids here at the hotel, you can take 'em to that," Grant said."

"You're just jealous 'cause I saw 'em first. Hey girls, Señor Grant and I have to go meet some folks for dinner now. We can play again later, OK?" Rex said to the girls.

"We want to come too!" Moll said.

"Yeah, we want to come too!" Mag followed.

"Not this time, maybe later, if I'm still able to stand up," Rex said, the last part low, so only Grant could hear. "Or tomorrow, for sure."

"What if we're not here?" Moll asked.

"Yeah, what if we're not here?" Mag asked.

"Well … when are you leaving?" Rex asked

"Sunday," Moll said, deliberately.

"Yep, Sunday," Mag added.

"Well then, you will be here, won't you?" Rex said.

There was silence. The girls looked at each other, then looked back at Rex, then at Grant, then back at each other. They then looked back at Rex, then at Grant.

"I guess we'll still be here then." Moll giggled.

"Yep!" Mag followed.

Grant looked back and forth at the group. "Oh, boy," he said, clapping his hands together. "Sort of like feeding time, eh, Barnum?"

The girls then clapped their hands together.

Rex placed his head on the table, laughing into his lap.

"Let's get a move on it. Leave them a treat and let's go," Grant said.

"Right," Rex said. He got out of his chair and walked over and put his arms around the two women, leaning over and whispering something in their ears. They giggled and poked him in the side. He reached in his pocket and put some money on the table for them to buy more drinks. They shook their heads, but he repeated the whispering and they finally said something, followed by "OK." He wanted their attention, but he wasn't going to leave the tab open for them to invite their family and friends to the Ritz while he went to dinner. They kissed Rex on the cheek.

"Let's go," Rex said, walking away from the table.

Grant was fixated on the spectacle, even though it now seemed to be over. "Right." Grant nodded at the women.

"Good bye, Señors Grant and Rex!" they said loudly, in unison.

Grant and Rex started toward the hotel. "You want to take a shower?" Grant asked?

"I do, but if I do, I'm gonna end up lying on that bed with the AC running and sleeping until Tuesday. So the answer would be no. Let's go. You know where the hell we're going? It would be a first if you did."

"I think I know. We can walk it, I think."

Rex noticed the man and the woman with the sunglasses that were in the bar earlier. They were sitting out of the sun, off to one side of the pool area, but still with a good vantage point of the pool.

"Were those two here earlier?" Rex asked.

"Who?"

"Those two with the sunglasses. They were in the bar earlier. They look like accountants. Or cops."

"You're drunk," Grant said.

"Not drunk enough."

"How about just drunk enough to be paranoid? You think somebody gives a shit that you're hanging out with a couple of dollies at the Ritz?"

"You would be surprised at the lengths these people go to, to find out everything you're doing," Rex replied.

"You are messed up."

"Not really."

"It looks like some guy, some woman."

"Why were they wearing sunglasses?"

"Because we're in the fucking desert and the sun is blinding? Just making a quick observation," Grant said.

"Not in the bar."

"Maybe they don't want to be recognized."

"Exactly," Rex said.

"No, like famous and don't want to be recognized."

"They stand out because they dress like they should be working at the FBI or something."

"Your goofy fucking paranoid imagination is as twisted as you are."

"If you had been through all the shit that I've been through, you'd think the same as me," Rex said.

"If I had been tossed in a cement truck filled with bricks, nails, and broken glass, I wouldn't think the same as you. Maybe if they took out three-quarters of my brain," Grant said.

"I'm serious."

"So am I."

They passed the front desk, and Grant left a note for Annie with the name of the restaurant. Once they got outside and started the walk, it didn't take long for them to realize how brutally hot it was, even though they were starting the walk on the steep downhill grade.

"At least it isn't an uphill," Grant thought, which, in this heat, would have been pretty miserable.

"Goddamn! It's hot out here! What the hell were you thinking?"

"You've only taken two steps. You need to get in shape," Grant said.

"Maybe I do need to get in shape, but not today. I need a cigarette."

"Oh, yeah, because that'll cool you down. You don't even smoke."

Walking down the hot road, it occurred to Grant that he really did not want to walk the reverse, uphill path of this trek. They continued their walk, talking about the day, about other days. Getting caught up on each other's activities would have been thoroughly enjoyable, had it not been for the fact that the walk down this road did not seem like quite as good an idea as when he had been in the cool air conditioned hotel lobby. After all the drinks they had, picking up all the rocks along the way probably would have seemed like a good idea as well.

"A little warmer than I remembered it being by the pool," Grant admitted.

"Probably because you're in the goddamn desert, walking down a steep-assed fucking hill after several cocktails. Maybe the heart attack will kill me before I tumble down into the highway, and get hit by a truck."

Grant unsnapped his cowboy shirt, pulling the shirttails out to let some heat escape.

Heat stroke occurred to both of them at roughly the same time. They heard a car pulling up behind them. They turned to look and saw that it appeared to be someone waving at them as the car pulled alongside. Grant saw that it was Fausto, from the hotel.

"Are you OK, sir?" Fausto asked, as he pulled alongside them.

"Fausto?"

"Yes Señor Grant, are you all right?"

"I was, but now … not so much."

"Sir?"

"Are you going that way?" Grant asked, pointing down the road, suddenly realizing it was a stupid question, as that was the only road to and from the hotel.

"That's why your name isn't Einstein, you moron," Rex said, pushing Grant to the side. "Que paso, chief? You wanna do dos gringos a biggo favoro, and take them for a ride in your car? Senior Grant would even pay you. Best do it now, before I kill him and keep all the money myself," Rex said, muttering the last part so only the two of them could hear.

"Yes, sir, how did you know," he replied smiling. "Would you like a ride? It looks like you are losing your shirt," Fausto said.

"You got that right, all the way around," Grant said, as they crossed the road to where Fausto's car was, getting in with a sigh of relief. "Glad you came by, I was about to take my pants off."

"That would not be good, sir. Where are you going?"

"Someplace called La Casuela's. You know where it is?"

"Sure. It is not that far, in the car, and really not that far when walking—when it is a different time of year. This time of year you would find it to be a very long ways. It is better that I came along, or you might have been very unhappy," Fausto said.

"Suppose you are right. I just felt like walking at the time … for six or eight steps, at least."

"Lucky for you I am here and you can still have the pants on."

"How far is this place?" Grant asked.

"Just a few minutes, and it is a good place too, Señor Grant, you will like it," Fausto smiled.

"Is this your friend here?"

"No, someone I just met today." Grant laughed. "Yes, it is my friend, Rex, Fausto. Fausto, Rex"

"You make friends quickly, Señor Grant."

"Thanks. I guess so."

They drove just a short distance and were at the place Isobelle had told him about. Grant hardly took notice of the distance or the roads, as the route and his current attention span were very similar in length.

"Here is the restaurant, Señor Grant."

"Not too far, under the right circumstances," Rex said sharply.

"Sir?"

"Thank you for the ride, Fausto, we really appreciate it. Probably saved me from killing this dumb bastard and dumping him off in the ditch, though he's been there a time or two," Rex said, smiling.

"You were going in the ditch? What does that mean?" Fausto asked.

"I'll tell you tomorrow. Here's something for helping us out and for your trouble," Grant said, and put five dollars on the dashboard.

"No, sir, it was no trouble, and I was going this way anyway."

"Us too," Grant said and got out of the car. "See you tomorrow."

Fausto pulled away and continued waving until he was out of sight. Grant and Rex stood there shaking their heads, Grant snapping his shirt, tucking it back into his jeans, Rex trying to cool down.

They stepped into the courtyard, which felt like a bucket of ice compared to the brief walk they had just been on.

"Hey, a little cool air in the desert sure makes things better in a hurry."

"You said it, chief. I'll pay for the taxi home, if I live that long. If I don't, you pay the goddamn cab fare yourself."

CHAPTER 12

"Ok, Casanova, who're we meeting here? Annie bringing a bunch of her friends? If I had more women to choose from, that would make it better still," Rex said, still wiping his brow from the walk, his face bright red.

"You sure you're not having a heart attack?" Grant asked.

"I don't get a cocktail soon, a heart attack is pretty much guaranteed. Who we meeting?"

"Women. You give a shit beyond that?"

"Always prepared, that's what I love about you hillbillies. Walk to the restaurant in a hundred twenty degree goddamn heat and you're hopin' there's a bevy of beauties waiting to give us a margarita sponge bath. We could have stayed by the pool and been comfortable. I'm only cutting you some slack because they got AC and, I'm assuming, booze. They don't have those things, I'm going to the kitchen, getting a knife, and stabbing you in the heart," Rex said.

"How about a nice cold glass of shut the fuck up before I kick your extra-large complaining ass?"

"Goddamn, it's hot. What's on for tomorrow, run through Death Valley?"

"Tomorrow I plan to get some new friends who don't bitch all the goddamn the time," Grant said.

"Good luck, I been looking for them for years."

This brought a laugh to both of them and they proceeded inside the courtyard to the bar. It was Friday evening, so the place was starting to jump.

They paid no attention to the activities, they wanted liquid.

"I think I'll have them make me a margarita in a five gallon bucket, stick my head in it and drink my way out," Rex said.

They found two seats at the bar and focused all their attentions on getting something cold in them. The scenery didn't matter at this point, they were in survival mode. Grant hated to admit it more than Rex.

"So, back to the 'who's meeting us' part," Rex said, his voice sounding dry.

"Busload of college cheerleaders," Grant said.

"Always the picture of preparation."

"Well, I would think Kat, but not sure. Annie said they are pretty close, and she seems to have your sorry ass figured out, so I hope she comes along just to get some jabs in at you."

"Wait, wait, wait, what makes you think the Greek has me figured out?" Rex asked.

"I'm smarter than you, and when you were starting the dolly-day-care center out by the pool, more of your brains might have gone where the rest of it has gone. How do you know she's Greek? She looks like she could be Annie's sister."

"Ballas. Kat's last name is Ballas. Kat, short for Katrina. Besides, I asked her, and she said she was. Probably half, anyway, cause she's blonde. She's smart and good looking, I don't give a shit where her family is from. Hah! Mag and Moll were something, those two, weren't they? " Rex said.

"I would expect nothing less from you. Nothing more, intelligence wise, either."

"High and mighty now, huh? Was a time, chief, you'd a have made a run at them too, right along side of me, flipping a coin, choosing sides, you remember the drill."

"Not sure I remember things quite like you do," Grant said.

"You never did."

"They're not my type."

"They used to be, and then Annie came along. So you traded up, but that doesn't mean you should forget your upbringing."

"Upbringing? Hah!" Grant laughed.

"You didn't always have the highest of standards."

"No law says a guy can't change his ways."

"You want to marry the doctor tonight, you go ahead. In the meantime, I'm not looking to settle down today … plus, up until today, you haven't exactly been on a hot streak with women, upstanding or otherwise," Rex said.

"Hola, Señors, can I get you a drink this evening?" They were interrupted by the bartender.

"Boy, are we glad to see you, boss. We almost died outside. My buddy here thought we should walk here from San Diego, almost killed us. Get me the biggest margarita you have, go ahead and make two of them. Oh, and bring my friend here a cup of hot black coffee," Rex said.

The bartender was unsure of what to do. He stood for a moment, looking back and forth at Grant and Rex.

"Two margaritas, two waters. Bring him a prairie fire," Grant said.

"Prairie fire?" both Rex and the bartender said at the same time.

"Tequila and Tabasco," Grant smiled.

"God, you want to kill me?" Rex exclaimed.

"All my life."

"I'll have same as him, two margaritas, two waters."

"Coming up, Señor," the man said, walking away.

"I like the lady bartenders better," Rex said.

"Why, cause they aren't as prone to kick your ass?"

"Maybe because the ladies are always looking after me?"

"Shit, I don't know about that. My luck, it's you, me, and that guy who just waited on us, 'cause the others came to their senses about what a dumbass you are," Grant said, relaxing a bit now. He started to look around the room and saw Isobelle and another woman entering the bar. "Was sort of hoping Annie would show up first," Grant whispered, elbowing Rex.

Rex turned to see Isobelle and friend. "Hey, she brought backup with her, all the better for me. Annie shows up with a pack of her pals, I'm set," Rex turned to see and waved at Isobelle, though she had already seen them.

The two women approached.

"Well, Señor Grant, I was not sure you would be here. I thought you would be meeting the blonde women first."

"You never know if anyone wants to meet Grant, that's the risk you take. Speaking of meetings, my name is Rex, Rex Schmidt." he said, extending his hand to the woman with Isobelle. She was of the same coloring as Isobelle, dark hair and olive skin, yet taller.

"Hello."

"Name?"

"Dawn. Dawn Mora."

"Word conservative, eh? You better sit with him," Rex motioned at Grant. "Oh, and his name is Grant. I thought I should tell you, because it might be an hour or two before he says anything. Takes him a while to warm up to people, unless he's walking here from Los Angeles, then he heats right up."

"Hello," Grant said.

"See what I mean? Have a seat."

The girls took chairs next to them at the bar, with Isobelle looking around the bar. "Is someone waiting on you?"

"Yes, but he's not as good as you, I'm about to die," Rex said.

Isobelle continued her search until she made eye contact and smiled at the man who had waited on Grant and Rex. He smiled and waved at Isobelle. She signaled, pointing at Dawn, Grant and Rex, then herself. He nodded, and went back to his business. Grant and Rex were watching the exchange.

"Friend of yours?" Grant asked.

"Oh yes, Jorge is a good friend of mine," Isobelle answered.

"Is he as good as you?" Rex asked.

"Probably not in the way you are thinking," she said.

Dawn laughed.

Rex laughed, looking at Dawn. "Good one. Hey, as long as he brings the cold stuff, I keep breathing."

"He will be quick, I promise you," Isobelle answered. "So, Señor Grant, are you enjoying your stay?"

"Of course he is," Rex responded, looking at Dawn. "What do you do?"

"I would like to hear Señor Grant's words when I am speaking to him. When I am speaking to you, I would still prefer to hear Señor Grant's words," Isobelle smiled at Grant, Grant smiling back.

"So Dawn, you were saying...." Rex turning his full attention to Dawn.

"You were saying for everyone, but since you asked, I work at Wally's."

"Where and what is Wally's?" Rex asked.

"Wally's Desert Turtle, it's a restaurant not far from here. You're not from around here, are you?" Dawn asked.

"No, but I could be."

"You're funny," Dawn laughed.

"Oh no," Grant said.

"Good to get an outside opinion, especially one that is so correct, so unsolicited, and from someone so delightful," Rex, said grinning at Grant and Isobelle.

"What do you do?" Dawn asked.

"I do a lot of things, most of them boring, but long as people pay me lots of money, I keep doing it," Rex said.

"Who doesn't, right?" Dawn said, agreeing with him.

Rex again turned and smiled at Grant and Isobelle, then back to Dawn. "Are you going to be staying here for a while? Please, say yes."

"Yes. You have nice friends, Isobelle," Dawn said.

"I know, that is important to the circle of life, it is not an accident. The light around this one shines from time to time," Isobelle said, looking at Grant. "I am uncertain about the light of the other one," she said, glancing quickly at Rex, then back to Grant.

"That's a bit above his level of comprehension, so you may just want to draw something on a napkin, or hold up something shiny for him to play with," Grant said, making Isobelle laugh. "But you need to elaborate on what we were talking about right before you left."

"So, you are enjoying your stay?" Isobelle asked, saying it low this time, so only Grant could hear. Rex was now no longer interested in anyone but Dawn, so he would not have heard it anyway.

"Well, it has been—"

"Here we are!" The bartender had returned, setting drinks in front of the entire group. He leaned forward, exchanging hugs and kisses across the bar first with Dawn, then with Isobelle."How are you? You both look wonderful, as always, muy bonitas."

"Jorge, my friend! This is Señor Grant and his friend Rex." Isobelle said.

"Hola Jorge, how are you?" Dawn asked.

"I am well, thank you. It is nice to meet you two," he said, extending his hand, shaking with Grant and Rex.

"Same here, boss," Rex said, grabbing the drink as soon as the glass hit the bar, shaking Jorge's hand with the other hand. "Sorry to douse and shake at the same time," he said, slurping the cocktail down, "but this cowboy tried to kill me earlier and, well, now I'm better," he looked at Jorge, then at Dawn.

"He's funny, Jorge," Dawn said.

"Oh, shit," Grant said under his breath, to which Isobelle elbowed him in the ribs. "Nice to meet you, Jorge. Maybe we should start a tab with you. My buddy here might—"

"Your money is no good here, Señor Grant. You are in very beautiful and very capable hands here. I will leave you now. You let me know if you need anything. Dawn and Isobelle, I love you both. I will be back to check on you," Jorge said, and walked away to tend to other customers.

"So, you were telling me about how you were enjoying your stay," Isobelle said, not missing a beat.

"I was?"

"Well, you hadn't told me yet, but I asked you right before Jorge came by."

"Oh, that's right. Well, I suppose I—you know, I just got here earlier today and, well I'm still a bit unclear on just how it is that you seem to know things, things about me without having been told the details."

"Hey chief, looks like we'd better get a bigger tent," Rex said, elbowing Grant from the other side, motioning his head towards the entrance to the bar.

CHAPTER 13

Grant looked towards Rex, annoyed, but then he picked up on Rex's head motion and turned towards the entrance to see Annie and Kat entering the bar.

"Déjà vu, seriously. That, or I'm really drunk," Grant said.

"Let us say déjà vu sounds more mystical." Isobelle smiled, looking at Grant until she followed his eyes to the entrance, when she turned to see Annie and Kat. Her smile dimmed.

"Hello again," Kat said.

"Hello again. It is nice to see you from the same side of the table. To be able to meet with friends of Señor Grant is a pleasure," Isobelle said, getting up from her seat.

"Señor Grant?" Annie asked, smiling, looking inquisitively at Grant.

"Yep, he's a legend in these parts," Rex replied, looking first at Dawn, then at Kat.

"Gosh," Annie said, "I had no idea." Her eyes widened.

"Please, sit down, be comfortable," Isobelle said. "I will ask Jorge to get us a table."

Isobelle looked up to find Jorge, but he had already noticed the additional women in the group, and was looking to see if they needed anything. Isobelle made a couple of head moves and Jorge nodded back, moving quickly from out behind the bar to get them a table.

"Kinda cool, isn't it?" Rex said, looking at Kat.

"She gets things done without talking … you may want to take some notes," Kat said, looking back at Rex.

"Annie and Kat, correct? This is my friend Dawn."

"Hello."

"Hello."

"Hello."

"Quite an echo in here," Rex said."

Grant shook his head.

"So, Señor Grant, is it now?" Annie asked. "How are you doing, Señor?" Her fingertips brushed his arm. "You look kind of flushed."

"It was the death march." Rex said.

"Death march?" Annie asked.

"Nothing. We got a little hot, it's all right now," Grant said.

"Son of a gun tried to kill me," Rex's eyes shot quickly around the assemblage.

"What stopped you?" Kat asked, looking at Grant.

"Fausto," Grant said.

"My Fausto?" Isobelle asked.

"Yes."

"Who's Fausto?" Annie asked.

"This is getting confusing. Does anyone have a program or a cast of characters? How long have you been in town?" Kat asked.

"He's been here for months, sleeping under a bridge. Just look at him, he's disgusting," Rex said, starting to laugh.

The group looked at Grant, then back to Rex.

"Don't start paying attention to him, it just makes it worse," Grant said.

"That's true, and he's bad enough now," Annie added quickly. The group all turned to look at her. "Sorry," she said, blushing.

"I have your table ready for you, right this way. Ladies, my name is Jorge, how can I be of service?"

"Oh, another margarita for me, and a program, please. Any chance of an understudy filling in for you tonight?" Kat said, looking at Rex

"Very good, and for you … excuse me, what is a program?" Jorge asked.

"We just like to give this one a hard time, everything's OK." Kat put her finger on Rex.

"Aw, come on, I had to get a hula-hoop," Rex said.

"I'm fine with the same as what they are having," Kat said.

"Very good. And for you?"

"Oh just water, water is good," Annie said.

"It's Friday night, Sims, live a little!" Rex exclaimed.

"Maybe later, back at the hotel," Annie replied.

"Take note, chief, this is going pretty fast for you," Rex said to Grant.

"What?" Grant asked.

"'Later at the hotel', the lady said. I can't keep having to tell you this stuff." Rex now turned his attention back to Dawn. "This kind of stuff happens to me all the time. What were we talking about? Something about turtles."

"Just water, I might have something later, thank you though," Annie said.

"Very good." Jorge said, leading the group to a table. Behind him, a staff member had collected their drinks, while another was right behind them with another tray of fresh ones.

"Please, sit," Jorge said.

"Thank you," Grant said, waiting for the ladies to sit.

"Do we have to wait 'til the music stops?" Rex said, looking at Dawn. She laughed.

"Come on, Señor Grant," Annie said teasingly, "that's what they are calling you here, right? Sit here and tell us how you know everyone in town." Her body language indicated that she was waiting for him to choose his place, so she could sit next to him.

"Yes, Señor Grant, please," Isobelle said, picking up on Annie's attempts to sit by him.

Grant glanced around the group. "Ladies first. Just because I'm on vacation, doesn't mean I don't have manners, or that I'm a slob like this one," he said, looking at Rex.

"Wow, Señor Grant is talking! Look out, ladies, he must be loosening up," Rex said, looking down at his pants, just to make sure.

The ladies smiled, getting seated, with Grant next to Annie, Isobelle across from both of them. Dawn sat, with Rex quickly sitting next to her.

Kat noticed that both Annie and Grant's body language had improved from the meeting earlier in the day. They were both sitting taller and less stiffly, and seemed eager, rather than apprehensive, to talk to each other. She looked at Isobelle, who seemed also to be noticing that whatever walls might have been up earlier were now removed.

Grant was relieved that Annie was next to him, though he had been perfectly comfortable with Isobelle when she and Dawn approached them a few minutes earlier, and was relaxed with the entire group at the table. Kat noticed that Grant's confidence level had already risen. He was constantly looking at Annie, but trying to engage all of the women at the table as well. Maybe he was a bit overwhelmed. He was happy, she could see that. He probably wished it were just him and Annie.

Isobelle was paying considerable attention to Grant. The fact that there were others seemed not to bother her. Isobelle was used to having to spend a great deal of time with strangers. The difference this time was that she wanted to be here. She was also very adept at picking out details, and conversely tuning out things that were of no concern to her. Isobelle did not seem pleased that Annie was there, but she was obviously determined to learn as much as she could about Grant and Annie, listening intently to what they said.

"So Dawn, is it?" Rex asked.

"Yes, Dawn."

"You from around here?"

"Yes, I am."

"Don't you think it's too hot here? I know that sounds like a stupid question, especially me not being from here. That didn't come out right. Do you think it's too hot here?"

Dawn waited until he had finished, even though the temptation might have been there to make fun of him like the rest had done.

"No, I don't. You just have to be careful about what time of day you go outside. I really like it here."

"I was just checking. I mean, I'm sure you hear people from out of town bitch about, well, probably bitch about everything, but they probably all say it's too hot."

"They don't say that in the winter, but as we are now close to summer, yes they say that."

"Do you just, I guess, get used to how hot it is?"

"Something like that, yes. Don't you get used to the weather where you are?

"I don't really pay attention to it."

"Then you must be adapted to the weather there, as well."

"Yeah, I guess so." Rex smiled at Dawn, and Dawn smiled back at him. The smiles were real.

Rex was making every indication that he wanted to leave with Isobelle's friend, Dawn, which made all three of the other women very happy.

Dawn was not as intense as Isobelle. She was pleasant, carefree, and not really concerned with anyone's past. She seemed content to just be with the group and hear the tales.

Rex clearly loved a crowd, but Kat thought she might have scared him off a bit. "I hope so," she thought.

After the first round of drinks arrived, everyone seemed more at ease. Conversation came easily and fluidly, and everyone was occupied sharing stories together, reminiscing about old times, and catching up on the new.

Kat was anxious to speak with Annie later, to see if her feelings for Grant had changed. She saw that Annie did not appear pleased Isobelle was there, probably because Isobelle was showing an interest in Grant. If that were not the case, Kat was sure that Annie wouldn't have been upset in the slightest that Isobelle was there. In her experience with Annie, she never seemed to show her real feelings, but had shown them twice today. Right now, she looked like she was struggling to keep her feelings in, which was out of character, because Annie was not a person who ever visibly struggled with anything. She was not perfect, but she knew how to minimize her mistakes and emotions when others were around.

"Annie, are you sure you don't want something to drink?" Kat asked Annie, not loud enough to draw the attention of the others.

"No, I'm fine, thanks," Annie answered.

"You know it won't be a problem getting back, I just want to make sure you are—"

"I know, I know. It's ok, really, I'm fine."

"I don't mean to bother," Kat said.

"You're not, don't worry, I'm glad you're here."

"Anytime, you know that."

"I know, and thank you." Annie smiled.

"Hey, no secrets down there!" Rex said, looking away from Dawn just long enough to see that Annie and Kat were talking to each other.

"Secrets? From you? How is that possible, you already know everything," Kat responded.

"You're a quick learner, I like that about you. You're quick to see my wisdom!" Rex laughed.

"Once again, it's all about you," Kat said. "How lucky we are to be in the presence of such greatness!"

"Exactly!" Rex followed.

"You know you shouldn't compliment or encourage him, ever, even sarcastically!" Grant said, looking at Annie and Kat.

"I'm not, he just thinks I am," Kat said.

"I don't think he's so bad," Dawn said, looking to where Kat was sitting.

"Oh no," Grant put his head down on his arms in mock exhaustion.

"No, really, I don't think he's so bad. He is kind of adorable," Dawn said.

"You only just met him," Kat replied.

"So did you," Dawn offered back.

"Well, yeah, but I know more about him," Kat responded.

"Well, everybody has good things and bad things about them, and sometimes people just need someone to talk to."

"Well, I would guess talking has never been a problem for Rex," Kat said.

"Agreed," Grant said.

"Agreed," Annie said.

"What do you think, Isobelle?" Dawn asked.

Isobelle had been watching and listening to the responses of Annie and Grant, not really paying attention to Dawn and Rex.

"What's that? I'm sorry."

"I said, what do you think about Rex?"

"He speaks a great deal."

This made Annie, Kat, and Grant laugh loudly. Rex made a dour face at them, and then looked back to Dawn.

"I like your assessment better," Rex said.

CHAPTER 14

With such an unusual mix of people and backgrounds, it was turning out to be quite a pleasant evening. Fortunately, everyone had something to say or an interesting story to tell, and the differences in occupations and upbringings only served to liven up the discussion. The pace at which the tequila drinks were arriving was brisk by any standard, but the abundance of active and lively conversation helped keep everyone at a steady pace and solidly in control of their faculties. The steady stream of food and drinks was coordinated by Isobelle and Jorge, who saw to it that no one lacked for anything.

Grant was trying to work up the courage to talk intimately with Annie, but he wasn't going to risk getting sloshed and losing ground. Besides, he knew that he had already had a substantial amount to drink that day, and combined with the painkillers from the accident, he was rather surprised he was still standing.

Rex didn't hold back, not that he ever did. He looked to be a bottomless pit in terms of food and alcohol consumption, so quantity really didn't change his disposition one way or the other. He was letting off a tremendous amount of steam that had been building over the investigation ordeal at work. He was still nervous about the couple with the sunglasses back at the hotel, but he felt great just being back with his old friends.

Kat wanted to hear it all, even though she had heard much about Grant from Annie over the years. She found Grant to be quite interesting, to be a good, albeit sad soul, and could see why Annie thought so highly of him. She could see his shyness and had a difficult time believing that he had done all the crazy things that Annie had told her about. She had not known him back then, but she saw him as a difficult person not to like. The idea of Rex getting into trouble seemed a given from the first.

Annie was not drinking, though she seldom did. Kat thought she seemed mostly comfortable with the conversations, and not confined by the past. She smiled often, watching Grant probably more than she realized. With Isobelle there, she wasn't as calm or relaxed as she might have been otherwise. Kat thought might have actually been a little jealous of Isobelle—though she was clearly doing her best not to let it show.

Kat could see that Isobelle was in complete control of herself. It was clear to Kat that Isobelle was interested in Grant and she was mentally noting all conversation about him. Kat detected a different energy about Isobelle. She did not run into that kind of energy very often, so whenever she was around it, it really stood out. She also felt that Isobelle knew that Kat could sense it, and as a result was trying to hide it.

Kat thought Dawn to be a delightfully simple person and who seemed to be having more fun than anyone. Kat was amazed that anyone could find Rex amusing, but Dawn seemed to be that exception. For some odd reason, Kat thought Dawn could have been Annie when she was younger, before career and the drive to be successful came to visit, and stayed for good, replacing playfulness with practicality.

"So, you must tell me how all of you met," Isobelle said to the group, no one in particular.

"Me first!" Rex said.

"I am not surprised in the slightest that you would speak first," Isobelle said, "So go ahead."

"Great. I met you and the Greek this afternoon, and Dawn a few minutes ago," Rex said, smiling and looking quite proud.

They all collectively shook their heads, while Dawn just laughed.

"Such a revelation! Can you tell us about your most memorable time together?" Isobelle said.

"I would have to say today was the most memorable, and I know you ladies have enjoyed spending time in my presence as well," Rex shot back.

"Aw, isn't that cute? Rex has taken in a large amount of alcohol and now he believes his presence to be meaningful. You just go with that," Kat said.

"I thought it was funny," Dawn said.

"You're just going to make it worse," Grant said to her.

"Aside from the meetings of today, how did the rest of you meet? Perhaps someone besides this one may speak to this," Isobelle said, pointing at Rex.

"We met in college," Annie said.

"In college. Where was this?" Isobelle asked.

"It was in Colorado, in Boulder, Colorado," Annie answered.

"So that would have been...."

"I met Grant and Rex in college. I met Kat a few years after that."

"Meeting us was the best thing that ever happened to Annie, 'cause I don't think she had ever had any fun before she met us," Rex added.

"That's not true, Rex. I had lots of fun before I met you."

"But not real fun."

"Yes, real fun."

"Like what?"

"Like lots of things!" Annie said, protesting, but unable to conjure up anything specific.

"Let's hear 'em."

"I don't keep a list, do you?"

"Yep, part of it is up in the room."

"Where's the other part?"

"In the Smithsonian," Rex smiled.

Everyone laughed.

"Probably the criminal wing of the Smithsonian," Kat offered.

That drew even more laughter.

"Were you in jail?" Dawn asked.

Grant laughed.

Rex started to move in his seat anxiously, like he had just discovered a tack in it. He started looking around the bar. "Not really ..." Rex said, looking around the room, to see if the people in the sunglasses were watching him.

"If they ever pass a law against coloring outside the lines, you're done," Grant said.

"Says Padre Grant, the man who never did anything that might be considered outside the law."

"I thought he was Señor Grant," Annie said.

"Just another alias—which brings us back to you, Annie, and the self-evident fact that you did not have any fun until you met us," Rex said.

"Well ... there were some fun things."

"Some fun things? You and your friends thought we were the funniest thing you had ever seen."

"You probably always think that," Kat said, coming to Annie's defense.

"Now, we are here to enjoy the company of friends," Isobelle said, trying to take control of the situation. Her bartending reflex was to diffuse anything that sounded like an argument. "We all have differences of opinion, no? That makes the past not right, not wrong, it is just the past. That we are all here together tonight, that means something, yes?" she asked, looking around the table.

"Always somebody bailing you out," Grant said quietly, looking at Rex. Annie elbowed him under the table.

"It's OK, she's right. We are all here tonight, so that means … I mean … it means something. Nothing bad. If it had been bad, we—well we would be somewhere else," Annie said.

Kat looked at Annie, then at Isobelle, then back to Annie. She knew that even though Annie's statement seemed disjointed, it was not, and the look in her eyes told her she meant something real.

"It was a long time ago," Grant said. "Back when Rex was funny. Not like now."

This brought laughter to the group, pulling them out of the seriousness that had crept in for just a moment, like a cold wind, but was gone again.

"He was just as ugly then, but at least he was funnier," Grant added.

"You think I'm ugly? I'm hurt," Rex said, feigning sadness, then looking at Dawn and smiling, "but I'm over it, right Dawn-to-dusk?"

"Yep, you are tough and funny. I don't think you are ugly."

"Hell…." Grant started.

"So you met in college and you have been friends all this time?" Isobelle said, wanting to get back on track.

"Well, I guess you could … there's been a bit of a break in the … well, Annie needed a break from … from … probably a break from me. And we all needed a break from that one," Grant said, pointing at Rex.

"Is that so?" Isobelle asked.

"No, it's not like that. We just needed different, I don't know, we wanted to…." Annie paused.

"They used to be together, and now they're not," Kat said, in attempt to rescue Annie from the statement she was struggling to make.

"And it has been sometime since you have seen each other," Isobelle said, matter-of-factly.

"Yes," Grant said.

"Well, I think that it is good that you did this, for whatever reason. The world puts many stones in the paths of those who have traveled far together. When others can help clear those stones, it allows us to see both the paths ahead and the paths behind more clearly," Isobelle said.

Kat was going to say something, but stopped and looked around the room.

"Yes, I think it does," Annie said, sounding relieved.

All of a sudden, they were surrounded by more food than any of them had ever seen on one table. Jorge was hovering above them, smiling.

"I hate to interrupt, but Isobelle and I took the liberty of ordering some food for you. Some are special dishes you will not find on the menu."

"I'm all for that, chief!" Rex said.

"Very good, my friend. It is not good to have a table with full glasses, without full plates to keep them company. The conversation is good, but will now be better with the food alongside it," Jorge said.

"I like this guy," Rex said.

"Thank you, Sir." Jorge had what appeared to be the entire wait staff behind him with virtually every Mexican dish one could imagine. "Crab enchiladas, chili verde with pork, chili rellenos, lobster tacos, scallop quesedillas, carnitas, tamales, chicken mole … have I forgotten anything?"

"I'm guessing not," Grant said.

"Is there a piñata?" Rex smiled.

"Hey!" Grant said, shooting Rex a harsh look. He didn't want to insult their generous benefactors in any way.

"No piñata. Very good, then. I hope you enjoy what we have prepared for you," Jorge said.

"Well, then we should do as Jorge tells us and assist our conversation with this wonderful food," Isobelle said, putting her arm around Jorge.

"Yes, please enjoy. We will bring more if this is not enough."

"Probably better, chief. Annie's a huge pig, and will probably eat all of this before any of us get a chance to start," Rex said.

Dawn punched Rex lightly on the arm. "I'm starting to think you never quit."

"I'm sorry. She just always eats a lot, she's not a pig," Rex said.

"I do not," Annie said.

Rex was laughing now, stuffing food into his own mouth, his response garbled by the sound of his eating.

"Always the gentleman. Thank you Jorge, and we apologize for that thing at the end of the table. If you have a place out back where we could tie him up to feed him, it would be easier on everyone in the restaurant," Grant said.

"I will see what I can do, sir."

"Call him Señor Grant, everyone else does," Rex shot back. "And I think I should have a nickname, too."

"Oh, I can think of several," Grant said.

"Me too," Kat smiled, and turned to Annie.

"I'm trying to be nice," Annie said.

"You always are, but you could make an exception this once, couldn't you?" Kat said.

"I'm sure your names for Rex would be good ones. I don't have to add to them," Annie fidgeted with her fork.

"Maybe it would make you feel better," Kat said."Here's a chance to let loose a little. Just give him a nickname, and we'll use it the rest of the night," Kat persisted. She took her fork and pretended to jab Rex with it.

"Do I have to?" Annie started imitating Kat with her own fork and knife.

"Yes."

"Hmmm, oh gosh, how about … piñata?"

Grant and Kat smiled like they had just found a great treasure.

"That's perfect." Kat held up her silverware.

"Yep." Grant added.

"I get a vote?" Rex asked.

"Nope, you wanted a nickname … Señor Pinata." Kat exaggerated the previous gesture, coming closer to Rex.

Annie laughed so hard her face turned bright red. "Guess that one works!"

CHAPTER 15

Kat, who had come along as the observer and for moral support for Annie, was amazed at how good a time she was having. She hadn't forgotten her duty, but that didn't mean she couldn't have a good time while she was here. Still, she thought she should probably offer Annie an escape rope, just in case Annie wanted a way to get out of the gathering. She didn't think Annie needed it, but her behavior had perplexed her ever since they got to town, so she figured she had better at least offer. They had been friends for a long time, and this was the first time she had seen Annie act like this. Kat could tell Annie was wrestling with some feelings she wasn't used to dealing with. Kat also thought Isobelle seemed to be able to tap in effortlessly to what everyone was thinking and feeling. She could have sworn that Isobelle already knew everyone's past, and could probably give anyone she cared to a glimpse of their future.

"We haven't heard from you, Kat, as to how you came to know these people," Isobelle said.

"She's been waiting her whole life to meet me," Rex said.

"That pretty much sums up my life. Waiting to meet the man of my dreams," Kat said, motioning towards Rex.

"I told you," Rex smiled.

"What else is there? What other goals could I possibly have? What mountains are there left to climb?" Kat said, extending her arms, her palms facing up.

"That pretty much sums it up. They do quickie weddings at the Ritz? I think we should get married tomorrow," Rex said.

"Do we have to rush it? Can't we wait until Sunday?" Kat asked.

"So aside from the potential wedding plans, how do you know these people?" Isobelle asked.

"Annie and I have been friends a long time. I just met these two today, but I've heard a great deal about them from Annie," Kat answered.

"Probably the most about me," Rex said.

"Yes, but again, probably not in the way that you think," Kat said.

"I think I understand," Isobelle said. "What about the quiet one, Señor Grant?"

"What about me?" Grant asked.

"You have not really elaborated on your relationship with your friends. I have a pretty good idea, but would like to hear you speak more about this," Isobelle said.

"Well…." Grant looked at Annie first, then Rex.

"Well…." Annie looked back at Grant.

"I've known Rex since high school," Grant said, "and I met Annie in college."

"And you two are very close, still," Isobelle said.

Annie looked down at her lap, and Grant stared at his now-empty plate of food.

"We, uh, haven't seen each other in several years," Grant said.

"And why is that?" Isobelle asked.

"Well, it is because—" Grant started.

"Do you want to hear my theory?" Rex cut in.

"No!" Annie and Kat said, together.

"It's either because Grant is a dumbass or because he was abducted by aliens," Rex said.

"Always the smart one," Grant said.

"So?" Isobelle continued.

"Things sort of … I sort of, well…." Grant was fumbling for words.

"It is not my place to pry," Isobelle said. "The important thing is that the friends are back together now, and everyone seems to be having a good time."

"Especially because I am here," Rex said, smiling.

"That's right!" Kat raised her glass.

"That's it!" Annie raised her fork.

"I knew it," Rex raised his glass and his fork.

"As much as I'm worried about Rex having to deal with the trauma of me leaving, maybe we should be going, Annie," Kat pointed her fork at Rex, but kept looking at Annie.

Annie looked at Kat, and paused. "Maybe I can get a ride back with someone if you need to go."

"That's right, I might kill myself if Kat leaves," Rex leaned toward Kat's out-stretched fork.

"No suicides, please. I'm going to call it an evening, though it has been a very interesting evening," Kat said, her eyes narrowing at Rex, looking at Rex as she slowly withdrew her fork from the cutlery wars.

"There it is again. I thought I behaved myself, pretty much."

"You did very well," Kat said, reaching over, touching Rex on his cheeks, then squeezing them together with her hands, until he looked like a fish. "But even I can only take so much good behavior. It was nice to meet everyone. Isobelle, do you think your friend can call me a taxi?"

"Most certainly," Isobelle replied. She looked up and caught Jorge's attention, making a gesture like she was on a telephone, then looking at Kat. Jorge nodded. "It was nice to meet you as well. I hope that I will see you back at the Ritz tomorrow."

"I'm sure you will," Annie said.

"What do you need a cab for? I thought you drove," Rex said.

"Oh, that's just what we told you. Probably not a good idea for doctors to drink and drive. They might have to dodge some sloppy drunk lawyers walking down the road on the way home," Kat smiled.

"She's pretty good, chief," Rex said.

"Hard to pull one over you," Grant laughed.

"How about Dawn and I share the ride with you? That OK with you, Dawn's Early Light?" Rex asked. Dawn smiled and nodded.

"Well, all right. But on one condition," Kat said.

"And that is …?"

"That only Dawn and I can talk. If you talk, you walk the rest of the way," Kat asked.

"No walking! I'll be quiet."

"I don't think that's possible, but good, let's go. Good night everyone.

Thank you for a really interesting evening. How much do I owe for my share of dinner and drinks?" Kat asked.

"That is not necessary, everything has already been taken care of," Isobelle said.

"Taken care of? You're not even finished yet," Kat responded.

"True, but everything has been taken care of. Thank you for joining us, and for allowing us to join you," Isobelle said.

"Well, thank you, that's extremely nice of you. Call me later, Annie, if you need anything."

"Thanks, Kat, I will."

The three departed, leaving Grant, Annie and Isobelle, which initially created a void of conversation, but they got over that quickly. They were all tired after a long day, and Grant and Annie were wrestling with the tumultuous emotions that seeing their old friends had evoked.

"That was something," Annie said.

"Which part?" Grant asked.

"The whole thing. It has been a long time since … you know, since … since I—"

"Since you had to hear the lowdown on the entire universe according to Rex?" Grant asked.

Annie just smiled, looking around the room. "Maybe. It was just something, all of it. I may not have heard everything Rex said."

"Difficult to believe," Isobelle said, "that you could not hear everything Rex said. I think the people on the other side of the restaurant heard everything he said," Isobelle laughed, looking back at Annie, then at Grant.

"Well, he got to relax, so that seemed to be good for him. We all still want to beat him up, though, right?" Grant extended his hand.

"Oh yeah," Annie shook her head.

Isobelle laughed. "He is not so bad, I have seen worse."

"We'll poll you at the end of the weekend to see if your vote stays that way," Grant said, weary but content. "Maybe we should go also?"

"Well, I can give you a ride, if you would like?" Isobelle offered.

"We can get a cab. Err—your pal could get us a cab. Don't want to…."

"It is no trouble, I will take you."

"You all right to drive?" Annie asked.

"Yes. I have not been drinking. Jorge made sure I was all right hours ago."

"Oh, gosh, I didn't know," Annie said.

"These desert folk seem to be on a different frequency than us out of town folk," Grant commented to Annie.

"If you say so. We may go, then," Isobelle gestured toward the door.

The three got up and left the table. Isobelle hugged and kissed Jorge on the way out, and they all thanked him for their very festive evening. They walked out of the restaurant and through the parking lot, looking up at the stars, which were as plentiful as the glasses and plates that Jorge had provided. There was almost a collective sigh from the three of them.

"The quiet is good, no?" Isobelle asked.

"Yes, it is," Annie said still looking up at the sky as she walked, hovering close to Grant.

"You think so as well, Señor Grant?" Isobelle was watching Grant.

"Yes, a little break is good. I might have eaten too much," Grant patted his stomach.

"You were supposed to, that is why we picked the dishes, so you would eat well tonight," Isobelle said.

"Well, they were great, and I did."

"I ate a lot too," Annie started to pat her stomach, but stopped as she noticed Isobelle looking at Grant.

"You never eat a lot," Grant added.

"It seemed like I did, lots of choices, you know," Annie looked back up at the sky.

Grant was now watching Annie as she walked. He wanted to say something, but he hadn't had so much conversation in years and he felt like he had run out of things to say. He was content to walk under the stars with Annie and Isobelle by his side.

"I feel like I've been here for several days already, but we just got here this afternoon," Annie said.

"Rex has a way of making hours seem like days," Grant said, not knowing what else to say.

Annie laughed. "I don't mean it that way. It was all, you know, good. Only, it was really concentrated, and I'm sort of exhausted now, but in a good way."

"When you do not see someone for a long time, seeing them again can have that effect on you, and I did not mean to bring up uncomfortable subjects. I only wanted to know how you met. It is none of my business, the details of your life. I am curious, but I do not wish to pry," Isobelle said.

"You weren't prying; I didn't take it that way."

"Maybe I should not have asked about how you met."

"No, it was all right. It made me laugh, actually. I hadn't thought about it in a long time," Annie said.

"How about you, Señor Grant? You were uncomfortable?" Isobelle asked.

"No, not at all. I don't get out much, probably should do that more. Annie didn't hit me, so that's a plus. She could have, but didn't."

"Why would I hit you?"

"Oh, I don't know. 'Cause I deserved it, maybe?"

"Maybe we should change your name to Señor Goofball." Annie said.

"Just more letters for the paperwork."

The drive back to the hotel was very quiet and very comfortable. Even though fatigue had set in, Annie and Grant seemed more relieved than tired, and Isobelle was content. She had set out to learn more about Grant, and though she had not learned as much as she wanted, she had learned a great deal just by being around him. They stopped at the hotel, and they all got out of the car.

"Here you are. I would like to thank you for allowing me and Dawn to join you and your friends this evening," Isobelle said.

"Well, thank you for a really great evening," Annie said.

"Yes, that was really over the top, thank you. Not sure what you have to thank us for. You and your pal Jorge took care of everything," Grant said.

"It was very kind of you to do that, and it certainly was not necessary. We would like to do something nice for you to return the favor," Annie added.

"That is not necessary. To get to know such nice people is a very good thing. Not all the people that come to the desert are as kind as you. Even the talkative one is interesting, in his own way."

"I hope that Dawn is still speaking to you after tonight," Grant laughed.

Annie rolled her eyes.

"Dawn is very capable of thinking and acting for herself. If the talkative one got out of line, and you find him missing, you might want to check the hospital," Isobelle smiled.

"Wow, can you imagine?" Annie said.

"I can, actually. I told you, the folks here in the desert are different than we are," Grant said.

"Did you tell me that?"

"Well, I told somebody that. I can't remember everything I say."

"You should, Señor Grant, because you speak very little," Isobelle, still smiling.

"Yeah, she's right, Señor Grant," Annie said, nudging him slightly.

"I hope you sleep well, and that I see you both tomorrow. Here is my number, if you need anything at all," Isobelle said, handing them a business card. "My home number is on the back."

"Isobelle Mendez," Annie said, reading the card.

"That is me."

"Gosh, you don't have to do that. We wouldn't dream of bothering you at home, we'll be fine. That's very nice of you," Annie said.

"It is not a problem. I do not give it to everyone, only the good people," Isobelle said.

"So, does the Plaid Platoon from this afternoon have your card?" Grant asked, smiling.

"No, they do not!" Isobelle said.

"Just checking."

"Who is the Plaid Platoon?" Annie asked.

"Nothing," Grant said. "Inside joke."

"Oh, I see," Annie said, slightly put out that Isobelle and Grant apparently had inside jokes together.

"Your friend is funny. It is nothing to be concerned about. He notices strange things, that is all," Isobelle replied.

"That he does, that he does," Annie said, looking at Grant and Isobelle.

"Well, good night to you," Isobelle said, hugging first Annie, then Grant.

"Good night to you, and thank you again," Annie said. She was moved by the gesture and looked at Isobelle as she hugged Grant, then looked up into the night sky.

"Thanks again," Grant said.

"Always talking," Annie laughed.

Isobelle got back into her car and slowly drove away. Grant and Annie stood together, looking up at the desert sky. The Milky Way looked like a giant, white paintbrush had made a swipe across the black spotted canvas. Annie sighed.

"You want to go swimming?" Grant asked.

"No! Are you serious?"

"No, just thought it sounded funny."

"Well, it does sound funny," Annie said.

"We could walk to the pool and look at it before … you know…."

"I'm really—"

"That's OK, it's late," Grant said, looking towards Isobelle's car as it was pulling away.

Annie changed her glance from the sky to Grant, looking towards Isobelle's car.

"No, you know what? Let's do that. Let's go swimming."

CHAPTER 16

Saturday Morning

Hummmmmmmmmmm.

The grass felt good beneath Grant's bare feet, and the sun was warm on his shoulders. There was a hum, but he didn't know the source of the sound. He turned around to see Annie walking ten feet behind him, at least. He walked on, back over to the swimming pool. The hum was still there. He came to the edge of the pool, ready to dive in. The humming was bothering him and he thought maybe if he dove into the pool it would go away. He looked across the water and now Annie was standing near the edge on the other side. He was trying to get in the pool and swim to her, but he couldn't get his feet to leave the pavement. It was as if he were cemented to the surface and he tried frantically to free himself and swim to her. Annie said nothing, but a voice beside him was speaking soothingly to him from not five feet away. He was about to dive in, he wanted to dive in, when—

Rrriiinnnggg!

The phone ringing startled him, making the swimming pool and Annie disappear, and the voice stopped speaking. He awoke with a jolt.

Rrriiinnnggg!

The phone rang again, and the low hum of the air conditioner was audible between rings. He had taken a deep breath, thinking he was about to dive into the pool. It took him several seconds to realize he was not gliding under the water, that he could let that breath out, that he was … in his hotel room. The phone rang again.

"Shit!"

"Hello?"

"Get the hell out of the sack, you sorry bastard!" It was Rex.

"What? What the hell time is it?"

"How should I know, I'm on vacation. Get your ass down to the pool and let's eat," he said, drawing the word out as long as possible, "'Cause I am starving to death! And you are wasting time, alone, just like always."

"What?"

"You are really on top of it today. You're not used to talking to people in person, and certainly not good looking women, so that must be what has you all messed up. Not that you're ever not messed up. Get the hell down here. Bye." Rex hung up.

Grant let out the breath, lying back down on the bed, his heart was pounding. He worked to get his breathing in line, to clear his mind. There was a great deal to clear.

"How far back did the dream go," he thought. This was going to take a few minutes. He took several breaths, in, out, slowly repeating. Now that the fog was lifting, he was able to piece together the events of the evening. The previous day had done a great deal to calm some of his demons. To think that he had held the attention of the woman he still loved, and for some strange reason, also held the attention of a woman he had just met, was quite a lot to be happy about. He stopped, thinking back to the dream.

"Now that was too damn obvious, even for me," he thought again. He stopped, listening to the hum of the air conditioner, lying back across the top of the bed. Spending time with Annie, as he had done last night, was something he had been imagining for a long time. He would have been content with the time they spent together at the restaurant, but the peacefulness of sitting by the pool with her afterwards was more than he could have hoped for. There, it was just the two of them, their legs dangling in the water, the conversation easy, when there was any at all. She was just easy to be around. He reluctantly got up from the bed, and quickly showered, shaved, dressed and headed to the pool.

The reflection of the sun off the pool made the day seem more glorious than it already was. Rex was holding court, and his bookends, Moll and Mag, were with him. Grant had hoped they would not be there, but knew they would be. Rex saw him coming.

"There he is, sleeping his life away, when he could be here having a great time with us!" Rex said.

"Hello," Grant muttered.

"Don't overdo it, chief, you got the whole day ahead of you and I would hate to have you run out of things to say."

"We always have you to talk incessantly if somebody should ever be at a lack for words…." Grant grumbled.

"We can talk too!" one of the women said.

"I'll bet you can. Which one are you?" Grant asked.

"I'm Moll, she's Mag," the woman said.

"Of course you are," Grant nodded once.

"Yeah, she's Moll, I'm Mag," the other one said.

"That's great, I remember now. I was in a hurry last night."

"And you are Grant," Moll pointed out.

"Yep, that pretty much covers it."

"That's Señor Grant, ladies, and I'm glad we got these introductions squared away. Now, can we eat? I'm starving!" Rex said.

"It's not my job to keep you fed, I'm not the zookeeper," Grant said, still not looking back at Rex.

"I got to do everything myself," Rex said, now waving at one of the staff members. The man came quickly.

"Hello there, could you—what's your name? Could you get us some menus?" Rex said.

"Certainly, sir. My name is—Señor Grant, good morning!" the man said, looking away from Rex and up to Grant.

Grant turned his gaze away from the pool to the staff member. "What? Oh, Fausto, hello."

"Is there anything I can bring you while I go get you some menus?" the man asked.

"Hey, I remember you from last night. You saved my life walking down that hill. Bloody Marys, all the way around," Rex said.

"Very good, sir, and it was my pleasure."

"Maybe your bartender girlfriend will be here this morning to take care of us," Rex grinned.

"Is his girlfriend the bartender?" Moll asked.

"No," Grant shot back. "I just met her yesterday."

"And she's your girlfriend already? Wow, you're fast!" Mag chimed in.

"She's not my girlfriend. I just met her."

"She wants to be his girlfriend, though," Rex said.

"When is it that you are fun to be around? I can't remember. I can see that it is not first thing in the morning," Grant said, looking back towards the pool.

"Hey, just cause you wore yourself out re-learning what it's like to be around people again doesn't mean you got to pee in the pool for everybody else," Rex replied.

"Did he pee in the pool? Yuck!" Moll said.

"Yuck!" Mag added.

Rex was laughing, looking at Grant, who was shaking his head, not bothering to look back towards the group. "No, hon, he didn't pee in the pool. It's just a phrase. In fact, he's so uptight that sometimes he goes days without peeing," Rex said looking first at Moll, then at Mag.

"Oh, I see," Moll said.

"I see," Mag said.

"But, are you sure…? Because we were going to go swimming later, and if he…."

"He didn't pee in the pool, trust me, it's OK to go swimming," Rex said patting her on the back.

"Two gals, one mind," Grant muttered, "or less."

Isobelle arrived back at work at the Ritz, feeling pretty good about the night before. She still wanted to get to know Grant better, but the time spent last night was progress. She was enamored with him and had decided he was worth the effort. The woman, Annie, seemed like a very caring person, and though she wished she were not here to compete with, Isobelle found it difficult not to like her. Isobelle could feel that Grant and Annie had been very much in love at one time. It seemed the break was hardest on Grant, but Annie's eyes told of much sadness as well. The entire thing was perplexing, but Isobelle was sure she would see Grant today, and that would allow her to discover more. Isobelle had been alone a long time. She was tired of the men who came to the bar and always tried to hit on her. She wanted someone of substance. Grant hadn't tried to flirt with her, and she sensed his pain, his loneliness. She could tell there was some great person inside of him, someone who had been sitting alone for a long time, alone in the dark.

"Good morning, Isobelle," Fausto said as he passed the bar.

"Good morning, Fausto. Isn't it a lovely day?"

"Yes, it is a lovely day. Your friend, Señor Grant, he is out by the pool."

Isobelle lit up. "Oh, very good! I understand you rescued him and his friend last night."

"They were walking down the road, and it was very hot. It was not a good time of day to be walking."

"Well, it is lucky for them that you came along. He had already had a difficult day as it was."

"Well, it was nothing."

"It was very kind of you. But he is not by himself at the pool, is he?"

"No. He is with the noisy one, and the two flashy women, the ones you do not like," Fausto said.

Isobelle's expression changed as soon as she heard the roll call. "How long have they been there?"

"Not long. The noisy one wants breakfast. The flashy ones want whatever the noisy one can give them."

"Are the girls sitting near Señor Grant?" Isobelle asked quickly.

"No. They might as well both be sitting in the lap of the noisy one, but you know them, it is probably just a matter of time before they try."

"Yes, I do not care for them at all."

"They are always a problem, if not for us, then for some poor fellows. Well they are poor after the ladies finish them off," Fausto said, shaking his head.

"That is true. How about the women from yesterday afternoon? Are they there as well?"

"I have not seen them."

"Of course, I … very well."

"How—"

"Nothing, never mind. Well, make sure they—er, that Señor Grant gets something to eat, so he does not get drunk with them, because you know they will try to get him drunk. When they start to drink, let me know which drinks are for the women. Maybe they will drink too much, too soon, and will have to leave early," Isobelle said.

"Of course. The noisy one and the women have ordered Bloody Marys. Señor Grant just wants water right now."

"Gracias, Fausto. I will take care of it. You are a good friend."

"As are you, Isobelle," Fausto said as he left to bring the water and the menus.

Isobelle continued doing her prep work for the day ahead, which helped her to focus. She wished she could be out there, but Fausto would keep her posted on whatever she herself could not see. She looked about the room as she did her work and saw Kat was walking through the hotel, heading her way. She liked Kat. There was something very deep about her, and Kat probably sensed that Isobelle knew.

"Good morning, Isobelle."

"Good morning to you."

"I just wanted to thank you for the really great evening last night. It could not have been better."

"I am glad that you had a good time."

"I had a wonderful time. You must come to La Jolla sometime and let me return the favor."

"It would be my pleasure."

"Have you seen any of our friends from last night?"

"Well, I have not seen all of them, but have it on very good authority that the two gentlemen are out by the pool," Isobelle nodded.

"Well, one gentleman, anyway. Is Annie with them?"

"I do not believe so."

"Oh."

"Is something wrong?"

"No, nothing is wrong. I just … you haven't seen her, er, seen Annie this morning?" Kat asked, looking around.

"No, I have not."

"Ok, well thanks. Just thought I would check."

"Would you like me to give her a message if I see her?"

"Just tell her to call me if you see her."

"I will do that. Are you sure everything is all right?" Isobelle asked.

"Just a little … no, everything is fine, I think. Thank you again for the wonderful evening."

"My pleasure. We will see each other again."

"I hope so," Kat said.

"I believe that you know it is so."

"What do you mean?"

"I believe that you see things, but you do not tell anyone that you see things."

Kat looked at Isobelle, but said nothing.

"It is difficult at times to see things, to feel things in such a way that others do not. It is not always comfortable. I know you have a gift."

Kat pressed her lips tightly together. "I don't know what to say."

"You do not have to say anything. Sometimes you probably joke with your friends, or give Rex a hard time because you see things and do not know if you should say anything. That is OK."

"I know you can do it." Kat's expression was very serious.

"I can, but you can too, and you are awakening to that ability even now." Isobelle raised her eyebrows, leaning her head towards Kat.

"I can't tell anyone that." Kat looked around.

"This kind of thing is to be as you want it, you should know that."

"The whole thing is confusing." Kat rubbed her eyes.

"It will get better. Enjoy the gift you have been given."

"Wouldn't that be wrong, to enjoy it, I mean?"

"Not at all. There is, as I said before, no right, no wrong."

Kat looked at Isobelle for several seconds. "I have to go, but maybe we can talk more about this?"

"I would welcome that."

CHAPTER 17

Kat left the bar and headed for the pool. Isobelle could tell something was wrong, at least in Kat's mind.

Grant was doing his level best to not go insane listening to the banter of Rex and his new friends. That was hard to do with Rex. He always wanted everyone to be involved, and this was no exception. Though Grant had sternly maintained his composure at the dinner, he still drank quite a bit yesterday, and had to deal with a bit of a hangover today. He was also still trying to sort out the dream from the actual events of last night. There were no bad parts to weed out, which made the mental inventory easier. His time at the pool with Annie, after they came back from the restaurant, seemed like a dream, but he knew that part was real.

"Hey, Grant," Kat said.

"What?" Grant startled out of his reverie.

"Hey, Greek, what about me? Wanna meet my two friends?" Rex asked.

"Hello. Nice to meet you," Kat said, quickly turning back to Grant. "Have you seen Annie today?"

"No, I haven't."

"Oh, good. I mean, me either."

"Something wrong?"

"No."

"You sure?"

"Yes. I think she said she was going to play tennis with someone this morning."

"Better be done soon, starting to get pretty hot already. You sure nothing is wrong?" Grant asked, moving in his chair.

Kat looked at Grant. She looked back at Rex and the two women. Rex was holding two fingers up behind their heads, grinning goblin-like back at Kat. Kat quickly looked back to Grant. "Maybe a walk would…."

"Yep," Grant said, getting out of his chair.

"Hey, I thought we were having drinks and breakfast!?" Rex said.

"In a minute. Be right back." Grant replied, as he and Kat moved away from the table.

"Ok, but if you don't come back, this is all going on your room, right girls?"

Moll and Mag started giggling.

"Yeah, yeah," Grant said.

He and Kat moved over to the pool.

"Ok, here's the deal. I just met you, but I know a lot about you," Kat said.

"Uh oh."

"Look, I would do anything for Annie."

"I would too."

"We agree on that, so … um…."

"What is it?" Grant asked.

"She has a boyfriend … well, not really a boyfriend. More like somebody she knows, spends a little time with. No, has spent some time with, and … he is a colossal asshole," Kat said the last part so Grant could not hear, but unable to keep herself from spitting it out.

"Shit."

"I'm not telling you this to … to get a response out of you, or to get, I don't know, to get you to back off. I actually think you are—"

"I am what?" Grant asked, nervously.

"Look, in my field, I am not supposed to be judgmental."

"What field are you in? I missed that part of the conversation."

"Psychiatrist, I'm a psychiatrist."

"Holy shit!"

"Yeah, I don't usually get that response, but OK. He called her last night and said he's coming here," Kat said, looking uncomfortable.

"It's a free country, I guess," he said, but his body language clearly showed that he was disappointed by this news.

"The deal is … the deal—"

"The deal is what?" Grant asked, leaning closer to Kat.

"The deal is he is just the most … that he's—that he's the most, biggest total asshole in the world!" Kat said, shaking her head.

"Really? Worse than me?" Grand said, straightening up, standing taller.

"I wouldn't say all the time, but some of the time he makes your buddy Rex there look really good. You're not an asshole, you're just lonely."

"How is it that Annie would be with someone like that? And how do you know I'm lonely?"

"His parents and Annie's parents are good friends. It's more a pairing of convenience," Kat said. "And with you, I can just tell."

"Pairing of convenience?"

"You really don't have to repeat everything I say. Anyway, Annie works all the time, never goes out—"

"I know that drill," Grant said, looking around the area.

"She doesn't get a chance to meet anyone, so her parents and Clement's parents, they set them up, and Annie has just been too nice to—"

"Too nice to tell them to fuck off! Excuse my language."

"Hey, it doesn't bother me. I think she should tell them all to fuck off. Her parents have always wanted her to have—"

"I know this part really well, you don't have to explain," Grant said, cutting her off.

"I know it's hard to tell her parents to, you know, fuck off, but she could tell Clement. She should tell him to fuck off. Maybe this is a way to do that," Kat said.

"I didn't know you back, you know, back then, and I barely know you now, but you … you are—"

"What?"

"You are so much better than this guy, I can't even tell you!"

"You still drunk from last night?" Grant smiled.

"No!"

"Just checking. I think I might be," Grant said, looking all around the pool grounds.

"Look at me," Kat said sternly.

"What?"

"Look at me!"

Grant looked at Kat. She grabbed his jaw, turned it side to side, and looked into his eyes. "Nope, you're fine, visibly anyway. I would have to sit with you and make some notes regarding the inside, but my instinct still says lonely."

"Not sure I would sign up for that one," Grant mumbled.

"You're fine, trust me."

"So what should I do?"

"Just being, you know, just being a good guy," Kat said.

"That's all?"

"Yes."

"Well, I didn't know I was."

"Shut up. You didn't do anything stupid after I left last night, did you?"

"Surprisingly enough, no. And for me, that is saying a lot," Grant said, looking proud of himself.

"Good. I am going to try to keep him away from her, from us, from you. I am not sure how yet, but I will think of something. You cannot tell her, you know, or that will just mess things up."

"You're going to keep him away from her, from me, what the hell is that?"

"So she can relax, be with her friends, and not get distracted by Mr. Wonderful," Kat said, letting out a breath.

"Mr. Wonderful? Does he have a name?"

"Yes, I said it already. Guess you weren't listening," Kat said.

"Don't suppose you would tell me again?" Grant asked.

"If his name was Grant, would it make you feel, I don't know, different?" Kat asked.

"Is his name Grant?"

"No."

"Then why did you say that?"

"Just trying to draw you out a bit. Look, let's focus on what I just told you, to which, if you had been listening, I wouldn't have to tell you his name again," Kat said.

"All right."

"Good."

"So what is his name?" Grant asked.

"Clement. His name is Clement. Do you feel better now?"

"No."

"Then it didn't make any difference."

"I guess not."

Kat took a deep breath. "So, can we do this?" she asked.

"You are going to keep Clement away?

"Yes. I think it's best for her."

"You do?"

"Don't you?"

"I don't know the guy," Grant said.

"You enjoy being with Annie?"

"What do you think?"

"I think that if you want to enjoy some more time with her, he doesn't need to get in the way of that right now."

"Right now?"

"Why do you repeat the last thing I say? Are you four years old?" Kat demanded. "It's really irritating."

"Force of habit, I guess."

"Well, right now means right now. I can't know where this—where you and her are going to go. What I do know is that it will go nowhere, and there will be no more of you and her, not even in the immediate future, if he's around."

"You think not?" Grant asked.

"I know not. Just one day, and she is already better. I can't say if it has anything to do with you or not. Maybe it was just her getting away to come out here that is getting her to relax, but she hasn't been this relaxed in a long time," Kat said.

"So...."

"So just do what you do, and try not to hold anything back for next time, in case there isn't a next time. Does that make sense?" Kat said.

"Somewhat."

"Good. I think it's worth continuing on with the vibes we're getting from the desert."

"I always did get good vibes from the desert ... this time, maybe more," Grant said, looking up at the sky.

"Exactly."

"All right."

"Hey, don't look so disappointed. You're not out of the running yet," Kat said, touching him on the shoulder.

"Didn't know I was in the running," Grant said.

"Annie was happier last night than I have seen her in, I don't know, forever. That doesn't mean that you are going to end up back together, but worse things could happen than the two of you seeing each other this weekend, or maybe every once in a while, right?" Kat asked.

"Right."

"Can I ask you a question?"

"Ask away." Grant said.

"What were you hoping to accomplish this weekend?" Kat asked

"Not sure what you mean."

"I mean, what were you, were you wanting to … what did you think would happen with you and Annie?"

"I didn't know," Grant said. "I didn't know what was going to happen. I haven't seen Rex in a long time."

"So that was…."

"That wasn't the only thing. I wasn't sure I believed him that Annie was coming here. This may surprise you, but Rex has been known to…."

"Has been known to be full of shit?" Kat said, becoming impatient.

"Well, I was going to say he sometimes adds or subtracts integral parts of his stories, but it sounds like you get the picture."

"Go on," Kat tapped her fingers on her leg.

"Well, I was just hoping that this time he was more accurate in his outline of the excursion."

"That he wasn't completely full of shit, and that Annie would be here."

"Something like that, yes," Grant said, looking away from Kat, and back over to the pool.

"And if she was here, you would…?"

"I didn't know what I would do. Why are you asking me this?"

"Because I care about Annie," Kat said.

"You think I don't?"

"To the contrary, I think you care deeply about her, or at least you do now."

"But you think maybe I didn't in the past?"

"No … I don't know … I … She told me about some of the shit you and skeezitz used to pull. I was intrigued by the dynamic of the whole thing, though dynamic might not be the right word. Rex starts calling her after how many years, and she doesn't really like him anyway, and then he asks her to come out here for a reunion with him—oh, and her former boyfriend."

"A might perplexing, ain't it?"

"No, it's a lot perplexing, clinically, or otherwise." Kat said firmly.

"So why are you quizzing me about it? I'm just as curious about this get together as you are. More, actually."

"But you still love her?"

Grant started to fidget. He rubbed his hands and arms, as if trying to get the skin to come off and grow anew. He looked at the ground, back to Kat, then back to the pool.

"Hey, I shouldn't have asked about that, I'm sorry. I don't want anything bad to happen to her, ever. Not that you would be bad. I actually think it would be really good for her."

"Yeah, well, thanks for the vote of confidence," Grant said.

"It came out wrong."

"Okay." Grant paused, took a breath, and looked around. "What about you?" Grant held his hand out to Kat.

"What about me?"

"What were you hoping to accomplish this weekend?"

"I wasn't, I just came—I was just here for…."

"That clears it up."

"A weekend in the desert, with my friend. Anything wrong with that?" Kat asked.

"You know everything about me, I know nothing about you. So you can ask me questions, and I just have to provide the answers. Seems a bit one sided to me. If it were Rex, well, that would be different."

Kat paused, and looked around the pool area. She looked back over to where Rex and the girls were sitting. Rex had an arm around each one of them, but noticed Kat looking their way, and waved back at her. Kat smiled, barely holding up one hand, waist level, to wave back. She looked back to Grant.

"That's fair, you're right. I've been hearing about you for years, so, I guess I have the advantage."

"Was it bad stuff?"

Kat could see Grant's point. She had been grilling him, and he didn't really know her at all.

"Of course not," Kat said.

"How the hell would I know?"

"Well it wasn't, it was all good."

"So back to you," Grant persisted.

"Me, back to me. What do you want to know?"

"Whatever you're willing to give up."

"Let's see ... Annie and I met in med school, and have been friends ever since. I seemed to fare better with the questioning to get inside of patients, rather than the cutting them open to get inside of them, so I went the psychiatrist route. I had always been able to tell ..."

"Tell what?" Grant interupted.

"We can talk about that another time."

"You mean on the clock?"

"No, not on the clock. Just when we know each other better."

"Sounds like you already know me."

"Goddamnit!"

"OK, OK. Back to you."

"Thank you. We, Annie and I, just have been really close friends since then, and I would do anything for her. We traveled some together; we live in the same town; we seem to share a lot of the same beliefs. I don't have to tell you how she is. She is a healer, I just interpret things. She would do almost anything for anybody, but she's a better person than I am."

"You're a bad seed, huh?"

"No, just not as understanding or as forgiving as she is."

"Where are you from?" Grant asked.

"Is this necessary?"

"You know everything about me...."

"Fuck! Sorry. Right, right. I am from all over. My family moved around a lot and that was sort of draining, so after I went away to school, I tried to be more grounded, if that makes sense."

"A lot of folks want to be more grounded."

"Right, some just aren't aware, and probably never can be," Kat said, as she looked back over to Rex, and he again waved back. "I started meditating, I started looking into energy work, I started yoga, positive affirmation...."

"You still do all that?"

"Every bit of it."

"So you are a person of commitment," Grant said.

"Absolutely."

"That's good."

"I think so. I enjoy what I do. I'd like to go out of the country someday to work in an underprivileged area for a while."

"That's quite impressive."

"Thank you. Feel better? I mean, now that you know about me?" Kat asked.

"I know very little about you, but I suppose that now I know more than I did, so it's a start."

"Good. You want to know more, just ask."

"You said this was good for Annie. Is it good for me?"

"You seeing anyone now? Not that it's any of my business."

"That hasn't seemed to have stopped you from asking everything else, but now that I know what line of work you are in, I guess it is in keeping with your profession. But nope, not seeing anyone," Grant said.

"Then this would be better, wouldn't it?"

"Yep."

"Good. I'll see you when I see you. Sometime later today," Kat said, turning to leave. She paused, not looking back.

"All right," Grant said.

"By the way, Rex was right," Kat said.

"About?"

"About you talking too much."

CHAPTER 18

Isobelle was still doing her prep work at the bar when she saw Annie walk into the hotel. She was wearing her tennis clothes, and she looked like she had been exercising. She walked by the bar and caught a glimpse of Isobelle, and stopped to talk to her.

"Good morning."

"Good morning, Annie. How is everything today? You look like you have had a workout, no?"

"Yes, I really needed it after the great dinner last night, which I want to thank you again for. That was so kind of you and your friend to do that for us."

"It was a pleasure. You were playing tennis, it looks like," Isobelle said.

"Yes, still chasing the ball whenever I can."

"It is a very good game."

"Do you play?"

"Yes. Not often, but I play."

"Well, we should hit sometime."

"Yes, that would be nice. You would undoubtedly win."

"We can just hit, we don't have to keep score. It's just to get out and get the exercise," Annie said.

"I can do that."

"Good. Say, have you seen any of our friends pass by here today?"

"Yes, Kat stopped by and we talked a little. She is a very nice person. There is a great deal of depth to her. Her comments mask a real understanding that she has of a great many things."

"Yes, she is a wonderful person. We have been friends for a long time, and she is very insightful … much more so than I am."

"You never give yourself much credit. She is your friend of many years, so she sees good qualities in you, that I know," Isobelle said.

"Maybe she just knows I need lots of help."

"That I doubt."

"Well, she is a great friend."

"And Señor Grant sees a great deal in you, so maybe you are too hard on yourself."

Isobelle could see Annie perk up when she heard Grant's name, but she started to fidget when she talked about his feelings. Isobelle knew Annie wanted to hear more about him, but for some reason was having trouble dealing with their past.

"I don't know about that. It was such a long time ago that …" Annie said, stopping before she finished the sentence.

"I apologize; it is not my intention to talk about matters that do not concern me."

"That's ok, you don't have to apologize. Speaking of Grant, have you seen him this morning?"

"I personally have not, but it my understanding that he is out by the pool, with the noisy one," Isobelle said.

Annie laughed when she heard Isobelle describe Rex that way. It was funny yesterday and seemed even funnier today.

"What did I say to make you laugh?"

"Your description of Rex," Annie smiled.

"The noisy one?"

"Yes, that."

"He certainly speaks more than the others, or anyone I know, for that matter."

This made Annie laugh even more.

"Do you not agree?" "I completely agree. He's always been that way, it is just funny to hear someone else notice and comment on it," Annie said, still smiling.

"You say he has always been that way?"

"Yes. Grant says that Rex's family was always sort of, I don't know if this is the right word, but that they were overpowering, overly controlling, and he rebelled against that by talking a lot … and being sort of crazy."

"I can see that about his family, but in what way do you mean?"

"They would always tell him to do what they thought was best for them, not necessarily what was best for him," Annie said, then wondering why Isobelle had said that she saw that in Rex.

"That is something, no?"

"Why do you say that?"

"I do not know these people, I am only commenting on what you tell me. A person this far along in his life should perhaps chose his own path, not one chosen by others. There is a particular school of thought that says that our paths have been chosen long before the lives we are currently in. We may still make choices, but those who help us along the way were meant to help us and not to dictate to us. We are not meant to do everything on our own, and our guides help us get to where we are going," Isobelle said, polishing a glass with a towel, holding it up to the light.

Annie looked at the glass Isobelle was polishing, the reflecting light moving across her face, down the bar and out of sight. She looked at Isobelle and felt a chill. She started to say something, but then looked back down the bar, to where the light had vanished. She started again.

"I can't…."

"You know better than I." Isobelle paused. "Whatever the case may be, I hear from my friend that they are out by the pool. Kat was heading out there to see them. I believe the women from yesterday are also with them."

"The women from yesterday?"

"Yes, the ones who were at the end of the bar when you were here."

"Oh, those women," Annie's demeanor changed.

"Exactly. Perhaps you and I can see them for what they are. I am not sure how the men see them."

"Maybe I'll go out there and check on Kat. She's not very tolerant of people like that. Thanks again for last night and I hope we see you later."

"You are welcome, and I hope I see you later, as well. Enjoy your day and just tell Fausto if you need anything at all."

"Fausto?"

"Yes. He is waiting on them out there. If you need anything at all, please let him know. It does not have to be on the menu, whatever you would like. Oh, I almost forgot—Kat told me she would like you to call her."

"Thank you, I will."

Annie left the bar and headed to the pool area. Isobelle could tell that Annie still had feelings for Grant, but she seemed to be having trouble coming to grips with those feelings and with her relationship to Grant. Isobelle thought that perhaps their past conflict might prevent Annie from fully showing her true feelings to Grant, which was all right with Isobelle.

Annie could hear Rex as soon as she stepped outside, and soon could see the girls from last night. The women were wearing bikinis, but there was not much material in the two garments combined. Annie dreaded conversing with the two, but she wanted to find Kat and to see Grant.

"Well, look who's going to join us," Rex said loudly enough for most of the pool area to hear.

Annie was far enough away that she was not going to answer back as loudly as Rex had greeted her. She blushed a little, smiling at Grant, not making eye contact with anyone else.

"What took you so long to … hey, you look like you've been, what, bowling?" Rex said.

"That's right, Rex, these are my bowling clothes," Annie said, shaking her head, still looking at Grant. Grant returned her expression of barely-contained laughter. "And you know how hard it is to find a good bowling alley that opens at seven in the morning."

"I didn't know you could go bowling at seven in the morning," Moll said.

"I didn't either," Mag added. "And I thought bowling clothes looked different."

"Yeah, me too. They look the same as tennis clothes. Who knew?" Moll shrugged.

"I can only stay a minute, I need to clean up after my bowling," Annie said, raising her eyebrows, smiling and looking at Grant. She sat next to him.

"I thought bowling alleys were air conditioned," Moll said.

"Yeah, me too," Mag followed.

"Yeah, me too," Grant joined in.

"Well, this one wasn't," Annie said, kicking Grant's foot under the table.

"That's too bad. Maybe you could jump in the pool," Moll said.

"Yeah, it would cool you right off," Mag said.

"Really? I mean, I would have to get a suit on first," Annie answered.

"You got one like these girls have?" Rex asked.

"I'm pretty sure I don't, they look pretty expensive."

Moll and Mag beamed at what they deemed to be a compliment. Grant looked down at his feet, which were now becoming sore because Annie had her foot on top of his, pressing down every time Moll and Mag said something.

"There's a great shop here that sells them, if you want to go get one. We could give you the name," Moll said.

"Yeah, they know us in there," Mag said.

"I'll bet they do, and thank you, I will keep it in mind," Annie said, pressing harder on Grant's feet. "Have you seen Kat?" Annie asked.

"She was here a minute ago. Said she had to, uh, take care of something," Grant said, rather off guard.

"Everything all right?"

"No, err, yes, fine. Just an errand or something. She's kind of a free spirit, isn't she?" Grant asked, trying to cover his stuttering.

"Yes, very much so, and I mean different from your friends here," Annie said, her eyes moving towards Moll and Mag, then back to Grant. The girls were now enthralled by some story Rex was telling them, no longer paying attention to anyone else.

"Rex found 'em, not me," Grant said.

"You're here."

"It's not like that."

"You sure?"

"Quite. They're too smart for me."

Annie could not stop herself from laughing out loud.

Grant smiled back. Annie let up the pressure on his foot.

"I have to go clean up," Annie said.

"You don't want to go in the pool?" Grant smiled.

"Later," Annie stepped on his feet again. "I have to change out of my bowling clothes."

"Thought as much."

"I need to have lunch or something with my friends I was supposed to see last night," Annie said.

"I understand."

"I'll see you after that," Annie said, standing to leave.

"You leaving so soon? The drinks haven't gotten here yet," Rex said.

"You can have mine, I'll see you later," Annie said, leaving the group, touching Grant on the shoulder before she left.

"Well, she didn't look like a bowler," Moll said.

"I didn't think so either," Mag added.

"You just never know," Grant said, getting up to go after Annie, pausing to stretch.

"Where you going?" Rex asked.

"Bowling."

"I didn't know bowling was so popular here," Moll said.

"I guess it must be," Mag added. "Are you going to take us bowling?"

"Sure, if you want me to," Rex said. "But you heard her say it wasn't air conditioned, so maybe we should go swimming instead. After the drinks come, of course."

"Well, OK, if it's OK with Moll."

"It's OK with me, if it's OK with you," Moll said.

Grant smiled at both women, finishing his stretch, looking around the area. He looked around just as the man and the woman with the sunglasses, from the night before, sat down, a couple of tables down from them. His smile dimmed.

CHAPTER 19

"Annie," Grant called. She hadn't made it back inside the hotel before Grant caught up with her. She turned, somewhat surprised. "Glad I caught you."

"Aren't you going to hang with the swim suit models?"

"Uh, let's see. No."

"Why not? They are amazing conversationalists, and they're almost naked. I thought you would like that."

"Well, I like part of that."

"Which part?" Annie said, looking angry.

"The conversationalist part."

"Right."

"No, really, they're fascinating."

"Uh-huh."

"Couldn't you tell?"

"I must have been too intimidated … you know, by their use of big words."

"Yes, they are much too sharp for me. Rex, however…." Grant said.

"They are right in a long line of caring, female, geniuses that he has surrounded himself with over the years. "

"I think he has a questionnaire that he gives them."

"Very in-depth, no doubt."

"I actually think it only has one question, maybe two."

"Usually it is only one woman. He must have gotten a buy-one-get-one deal somewhere. Where did he shop this time?" Annie asked, still not smiling.

"They were here, at the bar."

"At the bar, what are the odds of that?"

"Well, we were just talking and … wait, you were there, you saw them come in, I wasn't involved in that," Grant said.

Annie thought for a moment and looked back towards the pool where Rex and the women were still carrying on. She looked back at Grant. "I guess I wasn't paying attention to them when they came in, but now that you mention it."

"I do enough screwed up things on my own to get credited with anything that Rex does. That would make the tally awfully high, even for me."

"All right, I won't give you credit for this one," Annie said, relaxing a little.

"Thank you."

Annie looked back again to where Rex and the girls were and shook her head. "Do you think he's happy like that?"

"I don't know. Are any of us happy?" Grant asked.

Annie tilted her head and looked back to Grant, then down at the ground. "That's sort of hard to say. I mean, we all get busy and sort of do the things we do, I guess."

"I didn't mean it that way. I mean … I meant, hell, I didn't mean anything," Grant said, somewhat flustered.

"Are you happy?"

"Probably, yeah. Are you?"

"Yes. What is 'probably' supposed to mean?" Annie asked.

"Nothing. Nothing meant anything."

Annie was smiling a soft smile. "Nothing meant anything?"

"You know, we could …"

"Could what?"

"Well, for one thing, we could not be standing here while the circus is over there, that might help," Grant said.

"I thought you liked the circus."

"Clown tent is full, don't need one more."

"Kind of shorting yourself. I was thinking more ringmaster."

"Really?"

"No, but you made the circus analogy. I guess that's not asking a lot, let's walk. As long as you don't mind, you know, walking around with someone in her sweaty bowling clothes," Annie smiled.

They both smiled and began to walk around the grounds of the hotel, away from the crowd at the pool. The day was warming, but Grant had a t-shirt and shorts on, and of course, Annie was wearing her "bowling" outfit. They did not say much, as it was just nice to be away from the fray, and away from the parts of the past that neither one of them wanted to think about.. Grant pointed out the plush greenery, which he said he thought seemed funny to see in the desert, comparing it with the embellishments of the inside of the building. He did his best not to be tongue tied, and walking eased his mind, and seemed to make him stop pressing himself for some sort of atonement that he thought he had to make. She did not seem to be looking for an apology from him. He definitely thought she had a right to hold a grudge, though he sensed she had let go of any anger towards him a long time ago.

"Would you like to have lunch, or dinner?" Grant asked.

"Eventually, both," Annie smiled.

"I mean just you and me. No circus. Well, at least with just me it would be a smaller circus."

"You would play all the parts yourself?"

"Probably."

"Would I get a good seat, or would I have to sit in the back?"

"Your choice."

Annie pretended to be thinking hard, scratching her head, looking up and around. This made Grant nervous. "Gosh, I don't know."

"I understand if you don't—" Grant said, looking down.

"Of course we can," she said, laughing, shoving him a little. "I have to meet my other friends for lunch, but we can have dinner together, that would be nice."

"You sure? You're not just messing with me?"

"Do I usually?"

"No."

"Why would I start now?"

"To get back at me?" Grant asked.

"For what?"

"Oh, I don't know. For messing things up, I guess."

"What makes you think you messed things up?" Annie turned to face him.

"Twisted intellect, I guess."

"Do me a favor?" Annie asked.

"Sure."

"Don't think too much and we'll talk more later. You said Kat was taking care of something? I have to call her."

"Yep."

"But everything was OK?"

"Yep."

"You're sure?"

"I said it, didn't I?" Grant smiled.

"Funny. All right. I'll see you later," she hugged him and headed to her room.

Grant stood there for a minute. He was ecstatic that Annie had agreed to go out for dinner with him, just the two of them, but he was worried that this Clement character was going to show up and potentially sever what thin thread might have been reattached. As for Kat, considering that he had just met her, Grant had a good deal of faith in her pledge to steer this guy a different direction. This would have to do.

"Can't lose what you don't have," he said.

He walked back to the pool area, where it was obvious that the group was on consumption overdrive. He was a little nervous from his conversations with Annie and Kat, so maybe having a drink with them wasn't the worst idea.

"He's back! Where's the bowler?" Rex bellowed.

"Wanted to get in a few more frames before lunch," Grant said, sitting down.

Got to respect that kind of dedication."

"She went back to bowl some more? Wow, she must really be good!" Moll raised her eyebrows.

"Or she's trying to be really good," Mag nodded slowly.

"Well, You can stay here with us, we're having fun," Moll said, sidling up to Grant.

"There is no doubt in my mind that you are," Grant said. "I can see it in your pack leader's face. This is his kind of day."

"What about you, isn't this your kind of day?" Mag asked.

"Of course it is, but I'm not as smart as Rex, as I am sure he has told you, so I—"

"Watch it, chief. Don't be talking me up too much in front of the girls, you know how I get embarrassed about my many talents."

"He's great, isn't he?" Moll said, looking back at Rex.

"Yeah, he's great," Mag added.

"Boy, is he ever!" Grant said.

"You are very wise people," Rex laughed. "Hey Grant, you see that guy and that woman, over there, in the sunglasses? They were in the bar last night."

"Yeah, so?"

"I think they're watching me."

"I can pretty well tell you that no one is watching you. And I don't mean just them," Grant said.

Fausto came to the table with drinks.

"Welcome back, Señor Grant. Here are the drinks for the ladies and the gentleman."

"You had better bring Señor Grant a drink if he wants to be allowed to sit at this table," Rex said loudly.

"I would be happy to, but first, Señor Grant has a phone call inside. I will be happy to take you there, Sir."

"Gotta be a wrong number, the only friends he has are sitting at this table," Rex shot back, "and we're a bit iffy at that."

Grant quickly stood and followed Fausto back into the hotel.

"We'll be here waiting for you, but only 'til Sunday!"

"Great."

Grant couldn't think of anyone that would call him, except for maybe Kat.

"Maybe she had convinced the guy not to come, or maybe he's here now, or maybe…." Grant hoped he wasn't speaking out loud.

He and Fausto were back inside the hotel and at the bar in no time.

"Here you are, sir," Fausto said, leaving him at the bar, where Isobelle quickly appeared.

"Good morning, Señor Grant," she said smiling, "It is a beautiful day."

"Yes it is. How are you?"

"I am very well, thank you, and yourself?"

"Good, good. Fausto tells me I have a phone call."

"It was more of a rescue call, and I must confess that it is from me."

"Hah! That's a good one. Well, I guess thanks are in order."

"It is probably rude of me to interrupt you from your friends," Isobelle said, blushing slightly.

"Well I only know the one."

“The noisy one, Señor Pinata.” Isobelle smiled.

“Yes, the noisy one. I don’t know the other two.”

“But you know what they are after.”

“I think so, yes,” Grant said.

“Does that interest you?”

“Not really, no.”

“But it is all right for the noisy one to be out there by himself?”

“Well, strange as it sounds, he could use a bit of an ego boost,” Grant said.

“I find that very difficult to believe, but if you tell me it is so, then I will believe you,” Isobelle said.

“But you thought I needed to be rescued?”

“Not so much rescued, as given another option.”

“Another option?”

“Yes. Your other friends have both stopped by to speak with me this morning, but I understand they are no longer out there with you. I wanted to give you another option, in the event that the two remaining women were, how do I say, too intelligent for you, with no offense meant to you,” Isobelle said.

This put Grant completely at ease, and he laughed loudly. Isobelle did not seem to hold anything back. She was a joy to talk to and easy to be with. He had not experienced that with anyone since Annie. He could sit and talk with this woman and there was no pretense. The group at the pool would do fine without him, would probably not even notice he was gone. Rex may have been telling the truth and they might well be sitting in that same place until tomorrow. Sitting here talking with Isobelle would be better than fine.

“I had the kitchen make you this small quiche. I thought it would help if you had something to eat. It is nothing big, I hope you enjoy it.”

“Thank you, but you didn’t have to do that. Plus, after last night, I’m not sure I need to eat again until Sunday,” Grant said, rubbing his stomach.

“It is my pleasure to do this. Please, sit for a few minutes. It is quiet in here, and I would welcome your company.”

“You sure I’m not getting in the way? You’re not really open yet, it doesn’t look like.”

“No, but I welcome your company.”

“You don’t want to enjoy the peace and quiet, before the plaid people come back?”

“I would enjoy your company more.”

CHAPTER 20

The peacefulness of sitting at the bar while Isobelle did her prep work, having a small, quiet bite of breakfast was a good respite for Grant. She did not interrupt his breakfast, and went about her duties, seeming just happy to have him there. The sense of time, at a resort like this, was something Grant was unfamiliar with. There did not seem to be clocks anywhere, and time seemed to move very slowly, with the somewhat bewildering caveat that even with this leisurely condition, a great deal can happen. Isobelle would occasionally make a reference to desert time, and this seemed to be what she meant. Grant thought it odd that only the day before, he hadn't seen Annie or Rex in years. Today, here he was, Rex was out at the pool, Annie was upstairs, and he was sitting here with Isobelle, in complete peace. There was nothing in the mix that was not progress.

Fausto returned to the bar. "Excuse me, Señor Grant, Isobelle, but the people at the pool keep asking for Señor Grant," Fausto said. "I did not want to interrupt, but they are telling me they are going to call the police and file a missing peoples report."

"Missing person report, but that is quite all right, Fausto, you are not interrupting, we were just talking." Isobelle knew it was not Fausto's fault, but she was disappointed to have her time with Grant interrupted.

"And I thought they wouldn't notice," Grant said.

"Of course they would notice. You are not someone who can just fade away without notice. Fausto, please tell them that he is on his way. I will send some drinks with you to ease their frustration. Excuse me for a moment, Señor Grant, while I take care of your friends." she said, as she moved away to take care of the order.

"Perhaps you could put some of those little umbrellas you keep under the bar in the drinks for the women. They seem amused by everything," Fausto said.

"Good idea, Fausto." Isobelle said over her shoulder, then turning back to look at Grant. "They wouldn't really call the police, would they?"

"Not to be serious, but Rex would think it was funny to do it. We sort of differ on our sense of humor. It would take him a minute to remember he really doesn't want to have anything to do with the law right now."

"I thought as much," Isobelle said, returning to her task.

Grant was pleased at her comments, as he thought that no one ever noticed him. For Isobelle to take issue with that was a compliment. He wasn't used to compliments or attention, which he seemed to have been receiving non-stop since he got here. This was a drastic change from the rituals of his solitary life. To talk to so many women, which to him was any number more than zero, was, in his mind, astounding. He watched Isobelle prepare the drinks for Rex and his new campmates and again marveled in her movements, the blending of confidence and grace. His reflected that his life lacked any semblance of either. He thought it would be nice to have something, someone to make that possible. She returned quickly.

"I had better go and quiet them down before they get thrown out. I really don't want to change hotels."

"I would not like that either. Perhaps we could meet later, after work."

"Well … not sure. I am meeting someone for dinner, I hope, so…."

"Another time, perhaps."

"I'll get back to you. You were very generous last night, and this morning."

"It is my pleasure, just as it would be my pleasure to speak with you again tonight."

"Well, like I said before, don't be taking such good of care of me, or else I might stick around."

"That is my goal."

"I'm generally not a part of anybody's goal, so that's good that I finally got out of that rut. How long have you had this goal?

"Just since you got here."

"Well, not sure I can live up to that."

"You will do just fine."

Grant left the bar and headed back out to the pool. The group seemed now nearly drunk, and it was only noon.

"Spokesmodels for a drunk nation," he said to himself.

He didn't really want to be with them, but he also didn't want them carrying on about filing a missing person report, as Fausto said. Rex wasn't actually concerned that Grant was missing, but he would think about calling the police just to be funny. Grant thought he might try to finish the swim he started last night. Being in the quiet with Isobelle was much better than spending time with Rex and his two dolls. Walking the gardens with Annie was infinitely better than this.

"Just getting ready to call the police!" Rex shouted as Grant approached.

"That's what I understand."

"Who told you?"

"It was all over the hotel. Those folks in the sunglasses were hoping that you would, but I knew you wouldn't."

"Why's that? Wait, what? You talked to—"

"Because if you called the police, you would have to tell them who you are. I was kidding you about the people with the sunglasses. You are a paranoid bastard," Grant said.

"Just cautious, but good point about the federales." Rex said, letting out a slight sigh of relief. "Our man Fausto found you, I see. What were you doing, talking to the plants again?"

"No, talking with a woman. A really attractive woman, actually."

"Just 'cause I haven't seen you in a while doesn't mean you have to start lying on the second day. You don't have to try to impress these two with your tales of adventure—they're already impressed, right girls?"

"We're impressed," Moll smiled.

"We sure are," Mag added, also with a big smile.

"You sure are," Grant smiled.

"Great, aren't they?" Rex laughed.

"Just peachy, Leon. You going to sit here with them all day, or what, exactly?" Grant asked.

"Haven't decided. As you can see, the possibilities are endless, the world is our oyster."

"Are we having oysters?" one of the girls asked.

"If you want, sure." Rex responded to the girls.

"I would say the possibilities are mindless, but that's just me," Grant smiled.

"Well, this really isn't taxing for me, you know."

"It is costing you a fair amount."

"Like I give a shit," Rex said, tossing an ice cube at the girls.

"Well, as long as you get your money's worth."

"I already have. I got you off your sorry ass and out of whatever cave you were living in. Oh, and by the way, in case you didn't notice, I got your old girlfriend here too. Oh, and a good looking bartender who's ready to jump you at any second. Money's worth?"

"What about these two?"

"You want one of them too? Goddamn, you're greedy. Leave a crumb or two for Rexy, if you don't mind. I don't live in a cave, but I deserve some fun too, you know. But...."

"But what?"

"If you want 'em, I could let you take over the tab and I could call Dawn up, which I am probably going to do anyway, after these two become one massive, sweet, slurring slushy."

"Nice alliteration."

"What can I say, they are in the presence of greatness," Rex motioned towards the girls.

"College seems like the other side of the moon now, doesn't it?" Grant asked.

"Not sure what brought that up, but yeah. I don't think about it much, but on days like today I sure do. The weather's great, no immediate ambitions. Kick back, have a few drinks, wait for the women to show up. All the times we just went somewhere and started...."

"Started some shit."

"Something like that."

"You started most of it."

"Your memory has really deteriorated over the years, I meant to tell you last night, Rex said.

"You meant to tell me last night that my memory has deteriorated, but you forgot."

"Something like that. Look at those two. We don't even need to talk to them, and they are having a perfectly good time. I could give 'em a magazine, or a stuffed animal, or some car keys, and they would amuse themselves for hours. How is that possible?"

"You just always brought out the best in women," Grant said.

"Where were these two when we were going to college? It would have been a lot easier."

"You know that their goal is to get you to spend as much money as is humanly possible for you to spend on them?"

"Oh no! Oh my god! You mean someone is trying to take advantage of me?" Rex said, feigning fear.

"So how is it that these two are any different than what you always seemed to attract in college? The only difference is that the stakes are higher now. They don't just want a pizza and beer, they want jewelry and a trip somewhere. Play your cards right, you'll end up with a time share, maybe a couple of apartments you weren't really thinking about acquiring before this weekend," Grant said.

"You've been living in your head way too long."

"How's that?"

"You think I give a shit what these girls are after? Unless they are carrying guns, and I defy you to tell me where they would hide one in those bikinis, they really are of no threat to me. They're just company, in bikinis that are at least a size too small. You trying to tell me there's something wrong with that?" Rex said, not taking his eyes off of the women.

"Well…."

"Well, if you have to think about it, then you need more help than even I figured. Life is way too short. Try living a little, try not thinking about every goddamn thing under the sun. Right girls?"

"Right!" Moll said, raising her glass.

"You got it, chief!" Mag said, repeating the gesture.

"See, the experts don't lie," Rex laughed.

"Have they elected you king yet?" Grant asked.

"Becoming king is not an election process, as you should remember from your otherwise blurry college days. It is a birthright, which, according to these lovely ladies, I have."

"OK if I don't bow?" Grant asked.

"For now. But if you don't loosen up and have fun, you will have no choice but to bow."

"How's that?"

"You'll have to bow after I slug you in the goddamn stomach for being such a dumbass," Rex said.

"That a threat?"

"No, I think it's the promise one."

"Good to know."

"Now either get in there and get with Annie or Margarita."

"Isobelle."

"Right, Isobelle. Get with Isobelle, or get in here with us."

"Can I think about it?"

"You want to bow?"

"No."

"Then go find one of your girlfriends. You don't find one, get back here with us. Now go, I'm tired of talking," Rex said.

"I doubt that."

"I'm tired of talking to you. If you were here with a woman, I would talk to you."

"That the prerequisite?" Grant asked.

"It is this weekend. If I wanted to just hang out with you, I would have come to your place, and we could have been depressed together. But I didn't do that, did I?" Rex asked.

"No."

"No, I didn't. I set this up with your old girlfriend. Isobelle and the Greek, they're a bonus. These two here, they're another bonus. What the hell more do you want out of life? And by life, I mean life right now, not life two days from now, and for the rest of your life. I can't keep having to tell you this shit. You were pretty spontaneous in college, what the hell happened?"

"Trying to get serious, I guess," Grant said.

"Well, you over adjusted the meter and have moved it into the pensive zone. May want to think about dialing it back a turn or seven. Don't you? When was the last time you had any, and I mean any, goddamn fun?" Rex asked.

"Oh, I don't know...."

"Take your time, I'm not going anywhere, am I girls?" Rex smiled.

"No way, chief!" Mag said.

"Your ass belongs to us!" Moll said, putting her arm around Mag.

"When was the last time you had any goddamn fun?" Rex demanded.

"I went for a bike ride."

"What about last night, Einstein? Was that almost as much fun as a fucking bike ride?" Rex asked.

"Last night was fun."

"Why was that, do you think?

"Good food, good company, except for you."

"Then why are you thinking about a goddamn bike ride? You got something against people?" Rex asked, annoyed. "Being with Annie, being with whats-her-name, you don't think that had anything to do with the fact that you finally had a little fun last night?"

"Probably," Grant said.

"Shit. I'm starting to think you're hopeless. Girls, I want you to come give Señor Dipshit a kiss on the cheek."

"Ok!" Mag said.

"Ok!" Moll said, louder.

The girls both got up and came over and kissed Grant on each cheek. It was more difficult for them than it should have been, because they couldn't stop giggling. The girls then kissed Rex on each cheek and excused themselves to go to the ladies room. They left a small bag with their belongings, so Rex knew they would be back.

"You happy now?" Grant asked.

"No, dim bulb, it doesn't mean a shit if I'm happy! Of course I'm happy! I just dodged, or hope to hell I dodged a huge legal bullet, and I am going to let off steam, get drunk, be with good looking women, etc., etc., etc. I can't fucking believe I have to spell this shit out for you. Have fun!" Rex shouted. "Now, I'm gonna go through their stuff while their gone, so I know where they live if they steal my wallet. I want you to be happy! Go back into the hotel and find a woman. You don't find one, I'm gonna loan you one of these, your pick."

CHAPTER 21

Grant went back through the hotel to the front exit. He thought a short walk might do him good, before the day got scorching hot, and this time, no long treks like the ill-timed walk to the restaurant last night. Just a quick jaunt might be all right. He was tempted to go back and see Isobelle. He wondered if Rex might have been right about him needing some companionship, and his sense of contentment with Isobelle earlier certainly indicated that he did. It was always scary to think Rex was ever right about anything. Rex knew business, he knew the ways of the world, but relationships were not his strong suit. He generally thought relationships were a waste of time. Rex may have changed after his ordeal, and even though that seemed quite a jump, Grant at least now was considering it a possibility.

Grant made it to the front of the property. As he left the hotel entrance, he saw Annie sitting in her car, the engine running, staring out the window opposite where Grant was standing. He walked up to the car, but Annie was still looking out the other way. She hadn't noticed him. He tapped lightly on the window and she startled, but smiled when she saw it was him, and rolled down the window.

"Need directions?" Grant asked.

"What! Oh, no, I was just—" Annie started.

"Heading out into the desert?"

"Well, not out into the wild part of the desert. At least I hope not. Heading to meet my friends for lunch."

"Good. Hate to read about you in the papers getting lost out there in the wild part."

"OK, then let's say I'm not heading out into the desert. Where are you heading?"

"Oh, just going to walk a bit. Not far, I learned my lesson last night. Killing a little time," Grant said.

"Until?"

"Until you got back from meeting your friends."

"Well that doesn't sound so bad. How about I give you a ride?" Annie asked.

"You're not going to take me out and leave me in the desert?"

"Tempting, but no."

"Well, all right," Grant said, getting into the car.

"Where's your partner?" Annie said, pulling away from the hotel.

"Still with his harem."

"And you still didn't want to be in on that?"

"Not really."

"Are you sure? 'Cause I can take you back." Annie smiled, raising her eyebrows. "Maybe you can take them bowling."

Grant shook his head. "No, this is fine. You can just drop me somewhere and I can get back to the hotel. Not much of a bowler."

Annie chuckled. "Somewhere like?"

"I don't know. Somewhere I could eat later if I wanted, though I'm not that hungry, come to think of it. Air conditioning might be nice, but not a requirement."

"Dining by yourself?" Annie asked.

"Probably, I'm used to it. Less people to give me shit, when it's just me." Grant smiled.

"You didn't come out here to be by yourself, did you?" Annie returned the smile.

"No, I came out here to see you. Why did you come out here?"

"I came out here to see you."

"Really?"

"Yes. Is that bad?"

"It's not bad at all," Grant responded. "What did you expect?"

"I didn't know what to expect, and I didn't want to expect anything, I just wanted to see you, to see how you were doing, what you were doing," Annie drummed her fingers on the wheel.

"Well, I'm glad you did. It has been a while, since, you know." Grant glanced quickly at Annie.

"Yes it has. I still think about it." Annie said softly.

"You do?"

"Yes. You don't?"

"I think about it a lot, just not sure why you do, I mean, you're pretty busy, you don't have time to think about something that happened a long time ago." Grant looked out his window.

"You think because I'm busy, that I don't think about things that happened in my life before I got busy?" Annie gripped the wheel more tightly.

"I don't know."

"Well, I know. Of course I think about it. There were some really great times. I wonder sometimes if the good stuff went by too fast. Do you ever think that?"

"I think about that all the time. Like I should have been taking notes, or something," Grant gazed out the window.

"Me too."

"Really?"

"I know things, people, everything changes, but it just went so fast and now I, I don't know. Take notes, huh? Too bad you didn't, we could be reading those notes." Annie tilted her head.

"Are you feeling all right?" Grant pulled his head back.

"I'm feeling fine, why?"

"You're the smart one, so if you need my notes, well, that's not a good sign."

Annie laughed and smiled back at Grant. "It just went so fast," she said quietly.

"Sure did."

They sat in silence for a few minutes. They might have had separate visions of that time, or they might have had the same vision of that time. The expressions were a mixture of contentment and question, with neither seeming anxious to let the images vanish with conversation. Annie broke first.

"What about her?"

"What are you talking about?" Grant asked

"Isobelle. She likes you. Is that a bad thing?

"Having someone like you, is never a bad thing. Well, maybe if that person is Rex," Grant shook his head. "I guess I haven't noticed. I just thought she was being nice."

"Well, she likes you, so I was just wondering if you were thinking about doing anything about it." Annie said.

"Doing anything about it? I don't even know her. I just met her a little while before you did, just a few minutes, even"

"Well, she seems to have a thing for you."

"Did she tell you that?"

"She didn't have to. I see the way she looks at you," Annie said.

"I haven't seen anything."

"Well, it's pretty hard to miss."

"I haven't. I'm serious."

"You don't need to be defensive, I'm just making an observation."

"Well I haven't noticed. Pull over here." Grant said

"How could you not notice? What were you looking at, Rex?" Annie laughed, pulling the car over.

"You."

"What?"

"I was looking at you," Grant said.

The car got quiet. The resonance of the air conditioning and the engine were the only sounds. Even a very good ear would have been hard-pressed to detect any breathing. The pause was not that long, but it seemed like an eternity. Neither was sure of what they had just heard or just said. Annie was staring forward, Grant was trying to think of something, anything else but the silence, looking out the window of the door on his side. They had come to the parking lot of a country club, Rancho Las Palmas, the sign read.

"You … you come out here much?" Grant asked, trying to lighten the conversation.

"What?"

"Palm Springs … you come out here much?"

"Let's get back to the looking part. You were looking at me?"

Grant paused, not wanting to answer. He had told her he had been paying attention to her, and for him, that was saying a lot. He didn't want to elaborate, for fear he would just say something wrong. He thought repetition might save him from further explanation.

"Yes. I was looking at you. That's OK, isn't it?"

"Yes, that's okay with me." Annie smiled. She avoided looking at him for a moment as she took a deep breath. She let it out slowly and her exhale sounded as if she were refreshed. She paused, then took another breath.

"I don't, um, come out here much. Palm Springs, I mean. I've been too busy. My family used to come out here when I was little, and we always had a great time. I have some friends who have vacation homes out here. They're the ones I am going out to meet. They always give me grief because I never come out to see them." Annie seemed relieved that the subject had changed, but she knew their mutual feelings for each other were now out in the open.

"They probably don't live here in full summer, I'm guessing."

"No, it's too hot."

"Summer is just starting everywhere else, and it's already almost too hot here," Grant said.

"Yes."

"Probably why you got your tennis, er, your bowling in early this morning."

Annie laughed quietly. "Something like that."

"I really like the desert. Really liked it growing up. I don't remember it being as hot as this, though."

"I remember you used to tell me about it. I remember the time we stayed in that little motel here," Annie said.

"Yes, that was good, that time at the little motel here," Grant said, nodding his head.

"I thought it was a very good time, a very peaceful time," Annie said, pausing, catching herself. "You are very good at kicking up dust. Figuratively speaking. Do you come out here much?"

"Never."

"Really? I thought you would come out here at least once in a while. You live so close. You can stay out here pretty cheap, if you do it right, like you and I did back then," Annie said.

"Right, pretty cheap, like the Ritz?"

Annie laughed, "Not like the Ritz. But sometimes the Ritz really does the trick when you are in the mood for…."

"Kicking up opulent dust?"

"Yes, for kicking up opulent dust."

Annie pulled out of the parking lot and started down the road again.

"It really is nice, the Ritz, I mean. I must confess that I've never stayed in one before. They find out what a shit kicker I am, they'll probably throw me out."

"If they haven't thrown Rex out, they're not going to throw you out," Annie said.

"He's not a shit kicker, he came from money."

"He's not a shit kicker, but he is a shit, pardon my language. Money doesn't make him a better person. You are a much better person than he is."

"He's changed a little since his run-in," Grant said.

"I could see that at the pool earlier." Annie said, glancing at Grant.

"He's good, in his way."

"And that way would be?"

"He really wanted us to be here," Grant said.

"He had to have had an angle."

"Not that I can see, and believe me, I've been looking. He didn't know those girls were going to be here."

"You sure about that?"

"It's not like he's paying them."

"Not directly. Not yet." Annie shot Grant another look.

"He knows what he—what they are in for. He's OK with that. They're not hookers," Grant laughed.

"Not technically," Annie said, starting to laugh.

"Not technically, and for him, that's good. He did get us here, so I guess we have to give him…." Grant started laughing harder.

"What's so funny?"

"I was just thinking about the list of things you had him do. That was pure genius."

Annie blushed.

"I mean, it was hilarious, though it really didn't sound like you."

"Why not?"

"It was too nefarious for you. You were always good, and by good, I mean you would never have done one-tenth of the stuff we did. The list was just out of character," Grant said.

"Don't think I could do it?"

"I thought you could, but I didn't think you would."

"No?"

"No. When, and as the rest of the world falls into more atrocities put upon itself by itself, you remain the constant of how people should be. Decency, grace, and beauty, that's you."

Annie didn't know what to say. She smiled, her eyes glazing. "Thanks," she said quietly.

"Maybe the hula-hoop, but the others didn't sound like you," Grant said.

This made Annie laugh. "I remembered some of the things that you said you liked, so I put them on the list. I brought them here with me, to give to you. I also knew it would make him mad that I gave them to you, which is a nice bonus. The other stuff, Kat helped me with."

"The hula-hoop?"

"It was my idea." she said, very proudly.

"The hula-hoop, synonymous with chicanery," Grant said.

"Me? Never!"

"It looks to me like you have crossed over, and are now on the path to being a hellion. Never thought I'd see the day."

"Well, just goes to show that—"

"Show that what?"

"Show something, gosh, I don't know what it shows, but I did it." Annie was still proud of what she had done.

"Well, I'm proud of you. And…."

"And what?"

"And I'm sorry for all the crazy shit I did."

Annie was silent for a moment, before responding.

"That's OK."

"It's not OK, but I am sorry. I want to have dinner with you later and we can talk. We can talk about all the other potentially hellish things you might be thinking. Nothing like a reformed hell raiser to keep a neophyte from going down the path to ruin. I can tell you virtually everything in the world not to do," Grant said.

"You think that's necessary?"

"Well, if you don't want to become a screw-up like me, it is."

"I don't think you are a screw-up."

"I screwed up with you," Grant said.

"We were in college, how smart are you supposed to be? How smart is anyone supposed to be?"

"Hell, I don't know. Maybe that's why I went to college."

They rode quietly after that, and Grant had Annie drop him at a little sandwich place, the hum of the air conditioning and the engine now blending with full, easy breathing.

"Are you sure you want to stay here? Why don't you just come with me and I'll introduce you to my friends?" Annie asked.

"No, but thanks. I don't want to be an awkward show-and-tell for you. You haven't seen them for a while, you need to spend time with them."

"I haven't seen you in a while either."

"Well, then, let's just settle for dinner together. Just you and me."

"Let's do it. If it saves me from, what did you call it, being nefarious?"

"Nefariousness and chicanery, yes."

"If it saves me from those things, then of course."

"You sure?"

"Yes, I think it would be nice."

CHAPTER 22

Annie drove away, leaving Grant at the sandwich place. The shop wasn't fancy, but it had a view of the mountains. It was a relief to have had the exchange on the way there. She had actually given him the benefit of the doubt on how things had gone with them. He had beaten himself up over their ultimately failed relationship for more years than he cared to remember. He was relieved, but he couldn't help puzzling over Annie's comments about Isobelle. Annie was never jealous of anyone, but in this case, her behavior seemed to indicate that she was. She was so comfortable in who she was, comfortable about the right conclusions coming without intervention. Even if she was just being protective, that meant she had to care at least a little bit, or that she cared enough to want to be protective. If she were still upset with him, or indifferent, she wouldn't care if Isobelle was paying any attention to him. At this point in his life, the thought that anyone might like him made him feel pretty good. All this put him in such a good mood that he thought he could even tolerate Rex and his band of gypsy women, at least for a little while. He didn't eat. After Isobelle's quiche, he wasn't very hungry. He just sat at a table outside, sipping some iced tea and looking at the mountains. He felt better than he had in a long time.

Once back at the hotel, Grant saw no point in checking anywhere but where he had last left the group, so he went right to the pool area. He wanted to stop and see Isobelle, but thought he had better check to make sure none of the furniture had found its way into the swimming pool first. The noise level had shifted upward since Grant left them there, and he stood out of sight for a few minutes to get a reading.

The meticulously groomed area around the Ritz courtyard seemed even more so today, and the blue of the furniture and the umbrellas looked like giant sapphires sprouting in the desert. He hadn't noticed the abundance of blooms of the bird of paradise plants that seemed to frame the entire scene. The sky was a shade of blue that didn't appear along the coast, where he lived. The skies near the ocean were spectacular, but the cloud layer did not always completely dissolve like it did in the desert. There was a more complete melting away here that gave the sky a purity he was unaccustomed to. He hesitated before he took a step away from the calmness, hoping he could find that same calm again later.

"So we were in New Orleans and Señor Grant says … well here he is now! He can finish the story. Señor Grant, come over here and tell these beautiful girls about when we went to New Orleans!" Rex said, now even louder than he had been before.

"Yeah Señor, get over here and get to talkin'!" Moll said.

"It's your turn!" Mag said enthusiastically.

Grant approached the group cautiously, but with a newfound confidence. He had completely forgotten the taste of confidence. He also was very hungry all of a sudden.

"New Orleans, eh? Great food down there."

"Sit down, hillbilly, and delight these girls in your tales of adventure, you know, before the head injury. Sausto here can bring you some food. Bring him what we were having." Rex said, as Fausto approached the table.

"Fausto, you dumbass!" Grant said.

"What did I say?"

"Sausto. You are a putz."

"Head injury?" You didn't tell us he had a head injury? We thought he was just shy. Some handsome guys are, you know," Moll said.

"Not many of 'em are shy. Most of 'em are assholes," Mag added. "But you're not."

"Thanks, and you are sitting next to my biggest head injury" Grant said, pulling up a seat."

"Welcome back, Señor Grant," Fausto said.

"Hello, Fausto. Could I look at a menu?"

"Bring him what we're having. He doesn't like it, he can go have his new girlfriend get him something else," Rex said.

Fausto looked at Grant, and Grant nodded. Fausto quickly cleared a store's worth of empty glasses, wiping the table down.

"I will be right back with your food, Señor Grant."

"Everything all right? You do as I tell you, and find a pretty woman to talk to all this time?" Rex asked.

"I have been talking with a woman, yes, though I'm not giving you the credit, as it had nothing to do with you."

"Hah! You should have learned by now that everything has something to do with me! Right girls?"

"You bet it does!" Mag said.

"Yep! Let's toast!" Moll followed, as the two girls clinked glasses.

"Can you believe this admiration?" Rex said.

"Tell 'em you ain't got any money, we'll see which direction that admiration goes," Grant said.

"I have money."

"I'm making a point, dipshit."

"Why don't you make a point of having a drink with us," Rex said.

"All right."

"All right? No arguing, no rationalization? Are you sick?"

"Sick of you," Grant laughed.

"That's my boy, he's back! Get Frausto back out here and let's get you caught up!"

"Fausto, and I don't need to catch up. Plus, you are too far ahead."

"Right, Fausto. I have trouble with names. I've seen you catch up, you can do it," Rex said.

"Got a date tonight, need to be coherent, and the number of things that you have trouble with is a number with a lot of zeros after it."

"You don't need to be coherent for me," Rex said, unfazed by the comments.

"The date ain't with you," Grant said, flicking something on the table at Rex.

"You don't love me anymore?"

"I detest you as much as ever."

"Good, I don't want all these beautiful women to get in the way of deep seated torment," Rex said, flicking a scrap of paper back at Grant.

"Nor will it."

"Who's the date, anybody I know, or did somebody new find you irresistible?"

"It's with Annie."

"Once again, I remind you, you owe me big time."

"You take a post-dated, four-party check on a Louisiana bank?"

"Sure."

"Good, I'll make it payable to Dip Shit."

"I'll frame it and put it with the others."

"I have a suggestion what you could do with it...." Grant said.

"Ah, it's good to have you back, you poor, dumb bastard. Let's get your buddy back here to get us a drink," Rex said, his voice rising.

"You really think you need another?"

"Not really, but I think you do. You look happy, for once."

"Consider yourself an expert, do you?" Grant asked.

"Well, when it comes to you, yes. Have a drink, watch the show, have some fun."

"By the show, I assume you mean the bleach blondies here."

"Yeah, it's pretty funny."

"To you maybe," Grant said.

"Again, I'm not asking you to marry one of them, just enjoy the show."

"I got stuff to do later."

"That's fine, and that's later. Right now, you ain't got shit to do but hang out and enjoy the—enjoy the everything! Nice day, nice place, nice girls, nice best friend," Rex laughed.

"I was with you until that last one."

"I understand. I should have said nice only friend."

Fausto returned with plates of shrimp, stone crab claws, oysters, spinach salad, tomatoes with basil and mozzarella, and truffle french fries.

"Yes it does. Shut the hell up and have a goddamn drink. Try this food too, it's great," Rex said, grabbing for the just arrived plates.

Annie hurried into the restaurant to meet her friends. She was a little late because of the time she had taken with Grant. She didn't mind that she had taken the time to talk with him, but she was still a bit shaken by her loss of composure during their conversation. She herself didn't understand why she had taken him to task about Isobelle. That was none of her business. Grant and Annie had not been together for a long time, and Grant owed her nothing. If a good looking woman was interested in him, it was no concern of hers. The trouble was that she was concerned. She was bothered by someone else wanting to be with Grant, bothered by how good it felt to be with him again, after all this time. She was not ready for any of this.

Kat was waiting with the other women when Annie walked in the door. She could see that Annie was flustered, and wanted to ask her what was wrong, but she was not going to do it in front of the others. Kat had quickly become bored with the others while waiting for Annie. She had an odd feeling that the conversations were pointless, and it was apparent from the outset that she no longer had anything in common with these people she thought she knew. She was glad Annie was now here, but she knew that Annie would also quickly tire of conversation about Frette linens, trips to the Amalfi Coast, and granite kitchen counters. The women all stood and hugged each other.

"Sorry I'm late," Annie said.

"I was getting worried," Kat said. "Everything all right?"

"Yes, fine, Grant and I were talking."

"Grant? Wasn't that that guy you went with in college?" the first woman, Gina, asked.

"Yes, we dated in college," Annie said.

"What are you doing with him here?" the second woman, Melissa, said.

"Wasn't he kind of a loser?" the third woman, Rachel, asked.

"He was never a loser," Annie said, annoyed with the comment.

"Well, OK, he wasn't a loser, but what is he doing now? Didn't he drop out of law school?" Gina asked.

"He didn't drop out of law school. He graduated, passed the bar, worked with a firm and didn't like it. He's getting ready to start his own business," Annie said, defensively.

"Oh, that's nice. Did you just run into him here at the hotel?" Rachel asked.

"No, we … his friend, another friend, arranged for us all to meet out here." Annie said.

"Well, we were worried that maybe you found a rich one at the hotel and decided to run off and get married without telling us," Melissa said.

"Even though you're long overdue to find one, you still have to invite us," Rachel said.

"What do you mean I'm 'overdue to find one'?" Annie asked.

"Yes, clarify that one for me too," Kat said.

"I only mean that if the two of you could crank up the search a little bit, we wouldn't have to worry so much about you getting set up properly," Melissa said.

"Oh absolutely. You could both register at Tiffany's, and we could get the gifts in one fell swoop," Rachel said.

"Oh, that would be great. Maybe you could do a destination, double wedding sort of thing and we could all go to Hawaii together! Wouldn't that be great?" Melissa said.

"Oh my god, that would be so perfect!" Rachel said.

"So get on it, girls. We can't wait forever for you two to marry a couple of successful, great looking guys and settle down and quit the rat race," Gina said.

"Yes, you both need to get one of these," Melissa said, holding out her left hand to reveal what looked like a glass doorknob mounted on the ring on her hand. "Right?"

The others followed, holding up their hands with similar massive ornamentation.

"Are those real?" Kat exclaimed.

"Well, yes, they're real! If you knew about these things you would know that you have to have one," Rachel said.

"Why?" Annie said.

"Because, dummy. It shows commitment. Twenty-five percent of his yearly earnings," Gina said.

"You want everybody to know that you don't mess around when it comes to your wedding," Gina said.

"Absolutely," Melissa said.

"This shows more love than, say, a smaller one?" Annie asked.

"Oh, love doesn't have anything to do with it," Rachel said.

"It doesn't?" Annie asked.

"If he spends this much money on you, he has to love you," Gina said, and all three of them laughed.

Annie and Kat looked at each other. Whatever joke there was, they didn't get it.

CHAPTER 23

"Why the confused look?" Rachel asked, still laughing.

"Just not sure what the size of the ring has to do with anything," Annie said. "If you love each other, it shouldn't matter."

"Agreed," Kat said.

"You two have a lot to learn in a very short time," Melissa said.

"Why in a short time?" Kat asked.

"Because you need to get on with things," Rachel said.

"Get on with things? Things, what things?" Annie asked, disoriented, still wondering to herself why she had asked Grant about Isobelle.

"Life things! Marriage, picking a honeymoon and wedding location, getting a house, quitting your job, having a family, choosing a nanny, getting a summer home, that kind of thing," Gina said.

"We would hate for you two to get too far outside of your window," Rachel said.

"Window, what window?" Kat asked.

"Your window of opportunity," Gina said.

"Oh yes. You get outside of it, and you might not ever get back in … you might never get all those things," Melissa said.

"Which would be tragic," Kat said, smiling at Annie, who grinned back.

"You think we're kidding?" Gina said.

"No actually, I don't think you are … and that's what's funny," Kat said.

"Wouldn't you hate to miss those things?" Rachel said.

"I really don't care about those things. If and when I find the right person, we are going to be in love, and we might get married on a boat, or at the courthouse, or on a mountain in Nepal. And if we have bands of leather, silver or … or even tattoos, what the hell difference does it make?" Kat said.

"Well, you two are both doctors, and you want someone who's on the same level of success as you are, right? And with that comes all those other things, so there's no reason to miss out, just because you are being, I don't know, too picky," Melissa said.

"Are these the only things that are important to you?" Annie asked.

"They are all important things that you are going to miss if you don't get it in gear," Melissa said.

"Those things are not important to me. Finding someone to share my life with, that's important to me. Whether that takes me ten minutes or ten years doesn't matter. And the fact that we love each other, well, that's what matters. What the hell happened to all of you? You sit there with those gargantuan rings, your twelve names each, and tell me I have to go find somebody, anybody, as long as he's rich, and start accumulating? When, exactly, did you stop being people and become shopping carts?" Kat's voice trailed off as she finished.

The group was silent.

"You know we have worked very hard to get to where we are." Annie added.

"And it is admirable that you—"

"I'm not trying to be snooty about what we do, but, shit, I'm rather proud of what I do, Annie is proud of what she does. I don't think my success clock is ticking and that I now should rely on someone else to take care of me. You think I'm doing this for the money? I am *not* doing it for the money! I am looking into practicing out of the country, helping people who don't have good medical care. I'm not going to get rich doing that, but you know what? I don't care. I'm doing it to help people. You chose a different path, that's fine. Don't get in my face about why I didn't go the way you did, and I won't get in yours about why you didn't go my way.

"We just want the best for you." Gina said timidly.

"The best, like not having to work, or having to meet old boyfriends…." Melissa said.

"Wait a minute. I work because I want to. I love what I do," Annie said.

"Annie, dear, look at you. We haven't seen you in how long? You know we have homes out here, and you're only a couple of hours away. You work all the time, you aren't married, and you're here seeing an old boyfriend. We're just worried about you two," Gina said, with a fearful glance at Kat.

"This is the only iron you have in the fire, this guy?" Melissa asked.

"She's seeing someone else," Kat responded, "But he's an asshole," she said quietly.

Annie shot her a harsh look. Kat closed her eyes, patting Annie on the shoulder and whispered, "Sorry."

"Ok, so she's seeing someone else, that's good. Have you talked about getting married?" Rachel asked.

"No, we haven't," Annie answered.

"How long have you been seeing him?" Melissa asked.

"When did we step into the goddamn courtroom?" Kat said, starting to lose what little composure she had left.

"Easy, easy, there. She didn't mean anything by it, she was just asking." Gina said, trying to diffuse the situation.

"Let me ask you a question. How long have you been married?" Kat asked.

"What?" Melissa was confused.

"How long have you been married, and you are you still in love with each other?" Kat asked.

"What kind of a question is that? That's sort of personal." Melissa was still confused, but was becoming agitated.

"No more so than you questioning the choices Annie and I have made."

"So you don't approve of our—our lifestyle?" Rachel asked.

"I could give two shits about how you live your life, because it is your life. I don't judge it, don't condemn it. You're happy? I'm happy for you. We get together, talk about old times, new times, it's all great. But there was a time when you were all working to be what we are now. You chose differently, I respect that, I support you. But for you to not give me the same respect I give you, well, that just sucks."

"Sucks?" Gina asked, laughing.

"Yeah, it sucks." Annie said.

Everyone in the group turned to look at Annie. They had heard Kat say this before, but it was not something that Annie had ever said.

"OK, troops. We had better back off this quickly, because we have done the unthinkable: We've gotten Annie all riled up." Gina said.

"That was not our—"

"Let it go," Kat said.

"If he didn't want to stay with a firm, that's his decision. He's very talented and can do what he wants," Annie said.

"What are you talking about?" Melissa asked.

"Nothing, never mind," Annie said, realizing what she had said.

"Maybe we should order some lunch," Rachel looked at her nails.

"Good, let's do that. We can still plan a trip to Hawaii," Melissa giggled.

"Don't push it, Melissa," Kat narrowed her eyes.

The tone changed after that, the talk lighter than the initial confrontation. Annie was too polite to tell them she really didn't have time for such a ridiculous conversation, and Kat had made it clear that she thought the marriage discussion was a bunch of bullshit. Rachel and Melissa seemed to be able to talk endlessly, unfazed by Kat's and Annie's stance on the matter of marriage and career choices. Only Gina seemed affected. She was somewhat quiet for the remainder of the luncheon, and Annie thought that perhaps they had upset her. She was nice enough, but not as buoyant as when the gathering started. Annie and Kat got through the luncheon, but they both were extremely glad when it was over. Though they all promised to reconvene in a few months, Annie and Kat were in no hurry to enroll in another follow-up course on material acquisition.

"What the hell was that, what we just saw in there?" Kat asked, still a little riled, as she and Annie walked to the car.

"I don't know. I was hoping you would tell me," Annie answered.

"I mean, like I said, I really could give two shits about how they live their lives."

"I think you got that point across, with a nice turn of phrase, I might add. Where did you get that from, Rex?"

"I'm not sorry. They were pissing me off."

"I know. I wasn't too happy with it either."

"It's not like it's any of their business, or anything like that, but I don't think that's what bothers me."

"What bothers you?"

"Well the whole thing, but … but at one time, they were heading somewhere, they were going to make a difference, just like I think we make a difference." Kat sighed. "And now, they've just had their memory erased—or had it gold plated by Tiffany's"

Annie laughed. "I guess we shouldn't judge them, any more than they judge us."

"Well, they goddamned started it! They *were* judging us. They were criticizing our choices and saying that we ought to follow their paths instead of our own. I think it's nice that they are married, have kids, vacation homes, and whatever else it is they have."

"Whatever it is they have, you're not buying right now."

"Right, and that should be OK. It should be OK without having to give a dissertation justifying my life, with timeline of projected nuptials, honeymoons, and children. God, that pisses me off!"

"I have been thinking, though."

"Why do I think I'm not going to like the sound of this?"

"Don't worry, thinking isn't bad."

"What have you been thinking?"

"I don't know, I just … I've just been going nonstop for as long as I can remember."

"That's why we are here this weekend. To see what it feels like to not be going nonstop. Look at it as a test vacation. Not long enough to accomplish a major overhaul, not short enough to do no good at all."

"I don't know, I mean I'm not really getting any younger."

"Oh, Annie … God, those agitators put poison in your food."

"They didn't do anything to me, I've just been thinking…."

"Did you think seeing Grant was not going to elicit some kind of feelings?"

"I didn't know what seeing Grant was going to do. I just wanted to, I don't, I wanted, I really wanted to see him."

"All right, so now you've seen him, you know what he's doing, and how does that make you feel?" Kat asked.

"It feels good to be with him."

"Well then, just go with that."

"Just go with that?"

"Talking to you is like talking to Grant—hearing everything you say repeated. What about that jerk who's coming out here to find you?"

"You're a big fan of Clement's, aren't you," Annie said, shaking her head.

"It's not important how I feel about Clement, though, if you are asking, I think he's an asshole."

"He's not. He's just a little—"

"He's just somebody you let your parents set you up with so you wouldn't upset them."

"That just makes me sound like the people we just left," Annie said, sounding troubled.

"You are not like them."

"I'm not married; I just work and spend some time with a guy that you hate."

"Do you want to get married? I mean, because we never talk about it, and that's all right, but maybe I should have asked you before. Hey, maybe you should ask me, so you don't think I'm singling you out. I never talk about it either."

"Someday, maybe. I don't know, I ... I haven't been thinking about it."

"Until this weekend. That's probably natural," Kat said.

"Probably?"

"You saw your old boyfriend, you saw some old classmates, who are now married, and you may see the current man in your life. You may or may not get to see those two men together at the same time. Why should that bring out any feelings?"

Annie looked at the ground. "Gina sure got quiet."

"Maybe we got through to her. Maybe we saved one of them."

"That wasn't our intention, it just happened that way. They started it, right?"

"They started it, and it really sucked!" Kat said

"They're just different now, which is sad."

"Yep, it is sad." Kat put her arm around Annie as they walked. "I want you to do whatever you want to do, as long as you want to do it. You don't need to do anything, or not do anything, just because your parents or anyone else thinks you should. You are the best friend anyone could ever have, so you deserve to be totally happy. Forever. New guy, current guy, previous guy, whoever." They got to Annie's car, and Annie dug in her purse for her keys. Kat waited until Annie unlocked her door and then said, "Annie?"

"Yeah?"

"Maybe not the current guy."

Annie smiled and squeezed Kat's hand. "Definitely not the current guy."

CHAPTER 24

"Much as I hate to leave this festival of joy, I need to go meet Annie," Grant said.

"We'll come with you," Rex said.

"Yeah, we're coming too!" Moll said.

"You bet we are!" Mag said. "But where are we going?"

"You are going to stay here and keep an eye on Rex, to make sure he doesn't get into any trouble. Can I trust you with that?" Grant said, looking Moll directly in to her eyes.

"You sure can, chief." Moll said, in a serious tone.

"We'll keep four eyes on him." Mag said.

"I knew I could count on you, but you may want to get on the iced tea train, just so you can keep four eyes on him and not eight," Grant said.

Rex just started laughing. He said something, but no one could hear what he said between the laughter.

Grant lowered his voice, leaning down to speak to Rex's head on the table. "Good, then we're in agreement. Annie and I will be at Tommy Bahama's. I told her it would be just me and her for dinner. You want to come have drinks later, that's up to you, but try not to show up before about nine o'clock, if you have to show up at all, please. Ten would be better, again, if you have to show up. It wouldn't break my heart if you left these two behind, but that's up to you. You might be ready for some grown-up conversation by then, and you can pick this up later in the room with them." Grant patted Rex on the back and stood up to leave. "We'll see you ladies later."

"That's right, you will, chief!" Mag said.

"Hey, that's my line!" Moll said.

Grant left the flock laughing to himself. The fact that he felt fine when he sat down and no worse when he left gave him more confidence that the glacier he had been living under might just be thawing. He could tolerate Rex's circus so much more after he had been with Annie. He wondered if it had been a bad idea to tell Rex where they were going to meet, but for some reason, he didn't think Rex would mess this one up. Rex had arranged the weekend, so there was some merit in that. Maybe even Rex could not put a dent in things, once Grant and Annie had talked. That was hoping for a lot, though.

The bed looked too inviting to pass up. It was early, but he was tired. With Annie gone, and Rex making hand shadows, he had some time before he had to leave. The emotional log flume ride had tired him out. After his last session with Annie, being tired finally had a good feel to it.

"Even though you think we saved one, do you think you were a little hard on them, possibly?" Annie asked Kat.

"No. We weren't. It was really stupid. They have become mindless consumers of everything that makes them look like hangers-on of the spoiled rotten wagon. I don't begrudge anyone for having a good life, but to tell me—to tell us—that we need to get with the program and go get somebody to shower us with stuff that makes us look like them? That's bullshit!" Kat declared emphatically.

"It was pretty stupid. I knew them when they were driven, and now they're just … being driven."

"Do you know the difference between them and the two women Rex was with?"

"What?" Annie asked.

"These three were better dressed."

Annie started laughing.

"You like that?"

Annie was still laughing and having a hard time getting her words out. It was just spurts of words, with more laughter. She was even crying, she was laughing so hard.

"You like that? Kat again asked.

"Yes" was the only recognizable word Annie could get out.

"Well, it's true."

"I know it's true," Annie was regaining her composure. "It's pretty sad even though I'm laughing. It was just the way you said it, I don't know."

"It was pathetic. They sold out, and they think we should do the same. I like my life, I like my journey, your journey. Besides, you're closer to getting married than I am," Kat scrunched her shoulders.

"I'm not anywhere near getting married."

"You're at least occasionally seeing someone, which is more than I can say. Even if he is a prick." Kat muttered the last part under her breath, so Annie couldn't hear.

"But it's not like that."

"Well, you are at least trying to meet someone."

"I know, but I don't think—" Annie started, but Kat cut her off.

"What happens when he shows up out here, like he said?"

"I don't think he will."

"Clement is not a 'don't think he will' kind of guy. You need to say, 'Hey, honey, don't come out here! I'm fine without you!' Besides, what happens when Grant sees you with him? You think that's going to go well? It's going to break what's left of his already broken heart. I don't think you want that."

"You think his heart is broken?"

"Annie! You can't see the way he looks at you? The way he blames himself for every rainy day that ever happened?" Kat said.

"He's just, you know, quiet anyway, and I have been telling him to quit blaming himself for everything."

"Quiet? His heart is broken and he loves the very air that you breathe—it's more than just that he's 'quiet'!" Kat exclaimed.

"It's been a long time, I don't think—"

"You know it's true. I can't tell you who to love, or who not to love, but you are going to put this guy under if he sees you with … with—"

"With Clement," Annie said.

"Yes!"

"He wouldn't do anything crazy."

"He wouldn't do anything crazy, but he might never speak again, and he hardly talks now," Kat said.

"I—I can't control that, or what he says, or anything."

"Tell Clement not to come. Does he know where you are?"

"No. I told him we were staying with friends."

"Nice touch."

"It's deceitful," Annie said.

"It's the right thing to do."

"You think so?"

"Yeah, I do. I'm sorry, Annie. I just never thought he was right for you. He is what those girls want, and they don't have a tenth of the talent, a tenth of the heart that you have. You deserve somebody great."

"I … I—"

"I'm sorry, I'll shut up, you have to make your own choices. I love you and don't want to have anything bad happen to you, ever, that's all. I'll keep quiet from now on," Kat said, looking around.

"That's … don't … gosh, it's all right," Annie struggled.

"That made absolutely no sense."

"It didn't did it" Annie said.

"None."

"No, Kat, it's all right. I just don't know what to do. I don't want … I mean, it's nice to talk with Grant again."

"And you mean 'talk with' in the most liberal interpretation of the phrase," Kat smiled.

"He loosens up once he gets to know you, but it's not such a bad thing not having to wait for someone to shut up before you can talk. I've missed that, actually. He never focused on himself. He just always seemed to be glad to be with me, it wasn't important to be talking."

"Not like anybody else we know."

"Rex? He's always been like that. He isn't really a bad person. He just likes the sound of his own voice," Annie said.

"And he thinks that if he says it, or he thought of it, then it must be brilliant."

"Yeah, that's pretty much it. He was, and I guess is still an attorney, though practicing law might be an accurate statement in his case. He is really just sort of a power broker, working with select clients, big money clients, not trying cases, but more keeping them out of trouble in putting deals together. He was Grant's friend, still is, so I guess I … I … heck, I don't know," Annie said, shrugging her shoulders.

"We only touched on it last night, so I'm still not completely clear about how he and Grant, you know...."

"They met before they met me. When they were growing up, in high school."

"Again, you mean growing up, in the most liberal interpretation. They are nothing alike. Rex has that East Coast edge and dialect, and Grant, well, he should probably be single word subtitled."

"Funny, huh. Rex's family moved to Colorado, where Grant lived, and they got to be friends. Rex never lost the New York accent, or the attitude."

"I would never have put the two of them together as friends," Kat said.

"Well, they're both off-the-charts smart, so maybe that's it. That and they both liked to get into trouble, though Grant says that it's not at all like what they used to do, and I believe him. Funny thing was that they make fun of each other all the time."

"I hadn't noticed."

"Yeah, well, they constantly did that, do that, and it seemed to amuse both of them. Quite a foundation for friendship, giving each other a hard time. Anyway, it was pretty crazy in college, all the stuff they did. I probably can't even imagine all the stuff they've done that I don't know about," Annie said, shaking her head.

"You told me before that it was crazy."

"I'm not angry about any of it. Most of it was fun, or at least funny, actually."

"They didn't get you involved?"

"Gosh no! Most of the time I couldn't even believe the stories, but they all turned out to be true," Annie said, her eyes opening very wide.

"Everybody is young once," Kat said.

"Yep, everybody is young once. These guys did stretch it absolutely as far as they possibly could, though."

"Grant definitely has gotten that out of his system. Rex I doubt ever will."

"I think you're right. From the little that we've talked, it doesn't sound like Grant is doing anything even remotely crazy."

"Not crazy in that way. Sounds to me like he's a hermit."

"That's too bad. He has a lot to give," Annie said.

"He thinks he gave it all to you and blew it. And he feels that weight every day."

"How can you be sure?"

"I have a sense for certain things, and I sense he feels terrible about what happened," Kat said. "Why else would he come here?"

"To see Rex."

"To see Rex? At the Ritz-Carlton? Right, and I'm thinking about joining the country club with our friends back there. Don't you get it? He ninety-nine percent came here because he had a slight suspicion based on what Rex had told him that you were going to be here. The other one percent was because Rex was here. You don't have to reconcile anything, but just know that he is hurting, and is going to trip over himself trying to figure out how he is going to reconcile that." Kat gave Annie a quick hug. "Just listen to your heart, you'll be fine, you always are."

CHAPTER 25

The nap was a fine respite from the poolside carnival, and Grant's only worry was that he would sleep through until Sunday and miss the dinner with Annie. The nap wasn't as restful as it could have been, but nonetheless, he felt well-recovered and energized. The demons he had brought with him on the trip seemed to be checking-out early and finding different transportation to their next destinations.

He got up from the bed, stretching and still feeling some of the knots in his body from the accident. The people at the hospital had said that his body would probably feel a little tense for a week or so. It was impossible to avoid, when a thousand pounds of metal crashed into you. He put on his best white western shirt, a relatively new pair of Levi's, a woven horse hair belt with a silver buckle, and his handmade boots. This was as dressed up as he ever got. He called the front desk, asking them to get him a taxi.

Grant got in the cab to take him to Tommy Bahama's, the bar and restaurant that Isobelle had recommended. If she recommended it, it was probably very good, based on last night's experience. He continued to marvel at the aura she had about her. He had only met a couple of her friends, but they seemed to be people who would kill for her if the situation called for it. Grant thought this an admirable, yet all but vanished quality in people. He didn't usually think back about college, except for the parts with Annie, but he did remember the friendships they made at that time in their lives, and how everyone that you were connected with was of the utmost importance, and vice-versa. Now that he was away from that environment, he had found that people did not value friendship like they did then. Everything was a scheduled event, and if you weren't on someone's schedule, you didn't exist. The people he had dealt with in his short stint as an attorney gave the impression that they could care less if he lived or died. It was definitely not confined to the legal profession; it seemed more to be the business world in general. People would tell you how much you meant to them and to the organization, but given the chance, they would stab you in the back at the first opportunity. He missed the camaraderie that had existed in his college days. In times when no one had anything, there was a commonality of poverty and purpose. Everyone wanted to make it through school, and everyone seemed to know that it was going to take some getting along together to get it done. Isobelle's friends reminded him of that time.

His reflections on the past left him blissfully ignorant of the present, and he had no idea how far or in what direction the cab had gone. Only the passing golf courses and palm trees confirmed movement. The name on the sign out front of the restaurant told him he was at the proper place. He stepped out of the car and paid the driver, while the warm air quickly engulfed him.

He opened the door of the restaurant and the smells of the food and the air conditioning washed over him. The place had a good feel to it, a thought that came to him just as fast as the refreshingly cold air. He didn't care if it was wishful thinking. He moved inside and was greeted by a very good looking woman, about five foot ten, very slight of build. She had a look about her, a look that possibly her hair might be a different color every time you saw her. She looked to be incapable of gaining weight, and today her hair was reddish-blond. She appeared to be the hostess.

"Well, here's a fine looking fellow," the woman said.

"What's that?" Grant said, turning around to see if she were talking to someone else.

"There's no one back there, I'm talking to you," she said.

"You are?"

"Yes. I bet you probably get that a lot."

"Get what a lot?"

"Women talking to you because you—because you have a palm tree growing out the top of your head."

"Not that I recall, and I think I would have noticed if they did."

"Well, they must have been blind."

"I'm sure I don't know."

"You here to meet someone?"

"Yes, as a matter of fact," Grant said proudly.

"Well, my name is Savannah, so you just met me," she said with a laugh. "Hello."

"Hello. What is your name? We haven't officially met until we know each other's names."

"Grant."

"Grant. Well, Grant, I think you are going to have an exciting time tonight."

"Really?"

"Yep. You've already met me, so things are off to a good start, don't you think?"

"I'd say so, yes."

"Do you have a reservation?" Savannah asked.

"I don't think so."

"Tell you what I'm going to do. I am going to put you on the list here, like you had a reservation, OK?"

"Sure, thanks," Grant said.

"What time would you like me to put down?

"Oh, eight, I guess, it may run later," Grant looked around.

"Ok. How many?"

"Two."

"Two. Guy or girl?"

"Is there a line for that?"

"No, I just wanted to know, for curiosity's sake," Savannah grinned.

"Girl."

"Damnit! Wife, or friend?"

"Friend," Grant said.

"Yes! I've still got a chance."

"What?"

"Just kidding. You'll remember me though, right?" Savannah asked.

"How could I not, at this point?"

"What's my name?"

"Savannah."

"Good one."

"What's mine?"

"Greg."

"Nope."

"Damnit! Gary?"

"Nope."

"I'm just messing with you. It's Grant. I wrote Grant, right here in the book. Where you from?"

"Encinitas."

"Really? I want to move there."

"You get right to it, don't you?"

"No, silly, I really want to move there. I have a friend that lives there, and she wants me to move there. I like the desert, but I need a change. I've been looking into it. I actually have a couple of possibilities there, so we might be neighbors. Do you know my friend that lives there?"

"I'm sure I do."

"No you don't, I just think it's funny when people ask things like that. I get it all the time, people asking me if I know someone they know in the restaurant business, like we have meetings."

Grant was laughing to himself, not sure of how to respond.

"You go in to the bar, hang out with Mitch, wait for the other member of your party—a girl—to arrive, and we'll fix you up," Savannah said, emphasizing her disappointment that his dining partner was female.

"OK. Wait, who's Mitch?"

"The bartender."

"Oh, right. Do you need the name of the person that is meeting me here, or that I hope is meeting me here?"

"Nope, I'll know. Wait! You 'hope is meeting' you? That means I really do have a chance!"

"Never say never." Grant grinned at Savannah, and she returned a huge smile. He thought she was probably quite fun. She would certainly trade the cow for the magic beans because she wasn't really into cows anyway, whether the beans worked or not. Grant walked into the bar area, which was decorated in a sort of tropical-tobacco-sugar plantation motif, or at least what he believed those places would look like. He pulled up a stool at the bar.

"Hey, how's it going?" The bartender asked.

"You would not believe me if I told you," Grant replied.

"I'm not so sure about that. You forget where I'm standing. You have quite a list of stories to compete with. Perhaps a proper cocktail would help."

"What do you recommend, because I've sort of been on the tequila train since yesterday, may need to change cars. You can leave out hot drinks, please, and any goddamn pink drinks."

"Of course. Let's leave out the usual suspects, assuming they have already been interrogated today. Mojito is kind of different, yet still has a sense of decorum to it, not generally found at fraternity parties, and it's not pink. Sazerac more towards the classic side."

"I'm not a rummy, so Sazerac sounds good. Might have had one, but only in New Orleans maybe. My mind is shot, and decision making and memory are suspect."

"Good. My name is Mitch. Isobelle is going to try to be here later, so make yourself comfortable and I'll do my best to help you along that road."

"A couple of days ago I would have been surprised that you knew who I am without me telling you, but now, not much surprises me. Grant," he said, holding out his hand.

"I know, nice to meet you. Isobelle said you were a good guy, and if she says it, I believe it," Mitch said, shaking Grant's hand.

"You been friends long?" Grant asked.

"I would say long. Desert time is kind of unusual, so no one is ever really sure how long things really are."

"Interesting concept. I would have to agree with it."

Mitch turned away to prepare the Sazerac. Grant turned to survey the rest of the bar. He had a good vantage point and always found bar activity to be, at the least, mildly amusing, and sometimes completely hysterical. Mitch returned quickly with the finished product.

"Here you go, Grant," Mitch said, placing the Sazeracin front of him. Grant pushed back slightly from the bar, taking another look around the room, and let out a long breath.

He scanned the locale and started watching the other patrons. First up, a fashion-model-slash-actress-wannabe with an overly-amped-up-gym-focused date. She was clearly contemplating suicide because she had told him that she had cheated, having had more than just tofu for lunch. Her date reassured her that it was all right, all the while glancing at himself in the mirror to look at his own overly large arms.

A few tourist couples, with a fluorescent tint to their skin—a tint that made Grant's eyes hurt to look at them. Their obvious sunburns and the extra weight they had packed on over the years probably meant they had to bathe in aloe vera just to endure the pain of putting their clothes on in the morning. Their clothes might once have fit them well, but those days were long gone.

College guys ordering shots of liquor and quoting movie lines. An older couple commenting on the outdoor water misters on the patio and wondering if they really worked. Two guys watching the baseball game on the television, citing various statistical backgrounds on the players and the teams.

Except for supply chain duties, Mitch had pretty much left Grant alone during this time. He seemed perceptive and could see that Grant was deep in thought. The second that Grant seemed to break away from his thinking, Mitch was there with another drink, Grant had not made mention of a refill.

"Some sort of desert ESP that I don't know about?" Grant asked.

"Orders from the lady herself. I don't do my job, I have to answer to her, and I do not want to do that. She can be quite deadly when provoked."

"That seems hard to believe."

"Believe it. She can tear you, or me apart, and I don't even know you," Mitch said.

"You said you had known her quite a while. From the business?"

"Yes. We used to work together and became good friends from there."

"Just friends? I mean…."

"We are dear friends, and not, you know, anything beyond that. I can't date dark haired women."

Grant looked at Mitch as if he thought Mitch was crazy.

"Okay."

"I mean, she is a wonderful person and I love her to pieces, just not that way. She's not my type."

"Wrong hair color…." Grant was starting to shake his head and say something else, but thought better of it and didn't.

"She has been a tremendous friend and there is nothing I wouldn't do for her. She would do the same for me. I would hate to mess that up. Plus, I'm really not that into that big of a commitment."

"I used to be that way. She bring all her friends in here?"

"Her friend friends, not guys she's going out with, if that's what you mean. It's not that she wouldn't, she just doesn't date much."

"Hers isn't a hair color thing too, is it?"

"What?"

"Nothing. So she doesn't see many guys. None of my business," Grant looked back out to the patio.

"She is quite private, in contrast to her gregarious manner."

"It would seem that way. She also seems quite, I don't know, mystical. Has she always been that way?"

"As long as I have known her, which is quite a while. I am not really sure where the mystical comes from, but I know what you're talking about. It always kind of creeped me out, so we don't really talk about it. I suppose with the private side of her, there was some hurt somewhere along the line that set the tone for that, but we all have had that, right? The hurt, I mean," Mitch said.

"I'll drink to that," Grant said, raising his glass. "Buy you one?"

"Your money is no good in here, but thank you for the offer."

"My money doesn't seem to be good anywhere around here. Must have picked up a stack of Confederate script before I left home."

"Where is home?"

"Near San Diego. Encinitas."

"Been there, drank there, swam there, biked there, ran there. Not in that order. Great place. You a surfer?"

"No, too many old injuries from previous lives. Swim a lot."

"It's a nice spot. You drink at El Callejon ever?"

"Whenever I can," Grant smiled.

"Had a friend that used to work there. I still have trouble with tequila as a result."

"You probably just didn't drink enough."

"I really don't drink that much in general."

Grant in mid drink, choked and almost spat out his Sazerac.

"You okay?" Mitch, responded, to Grant's nearly spraying the bar.

"You're kidding, right? About the not drinking much part?"

"No, I don't drink that much."

"You're a bartender, for shit's sake." Grant said, clearing his throat.

"That doesn't mean I have to drink a lot."

"Suppose not, but there's no reason not to use it to your advantage." Grant said, knowing this was going to hang Mitch up.

"To my advantage?"

"Forget it, just a stupid theory of mine, probably concocted while concocting concoctions … something like that…." Grant said, looking back out towards the patio.

Mitch was totally perplexed now.

"How about I just get you another drink?"

"That works, too."

Mitch moved away from Grant to tend to some other patrons and to get Grant another drink. Grant didn't want to get into a deep philosophical argument with him. He obviously was a close friend of Isobelle's, and he didn't want to seem ungrateful by disagreeing with his point of view, however twisted it was. The baseline that Mitch would not date dark-haired women as a matter of principle, and that he was creeped out by Isobelle's mystical nature made further discussion seem pointless. He was content to sit there, hoping Annie would eventually show up and that she hadn't changed her mind. Grant looked around the bar again and caught a glimpse of himself in the mirror. For once, he thought, things might just be all right.

CHAPTER 26

Grant saw Annie the minute she walked into the bar. Her blond hair looked iridescent, falling around the shoulders of the pink blouse she was wearing. Her tanned skin made the pink seem warmer than the air outside. She normally always dressed in sports clothes with her hair tied back, but not tonight. Her untucked blouse fell on her black slacks. The dark mahogany wood of the bar blended in with her dark pants, making it seem like she was floating from the entrance to where he was sitting. The smile she gave Grant when she saw him was the biggest smile he had ever seen on her face. He thought her beauty radiated from the caring that was attached to that smile. She brought an unknown, unfamiliar confidence with her wherever she went, and it seeped into the room, mixed with a compassion and a calmness that swept over whoever she was with like the desert breeze. If a person ever felt it, he would be changed for life, and would want to be around it as much as he could. He would curse the winter because it was void of that wind, that gentle breath of air, touching him ever so slightly, warming and letting him know everything was more than all right. Strangers and old friends alike could not help but sit in awe, as near to being fulfilled as they could ever believe possible. Grant thought this fresco could make him happy the rest of his life.

"This seat taken?" Annie smiled.

"Uh, no. I was just sitting here, talking with the bartender, waiting to meet someone for dinner."

"Well, I could come back later."

"No, no. But since you are here, maybe you and I could have dinner together."

"Well, I don't want to interrupt your plans—"

"Nope, this will work perfectly. See, I had planned to have dinner with you, but…."

"But what?"

"But I thought you might come to your senses and decide against it. Though I was hoping you wouldn't," Grant said. "Well, here you are, you might as well stay."

"Well, I seem to remember saying that I would have dinner with you," Annie cocked her head to one side, a crooked smile played on her lips.

"You did, but you could have won the lottery on the way here and decided to go buy Rex the monkey he's always wanted." Grant looked at his empty sazerac, then exchaled. Now that Annie was here, he couldn't believe he was so nervous, like a teenager on a first date. And yet, talking to her felt so ... so right.

"Winning the lottery would make me go back on a promise? And go buy a monkey?" Annie raised an eyebrow and laughed softly.

"Well, you said you would, you didn't promise you would."

"Oh, well that's different! I should get going then, I mean to go buy the monkey."

"See, I figured you had somewhere else to go."

"Why did you think that?"

"Because of the way you're dressed. You must be meeting someone other than me, because you … you, uh, look great," Grant said.

"It's nothing, really," Annie started to blush, though it was hard to tell with her tanned skin.

"No, trust me, it is. You really look great. Not that you don't all the time, but…."

"Well, thanks. I don't know that my 'bowling' clothes look all that stylish. You look pretty decent yourself," Annie said shyly. "Maybe it's the smile you're wearing that really makes it."

"I was thinking the same thing about you."

"Well, that can't be a bad thing, now can it?" Annie asked.

"Not if they're not painted on. You want a drink, or just head to dinner? What would you like?"

"Dinner sounds good, but we can stay here if you want."

"This fellow brings you drinks almost before you think about them, so unless you're wanting to just get sloppy," Grant said, rustling in his seat.

"You can if you want, I don't mind."

"Well, see … I, uh, haven't made a fool of myself around you in a long time."

"So?"

"So I actually thought that I didn't need to do that tonight, seeing how as I have quite a large number of marks against me already. I thought I would break with tradition and be maybe more like a normal person."

"But I never thought you liked being normal."

"Well, see, I wasn't normal for a good long time, so it's not like I missed the grade. So much so that maybe it's all right to be normal now, or as normal as I get, you know," Grant said.

"Well, if you say so. We'll see how I like the new normal you, and if I don't like it, we can try something else."

"Good. Let me square up with Mitch here, and we'll get Savannah to get our table."

"You seem to know everybody in town," Annie looked around the bar.

"No, not really. They seem to know me, which I'm not really sure about, but it's nothing to be worried about."

"How did they get to know you?"

"It seems to be a desert phenomenon," Grant said, liking the phrase.

"How does it work?"

"You come to town, everybody knows you, pretty simple."

"I came to town, everybody doesn't know me."

"They might."

"Well, they don't seem to all know me," Annie stuck her chin out.

"Maybe they just know the ones that need the most help, which would put me at the front of the parade," Grant said.

"Well, I don't think that's it."

"Well, I don't have an explanation for it."

"I could guess."

"And that guess would be…."

"It's an Isobelle thing," Annie tapped the bar lightly, in syncopation with the syllables.

"We talked about her earlier, so there isn't any reason to talk about her now, though she is a very nice person."

"A very nice person who happens to be very good looking and very attracted to you," Annie smiled, tapping him on the arm with her finger.

Grant quickly motioned to Mitch to get him to come back to where he was sitting. Annie was still standing, very close to Grant. Mitch saw the signal and came back their way.

"Ah, this must be Annie. Hello Annie, I'm Mitch."

Annie smiled and raised her eyebrows at Grant. "Hello, it is nice to meet you."

"Can I get you anything?"

"No, thank you. I think we're going to have dinner now."

Very good. Well, I'm sure you'll like it."

"Just bring me the check, and we'll get out of your way," Grant said.

"The check has already been taken care of. And please, stay as long as you like, you're not in my way."

"Who took care of the check?" Grant asked.

"I told you, your money was no good here, so you will have to take that up with someone else," Mitch said.

"Who do I take it up with?"

"I am not at liberty to say, just know all is well."

"Hum. Well, thank you. You ever get back to Encinitas, we'll go to El Callejon for tequila."

"We can go there, but you will have to do the tequila by yourself."

"Well, something to, to return the favor."

"I'll take you up on your offer sometime. Nice to meet you, Annie. I hope you two have a good time," Mitch said, shaking hands with both of them, and then heading off to take care of other customers.

"Well, thanks again." Grant stood up to go back to where he had met Savannah. He reached in his pocket and pulled out some money and put it on the bar after Mitch had walked away.

"You want to tell me about that?" Annie asked.

"Well, I do, but let's go talk to Savannah and get our table."

"Tell me again how you know Savannah."

"I don't know her, I just know her name and that she's the hostess."

"And that is how?"

"We could talk about it over dinner. Or not," Grant said, his voice trailing off.

"No, I would like to talk about it. If you are running for mayor or something here, I want to know about it, maybe get in on the campaign."

They moved back towards the hostess stand, Annie had her arm inside of Grant's arm as they walked. Grant could find no reason to discourage her from doing that, and if it were cooler outside he might well have continued the walk for an entire city block, or maybe all the way back to the hotel. They returned to the hostess stand.

"Well, he's back! Your table is ready. Mitch called and told me you were coming. Is this your sister, or a cousin, maybe?" Savannah said.

"No, this is, um … this is my—this is Annie."

Annie shot him a perplexed look.

"Not related, huh? Shucks."

"What was that?"

"Nothing. I have a table ready for you. If you and Annie would follow me, I'll take you there. Oh, and it's nice to meet you Annie, I'm Savannah." she said, grabbing a couple of menus and moving them through the restaurant towards a table.

"Yes, I know. Grant and I were just talking about you, and it is nice to meet you," Annie said, looking back at Grant.

"You were?"

"Yes. I was trying to figure out how it was that he knows so many people, and he's only been here since yesterday afternoon."

"Does he know a lot of people?"

"He knows you."

"Oh, that's because I introduced myself, flirted with him, actually," Savannah smiled.

"Really?"

"Yes."

"Because you do that with all the guys?"

"Heck no, are you kidding? I mean, look at him! Are you his girlfriend?"

"Uh … "

"Hey sorry, it's none of my business. He's just a really good—you know."

"Do you think I should be trying to be? His girlfriend, I mean," Annie asked.

"That's up to you. But if you aren't going to try to be, let me know."

"I'll do that."

"Enjoy your dinner; the food is really good here, so I think you will. Nice to meet you," Savannah said, turning to go back to the front. Annie and Grant sat down at the table.

"So maybe we had better talk about all this, you know, so I can let all these women know my intentions, as they seem to be lining up," Annie said.

"That's crazy," Grant said.

"Seems to be accurate, you heard her."

"I just met her!"

"And yet she wants to know if I am trying to be your girlfriend," Annie said, tapping one finger on the table.

"I could have, or should have told her."

"What would you have told her?"

"That you are a great soul, and that there is probably no chance in hell that you are trying to be my girlfriend, even though…."

"Wow!"

"Maybe we should eat."

"I can always eat, I can't always listen to you talk like that," Annie said. "You were saying?"

"Jibberish was what I was saying. That bartender…."

"Your friend, Mitch, go on."

"He was intentionally trying to put me at a disadvantage," Grant said, watching Annie drumming her finger on the table.

"Because he's friends with Isobelle, and Isobelle knows you're here with me."

"How would I—I don't know, he just was quick with the drinks."

"So Isobelle likes you, Savannah likes you. Maybe you should move here," Annie said, with a partial smile, making it hard for Grant to tell if she were upset, or just messing with him.

"I don't want to move here."

"But they both seem to like you a lot."

"So?"

"You can't tell me that it isn't flattering," Annie said.

"I don't know what it is."

"Come on, what's wrong with it?"

"What's wrong with it?"

"I just said that. Yes, what's wrong with them liking you?"

"What's wrong with…."

"No more of this repetition … just answer the question."

"What's wrong with it … is ... is that they're not you."

A waiter came up to the table. "Good evening, how is everything tonight?"

Annie and Grant held each other's eyes, not looking at the waiter.

"They're not—" Annie's smile was now full.

"No, they're not you."

"Maybe I can come back in a little while," the waiter said.

"Nope, please just bring us two of the specials."

"Well, we have several that—"

"Just bring us the two best ones, not the same," Grant said, trying not to look away from Annie, somewhat relieved by the distraction of the interruption.

"And for the lady?"

"I'm not eating both plates, she can have her pick," Grant gestured with his hand.

"That will be fine," Annie did not look away from Grant, and she now seemed annoyed by the interruption.

"Very good, and to drink?" Grant finally broke Annie's eye contact, eyeing the waiter, who looked very uncomfortable.

"Bring a really nice bottle of red wine."

"Any particular...."

"Nope, just a good one that goes with what we're eating. I really like Pinot Noir, so make it your best one."

"I probably shouldn't drink," Annie said, still not looking away from Grant.

"I probably shouldn't talk," Grant said, now looking everywhere but back at Annie.

"I can just bring one glass."

"Bring two"

"Very good, I'll be right back," the waiter said, leaving quickly.

There was silence at the table. Annie kept looking at Grant, and Grant was looking everywhere around the restaurant. It was Saturday night, so the place was filling up. Grant now started looking at every person that came into the dining room, following them with his eyes until they sat at their tables, watching them settle.

"It's supposed to be a good place."

"I didn't think you'd take me to a crummy place."

"I have before."

"I wanted to think it wasn't intentional."

"It wasn't."

CHAPTER 27

"Let's go back to the—" Annie started.

"I shouldn't have said anything," Grant said, cutting her off.

"Why shouldn't you have said anything?"

"It serves no purpose."

"Well maybe not, but it is nice to hear."

"Nice to hear what?"

"That you wished I was trying to be your girlfriend." Annie pursed her lips together.

"I didn't actually say … I probably blew any chance of that, a long time ago."

"Things change sometimes."

"Not when I'm involved," Grant said.

"Well, maybe you're wrong. Maybe things are changing"

"I would be lying if I said I don't think about you."

"And I would be lying if I said I don't think about you."

"Really?"

"Yes, really. How could you think I don't?"

"I just sort of figured after all that happened, that maybe you wanted to put that behind you," Grant said.

"And maybe I thought you were into less commitment." Annie stopped, looking up at the waiter who had just returned. This time Annie seemed to be glad for the interruption.

"How does this wine look to you?" the waiter asked, proffering them a bottle.

"Is it open?" Grant asked.

"No."

"Well, it would look better if it were in those two glasses you have in your hand."

"You want to try—"

"Nope, open it and pour it."

"Sounds good. Are you folks visiting from out of town?" the waiter asked.

"Yes," Grant said.

"But he's thinking about moving here," Annie said, starting to laugh.

"Oh, really?" the waiter said.

"Never say never," Grant said, also starting to laugh.

"Would you like to—" the waiter started to ask.

"Nope, pour it."

"Certainly. Both glass—"

"Yes, both glasses."

"I probably shouldn't," Annie said.

"Afraid you'll put your guard down?"

"No."

"Then have some. I hate to drink alone, especially with a beautiful…."

"Beautiful what?"

"Night. On a beautiful night."

This made them both laugh. The waiter seemed to not have recovered from the awkwardness of his first interruption and hurried away to check on his other tables.

"I'm sorry," Grant said.

"Sorry for what?"

"Sorry for all the stupid things I did when we were together. Here's to better days," Grant said, raising his glass.

"You don't—you didn't, aw, gosh. To better days," Annie said, raising and touching his glass.

They both drank, both took in the wine, the smells, the view of the evening desert sun, the softness of the moment. It seemed as if they were both holding their breath and then let it out at the same moment, at the same unhurried velocity, both looking at some far-off vision. The waiter started back over to their table, but after seeing them, thought better of it.

"Where's Kat?" Grant asked.

"What?" Annie still seemed drawn to her vision.

"What's Kat up to tonight?"

"Oh, she's just hanging out, she said. She told me she might meet us later, if that was OK."

"Sure. You can probably only stand me for so long, so a little reinforcement might…."

"Just stop, will you? Why do you keep beating yourself up over this thing? I'm here, you're here, can't you just leave all that other stuff alone? I came here of my own free will and I would like to think that I did the right thing," Annie said.

"Do you think you didn't?"

"See? Like that! Would you just stop that! Please?"

"I just should have done things differently."

"You don't have to—"

"Yes, I do. I have been thinking about it for a long time," Grant said.

"How about we just—why are you telling me all this?" Annie asked.

"I wanted to get it cleared up, see what you thought."

"Well, you never were much for talking."

Annie's expression was starting to change; she looked outside, looked down at the table. She was not used to this much conversation from Grant, certainly not this pointed.

"Okay, you're right, you know what? You do owe me an apology. Why did you guys always have to do all those … those … those stupid things you were always doing? That time—that time should have been for us, for you and me. My parents always wanted me to do the right thing. There was a future for us, and your behavior just messed that up. You made them right. I didn't want them to be right, not about this, not about you. I wanted to be right!" Annie was always composed, but it was challenge for her now. Her eyes were glassy, and she was having trouble making eye contact.

"I am sorry."

"You should be! All the time wasted with that knucklehead Rex, my parents saying they told me it was going to go … and now we're here, and you have women lining up around the block who want to be with you." Annie was having trouble getting the words out, and her jealousy and frustration were showing through.

"I just—"

"Everything could have been fine."

"I know. Your parents still didn't like me."

"Just a couple of things, and everything could have been fine," Annie said, taking a drink of her wine, not wanting to continue the conversation about her parents. "This wine, it's good."

Grant was thinking about asking the waiter to bring a booster seat for him, as he no longer felt tall enough to see over the table.

"I knew it," Grant muttered guiltily, half to himself.

"Well, why didn't you do something about it?"

"Because I didn't know how. I was younger and stupider. Now I'm older and still stupid. More than anything, I want to make it up to you, but there is no goddamn way to make it up to you. I wish I had it back. I raised enough hell in my life," Grant said, disgusted with himself.

"You still might have had some fun," Annie smiled.

"I don't know these two women here."

"What?"

"I just met them, like you did. I didn't come on to them," Grant said.

"That's none of my business, I shouldn't have said anything."

"I didn't come here to be with them, I came here to be with Rex … I mean, to be with you," Grant said, really feeling like he needed the seat booster now.

Annie laughed quietly, to herself, and looked out the window.

"Well, getting to replay the point is always tough. Most of the time you never get to. I'm not saying we can replay the point, but maybe we should just let that one go. We could just enjoy some court time this weekend, and leave it at that," Annie said.

"That would be … that would be pretty great."

"Okay. But I'm not sharing my court time with all your new girlfriends."

"Agreed."

"Some folks show up later, that's OK. We owe Isobelle that much for last night. She just needs to, you know—"

"Not a problem. And they're not my girlfriends," Grant said firmly.

The waiter had pretty much gone into hiding, based on his lack of timing so far. He saw that it looked like things might be all right at the table now, so he took his opening, and approached the table.

"Here are some plates to start with. I hope you are enjoying the wine I selected. I brought you some goat cheese, crusted with macadamia nuts and some habanero pineapple salsa on the side. Also, some coconut shrimp, with papaya mango chutney to start. Your entrees should be along shortly, but take your time and enjoy yourself. I've also brought two glasses of champagne, compliments of our bartender."

"Gosh, this looks great," Annie looked at Grant.

"I hope you enjoy it," the waiter said, and departed quickly.

"Kind of a jumpy guy, isn't he?" Grant looked at the waiter as he left.

"He's afraid of you."

"Maybe he's afraid of you, ever think of that?"

"Nobody's afraid of me."

"You mean besides me?"

"You're not afraid of me, are you?" Annie looked like she had eaten something sour.

"Well, not after the Sazeracs, but I'm also not going to run away and leave all this food and champagne behind."

CHAPTER 28

"For the lady, seared rare ahi tuna, crusted with lemongrass and sesame seeds, sauteed bok choy and shiitake mushrooms. For the gentleman, island cowboy steak, medium rare, with garlic and Maytag blue cheese, and some asparagus with lemon-garlic oil," the waiter said, placing the plates on the table.

"You were supposed to let her choose," Grant said.

"My apologies, I…."

"That's all right, this looks fine. I'll let her have her choice after you leave."

The waiter was greatly relieved. "Whichever you choose, I hope you both enjoy your meal."

"I'm sure we will, thank you," Annie added.

"Very good," the waiter said and left the table.

"I still think he's kinda jumpy."

"You bring that out in people," Annie said.

"When?"

"When, like, all the time."

"Me?"

"Yes, you. If your knucklehead friend was here, you would both tee off on the poor guy I've seen your work before."

"That's a bit harsh, don't you think?" Grant asked.

"Actually, I think I am understating it by a long ways. And I'll take the tuna, unless you want it."

"The what?"

"Dinner, we have dinner in front of us," Annie said, spreading her hands over the plates as if she were presenting the grand prize on a game show.

"Oh, right. Good. You can have part of this, if you want."

"Maybe."

"Good. Well, uh, we should drink the champagne, I guess. What should we drink to?" Grant asked.

"Let's drink to, to … I don't know, I never make toasts."

"Well, make one now."

"Gosh, all right. Here's to the day we met."

"Going for the funny stuff, huh?"

"It was a good day," Annie said, nodding slowly.

"You think so?"

"Well, I didn't run you off, did I?"

"No, but maybe you should have," Grant said, smiling.

"Why? Because I should have known that somewhere along the line it was going to lead to you asking me something about lotteries and buying monkeys?"

"Might have been easier for you in the long run. You would have to transport the monkey. Not as much fun, but easier."

"Maybe, but I like a challenge."

"Now you're just drunk. What have you had, a half a sip? You'd better slow down."

Annie laughed. "I am not!" she said. "All right, then, here's to us."

"OK. Easier for me to say than for you."

"Shush!" Annie said, as they touched glasses.

They ate dinner peacefully, enjoying the view of the waning sun on the mountains, casting long shadows on the desert valley. They both were happy and their words unforced. Grant was content, and had evidently forgotten or no longer cared that Annie's current boyfriend was possibly going to show up. In two short days, and he had had a chance to have a couple of conversations with Annie, which was much more than he had anticipated, and what they said to each other was much more pointed and constructive than he had thought possible. She owed him nothing, he knew, so he was pleased that she had gone well beyond what he had expected.

Annie saw Isobelle and her friend Dawn out of the corner of her eye. They were heading into the bar, but Annie said nothing. She knew Isobelle was interested in Grant, but that she was extremely polite and would not come and interrupt their dinner. It was more likely that she would wait until they were done and catch them on their way out, or that she would send drinks from the bar, something like that. Annie didn't feel threatened, not after what Grant had told her. She was enjoying herself. She had learned a long time ago that Grant was going to do what Grant was going to do.

"This is nice," she commented.

"Surprised you didn't jump up and run out the door before the food got here."

"I thought about it, but I was curious about the food, so I stayed," Annie said.

"Wanted to see if I was going to order scrambled eggs and hot dogs?" Grant asked.

"Something like that."

"Or Jell-O salad with mixed vegetables in it."

"That is just the weirdest thing," Annie said, making an expression like she had just eaten something very sour.

"I don't even think Rex would eat it, and you know he eats pretty much everything."

"He always manages to find the trough."

"Good point."

"Are you going to work with him?" Annie asked.

"I don't know. I haven't thought about it that much."

"Well, you need to do what makes you happy, as long as it doesn't make you crazy."

"You think I would go crazy working with him?" Grant asked.

"That's not for me to say."

"It is if I ask you."

"Then yes, I think it would make you crazy," Annie said quickly.

"You don't want to think about it—"

"No!"

"Maybe he's changed," Grant said.

"Maybe he's toned down."

"Same thing."

"No, it isn't."

"Improvement is improvement."

"Like a Category 4 hurricane is an improvement over a Category 5?" Annie asked.

"Something like that."

"So you understand the concept."

"Yes. But hey, he put this thing this weekend together, didn't he?" Grant asked.

"Yes, and I'm still waiting for him to try to sell me something."

"Yes, it's tougher for you; I can just slug him."

"So if you worked together you could have that feeling every day," Annie said.

They both laughed at the thought.

"You must have been thinking about me, 'cause you're both smiling," Rex interrupted. He was somehow now standing beside their table.

"Oh shit!" Grant said.

"If you spell shit, a-n-g-e-l, then yes, that's me."

"Oh gosh," Annie said quietly, surprised at Rex's appearance.

"Hey, watch the language, lady! There are young, impressionable minds here," Rex responded.

"You got the young mind part covered—or almost covered. No, wait. You don't have anything covered, ever," Grant said.

"Come on, it looks like you were done eating anyway, so it's time to play. You've both been missing me, Annie especially." Rex said, pulling up a chair next to Annie. "Hey, what are you havin' here?"

"Jell-O with mixed vegetables," Grant said.

"Yucch! I had an aunt who used to bring that to my parents' house for every holiday when I was a kid. I hate that shi—that stuff," he said, looking at Annie.

"Geez, Rex, I've never heard you curse before," Annie said.

"Geez? Annie, if you are going to continue to use that kind of language, I am going to have to take my young friend here away from the table. He's younger than me, you know. Next thing you know, on the way home, he'll be saying gosh, and golly, and all sorts of filthy words. Not sure how I would explain it to his mother." Rex said, looking at the plates, then towards the bar.

"You'll make up something," Annie said.

"Tell you what. You buy me a drink, I'll forget the transgression."

"Maybe we could finish our dinner while you wait in the bar," Annie offered.

"Didn't you miss me?" Rex tilted his head and batted his eyes.

"No," Grant replied.

Rex looked at Annie, feigning a sad expression. "And you, Goldilocks, didn't you miss me?"

"No," Annie said, smiling.

"That sound you hear is my heart shattering from the lack of love."

"That would mean you had a heart to begin with," Grant replied.

"I had an electronic one installed when I was younger, just so it would not be subject to this sort of disappointment. You going to eat that?" Rex said, pointing at Grant's plate.

"I'll tell you what you can eat," Grant said, starting to rustle in his chair.

"Easy, cowboy. No sense gettin' yer spurs all sharpened up. Listen to him, Annie, ain't he something?" Rex was still eyeing the food, then the bar.

"I … guess, yes, he—" Annie seemed flummoxed by the question.

"Hey, I didn't mean to hang you up with that question, though I certainly would have thought it would have taken a lot more than that to perplex the great Annie Sims."

"Just go have a drink in the bar, and we'll come get you when we are done, if you're lucky," Grant pointed to the bar with his middle finger.

"Ok, but I'm telling them it's on your tab, unless you stop by. You stop by, all you got to do is buy my drinks. You don't stop by, I'm buying rounds for the whole bar."

"What makes you think they'll believe you?" Grant held his middle finger up to his head to hide it from Annie, but so Rex could still see it.

"It's me, for God's sake, of course they'll believe me!"

"Maybe not. You might get to go to jail after all."

"Ooh, that was pretty cold. That may cost you several rounds for the bar … and … several rounds for the dining room. You think all these people out here would like a bottle of champagne after dinner, or do you think a shot of cognac, maybe a little Louis the Thirteenth would be a nice capper for all these swell folks? What do you think, Annie?" Rex turned to Annie, as if really asking a serious queston.

"What's Louis the Thirteenth?" Annie asked, confused with the direction the conversation had taken.

"Don't—you're just encouraging him," Grant took his finger away from his head.

"Not a big cognac fan, eh? Well, maybe I should go in there and order you some, tell them to get ready to send out more—a lot more."

"Why don't you go in there and have a drink, be a nice little Cro Magnon, and try and not to carry off any of the women over your shoulder or drag them out by the hair. When we're done, we'll come check on you. We'll be sure to ask them what police station they took you to, I promise," Grant held his hand to his heart.

"All right. Do they have food in there? The bar, I mean, not jail." Rex asked, craning his neck to look in the direction of the bar.

"I'm sure they do. Didn't you spend all day eating?"

"Eating and drinking. What kind of a barbarian do you think I am?"

"Do we really want to get into that now? And where's your entourage?"

"I think they had to go sleep it off. I think your girl … er, your buddy, sent out a couple of ass kickers and put them under," Rex yawned.

"What a shame."

"Yes, it is. I know Annie would have loved talking with them." Rex smiled.

"I'll be in the bar, running your tab, so just come by in a little bit, or—"

"I got it. Get the hell out of here, and try and not tear anything up," Grant said firmly.

"You got it, chief. Keep an eye on this one. My mother warned me about girls like her, using foul language. Speaking of that, where's the Greek girl?"

"Go to the bar, we'll talk about that when we see you."

"Right, chief. Still, keep an eye on the girl," Rex looked at Annie.

"Good advice, but don't need it."

CHAPTER 29

The mood was not completely broken, but it certainly had changed. With Rex now here, Annie and Grant would have to go check on him when they finished. Rex would run into Isobelle and Dawn in the bar, so he would insist that the two of them join him. As things appeared to be falling into a similar set up as last night, and there would be no shortage of drinks.

"Well, I guess we had a few minutes," Grant looked at his wine glass.

"We had a few minutes," Annie touched his hand tentatively.

"It can still be fun."

"Hope so."

"I would hate to let Rex derail the evening."

"We can savor the peace until—"

"Until he starts sending waiters with trays full of drinks for the dining room?" Grant held his wine glass up.

Annie laughed, though she knew the scenario was not a stretch of the imagination.

"Maybe we shouldn't wait that long."

"Probably not."

"It was a nice dinner, though. I enjoyed it," Annie nodded her head.

"Would you do it again?"

"I think I would."

"You think?" Grant asked.

"No, I would," Annie said, laughing quietly.

"What's funny?"

"How whenever we are together, there is always something keeping us from being … you know. From being just the two of us," Annie drummed two fingers on the table.

Grant stopped, looking into the distance, his eyes narrowing, a half-happy, half-wry expression on his face.

"You know, I have thought that more than once. I live alone, don't go out much. I come here, you're here, and all of a sudden we need a docent."

"Maybe someone is trying to tell us something," Annie said.

"I don't think so. I don't think that has anything to do with it."

"What do you mean?"

"I think it just works out that way. I don't think anyone is trying to keep us away from each other. The others, I think they like being around positive things, and you and I are, or seem to be … hell, I don't know."

"Seem to be what?"

"We seem to be—"

Kat was standing next to their table before either one of them saw her approach.

"Kat!" Annie said, surprised.

"How are … I'm sorry to—how are you doing? Annie, could I talk to you for a moment? Grant, I am so sorry. I just need to talk with Annie and then I will let you two enjoy your evening."

"Is everything OK? Are you all right?" Annie asked.

"I … I'm fine, everything is fine. Just that thing we talked about last night. Grant, I am so sorry to interrupt. We'll just be a minute." Kat said, sounding flustered, which, like Annie, was not often a part of her state of being.

"Sure. We'll be right back, Grant," Annie said, getting up from her chair, grabbing his arm gently, but firmly enough to show him she was serious.

"OK." He didn't know what else to say.

"We'll be right back, I promise," Kat said.

The two women walked away from the table and Grant watched both of them, every step. He picked up his wineglass, drained it, and poured himself another glass. He looked out the window and saw that it was full-on dusk now.

"I'm sorry, Annie, I think Clement is in town, I just don't know where," Kat said.

"How do you know?"

"I just do. I didn't want to bother you, but I wanted to let you know."

"Well, if he's here, I'll deal with it," Annie said, her smile diminishing. "Grant will be crushed."

"I don't want him to be crushed. He seems to be getting to a very good place right now."

"That's because he's here with you," Kat said.

"That's not the only reason."

"Well, let's say it's in the top … one."

"Well, I'll just spend the time with him, and hope that Clement doesn't show up," Annie said.

"Nice optimism. You know what happens after optimism?"

"What?"

"Reality," Kat said. "The reality of you introducing Grant to Clement and saying: 'and this is my—my what?'"

"Maybe he won't find us."

"By us, you mean you and Grant."

"You could stay here," Annie said.

"Getting kind of crowded, isn't it?"

"It's already beyond crowded. Rex is waiting for us in the bar, and I saw Isobelle and Dawn go in there too. Grant didn't know Isobelle was in there, but he probably does now."

"It bothers you that she…."

"That she what?"

"It bothers you that Isobelle likes Grant," Kat said.

"It's OK, she's allowed, he's allowed," Annie said, looking like she needed a place to put her hands. "I just want the best for him."

"The best for him is you. I don't know that he is the best for you, but you can do a lot worse than him. You already have," Kat said, her voice almost a whisper.

"Let's go back out there and tell Grant we're going to the bar," Annie said. "Maybe if we keep moving … hell, I don't know. We can go in there, maybe go somewhere else."

"Wow! You are really getting worked up," Kat said, smiling, and turning her head to the side.

"Very funny. Let's go."

Grant had the waiter bring the check, not missing the chance to make him feel uncomfortable one last time before he did. Grant thought there was really nothing to be upset about. It had been a pleasant, albeit short dinner, but it was a dinner with Annie, and if he never had another one with her, this one had been a good one to remember. He drained his last glass of wine.

"We're back!" Kat said.

"Yep, it looks like it," Grant said.

"How about if we check on your tab at the bar?" Annie asked.

"I'm sure it's pretty large."

"You have a tab at the bar? Didn't they bring it to you—" Kat started to ask.

"Rex, he's talking about Rex. Rex said if we didn't come in there, he would start ordering drinks for the—"

"Got it. Forgot who we were dealing with. Well, I could come and keep him out of your hair for a few minutes, until you settle the bill, and maybe you could sneak out while I open him up on a table with a dull butter knife," Kat smiled, trying to ease the tension between Annie and Grant.

"So back to the bar we go," Grant said.

"It was a very nice dinner," Annie said. "Maybe we could do it again?"

"I'd like that, but we have to survive tonight first," Grant said.

"We will," Annie smiled.

Grant had a lady on each arm as they walked back to the bar from the dining room. Savannah was on the phone at the hostess stand, with people waiting in line, and when saw Grant, her face lit up and she put the person on the phone on hold. Then she saw that he was with two women, at which point she saddened. She waved at him, and he waved back, which caused her to brighten up again. She waited until Annie and Kat looked at her, then she shot back a scowl in their direction. Kat looked at Annie, but Annie just shrugged. The three were almost into the bar when Annie heard familiar voices from behind them.

"Annie and Kat, twice in one day. Maybe they found husbands since we saw them last time!"

"Well, it looks like they're with someone—or at least with the same someone, from where I am standing."

They turned to see Gina, Melissa and Rachel. Neither Annie nor Kat wanted to see them right now. Grant had been spotted by the newly forming group inside the bar, and a yell rose up from inside calling: "Señor Grant!"

"Great," Grant said.

"Annie, Kat, aren't you going to introduce us to your friend?" Gina asked.

"This is—" Annie started.

"Are you ladies looking for a table in the dining room?" said a voice from behind them. It was Savannah.

"Maybe later, but no, just heading into the bar, thanks," Melissa replied.

"Oh, good, cause we're full. If you want to get in, you may want to get on the list. Everything all right, Grant?" Savannah smiled.

"Oh yes, just fine," Grant answered.

"Great. Mitch will look after you, but you let me know if you need anything. Gotta go!" Savannah sang, more than said, to the group, as she turned and headed back to her station.

"Who was that?" Rachel asked.

"A friend of Grant's," Annie smiled.

"Who's Grant?" Gina asked.

"Great," Grant ran his hand through his hair.

"Hey, it's my old buddy Kat!" Rex's voice bellowed from around the corner, inside the bar.

"Great indeed." Kat shook her head. "I have the feeling this is going to be a very interesting evening."

CHAPTER 30

"What was it you were saying about us just being us?" Annie frowned.

"I think it was some sort of dream. I don't think I really said it, or that you really heard it," Grant said, as they walked into the fray.

"Am I asleep now?" Annie held her eyes open with her fingers.

"I am not sure. If you are, pretty soon you won't be. There's a guy in here that'll wake you in a few seconds. He's probably been waking half the desert already."

"Good thing you're here, I was getting ready to send a little Lew-ee out to the dining room. Besides, look at all the girls I got," Rex said, motioning to Isobelle and Dawn.

"Hello," Grant said.

"Good evening Annie, Kat. Good evening, Señor Grant," Isobelle and Dawn greeted them.

"Isn't it great having all the kids from the tour bus together again?" Rex smiled. "Hey, Mick, better get a bigger round of drinks for the party this time. And based upon the three unidentified ones standing behind them, we may want to put on some additional staff. Come on over, ladies, let Rex get a good look at you, we won't hurt you."

"The others are OK, but he might bite," Kat said to the three women.

"Who's he?" Gina asked.

"The answer to all your dreams and prayers. We're going to raffle me off at the end of the night. Come over here and tell me how many tickets you want,"

Rex grinned.

"What is this?" Melissa asked.

"Just another great night in the desert," Kat answered.

"Just another night?" Rachel asked.

"Pretty much," Kat said.

"It's not like this all the time, just the last couple of nights," Dawn said.

"Really? And who are you?" Gina asked.

"We can make proper introductions, so that perhaps it seems less like an interrogation of my friend Dawn, here." Isobelle said to Gina.

"I'm Rex, ladies. That's all you need to know, but if you are sticklers for names—"

"If you are sticklers for names, you can call him Señor Piñata," Kat added.

"This is Isobelle, this is Dawn, behind the bar is Mick," Rex paused, looking at Kat.

"Mitch, dumbass," Grant corrected him.

"Names, I have trouble with names. Sorry Mitch. And this is Kat, this is—"

"We know Kat and Annie, and I'm not sure we are—"

"Well, then, that pretty much sums it up. Who are you ladies?"

"We're friends of Annie and Kat, and we're all married," Rachel said stoutly.

"The three of you are married to each other?" Rex asked. "This is interesting!" This evoked laughter from everyone but the Rachel, Melissa, and Gina, who were clearly not amused.

"Not to each other," Melissa said.

"I know, I was just breaking the ice. You can come over here and sit by me, too. Just watch out for Dawn and Kat, cause I think they kinda like me, don't you, gals?"

"I could not be more enamored," Kat said, deadpan.

"I can't help it, I like him," Dawn said smiling.

"We all have very successful husbands," Rachel said. Kat almost choked at the declaration and glanced at Annie who looked equally mortified.

"I'm successful, maybe they know me," Rex laughed.

"I doubt that," Melissa said.

"Why would you doubt it?" Dawn asked.

"Because you're obviously not from around here," Rachel said, looking at Rex.

"Success limited to the greater Palm Springs area, is it?" Rex laughed. "I'll be sure to let my buddies back in the Big Apple know they're all failures."

"No, of course not," Rachel stuttered. "That's not what I meant, but I—I just don't think we travel in the same circles."

"Well, get over here, get your tickets, and we'll drink until we walk in circles," Rex said. "Mitch! Get these young ladies some of your best ... your best—hold on. What do you snooty ladies like to drink?"

"Snooty?" Melissa said.

"I'm kidding. I meant alluringly aloof."

"Oh! Well, I'll have some champagne," Rachel said, pulling up a chair. "But we can't stay."

"Alliteration. Gets 'em every time," Grant quietly said, shaking his head.

"So I believe we have all been introduced," Isobelle said.

"You can have champagne, or whatever you would like," Rex replied.

"But we're married, as we mentioned before," Rachel said, "and won't be staying."

"You said that before, too. They all say that, at first. Your husbands show up, they gotta buy their own. Grant can't be buyin' drinks for everybody in town."

Mitch moved back over toward where the group was sitting. He was never far, but with Isobelle here, he was certainly not going to let the group run dry. He had a rather astonished look on his face, wondering how so many good looking women could be in one group.

"I knew you couldn't stay away from me, Kat." Rex pointed at Kat, then, as the bartender approached, he clapped Mitch on the arm. "Mitch, old friend, here's the drill. Get this alluringly aloof one champagne, and get the other two married ladies whatever they want. If their husbands come in, ask 'em if they know me. They give the right response, I might buy them something too. Get Kat and Annie each a daiquiri. Real ones, not any of those fruity flavored crappy things. Get Grant some good bourbon, unless he's drinking fruity shit now, in which case throw him out of the bar. Oh, and better freshen us up here too. Watch out for Annie, she gets a few in her and wants to fistfight everybody."

"Coming right up," Mitch said, as he hurried away.

The ladies seemed confounded and began pulling up chairs with the rest of the group. Rex was exultant. Grant, Annie, and Kat seemed dumbstruck that this was all taking place at Rex's urging.

"This is unbelievable," Kat whispered to Annie.

"No secrets!" Rex shouted. "Everybody sit before the music stops or you're out!"

"I couldn't be that lucky," Grant rubbed his hands on the thighs of his jeans.

"If you're out, you buy for the whole dining room," Rex followed.

"Right here will be good," Grant said, pulling out a chair for Annie first, sitting down after her.

Annie sat next to Grant, with Isobelle on the other side of him. Kat had more than she wanted of Gina, Melissa, and Rachel at lunch, so she sat by Dawn, who was sitting by Rex.

"See that wasn't so hard, was it?" Rex slapped his leg.

"But for some odd reason, nothing is ever as easy as you say it's going to be," Grant tugged at the front of his shirt.

"I can believe that," Kat nodded.

"Come on, don't side with him, you're supposed to be on my team," Rex turned his head, raising his shoulder to touch it.

"Since when? Just who is on your team, anyway?" Kat looked around.

"I'm on his team," Dawn grinned, "And I'm OK with that."

"Are you sure you are feeling all right?" Kat looked at Dawn from side to side.

"I feel just fine. I think he's funny. I could use some funny, right now."

"See, she thinks I'm funny." Rex pointed gently towards Dawn.

"We all do, dear, just not in the same way," Kat pressed her hands together.

"Well, whatever, we're all here now, so that is what counts," Rex said, pressing his hands together in the same fashion, imitating her.

"He is always this way, your friend?" Isobelle leaned over, touching shoulders with Grant.

"This is pretty tame, actually. You should have … no, wait, you probably wouldn't have wanted to see him years ago. You wouldn't be sitting here next to me if you knew him then," Grant replied.

"I think I would like to sit next to you, no matter the situation." Isobelle turned to him.

"Really? Well, you don't know me very well, so you may have misjudged me."

"It has been a very long time since I misjudged anyone. I can see things about people now. I did not always have that ability."

"That sounds rather … I don't know, rather mystic, I guess. You know, we never got a chance to finish the conversation from earlier about this mystic thing," Grant moved slightly in her direction.

"You can call it what you will."

"What do you call it?"

"I do not have a name for it, I do not talk about it much," Isobelle set her jaw.

"Then why did you tell me?"

"Because you are worth telling."

"Did it come from family members?" Grant asked.

"Yes, my mother, among others," Isobelle loosened slightly.

"Really?"

"Yes."

"That's quite a deal."

"We are all given certain gifts, but not everyone is open to the possibility, so they completely miss that they have the gift. Are you open to the possibility?"

"I'd like to think so, but I really don't think I have a gift. Am good at a couple of things, but I don't know," Grant said.

"If you say you have no gift, then you are not open to the possibility. I was like that once."

"But not now?"

"Not now. I treasure the gift."

"And this gift tells you I'm OK?"

"Yes."

"What does the gift tell you about that one?" Grant pointed at Rex.

"The one we have all called the noisy one?"

"Yes, the noisy one. I like that name by the way."

"It tells me the same thing that the rest of you feel," Isobelle looked at Rex then back to Grant. "Even though he is noisy, he dearly loves his friends. He does not have many, but he loves them. He still has some difficulties ahead of him, though I cannot see what they are."

"What about her?" Grant asked, moving his eyes towards Annie and back, so as not to alert her to the conversation.

"She is a very good person," Isobelle said.

"Everyone knows that."

"I just met her yesterday."

"Good point. What else?"

"There is a sadness about her."

"You met her yesterday and you know this?" Grant asked.

"Yes, but please do not tell her this," Isobelle gently touched him.

"All right. Why the sadness?"

"She is very successful, very driven, but there is a large void in her life," Isobelle nodded.

"Void, what kind of void? She has everything."

"She does not have someone to share her life with. Though she spends time with someone, someone more like the noisy one, she is not comfortable with him."

"You know … you see all of this?"

"Yes, but perhaps I should not have spoken of these things."

"I … I—no, you should tell me, err, speak of these things," Grant motioned towards her. "What about her?" Grant moved his eyes towards Kat, then back again, trying to get his equilibrium back, as he thought it now shifting.

"She is quite at peace, and deeper than she lets on."

"She seems to be."

"She is going on a long journey."

"Hey, you two, what's going on over there?" Rex interrupted.

"Nothing, just talking." Grant said, shuffling in his seat. "About all the folks here," Grant said, acting embarrassed.

"Probably saying that it could become a lynch mob, given the right motivation," Kat said, flicking Rex on the shoulder with her finger.

"You live to break my heart," Rex responded.

"Who's going on a journey?" Annie turned towards them.

"Kat is going on—" Grant said, before he knew the words were out of his mouth.

"Kat, are you going on a journey?" Annie asked.

Kat stopped, dumbfounded. "What?"

"Grant said you were going on a journey," Annie said. "Are you?"

"I don't know what I'm talking about," Grant tried to interrupt.

"Ever, he forgot to add the word 'ever,'" Rex said to the group.

"Well…."

"Well what?" Annie turned her head closer to Kat.

"I'm going to practice … in India," Kat replied, a little flummoxed by the attention. This was not how she wanted to announce her plans.

"May want to call off the quickie wedding, or speed it up," Rex looked at his watch.

"Shut up, Rex! India?" Annie closed her eyes for a second, and then returned to looking at Kat.

"Yikes!" Rex said loudly.

"You know I've been trying to put that together."

"Yes...."

"Well, it ... it got put together, just the other day" Kat said. "I was going to tell you, after this weekend,"

"Wow!" Grant said, glancing at Isobelle.

"We should probably leave you all to talk, and we'll go check on a table," Gina started to get up.

"That is not necessary, please join us," Isobelle insisted. "There is space there by Annie."

"We don't want to interrupt...."

"It is I who am interrupting. You have been friends for a long time, so you should be here, especially if your friend is leaving on a journey," Isobelle said, looking somewhat embarrassed.

"How did you know about Kat going away?" Annie asked.

Isobelle looked away, turning her gaze instead towards Mitch, who moved quickly towards them to bring more tables and chairs.

"Here we go, let's get you all a little closer together," Mitch said.

"But we don't—" Melissa was trying to say.

"Oh, but of course you do. Everybody says they don't, but they really mean they do," Mitch said, continuing to set up the chairs.

"Have I seen you here before?" Melissa asked.

"If you were here, I was probably here," Mitch replied.

"No, really."

"No, really. I work here, so it's not a far-fetched concept," Mitch laughed.

"That would make sense," Melissa shrugged.

"Isobelle taught me that the bartender should make sense, even when nothing else does." Mitch stood up tall.

"I like that," Gina nodded.

"Me too," Melissa said, "so maybe we can stay for a few minutes, 'til we get a table, though after talking with that goofy girl at the front, I'm not sure if we're going to get a table or not. This is getting confusing."

"Good, I like the idea of you staying here better," Mitch said, "so I'll be right back with your—wait, what would you like to drink?"

"What would you suggest? They all seem to be in very good spirits, no pun intended," Rachel said.

"I think a Jack Rose would be good. Be right back," Mitch said, heading back towards the bar.

Rachel smiled and watched Mitch all the way back to behind the bar, blushing slightly. "A Jack Rose," she said softly.

The three new women settled in, doing their best to survey the others without making it completely obvious what they were doing. Everyone seemed to be a bit on their heels, so Rachel, Gina, and Melissa were a little confused about the set-up, but they could see that at least a few of them were primed for the occasion—certainly Rex was, anyway. The newcomers did not feel awkward Isobelle and Mitch had quickly disarmed them and made them feel welcome.

"I do think we should get our name in for a table," Rachel said.

"I need to go out there anyway. I'll tell Savannah to get a table for you. Be right back," Grant said, getting up quickly from the table and leaving the bar.

"How do you know so much, in such a short time?" Annie asked Isobelle, turning away from her college friends.

"It is difficult for me to explain, not that you would not understand, but more that I do not know how to express it," Isobelle said. "Different people make different impressions," she added.

"I suppose, though if your first impression was from—" Annie looked down towards Rex.

"It was not."

"Good."

"My first impression was from the other one, and I mean that respectfully."

"I, well … I guess he—he is taller." Annie was at a loss for what to say.

"Yes, he is taller, but that was not why."

CHAPTER 31

"So all you girls scared Grant off? Damnit, we just got him housebroken!" Rex said, rubbing against Dawn, smiling at her. "A damn shame. Now I have to start all over again with him. Might have to take him back to the pound."

"I don't think he belongs in a pound," Melissa beamed.

"Me either," Gina said.

"So Annie, are you enjoying yourself here in the desert?" Isobelle asked, trying to change the subject.

"Yes, very much, thank you. You and your friends have been so good to us." Annie replied, still looking at Kat.

"Well, you are good people, so it is easy," Isobelle said.

"Not all of us are like that one down there," Annie said, pointing at Rex.

"Yes, Señor Grant is very different. He is still in love with you. I can feel it," Isobelle said.

"You could feel it?"

"Yes."

"And what about Kat? You could feel that, as well?" Annie asked.

"Yes, I could," Isobelle said.

There was a commotion at the other end of the table, as Rex noticed that Moll and Mag had entered the bar and was calling to them to come and join the group.

“Great,” Kat said, looking back at Annie. She shrugged her shoulders, mouthing the words, “I’m sorry, I was going to tell you,” without actually speaking them.

“Your friend, she does not like these women,” Isobelle said.

“Does anyone? “ Annie deadpanned.

“Besides Mr. Fabulous there?”

“Yes.”

“No.”

Both Annie and Isobelle laughed when Isobelle said it. It eased the tension they were feeling. Annie did not know what to make of Isobelle’s insights, and Isobelle felt she had probably said a great deal more than she should have, but she had strong feelings, and she did not wish to hold them back. She could tell that everyone there with them, with the exception of Rex, was holding back feelings.

“There is much here that you all are keeping from each other, although not in a deceitful way. I think each of you, in your own way, love each other very much. You are all just having a difficult time expressing that.”

“Yes, I think you are right.”

Moll and Mag were trying to find chairs to add to the group. Isobelle looked at Mitch, and he quickly came to her side. She whispered something in his ear, and he nodded approvingly. Gina, Melissa, and Rachel were puzzled by the short-skirted, tight-bloused new additions to the group. Dawn seemed to be a bit dismayed, and was quizzing Rex about the two arrivals. Her questions were inaudible, but the others could hear Rex saying something to the effect of, “old school mates,” and, “leaving soon.” Kat just put her elbows on the table, her head in her hands, and shook her head.

“I will make this up to you, I promise,” Annie said, looking at Kat.

“You don’t have anything to make up for. This is fine. Fun, even. I just should have told you about, you know, leaving,” Kat said.

“It’s what you have wanted to do.”

Isobelle was unfazed by the new distraction, as she had been dealing with these two women for far longer than this. They were just flies around the picnic table for her.

“I will take care of them,” Isobelle whispered to Annie.

“Oh, you don’t have—”

"Yes I do. I know from previous experience that there is nothing interesting that these two can add to the conversation or dynamic. Later, you must tell me about your other friends here," Isobelle said.

"Maybe you should tell me about them, is more like it—and how are you going to take care of them?" Annie asked.

"Even though you do not know me very well, you should trust me on this," Isobelle answered.

"Well, for some reason, I do trust you."

"To send these two on their way will not affect your weekend. It will only eliminate further disruption for someone you care about, though I do not believe they pose a problem for him. It is more that I fear that the loud one would make some arrangement that might put Señor Grant in an awkward situation. It is my understanding that this has happened before," Isobelle looked at Rex with Mag and Moll.

"Awkward situations? That would be like saying a tornado is a dust storm," Annie squinted.

"You know him better."

"Grant never lets himself get into situations with the women Rex always manages to dredge up."

"No, he is very trustworthy in that regard."

"How would you know that?" Annie asked.

"Because I can see it, I can feel it." Isobelle looked at Grant.

"But again, you just met him."

"That is true, but a person of his character is not often met. He stands out, even though he does not mean to.

Moll and Mag were happy to see and be seen, both by Rex and his friends and by the rest of the bar, though they had no idea who anyone was, that did not seem to bother them. They were fawning over Rex, which was all right with him. Dawn, however, was hardly enthused. Kat wrinkled up her nose, and looked at Dawn.

"I think I'm tired, are you tired?" Kat asked.

"What?" Dawn turned to her.

"Tired, are you tired?"

"No, why?"

"I'm not used to these kind of hours."

"It's not that late."

"You are in the restaurant business, so I guess it wouldn't be for you."

"Doctors have to work late sometimes, right?"

"Yes, but not every night … and drinking isn't usually involved," Kat said, taking a drink.

Dawn laughed. "So you are going to India? You must be excited."

"I was, I am … I don't know. You—are you actually attracted to that one?" Kat asked, pointing to Rex, who was only halfheartedly trying to fend off the advances of Moll and Mag.

"Funny, huh?" Dawn laughed.

"Well, funny wasn't the word, really. What about those two?"

"They will be gone soon."

"You seem to be, well, you're not … you are nothing—"

"Nothing like those two?"

"Yes, that is what I was trying to say. You are nothing like them," Kat said.

"And I am very thankful for that."

"And you are OK with that? With him?"

"He makes me laugh," Dawn said, turning to face Kat.

"I don't—"

"You are a doctor. Your work is based on extensive training, extensive knowledge, and the serious business of saving lives. Of course he wouldn't appeal to you."

"And why does he appeal to you?"

"I just told you, he makes me laugh."

"Sorry, I just was trying to clarify."

"He talks a lot, but that is not that much of a problem. He is used to being the big man when everyone is around. But you know, when just the two of us are together, when he is not talking to everyone at once, and is just talking to me, it seems to be all right." Dawn looked at Rex.

"When is he ever not talking to everyone at once?"

"Maybe that is the key. To avoid getting him in a bunch of people."

"Good luck with that. Our numbers seem to grow every time I see him, and I've only seen him a couple of times. If we were here a week, we would have to find a convention center to meet at," Kat said.

"Maybe we had you and Annie figured wrong, Kat," Gina chimed in.

"Yes, this is quite a gathering." Melissa said.

"Do you always party like this?" Rachel asked.

"Pretty much," Kat said, winking at Dawn. "We just love to party, right, Annie?"

"What?" Annie was not used to Kat using the word party.

"She's always so modest, you know how she is." Kat nodded at them.

"Well, when do the rest of the guys get here?" Gina looked around the room.

"And where did the good-looking one go?" Rachel looked back towards the exit into the dining room.

"I sort of like the bartender." Melissa smiled.

Kat looked at Annie and said quietly, "Those three women we had lunch with today, where did they go?"

"What guys?" Kat held her hands up off the table.

"Well, there are a lot of women here for just these two fellows, so I just assumed there were others on the way."

"It's not really like that." Kat responded. "We're all just friends. Besides, didn't we just have a conversation about how Annie and I were missing out, or missing our window, or bus, or something?"

"I'm sorry about that, Kat. I had—we had no right to challenge you on that. If you're happy, that's all that matters. Maybe I'm the one that has her priorities out of whack. Maybe I should have kept on, like you. I would probably be happier. I don't know." Gina said, looking around the room.

"Are you not happy?" Kat asked.

"I thought I was until I saw you two today. I haven't had your confidence since … since I knew you in school."

"Well, I chose my path, though it may not be for everyone." Kat answered.

"No, I think it should be everyone's. I think what you do and how you do it is admirable," Gina responded.

"All this since lunch?"

"More like, all this since I saw you last. Maybe today just jarred it loose."

Mitch and another member of the staff returned with two large trays of drinks for the group. This seemed to delight everyone except Annie and Isobelle, who barely noticed. The only one missing was Grant. He had gotten up to go to the restroom and had been snared by Savannah. With so many people there, his absence was not obvious to anyone but Annie and Isobelle.

"Are you having a good time?" Savannah asked.

"Yes, I think so," Grant answered.

"Good. That's what we're about here, fun." Savannah smiled.

"It's a nice place. You work here long?" Grant asked.

"A while. I like it, but it's not forever."

"What is forever?"

"Forever is something that makes your heart sing every day. This is fun, but it doesn't make my heart sing every day," Savannah said.

"Are you a singer?"

"Singer and songwriter, but that's not what I meant. Everyone can sing, just not everyone can sing well."

"Singer and songwriter. Do you sing well?" Grant asked.

"You ask a lot of questions."

"Sorry, didn't mean to."

"Sure you did. I think you secretly want to know more about me."

"That so?"

"See, there it is again. I think I should write a song about you."

"What would you call it?"

"You just can't help yourself, can you?" Savannah smiled.

"Based on previous experience, the answer would be no." Grant said.

"OK then. The song will be called Graham, the question man."

"Grant."

"I know, I'm just messin' with ya. I have it written down, remember?"

"You keep saying that."

"Maybe I'm going to—wait a minute, you came out here for something, are you leaving?" Savannah asked.

"Nope, restroom, and to see if those three who joined us are on the list for a table."

"I'll put them on the list. Restrooms are over there," Savannah pointed, "and stop back by here and I will give you a little something."

"What might that be?"

"You will have to stop back and see, won't you?"

"If you say so."

"Can I ask you something?"

"Sure."

"Are you sure you are having a good time?"

CHAPTER 32

"You certainly have fascinating friends," Isobelle said to Annie.

"That's for sure."

"It is nice that you and Grant are friends. It would be a shame not to be."

"I've been thinking the same thing lately." Annie looked at Grant. The smile that painted her face was simple and contented.

"Sometimes it is difficult to get past the hurt. Do you feel that you might return to how you felt for each other before? And I only say that, because I have never been able to do that, with someone I was very close to. I have wanted to, but have been unable. I always am interested to hear from others about such things. I want to be like that, yet there are some things that I just could not get past." Isobelle's gaze seemed to be looking well beyond the now boisterous bar.

"Maybe you weren't with the right person," Annie responded, taken aback by Isobelle's previously unseen vulnerability. "Based on what little I know about you, and what Grant has told me, maybe you should tell me what's in store for us."

"Did Grant say something to you about this?"

"Of course not. He is not someone who speaks of such things with people he has just met."

"He isn't someone who speaks of such things with people he has known for a long time," Annie said, smiling slightly.

"He is kind of a puzzle, is he not?"

"Yes, I guess you could say that about him."

"You still see things in him, but I do not see you carrying the light for him as much as he does for you. You do still carry some feelings for him, however," Isobelle said.

"How long have you been able to do this?" Annie asked, as if she were asking anyone a very simple question. She kept her focus on Grant, not looking away as she spoke.

"A long time, since I was very young. Others used to make fun of me, so I do not always speak of the things. You two just seemed like people worth speaking to. I do not always get it right, and I could be mistaken, but in this instance, it is not likely."

"You, your confidence is, it's not forced, and it's not arrogant. It is refreshing," Annie smiled, speaking to Isobelle, but still looking at Grant.

"Well, I think a great number of people have the ability, they only choose not to pay attention to it, or they choose not to believe it. You are very sure of yourself, but in a different way. You are caring, you want to help everyone always, yet you will sacrifice joy that might come your way, because you want others to be taken care of first. As for me, I have to balance what I see, with who I can speak with about what I see, and how the regular world operates, as opposed to the spiritual world. Harmony can be difficult in that regard. " Isobelle closed her eyes for several seconds.

"This is all new ground for me, so I apologize if I am not asking the right questions." Annie paused. "That's not really how I wanted to say that but I think you understand. Where are you from? I mean, where did you come from?"

"I am from many places, just like you are."

"I'm not from that many places."

"You might not think so, but your soul says otherwise."

"Fascinating." Annie nodded gently.

"I speak only as someone that sees a small light shining that is about to go out. I think there is still something there for you, but you do not trust your feelings enough to let them be known to others, and maybe that is as it should be. But know this: You should tell him soon, before the trouble with your other man starts. I fear this could be very bad if you do not say something."

Annie was having a difficult time bringing words to her lips. She leaned forward, then back, looking at Isobelle, then around the room, then back to Isobelle again.

"Come on, Rex, you promised you were going to take us somewhere!" Moll pleaded.

"You sure did, chief!" Mag followed.

"Just settle down, we're all having fun here," Rex made a settling motion with his hand.

"When you say 'we' you are actually speaking of yourself, as always," Kat made half circles of her hands, vaguely illustrating her point.

"Does this woman like you?" Moll asked Rex.

"Of course she does, all women love me, but that is a burden I have to bear." Rex held his hand to his heart.

Kat rolled her eyes.

"That must be tough when they all love you," Mag added.

"It is babe, it is. Luckily, I just deal with it as best I can."

"Well, here's to you then," Moll said, raising her glass.

"Here's to you, as long as you take us somewhere like you promised," Mag followed.

"Hey, we're here, aren't we?" Rex gestured around the room.

"This isn't out of town, and you didn't bring us here, we had to find you." Moll reminded.

"Yeah, we had to find you," Mag scowled.

"Well, I was just getting ready to call you," Rex held his hand up to his head, as if he had a phone.

"Call them what?" Kat said, looking around the room.

"Hey, take it easy. I'll get back to you in a minute" Rex pointed quickly, looking at Kat.

"Take your time, tend to your new guests here," Kat put both of her hands up to her heart.

"Here's to Rex, finish your toast," Dawn said, raising her glass and looking at Moll and Mag.

"OK," said Moll.

"OK," said Mag.

Dawn touched glasses with the other two, then drank hers down until it was empty. Moll and Mag followed her lead.

"Now that's what I like to see, girls drinking to me!" Rex asked.

"So when are the rest of the guys going to get here?" Gina asked.

"I thought we covered that," Kat said.

"I would take a run at that bartender … well, maybe," Melissa said.

"I want the good looking one to come back, where did he go?" Rachel asked, looking around.

"What are you talking about?" Annie asked, somewhat frustrated.

"We are talking about getting some good looking men to this table. This one is the only man here, and he never shuts up," Gina said.

"Get that goddamn bartender back here, I want to talk to him," Melissa said, surprising herself that it came out that way.

"Well, looks like somebody's getting their money's worth from these drinks. Where's the good looking guy, I want to talk to him," Rachel gently slapped the table.

"You can't Rach, he's Annie's ex-boyfriend," Gina responded, very deadpan.

"You're right. I'm sorry, Annie," Rachel said, raising her glass in Annie's direction, spilling some of it on the table, "but he is one hell of a handsome man."

"I'll say," Melissa chimed in, "almost as good looking as the bartender."

"Listen to you three! Is this the first time you have been out on your own, without your husbands?" Kat asked.

"Nope, second," Rachel laughed.

"Yep, second. Just kidding, this is the first time we've gone out all together. Just the three of us," Melissa laughed.

"We're loaded and ready," Gina added.

"I can see the loaded part," Kat said.

"To tell you the truth, we did have a few drinks after you left us this afternoon."

"And then a couple more before we headed out tonight," Rachel admitted, giggling."

"Not nearly enough, though. Get that son of a bitch bartender back here, stat!" Melissa said loudly.

"Easy girls, no fighting over me," Rex said.

"Oh, shut the hell up! Please?" Kat shot back.

The table went completely silent, and even Rex acted surprised that Kat had said what she did. Moll and Mag appeared to be the only ones at the table who hadn't heard. They looked like they were ready to crawl under or on top of the table and go to sleep.

"Who pissed in your—"

"Hey sweetie, there you are!" A voice rang out from the front of the bar. Annie, recognizing the voice, turned and looked.

"Clement?"

"Shit!" Kat scowled and slammed the table with her palms.

"Who is—" Rex started.

"Shut the hell up!" Kat shot back.

"I been looking all over town for you, sweets," Clement declared.

"So I'm back, what were you going to give me?" Grant said.

"Hey Tex!" Savannah said.

"Grant."

"I know, I'm just … you don't take jokes very well. See this?" Savannah said, holding up the book that was in front of her "This line where it says G-R-A-N-T? Well, that's you, so just lighten up."

"What were you going to give me?" Grant looked around to see if anyone was watching.

"A phone number."

"A phone number?"

"Not this again!" Savannah said, rolling her eyes. "Yes, a phone number. Here it is."

"Whose number is it?" Grant asked.

"The church down the street. I thought you might need to get religion before you go back to whatever planet you are from."

"Really?"

"No, you knucklehead, it's my phone number!" Savannah said, punching Grant in the arm.

"Your phone number?"

"Does this ever stop?"

"Eventually."

"Well, how about having it stop right now, or I take my number back?"

"You can't take it back, you just gave it to me," Grant said.

"I can choose to give it or not to give it at will, and I can certainly take it away."

"You wouldn't want to do that," Grant smiled.

"I might, if you didn't stop making me crazy by turning everything into a question," Savannah sang.

"Ok, just one more question."

"And that is?"

"Where's a good place to go listen to some music around here?" Grant asked.

"That's a normal question."

"I have them sometimes."

"You could have fooled me," Savannah said, raising her eyebrows.

"Maybe I already did."

"How did you already fool me?"

"You gave me your phone number."

"That was my choice, not trickery on your part." Savannah smiled.

"How do you know?"

"Agggghhh! Muriel's!" Savannah exclaimed in mock desperation.

"Muriel's?"

"Muriel's Supper Club. It's a ways from here, in old Palm Springs. You want me to call you a cab? You look pretty drunk."

"I'm not drunk!" Grant said.

"Sure you are, your whole group is sloshed in there, except for the athletic blonde one and that mystical-looking dark haired one. They've been talking and I don't think they are drinking anything."

"Annie and Isobelle? They were talking?"

"Would you like me to call you a cab to go to Muriel's to listen to some music?"

"Annie and Isobelle were talking?"

"Do we really have to talk about them? I get off work in about an hour, I could meet you there."

"Meet me where?"

"At Muriel's. Go back in there, tell them you got a better offer and are going to go have a really good time, and that you might be back in the fall. Or tell them you have a stomach ache and that you have to leave. Are you OK? You didn't have that much to drink, did you?"

"Hah!" Grant said, loudly.

"You're OK," she said.

"I'm glad you think so, because I'm not so sure. My uncertainty is not a revelation."

"Maybe you just think too much. I don't have that problem, so that's why I can tell you that. Most of the time I don't think at all."

"Really?"

"I don't mean like I'm stupid, I just don't think about things. I just do them," Savannah said.

"I do things, and think things, and most of them are stupid," Grant responded.

"Don't worry about it. You're not stupid; you're just in the desert. It's different here."

"Boy, is it ever. Savannah, right?" She smiled.

"Yes, that's right. You're funny."

"Wait 'til you get to know me, you might not think so."

"I think I will.. Most guys try to be funny to impress me, to pick me up. Thing is, they are not funny at all. I think you're funny, and you are not trying to be funny," Savannah said smiling.

"Well, that's me. Always doing what I'm trying not to do, or trying to do what I'm not managing to do."

Savannah was now laughing harder. "Where did you come from?"

"You mean today?" Grant asked.

Savannah could hardly speak now, she was laughing so hard. "Well, my question was more, 'where are you from?' You said you lived in Encinitas, is that right?"

"Right, Encinitas, near San Diego."

"Right, I was just testing you to see what you would say this time. I could use a break from this hot plate, so that might be just the place to be."

"Whatever works for you. They got a big lake there, too."

"I don't remember a lake."

"Big son of a gun, runs all the way to China, I hear." Grant said, smiling broadly like Savannah was.

Savannah looked at Grant, pausing, still smiling, but her smile faded to a blank look, as if deep in thought. They both looked at each other, and then there was a long silence. Grant raised his eyebrows. Savannah looked back at him, her head turned slightly to the side, with a look of disbelief. Suddenly her eyes opened wider, and she leaned toward him. She slugged him in the arm again.

"The goddamn Pacific Ocean! I'll say it's a big lake! You are evil funny now," she said, again smiling and laughing.

"That bad?"

"I'll overlook it this time. Hey, I've got to get back to work. As I think I said before, I don't generally do this, but you now have my phone number. Maybe we could get together sometime and not think too much. Tonight would be a good time to start, 'cause I don't know when I'm going to get to Encinitas, and you have obviously been thinking way too much,"

"You don't generally do this?"

"Well, maybe a couple of times, but not all the time."

"Must be something in the air," Grant said.

"Call me," Savannah said, and then turned and walked back towards the bar. Grant watched her as she walked, all the while shaking his head. He noticed she seemed taller, more muscular than when he first met her. She was probably as tall as he was. She had a freckle or two, and she had clearly been outside a great deal. She wore no make-up whatsoever. This was a person who had no footnotes. You were getting the entire story, as you saw it, with her. She had a bounce in her stride. She was going to stop and smell the flowers, but she was not about to contemplate or philosophize about the flowers. She saw things for what they were, and she was not going to get into a long conversation on why something was here, or not here. With her, the world was simple, straightforward, and magnificent.

CHAPTER 33

"I been looking all over for you!" Clement said.

"I told you not to come," Annie said quietly.

"I know, but you know me, I do whatever I want, whenever I want. I'm a big horse, I can't be kept in a little pasture," Clement replied with a frat-boy grin.

"I think he got his sizes mixed up," Kat scowled.

"There's Katty. Hey lady," Clement said.

"Uh-huh," Kat mumbled, still scowling. She hated how he talked.

"I just missed you so much and had to come and check on you. Hey, aren't you going to introduce me to all these hotties?" Clement asked.

Annie looked uncomfortable. All the things that had transpired over the past day and a half, none of them made her feel as awkward as she did right now. She looked around, then up, as if she wished she could fly to a place that made her feel safe. Kat knew this was not a feeling Annie was used to dealing with.

"Hey chief, you thinking about taking one of our guests somewhere?" Rex said, standing up. "We might want to discuss that over a drink first. Maybe you could pick one of these other ones."

"Who the hell are you?" Clement asked, turning to look at Rex.

"Nobody in particular, but I have been tasked with the welfare of these ladies, so, you know. . . ."

"No, I don't know. This one belongs to me, so why don't you go back to drinking and mind your own business?"

"Clement!" Annie said.

"It's all right sweetie, this drunk isn't going to get himself into trouble, are you, sport?"

"No trouble, chief. You just may want to take it down the road to a little younger crowd. Find some girls whose standards are a little lower. These are all decent people here. We just want to have a good time without, you know, any bullshit. Coming from me, that's saying a lot." Rex said, looking around the group, moving a step closer.

"Who is this, sweetie?" Clement asked Annie.

"Clement, I—"

"Rex is probably right—God, I can't believe I just said that," Kat said, her eyes opening very wide.

"You tell him, girl!" Moll said, motioning with a fist in the air, though she was clearly having difficulty staying awake.

"Yeah, you tell him!" Mag seconded, putting her arm around Moll, in part to congratulate her, in part to keep the two of them from falling out of their chairs.

"Who are these two?" Clement asked.

"They just graduated from Harvard, and they think you should move on down the road, too," Dawn smiled.

"What?" Clement said.

"We all just graduated from Harvard, that's why we're celebrating," Rachel held up her glass.

"Yep, every damn one of us," Melissa extended her arms.

"And he paid our tuition, so you might want to cut him some fucking slack." Gina said, motioning at Rex.

"Looks like you're outgunned, Clement," Kat smirked, "as usual," she murmured.

"This is a nut farm. Let's get out of here, sweets. I can tell you about all the cool stuff I've been doing since you were gone," Clement patted his hair, making sure it was in place.

"I only left yesterday," Annie said, still looking like she wanted to drift out of the room.

"I know, sweets, but you know how talented I am. She's always telling me how talented I am," Clement turned to no one in particular.

"I believe that this may not be a true statement," Isobelle raised her head slightly.

"And who is this?" Clement pointed.

"I am the one who knows that you do not belong here. You can meet up with Annie later, though I doubt she will want to do that," Isobelle said firmly.

"You some sort of clairvoyant, are you?" Clement asked.

"Perhaps, though I think you would get the same opinion about you from everyone here," Isobelle replied.

"Well, isn't that just the most amazing thing. Almost as amazing as a bunch of female Harvard grads."

"What did you say?" Kat asked, leaning forward in her chair.

"Easy Katty, I don't mean anything by it. I'm sure there's a Harvard community college around here. Come on, sweets, let's go get grab the Ferrari outside and go home. And by the way, I think we should get married when we get back. Maybe fly to Vegas tonight and do it, what d'you say?"

"Always the car," Annie said softly. She then realized what he had said at the end. She was unable to speak.

"You and I could go outside and you could show me the car, I really like cars," Mitch cut in unexpectedly, having shown up without anyone noticing.

"OK, who's this guy? You guys should print programs," Clement said.

"I've been saying that all weekend," Kat said, taking a large drink.

"I'm a little sketchy on who everyone is, myself," Melissa scratched her head.

"His family is friends with Annie's family," Kat said, nodding glumly at Clement. "Her parents like his parents, the usual story. Two families tying to get their kids together. More money than sense, a hereditary trait, passed down for generations, near as I can tell. It makes me ill," Kat said, shaking her head.

"I'm Mitch, I'm one of the bartenders here. I've been taking care of 'your friends'"—he said this with a bit of a lilt, so everyone but Clement realized he was being sarcastic—"all night, and I just happen to love Ferraris. So, let's go have a look at the car, she can stay here."

"That so? Just happen to have one outside," Clement said, with a smirk.

"That's what you've been telling everyone in the bar. Why don't we check our watches, and you leave, and call us when you get home, you know, to see how long it takes you," Kat smiled.

Annie was now looking so despondent that Isobelle put her hand on Annie's shoulder to try to comfort her. Rex took another step towards Clement. Mitch was smiling genially, but his posture showed he realized this situation could turn dangerous at any moment.

"I'm not … going to marry you," Annie said slowly.

"What the hell is this?" Clement asked, noticing Rex coming closer.

"Whatever you make of it, chief," Rex said.

"He's not chief," Moll mumbled, her head resting on the table, her eyes closed.

"You're chief…." Mag said, her arm around Moll, her pose the same as Moll's.

"This is crazy! Annie, sweets, how did you get hooked—did these people kidnap you and brainwash you?" Clement asked.

"I can't bear to see her like this. If these guys don't hit him, I'm going to," Kat said, starting to get up.

"Violence is not the answer. You need only be strong, to help your friend. She is in pain," Isobelle whispered to Kat.

"Sweetie, you cannot want to be with these people! Come with me, we can talk about the new house I looked at for us. We can sign the papers right after the wedding."

"I'm going to be sick." Gina turned up her lip.

"Us too," Moll said, not lifting her head from the table, not opening her eyes.

Mag said nothing, as she had passed out.

"Rex, why don't you sit down and let Mitch go out and see the car with Mr. Fabulous. You don't want to ruin a good night just because he's a prick," Dawn said, tugging at Rex's sleeve.

"Which one is she?" Clement said, looking at Dawn.

"She is my friend, and I think you should go," Isobelle said.

"Second that," Gina raised her hand.

"Yep, me, too," Rachel raised her hand.

"I concur, motion carried." Melissa added.

"You are all drunk. Sweetie here loves me and my car, and she has missed us both, and I think I just asked her to marry me," Clement said. He turned towards Annie, grabbed her and kissed her.

Grant walked back into the bar, just in time to see Clement kissing Annie. He did not know what to expect when he came back in, but he had counted on any trouble being a byproduct of Rex's presence. He pictured dogs wearing Rex's clothes, people standing on tables, some modest nudity, or maybe even full nudity. Grant was no more ready to see what was in front of him than

Annie was ready to have it happen. He stood there for a moment, then turned around and went back out of the bar. Isobelle was the only one who saw him leave, and she caught only a glimpse as he disappeared out of sight.

Grant stopped walking before he got to the door to exit the building. He started to turn around and go back when Savannah spoke to him.

"Leaving so soon? Did you have a good time?"

"Pretty good, up until now," Grant replied, moving away from the bar, towards Savannah.

"Tired of the circus?" Savannah said.

"Something like that," Grant said.

"You don't have to explain it, just go with your instincts."

"I will. I need to—to get away from here."

"Well, don't leave town yet."

"May have to."

"Wanted by the law, are ya?" Savannah asked, trying to get Grant to smile.

"Not yet, but it's still goddamned early."

"You go to the Supper Club, I'll meet you there after I get off work. Why don't you take this taxi I just called for someone else?"

"I don't want to cut in line."

"Such a gentleman. Nah, he went back inside to find somebody, go ahead."

"You sure?"

"That's the story I'm going with." Savannah said, hardly able to hold back her excitement.

"All right."

"Great! What's my name?"

"Savannah. Thanks for everything."

"I'll see you at the club later, maybe Encinitas soon. This is exciting!"

Grant walked out into the warm desert night air. A breeze touched him as he walked down the stairs towards the street, but it felt harsh this time. Savannah called from behind him, "I know your name is Grant!"

The desert air that had always given Grant a lift had too heavy of a load this time. The sight of Annie with that man at the bar had drained him completely, and not even the smell of the desert could help to fill him back up. He was doing his level best to push what he had just seen out of his mind. In the past, thinking about Annie had always made him feel good, and he did it often, but now those happy thoughts and memories had been taken from him in one fell swoop. He had been trying for years to forget that last day they were together, but still it stuck with him. He could still see her walking away from him, the sidewalk dark under her feet, and the night weighing in on him like iron. It pained him to recall it, and now, here it was, all over again. He had had enough. It was time to push all of these memories out for good. He turned back towards the sidewalk. A taxi pulled up and the driver looked at him.

"Headed to Muriel's?" the driver asked.

"What's that?"

"Somebody call a cab for Muriel's?"

"Oh, I guess that could be me. I don't know."

"Well, I sure as hell don't know, so if you don't, then I'll go pick someone else up that does know."

"No, no, it's me." Grant said, looking back up the stairs, then back at the driver. He let out a long breath, opened the door to the taxi and got in.

"Sure, let's go." A blast of air-conditioned, cool air smacked him in the face as he opened the door. He got in the taxi and they moved down the street.

Chapter 34

Sunday, After Midnight

"What are you doing?" Annie said loudly, as she pulled away from Clement.

"Just showing everyone here how much we're in love, sweetie," Clement said with a J. Crew grin on his face.

"I have never said I loved you, ever," Annie said, looking ashamed that this exchange was taking place.

"I know it's hard for you to say, but I know you do. Let's leave these nuts and go home."

"They are not nuts, you bastard, they are my friends!" Annie said, louder than before.

"You can't be serious. I mean, I know Katty, but these others, these 'Harvard grads', I don't think so," Clement said, checking to see if he could see himself in the bar mirror.

"I want you to get in that goddamn car, and I would appreciate it if you … if you would get—get the hell out of here. And I don't want to marry you," Annie said quietly, not looking up.

"You don't mean that," Clement said, matter-of-factly.

"I think she does, chief," Rex said, taking a step forward defensively.

"Chief…." mumbled someone, from the heap of Moll and Mag.

"You going to do something about it, are you?" Clement challenged.

"Well, it would save you a lot of explaining to your pals back home if you only had to tell them how I kicked your ass instead of having to explain how Kat kicked your ass," Rex smiled.

"That's funny," Clement said.

"It's really not, either way. I honestly think Kat is tougher than I am, so I might be the best alternative all the way around, if you choose to go down that path. Getting in the car and leaving is the easiest, though, I think," Rex said, still smiling.

"This is so fucking nuts!" Clement said, turning to look at Annie. "I drive all the way up here to propose to you, and you're hanging out with a bunch of nutscases."

Annie stood there, looking like someone had poured grease all over her and she didn't know how to get it off. She looked up at Kat.

"Where's Grant?"

"I don't know where he is, Annie," Kat said slowly, trying to process what was going on in front of her.

Neither Annie nor Kat was prone to crying, but right now, each one looked like they could at any minute, though Kat's seemed more out of a building anger than pain. Annie was disgusted with the behavior of this terribly self-centered, and obviously sexist reprobate. She had never once told him she loved him, let alone really liked him. And now he was proposing? She couldn't wrap her mind around it. And where was Grant?

"I really do not want to be the one to tell you this," Isobelle said.

"Tell us what?" Kat asked.

"Grant must have walked in just as—"

"Just as what?" Annie pressed.

"Just as this awful man was kissing you," Isobelle said.

"What?" Annie, said, looking at Isobelle, then at Kat.

"I did not see him come in, I only saw him leaving," Isobelle said.

"Who the hell is Grant?" Clement asked.

"Go … just go," Annie said, barely getting the words out.

Tears started running down her cheeks. She looked at Kat, then again lowered her head back down. The scene was too much for Kat, and tears of anger balled up in her eyes. She clenched and unclenched her fists, blinking her eyes, but was unable to hold the tears back.

"What is it with the waterworks?" Clement asked.

Kat stood up, grabbed two drinks off the table, turned and threw them in Clement's face.

"Do we look like this, you son of a bitch?" Kat responded.

"Oh yeah!" Rex howled. He turned to Dawn. "He looks like he's going to shit himself."

Clement's mouth hung open, his face turned slightly to the side, but his eyes were squeezed shut, probably stinging from the alcohol. His blue button-up shirt was drenched from the shoulders up, and he seemed frozen in place, as though he had to process what had just happened before he could move again. Alcohol dripped slowly, comically, off of his nose, Annie did not even look up, and started moving towards the door. Kat following after her.

"Fuck!" Clement finally said, wiping his shirtsleeve across his face. "What was that for? I just said—ah shit, wait, I'll take her—" Clement was not able to finish his sentence before Kat turned and punched him right in the face, sending him tumbling backwards and chairs, glasses and tables flying.

"You will do nothing of the kind!" Kat shouted.

The bar became extremely silent. Kat stood there, her hands still clenched into fists, her body shaking, tears streaming down her face.

Tears of admiration flooded Gina's eyes. "That's the coolest fucking thing I have ever seen." The rest, their mouths open, said nothing. Isobelle glared down at Clement, who was lying in a pile of barware on the floor, a most surprised look on his face.

"So we going to go out and see you get in this fancy car, or what?" Rex said, standing over Clement. "I told you it would have been easier to explain if I had done this."

"Can we go back to the hotel, chief, I'm tired…." someone from the Moll and Mag scrum asked.

"I'll get you there in a minute, baby. I have to help this poor fellow to his car. Mitch, could you call a cab for my sleepy pals over there. I'll help clean up this mess when I get back. I'll pay for everything, too," Rex said.

"No worries," Mitch said. "We can get this cleaned up, no problem, if you can take out the garbage."

"Deal," Rex replied.

"You are a bunch of goddamn nuts!" Clement said, still on the floor, holding his nose, which was starting to bleed.

"You want some more, you son of a bitch?" Kat said, moving towards him.

"Of course he does not," Isobelle interrupted, getting up, and putting her hand on Kat's shoulder. "You just go tend to Annie … before she gets away."

"You're right, I'll do that," Kat said, taking a deep breath. Isobelle's touch was somehow calming, and Kat spun abruptly and moved quickly towards the entrance to the bar.

"Kat," Rex called to her, chasing a few steps after her.

"What now, Rex?"

"Are—are you all right?"

Kat stopped, looking back at Rex. "Yes. No. I don't know."

"Not that you give a shit, but I think you're great."

"Thanks," she said, trying to manage a smile as she left, but at least the tears were under control.

Rex shook his head, looking around at the scattered chairs, the women of their group, the other customers settling back to normal.

"Show's over, folks." He grabbed a drink off the table, tipping it up to finish it.

It was then that he noticed the man and the woman with the sunglasses that he first saw at the hotel bar yesterday. They were sitting at a table in the corner. Rex moved over to them quickly.

"Why the fuck are you following me?"

The man stood, speaking to Rex in a language he did not understand.

Rex repeated the question. The man repeated his response.

"I believe they are from out of the country, Señor Piñata," Dawn said. "Are you paranoid, or something?"

Rex shook his head, and shrugged his shoulders.

"It's a work thing, Dawn, dear. Long story. Tell ya sometime."

Rex turned back to the man.

"Sorry for the intrusion, Gustav. I thought you were, ah … I thought you were, ah hell, I thought you were somebody else."

The man replied, again in a language Rex did not understand. Rex stood there for a moment, not sure what to say. He seemed relieved.

"Good evening, ladies, Rex is calling it a night. Been a full day. Come on, Dawn, how about giving me a ride home, I have a headache, several, actually. How about we go get some aspirin, then some ice cream?"

"I think the ice cream places are closed."

"Come with me to a magical place where I bet they will bring us all the ice cream we want. Now and for breakfast."

Grant thought the ride to the supper club seemed longer than it actually was. The driver made some polite conversation about how hot it was going to get, how slow the desert business is in the summer and how he moves to LA in the summer because there wasn't enough going on there to keep him busy. Grant really wasn't paying attention to the conversation. He was trying to figure out how to get the line on his emotional fly reel wound back in. He had let too much of it out, and the current he just encountered had taken it fast. "Should have gone fishing instead of coming here." One weekend. He came here for one weekend. His entire existence seemed to be flying away from his body, and he could do nothing but try to hold tight to rod and reel and hope it wouldn't break. There was no line left on the spool. His own mind was wearing him out. Maybe that was what Savannah was talking about.

The cab arrived at the supper club. He shoved some money in the driver's hand without bothering to look at the bills, but based on the rousing chorus of, "Thanks, buddy," he received as he exited, it must have been more than enough. He took a deep breath, closing his eyes, trying to take as much of that desert air into his lungs as possible, trying to get every molecule of the air to wash through his entire body, inside and out.

He exhaled and walked into the supper club, feeling like he had walked into some sort of cartoon, or that maybe his life had become a cartoon. The furniture and decor looked like something from another planet, and based on how he felt, he would not have been surprised if the place was populated by aliens. Lots of plastic, strange colors, strange shapes. A small band was playing, and the singer was attempting to channel every crooner that had ever lived. He moved further inside, making his way to the bar. One of the bartenders came over to take his order. In his mind, all he could see was a heap of fishing line in front of him.

"What is it with this place?" Grant asked, barely audible.

The bartender could have been one of the characters in the cartoon with her attire, but Grant was exhausted and barely paid attention.

"Hello," the bartender said.

"Hello," Grant replied. "What is it with this place?"

"What is what with this place?"

"Yeah, what is it with this place?"

"That's what you said, I'm just looking for clarification," the bartender said.

"Of what?"

"Of what you said."

"Of what I said about what?" Grant asked. His head was spinning.

"Is this something that we are going to have to do all night until I say the secret word, or may I get you something?" The bartender asked.

"Did you have something in mind?"

"I didn't have anything in mind. It's your drink."

"Pretty bad, is it?" Grant asked.

The bartender had become annoyed by this point.

"I've had worse, but don't try to outdo yourself."

"What do you recommend?"

"Our special tonight is a Grape Martini."

"That sounds … perfectly disgusting, so maybe just shoot me. Get me out of my misery."

The bartender turned her head, looking at him sideways. "Don't tempt me. Something less adventuresome, perhaps?"

"What would be a good drink for, for…."

"For what?"

"For when you think you might be losing your mind."

"For when I think I am losing my mind, or for when you think you are losing your mind? Though I think I know what you are going to say."

"What?"

"Listen, why don't you leave your name and number and I will have a good psychiatrist call you," she replied.

"You know one?"

"What do you think?"

"OK. You tell—you tell them Señor Grant was here, and he's not having any grape or banana split martinis."

"That sounds fine, Señor Grant, if that is your real name. Is there a number where the doctor can reach you, or do they all have your number already?"

"I'm at the Ritz, but I don't think I am going to be there much longer."

"You're kind of full of yourself, aren't you?" The bartender asked.

"Me?"

"Not talking to anyone else, so I must be talking to you."

"Right now, I'm not full of anything. Fishing line, maybe." Grant said, his voice trailing off.

"What?"

"Nothing."

"Well, that's great to know, but I don't think you're going to have much luck with me."

"I wasn't looking for—never mind."

“No. No offense, but your batting average is going to take a dip here.” the bartender said.

“I really wasn’t keeping … I mean, that wasn’t what I came in here for.”

Chapter 35

"Got to hand it to her … she packs a hell of a punch. We pick sides for bar fights, I'm picking her." Rex said. "Let me just tidy up a bit here."

"I'm leaving, don't bother," Clement said, picking himself up.

"You go after Annie, and I will personally hold you down."

"Hold me?"

"Yeah, while the Greek there beats the living shit out of you, or worse," Rex smiled.

"This is so fucked up," Clement said. He looked at Rex as if he wanted to deck him and then turned abruptly and stomped out.

"I concur," Rex said.

"Listen. Rule number one is: no pissing off the bartender," the bartender said.

"So I suppose that means rule number two is no pissing off the bar," Grant said, acting like he was going to get up on the bar and do something disgusting.

The bartender was only mildly amused.

"Had a hard day, did you?"

"I really don't want to go into it."

"Thank God for both of us. Women problems?"

"Yes."

"Lost or found?"

"Both?"

"Hmm."

"Aren't bartenders supposed to be understanding?"

"Aren't customers supposed to come in and order a drink without their life story somehow attached to the completion of the transaction?" The bartender said.

Grant was trying to laugh. It was a defense mechanism, as he didn't know what else to do. "You had me at pissing off the bartender. I promise I'll behave."

"Good."

"Not so fast. I didn't say how I would behave."

"Aw, you seem like a nice, misguided guy. Don't make me call the police," the bartender said.

"You wouldn't do that to a guy that just got out of prison."

"Well, since you put it like that, yes, I would."

"Wow! No break for an ex-con? You don't believe me?"

"Of all the gin joints in all the world, you gotta walk into…."

"Must be fate. Or luck. Could be … I don't have a clue where to go," Grant said.

"What's that old saying about the luck of the convict—er, ex-convict?"

"You said you didn't believe me."

"I don't."

"Basil Hayden's, on-the-rocks."

"Progress!" The bartender said, and walked away to prepare the drink.

"Whatever works," Grant said.

Another patron had come into the bar and took a seat next to him. Another bartender waited on him. Grant thought the man looked a bit disheveled, but he was in no position to talk.

Grant again tried to laugh, slapping the top of the bar. He was having trouble laughing. He felt like someone had kicked him in the stomach. The bartender smiled at him as she made her way to the bottles positioned on the back of the bar. Grant attempted a smile back at her, but it was weak. He lowered his head. He was having trouble breathing as well.

"I have to get away from here."

"What?" the patron said.

"Nothing, just thinking out loud."

"I'd say. Maybe thinking a little too much out loud."

"Is there a problem with that?" Grant turned slowly to view the source of the voice.

"No, guess not. Unless you were telling me to get out of here. Then there might be a problem." The patron's voice was getting a little louder.

"No, I don't believe I was."

"As long as you weren't, 'cause that would be bad for you."

"I said I wasn't."

The patron turned to look at Grant. "You have something you want to say?" the patron asked.

"Not to you."

"Not good enough for you to talk to?"

"Oh, shit, this is going to hell in a hurry," Grant mumbled.

The bartender returned with Grant's drink.

"Here you go," she said.

"You telling me to go to hell?" the patron said, now standing up.

"Oh, this isn't going to work," the bartender said. "You guys want to mix it up, take it somewhere else, starting with get the fuck outside, right the fuck now!"

"Hey, I'm just here looking for a drink, nothing else," the man said angrily.

"So you getting into it with this guy going to get that done?" The bartender asked.

The patron just scowled.

"Makes not a bit of sense to me. Why don't you try one of the bars over in La Quinta, I heard they drink and fight over there." The bartender froze, looking at the patron, not blinking, her index finger flicking back and forth towards the door.

The patron looked back at the bartender, then at Grant.

"Hey chief, I'm not saying anything and I don't want to start anything. I'll just finish my drink and be down the road," Grant said, disgust in his voice

"That's a good idea, except for the finish the drink part. Kind of think you should go now. Hey wait, what did you call me?"

"Nothing, forget it. The end of paradise, at last. Forget it, I'm leaving," Grant got up, put some money on the bar and headed for the door.

The man watched him and waited until he was almost to the door before he got up to follow him outside. Grant had been in similar situations before, usually because of Rex, and he had an idea that this might go this way. He stepped outside, taking a deep breath to relax himself, but was interrupted by the other man's voice yelling at him.

"You think this is done?" the patron asked.

"I don't think it ever began. That was your deal. Let's call it a night, shall we? I don't need any more shit tonight."

The patron moved closer.

"You some big deal!" the patron asked, screaming, as he reached back to take a big swing at Grant, as if hoping talking would confuse him, and keep him from noticing a punch was coming his way. Grant had seen this before. It was a long, loopy swing, which he easily ducked and responded with a short, powerful right hand punch of his own, moving upward into the patron's midsection. He threw his entire body weight behind the punch, and he heard the groan heavily as his fist connected with the man's midsection, punching all the air out of his lungs. The man immediately dropped to one knee, gasping for breath. His gasping was a terrible sound and Grant grabbed his arm as he went down.

"Easy. You'll be OK in a minute or two. Try some shorter breaths," Grant said, as he half-helped, half-dragged the man to let him lean up against the building.

"Whoa," the patron whispered, as there was no wind in his lungs to give force to his voice. "OK …." He got a few more words out, none of them understandable.

"I'm going to leave you here to try to get your air back and that'll be the end of it. Go back in and pay that surly fucking bartender for the drink of mine you interrupted, and be sure and leave her a nice tip, 'cause she acts like she could use some cheering up. You got that?" Grant said as he took his hand and pushed on the man's chest, forcing what little air he had recaptured back out again.

"Gaa it," the patron whispered.

"Good. A shitty way to end what started as a pretty goddamned good day. Un-fucking-real!"

Grant started walking down the sidewalk, away from the patron and into the night, shaking his head and talking to himself as he walked.

CHAPTER 36

Grant walked on in the desert night air. The confrontation with Annie's current fling was one more goddamned fly in a glass of good bourbon. He was pretty sure he couldn't take another. He kept walking, hoping for some clarity. Walking had always helped before.

He noticed a couple of Mexican women yelling at a bus, as they ran to the stop to catch it. They both had bags in one hand and hats in the other. He saw a drunk leaning against a light pole, smoking a cigarette, motioning to no one in particular, saying that he really would like some spare change to buy something, Grant was not sure what. Dogs barked in the distance and there were beacons from what he assumed was the airport. The lights seemed terribly foreign in this setting. The dogs barking made him feel empty, and he tried his best to tune out their lonely song and concentrate on not concentrating on anything. He passed a boarded up building that looked to have been a gas station at one point, though someone had evidently turned it briefly into a furniture store. It was now awaiting a new facelift and would have to endure it with plywood attached and sand piling up in its corners.

"Hope I don't look like that," he said as he paused in front of the building.

A motorcycle on the street caught his glance, as it was loud and was surrounded by green neon lights, something he was not accustomed to seeing.

"Sazeracs," Grant said.

A Rolls Royce moved past him, and he wondered if the neon motorcycle was the escort vehicle.

"Probably not."

He heard a train in the distance. He stopped, closing his eyes to better listen to its distant clatter. It was as if it were asking him to remember something almost gone. He recalled sleeping out in the backyard when he was young, hearing that same sound in the night.

"Where's that sleeping bag now," he thought. He thought he had a sleeping bag in his truck, but his memory was weak. The truck was being repaired after the accident anyway, so it wasn't here, so it didn't make any difference. The sounds of the train quickly disappeared, an airplane engine in the sky stepped in to take its place, disrupting the normal desert sounds. Grant started walking again. He looked into the sky, awash with stars, though the Milky Way wasn't as striking as the night before, as when he was with Annie

A siren, far off, but still too close for his taste. A coyote cried in the distance, a sound more to his liking, more normal to him. He clapped his hands together, picking up the pace of his walking, still doing his best to try to smile. The cry of the coyote seemed to give him strength and even produced a chuckle, of sorts. Annie had always thought he was crazy to get excited when he heard coyotes. He walked several blocks after the coyote's howls disappeared, thinking less and less about the sights and sounds of the night. He now heard only his boots making contact with the hard sidewalk under them. He tried to move with no sound, as if the clacking of his heels against the pavement was more penetrating than before.

He stopped in front of a car lot, pausing to look at his reflection in one of the shiny new vehicles. He put his hands in the back pockets of his jeans, standing there looking at his reflected self looking at back at him, wanting to say something, but not really sure what. The light of the street lamp and the curves of the car made for a distorted image, which didn't help his already shaken confidence. He looked again in the night sky, noticing the moon, beginning its evening saunter across the sky. He moved away from the odd reflection of himself, walking with his hands still in his back pockets and continuing his gaze upwards at the moon. He lost track of how far he had been walking, and time and distance lost focus and grew fuzzy, like everything else that had happened since he had arrived.

He had no idea where he now was, in relation to the hotel or the previous two bars he had visited. He thought it was only two; he hoped it was only two. He had always been a fan of walking, so the distance back to the Ritz didn't bother him. It was more the fact of having no idea where he was or where he was going that was unsettling. He thought about asking someone for directions, and then about how much people love giving a lone guy directions, especially in the middle of the night. Rex would love to see him right now. He would be laughing and rolling on the ground.

"Son of a bitch," he said out loud, loudly enough that a rabbit on the other side of the road burst out of its hiding place and into the dark to find another.

Grant remembered seeing a sign that read, "Highway 111." He was pretty sure that if he stayed on this road, it would take him to the road that then became that "steep-ass" hill up to the hotel, where he and Rex had almost gotten heat stroke. The two of them walking together yesterday evening now seemed like a month ago.

He wished he were back at the hotel, as he was now starting to get very tired. The events of the night and the last few days and the car wreck from the day before all tumbled around in his mind.

He was making every attempt to not think about Annie, about what had happened tonight. It occurred to him that if that were an easy task, he wouldn't be walking around Palm Springs by himself in the middle of the night. Things had gone so well until the kissing scene, if he didn't count the wreck that christened his arrival in Palm Springs. He should have asked Isobelle what she saw in store for him. Her gift was really something. Her ability to sense things about people and see the hazy outlines of events in their pasts and futures was something new to him. He still was baffled by it.

"Isobelle," he asked the night air, "do you see me, wandering around in the dark, talking to myself?"

He found himself at a bus stop bench, where he slumped down, his weight heavy upon it. He put his elbows on his knees and leaned forward, letting his forehead rest in his hands. He sat like that for a long time, trying to gain some semblance of clarity. All the night sounds suddenly seemed to have been dumped together to form a jarring auditory stew pouring over him. He was defenseless against the onslaught. The noise, the emotions, the conflicts, the heat—they were all weighing down on him, pressing him further and further into that bench. That warm desert breeze he had always counted on to refresh him was now just wave upon wave of hot grit. It no longer contained the normal desert matter; it was loaded with spent tire tread, newspapers, fast food wrappers, plastic bags, and foul air from passing vehicles.

The streetlights overtook the stars and made for a dirty gray, gauzy canopy overhead. This was no longer the desert. This could have been any overheated city in America; there was just less foot traffic on the sidewalk and a sense of desolation and emptiness. He had it to himself, and he despised it. For the first time since he had left his home a couple of days ago, he felt totally and inexplicably alone. He had tolerated this loneliness in the past; he abhorred it now. There was no sun sinking behind the mountain. No smiling, welcome face behind the bar. It was just him. He sat back, letting his head slowly fall with the motion, resting it on the back of the bench. He opened his eyes and looked again at where there had previously been a sky full of stars, looking hopefully at where the moon might be. He stretched his arms across the back of the bench and closed his eyes. All the time he had been contemplating his mistakes had been a complete waste, giving him only pain. Now, he was going to get on with his life. It was time to move on. Just as this mildly positive thought had occurred to him, a bus arrived. He knew he was nowhere yet, but he also knew that was about to change.

Chapter 37

The bus rumbled to a stop, and he squinted at the sight of the large, noisy, smoky thing, its doors directly in front of him. It looked like some strange gigantic lizard, its mouth gaping. A very large man wearing headphones was driving, and he looked out expectantly through the open doors. Grant forced his tired body out of the hold the bench had on him and moved into the bus.

"This go anywhere near the Ritz?" Grant asked, leaning inside the large reptile.

The driver looked at him blankly.

"The Ritz Hotel?" Grant asked again.

The driver pulled one of the headphones away from his ear.

"Ritz?" Grant asked a third time.

The driver nodded once and pointed to the sign next to the doors that said: "Tickets."

Grant closed his eyes, dug his hand into his jean pocket, pulled out a ten dollar bill and held it out to the driver. The driver looked in his interior mirror, verifying that no one was on the bus except he and Grant. He reached for the bill and Grant pulled it away.

"The Ritz?"

The driver nodded once again and Grant gave him the money, which was promptly tucked away in the driver's shirt pocket. Grant swung down onto the first row of seats as the driver closed the doors and pulled away, fitting his headphone back on. Grant looked back out the window to the bench as the bus moved away. He hoped never to see that bench again in his life. Grant thought he had done a good job of removing the obstacles from his life, but he had taken most of the emotion out as well. He missed the feeling of having someone close to him. Since he and Annie had been together, no one had been close to him like that. He wondered if he would now be able to build the bridge that was needed to cross the river, to cross over to a land where he could share his feelings with someone else.

He doubted he would ever see Annie again. He was having trouble thinking of much more right now. The car wreck, Rex, the weekend of drinking, the intoxication of being with Annie, of dropping that guy from the bar who may or may not have been the man kissing Annie, but who deserved what he got just for being an asshole—everything that had transpired this weekend had made him incapable of rational thought. He tilted his head back and rested it on the bus seat. "More comfortable than the bench," he thought, drifting off to sleep.

His rest was short; he was awakened by something poking him in the side. He opened his eyes and turned his head to find that it was the bus driver prodding him with what appeared to be a length of sawed-off shovel handle. Grant looked at him, through one partially opened eye. The driver pointed the shovel handle at Grant, and then motioned at the door. Grant looked out the window to see they were now at the street that led up the hill to the hotel. He got up slowly, waiting for his body parts to perform in unison with the messages from his brain. At this point, they weren't operating well together. He dug himself out of the seat and limped off of the bus. The driver looked at Grant and saluted with the shovel handle before he pulled the lever to close the metal reptile's giant mouth and pulled away, its foul breath pushing at Grant.

Grant started the walk up the incline, the road black and hot. He cleared his mind just enough to vow to himself that he would not try to decide anything until he had slept. He just wanted to get up this hill, get back to the hotel. He didn't have a vehicle, so he couldn't go home tonight anyway. He looked again, up the road in front of him, knowing how good it would feel to be at the top, inside, resting in bed. As painful as it had been, he thought the events of the evening may have given him the closure he needed. He was beginning, at long last, to see that he should no longer think about Annie. It was useless to think they might see each other again, let alone get back together as a couple. He saw car headlights up the hill coming in his direction.

"Hope it's Fausto, again, he can give me a ride." he thought. That thought lifted his worn spirits somewhat and he proceeded up the steep road, continuing to look towards the top. The vehicle coming his way seemed to be having difficulty staying on the road. Grant knew that feeling. He peered into the headlights, trying to see if it was Fausto's car. It wasn't; it appeared to be a red sports car of some sort. Grant sighed, giving up hope of Fausto giving him a ride up the hill. Suddenly, though, the headlights veered in his direction. There was no time. The car was going to hit him. Grant dove to the side of the road, hoping there was a ditch there, but he never found out. There was only a harder darkness there, filled with jagged objects.

He evidently hit himself in the head pretty solidly, as he had passed out and woken up several seconds—or was it several minutes?—later. He assessed his wounds quickly, if not coherently: his left knee was clearly bunged up, a gash over his left eye was bleeding down his face, and there was a powerful pain in his left side every time he took a breath. He unbuttoned and peeled off his shirt, then ripped off one of the sleeves, tying it around his head to staunch the bleeding above his eye. As he looked at his bare chest, he noticed a number of minor scrapes and scratches that would undoubtedly need cleaning. He swore violently, which ironically helped calm him down. Thus bandaged, he clutched his now-ragged shirt and started to stumble up the remainder of the hill.

"Probably look like some demented pirate," he thought to himself. "Hope I don't run into any kids. They'll prob'ly piss themselves."

Dazed, cut up, and brutally bruised, Grant somehow made it back to the hotel. There was a commotion out front, looking like someone, maybe one of the overweight, sunburned people he saw earlier at the bar, had eaten too much, and thought they were having a heart attack. There was an ambulance at the entrance, paramedics and several employees tending to a very loud woman, who was probably the wife of the man on the gurney. With all the disorder, he was able to slip in unnoticed, which was a first for his visit to the hotel.

Grant really did not want to go to the hospital right now, and he certainly didn't want a bunch of paramedics poking him and shining bright lights in his eyes. He'd already enjoyed that once this weekend and once was more than plenty. He cut down along the side of the hotel towards the pool area. In all the commotion, he found that one of the gates to the pool had been left open, and he slipped through the gate and took a back elevator up to his floor.

Once inside, he made for the bathroom, thinking to examine his wounds.

His head felt as if someone had been using it to block the wheels of a jetliner. He was having tremendous difficulty moving. He focused on, or tried to focus on the headwaters that led to his blood-soaked shirt. He peeled the makeshift shirtsleeve-bandage off of his eye, eye and brought his hand up to feel what was a huge bump on his head, and the wet, sticky gash above it.

"Shit."

He barely touched the area around his eye and it sent an electric shock throughout his body. His jeans were ripped out at the left knee, his knee cut and swollen. He reached for it, but was stopped short by the pain that now emanated from his left side. He was covered in dirt and gravel, and could see bits of grass and dirt and twigs sticking out of his disheveled hair.

"Hell."

He managed to sit down on the edge of the bed, groaning, and glanced at the blinking red message light on his phone. The pulsation of the light made his head hurt all the more. He did not want to talk to anyone. No one could possibly care about him—or at least, that was the thought running through his head. He lay back slowly on the bed. He did not want to get up. This time, at least, it wasn't Rex who had caused this. This had just *happened.*

The phone rang, and it took every effort for him to bring himself to an upright position, to reach over to the phone. The ringing sounded like someone spilling a large box of pots and pans on a concrete floor.

"Hello?"

"Where have you been? Didn't you get my messages?" Annie's voice demanded to know. There was urgent concern in her voice.

"I, um, just got here. I hadn't had time to check."

"Are you—I have been worried about … are you all right?"

"Nope."

"What's the matter? What happened? Where did you go?"

"Long story." Grant winced.

"You can't tell long stories."

"I probably can't tell this one either, then."

"Can I see you? I mean, I know it's late, but I can explain—"

"You don't need to explain anything to me, ever."

"I—I'm sorry, I didn't know he was coming here … I mean, I didn't want to think he … I knew, but—I didn't want him to come here!" Annie said, her voice starting to fail her.

"I'm not sure what you're talking about."

"What's the matter?"

"Just tired."

"I'm coming to see you," Annie said, trying to get her voice back.

"Ok, but I'm not much to see. You got any of your doctor stuff?"

"Oh God! I knew you weren't all right. I'll be right there," Annie said and hung up the phone.

Grant hung the phone up on one of the pillows. He looked around the room, his vision blurred, his head throbbed. He couldn't handle all of this thinking right now. Stringing thoughts together was impossible at this point. He lay back on the bed, wanting to sleep until his next birthday. Maybe he could tell the front desk not to bother him for a few days and that he would be all right. He just wanted to rest. He didn't remember how he came to be in the condition he was in, and he couldn't figure out what was the last thing he did remember. Remembering things had been always tough in the past, but this was a little scary. He wasn't going to attempt any major mental gymnastics just yet. He felt like he had nothing left to give, and going beyond empty was just not physically possible. Empty of emotion, hollow of head and heart. Maybe Annie wouldn't come, and he could just sleep until he couldn't sleep anymore. He couldn't remember if he had called her, or if she had called him. It didn't matter.

He wanted to dream, but a black cloth had been thrown over his imagination, and he was just too weary to check if anything else was broken. The short inventory he had done was enough. He was pretty sure the cut on his head, above his eye, was leaking. He was too tired to check. He would try to get the rest of him under that black cloth, so nothing else could get at him.

The knocking was very gentle and very far off. Grant had no idea where it was coming from. He had no idea where he was. Annie's soothing voice on the other side was the only thing that called him back from the blackness. He tried to sit up, but that wasn't working. He slid off the bed, onto the floor to his good knee, pausing for a moment to let things settle. One knee hurt badly, so he would not be putting weight on that one. He leaned back into the bed with the closest arm, bent at the elbow, using it as a pry bar to lift himself off the floor. The knocking got louder. Annie's voice was still soothing, though now it had more of a tone of urgency to it.

"Coming … coming," he moaned. Suddenly there was a stabbing pain from his ribcage.

The light he had left on at the room entrance was the only way he would find the door.

"How in the hell did I get in here?" Grant leaned against the door.

"Open the door, Grant." Annie was speaking louder than she ever did.

"Yep."

He finally made it the short distance from the bed to the door, fumbling with the knob, struggling to get it open. Beyond the door, there in the hallway, Annie's golden face shone like the dawn. He thought it was a dream.

Chapter 38

"You make me laugh." Dawn looked up at the stars.

"Really? Well, I am pretty funny," Rex replied.

The two were sitting on the edge of the swimming pool at the Ritz, their legs dangling in the water, their hands touching briefly, moving away, and then touching again. The night was still, though the occasional brief wisp of wind showed itself across the water, it went unfelt by the two. After the excitement earlier in the bar, the warm air, the cool water, and their gently grazing hands all combined to soothe their nerves.

"You never lack for confidence, do you?" Dawn smirked.

"You do that, and they're on you in a second," Rex looked down at the water.

"Who's they?"

"They is everybody. Anybody."

"So you are afraid of that?"

"Who said I was afraid?"

"No one, but just what you said means there is a fear."

"Not necessarily. I'm just cautious."

"I'm not looking for anything, you know."

"Everybody's looking for something."

"Not me. You're here, I'm here, and that's that." Dawn leaned closer.

"Yeah?"

"Yeah."

"Why do you think you're here?" Rex was still looking up at the sky.

"I have no idea, but I'm OK with that. A reason will present itself in this lifetime, maybe the next. Why do you think you are here?" Dawn looked up, as if to find where he was looking.

"Why do I think I am here?"

"That is what I asked."

"Well, I can't say as I subscribe to the different lifetimes thing, but for now.... "

"For now?"

"For now, I'm here to try to get that dipshit friend of mine to relax and learn to have fun again. I guess I have been missing out on the fun myself lately, so getting wired back in doesn't hurt," Rex said, looking down from the sky and now at Dawn.

"Those are good reasons," Dawn lowered her gaze to his. "It is very good of you to do those things for your friend."

"You think so?"

"Yes, I think it is. I think because of that, good things are going to come to you."

"Really!"

"Yes."

"Careful, I'm not used to hearing good news. I'm not sure I helped him much tonight. Probably would have been better if that douchebag-asshole, what's-his-name, hadn't showed up. I think Grant was rolling before that."

"You can't control everything. Anyway ... well, if I'm around, you should get used to good things, and hearing good news."

"Those are pretty good offers," Rex smiled.

"I think so," Dawn said, placing her hand back on his.

"I didn't think I would see you again. Sort of was iffy about seeing anything again. Come in. Can I get you something?" Grant said, turning to go back into the room.

Annie's face shifted quickly from glowing to concern. She grabbed his arm, gently, but with purpose.

"Grant, let me look at you," Annie said, entering the room, closing the door behind her.

Grant turned back around. Annie squinted to survey what damage she could see in the poor lighting, the cut on his head quite visible, even in the near darkness. She squeezed his arm.

"How'd I do?"

"Great, as always," she said, fighting back tears.

"Well, anything worth doing—"

"Shut up." She placed her small but strong hands to the wound on his head, and then gently put her arms around him. "Why do you always…."

"I couldn't tell you."

"One of these days," Annie sniffed, hugging him.

"That's what I always say," Grant winced, doing his best to hug her as hard as he could, considering all the areas of his body that weren't working.

"What is that beeping?" Annie looked around the room.

"I don't hear anything but hundreds of people marching in my head. Maybe on my head."

Annie released her soft embrace, though not quickly, letting her hands trail down his back as she let go.

"You hug all your patients?"

"Just the troubled ones."

"How do you make that determination?"

"If I have known them for a very long time, and if they look like they just fell off of a cliff," Annie said, waiting to wipe her eyes after Grant had turned to go back into the room.

"Sorry, I'm not really set up for entertaining," Grant said sitting back down on the bed.

Annie saw the blood soaked towel on the bed, saw the phone, hung up on the pillow next to the towel, rather than its cradle.

"You got this pillow on hold?" she joked, working to get herself ready to deal with Grant's injuries, and hanging the phone back in its proper place, the beeping stopping when she did.

"I didn't even know there was a phone in here."

"Somebody else staying with you?"

"Lots of folks, lots of women. They must have just stepped out," Grant said, lying back on the bed.

"I'm serious."

"I'm done being serious."

"Do you remember talking to me on the phone?" Annie asked, looking him over.

"When?"

"Just now."

"Did I?"

"Yes."

"I don't remember," Grant gently scratched his head.

"OK, sit up. I need to take a check you out."

"Might be scary what you see."

"Are you a doctor?"

"No."

"Then maybe you ought to let me be the judge of what I'm going to see."

"If you use a flashlight, you're going to see it shining on the wall—out the other side of my head."

"I'm prepared. Tell me what else is bothering you," Annie said, continuing her examination.

"How did I get here tonight?"

"You don't know?"

"I don't have a clue, but that's not unusual," Grant squinted his good eye.

"Was drinking part of the curriculum after you left me tonight?"

"Not enough to not know how I got here."

"How much did you have after…?" Annie paused, noticing that she was having to be more forceful to keep him focused.

"After what?"

"After you, you know, left me," Annie looked at the floor.

"I think I almost had one."

"One what?"

"One drink. Maybe not even," Grant said, unsure of himself.

"That's not like you."

"Well, I was saving myself for later in the evening. Knew I wanted to be able to clot better."

"Let's look in those eyes."

"What are you looking to find?" Grant asked, looking around the room like he had not seen it before.

"Signs of a concussion, but I think I have found them already, it's only slight, so you don't need to go to the hospital, at least not for that. What else hurts?"

"Knee, ribs, pride."

"I'll check the first two."

"What about the last one?"

"You do well with these, maybe we'll work on the other," Annie said, not delaying in the procedure.

Grant was not really keeping up with what Annie was doing. He was doing everything he could to focus with a severely dilapidated attention span and limited memory. He just looked at her, enjoying her being this close to him.

"How do I look?"

"Going to need stitches above that eye," Annie said, her lips tightening as she said it.

"OK. You do that?"

"You're not going to like it," Annie said.

"I bet I'll like it more if you do it."

"You won't like it regardless. Let's have a look at those ribs and that knee."

"I don't think I can get this stuff off."

"I'll help you," Annie said, slowly and deliberately.

"See, somebody else probably wouldn't make that same offer."

"Hmm," Annie said quietly. "I wish you hadn't left," Annie said, going back to examine his ribs. "I'm really sorry you left, actually."

"Not as sorry as me," Grant said, showing signs that breathing was paining him.

"I'm pretty sorry."

"Things happen."

"None of this should have happened. Your ribs are probably making breathing a bit difficult," Annie said. "Let's look at the ribcage." She put two gentle fingers to his side, putting slight pressure in a few different areas. She watched his reaction, noting when he winced from the pain.

"You're pretty bruised, and looks like you might have a few cracked ribs. What's the pain like when you breathe?"

"Like someone sticking a fucking red hot ice pick that's hooked up to a car battery into my side."

Annie paused, tilting her head, then returning to her task. "Doesn't look like there's any blood coming up when you breathe, so no punctured lung. Let's look at the knee,"

"You going to cut my pants off of me?"

"Yep," Annie said, quickly cutting the torn jeans away to expose the knee.

"You're pretty good at that. Was it in one of your medical textbooks somewhere? How to cut pants off of guys?"

"Yes, I think that was the title of the book, in fact."

"Have you practiced much?"

"Not in hotel rooms. It looks swollen, hard to tell if you tore something. When you go for the x-ray for the ribs, might as well have them check out the knee. We should get some ice on this knee. If it's not better tomorrow, you might need to have it drained. Maybe we should go to the hospital now."

"I've had messed up ribs before, they can't do anything. Did you say the knee drained?"

"You're not going to like that either."

"There are a lot of things I don't like and normally I would say OK, but I really don't think I can make it there tonight. I did see an ambulance out front, but it was full. How about I catch the next one tomorrow? Believe it or not, I have actually had much worse happen, and I've survived, been just fine."

"Did you have a doctor look at you then?"

"No, but Rex said I was OK."

"Perfect." She let out a loud sigh. "Nothing like an expert opinion. This is not real good, but I don't think you need to go to the hospital tonight. Just promise me you will go for a follow up visit in the next few days. And by follow up, I mean with someone from the medical field, not from Rex." Annie moved over to one of the chairs in the room, sitting down heavily. She put her hands on her knees and sat, looking back at Grant.

"What's the matter?" Grant asked.

"Not used to being up this late."

"Sorry for contributing to that."

"Up until now, you contributed the good part. This part, not as much."

"I'm usually only about half good, you know that."

"No, I don't know that."

"You've known me a long time. You know I always manage to put a different spin on things."

"I don't know anything of the sort. You always think you've messed everything up. If you were just thinking about the moment itself, instead of how you were going to potentially mess it up, maybe you wouldn't mess it up."

"I don't know about that."

"The number of things about you that you know nothing about is a very large number," Annie said, looking fatigued.

"I don't know about that either."

"Why did you leave?"

"Things are a bit hazy. I want to say—err, I mean, I don't want to say, but there was a guy … kissing you."

"He wasn't supposed to be."

"That's sort of what I—that's what I thought," Grant said.

"You just left! Why did you leave?" Annie put her head down, wiped her eyes. "I didn't want you to leave. I wanted you to stay. He was here, but I didn't want to be with him. I wanted to be with you. I came here because I wanted to be with you," Annie said, putting her head in her hands. "I wanted to be with you…."

Grant had never seen Annie like this before. But then, the pain in his head made him unsure that he was seeing her like this now.

"It shouldn't have surprised me, but it did."

"It surprised me too," Annie said, not looking up.

"I've been telling myself that I'm tired of trying to be perfect and I need to be more about having fun. Perfect is too hard."

"Perfect—what? Well, it wasn't like you didn't know the guy."

"Yes, I know him, and we have been seeing each other, but it's not like that."

"Not like what?"

"Not like a big kiss in public, what. We are not that close. I told him not to come. I didn't—I didn't want to … why would I have gone through that exercise with Rex if I didn't want to see you?"

Grant struggled to raise himself off the bed. Annie looked up at him, she sniffed.

"Maybe you could help me here?"

"You don't need to be moving around," she sniffed again, then started to snicker to try to take her mind off of things. "Just lie back down." She moved towards him, in the hopes of getting him to abandon his feeble efforts to try to stand.

"Nope."

"I'm serious."

"So am I," Grant said, struggling to stand.

"Just for a minute, then you have to lie down."

"I will," Grant said, putting his arms around Annie, "I just need a minute," he said. He held her like that for a moment, and then kissed her.

His head hurt, and he didn't want to upset her any more than he already had. He didn't want her to have to deal with two guys she didn't want kissing her in the same night, but he had to do this. After a few seconds, he started to pull away, but she pulled him back. Grant thought he could feel the soft desert breeze on him again.

"Should probably put a couple of stitches in that cut." Annie mumbled, taking a breath from the kiss, then returning to it.

"Would you mind?" he paused.

"No, I don't mind. I don't want you bleeding all over these sheets, or all over me in them."

CHAPTER 39

Grant had a difficult time waking. He had experienced foggy mornings before, but this one was thick. There was tremendous pain in his head. He was pretty sure the jackhammers had been called in, and were now adding additional personnel. His ribs and knee were no better than his head. In spite of all this pain, he could have sworn there had been a woman in his bed last night. Not just any woman, either, but Annie. He tried his best to move in the bed without having hot knitting needles embed themselves in his trouble spots. He looked around the hotel room. He knew where he was; that was a good sign. He looked towards the nightstand to check the time, and there was Annie, sitting by the bed. He wasn't sure, but through his good eye, it looked as if she were wearing one of his western shirts, and nothing more. He wondered if he had lost consciousness. The sight of Annie sitting there wearing nothing but one of his shirts made him hope that he wouldn't be regaining his facilities anytime soon.

"I was getting ready to wake you," Annie said.

"Why?"

"You have a concussion; I need to check on you."

"How did I get it?"

"That's a good question. Are you any more clear on that today than you were last night?"

"Not so far. How long have you been here?"

"A while."

"I wasn't dreaming?" Grant asked.

"That depends on the dream."

"That you stayed here, with me, last night."

"No, I was here." Annie smiled.

"Good. But how do I know you are really here now?"

"Guess you are going to have to trust me on this one."

"I liked having you here. If you're really here."

"Like I said, the trust thing. And I liked being here, except for the stitching you up part."

"Oh, that's right. Wasn't too crazy about that myself."

"I did warn you."

"You were right. You get tired of always being right?"

"I'm not always right. I'm wrong about a lot of things."

"Not that I see."

"Just rest. I have to go for a few hours. There are some relatives that I promised I would stop by and see. I called Isobelle, and she's going to come look after you while I'm gone. That's very nice of her, don't you think?" Annie asked.

"Nice of you to, you know, patch me up."

"I didn't do it to be nice. Any of it."

"Aren't you leaving today?" Grant asked, slowly.

"I was, but not now. We'll still have some time when I get back."

"I'd like that."

"Me too," Annie said. "I need to get ready. They might not understand me showing up with just your shirt on."

"I'm all right with it."

"Well, you live through the afternoon, and maybe...."

"Maybe what?"

She stood up, leaned over and kissed him, running her fingers through his hair.

"What about the others?"

"What others?"

"I'm a bit sketchy on last night, but it seems like there was quite an assemblage of characters at the bar."

"There was at least that."

"What can you tell me?"

"Not much. I sort of faded," Annie said, putting her head down.

"Me too."

"Let's see, oh, gosh. Kat is going back today. Your boy, who the heck knows. His girls were passed out on the table. Gina, Melissa, Rachel, not sure. And Isobelle you know about, you can ask her yourself when she comes to gets you. Oh, and Dawn, not sure about her either."

"I was wondering about the names of the three."

"You don't remember?"

"No, but that might have just been a group name thing. Wouldn't read anything into it. What about what's-his-name?" Grant asked.

"Pretty sure he didn't stick around too long. After Kat punched him, I left pretty quickly, to try to find you."

"What?"

"Wild, huh?"

"I hate it when I miss the good shit. Would have liked to have seen that."

"No, you wouldn't have."

"You sure?"

"The whole thing made me sick to my stomach. It still does," Annie said, looking away.

"Sorry."

"You focus on trying to rest, not on what happened. Isobelle will come get you and I'll see you later. Do me a favor?"

"What's that?"

"Try and still be in town when I get back," Annie said, kissing him.

"Don't want to piss off the doc."

"That kind of attitude might be good for your health."

"I'm always looking to improve my odds," Grant said.

"Well, here's your chance."

"I'll do my best."

"Best to—?"

"Not piss off the doc."

"Good."

Grant made his way out of the hotel, slowly dragging a bad knee and navigating with one eye. He avoided engaging anyone in conversation. He got out the main entrance and across the street to the tennis courts, where Isobelle said she would be. She saw him and pulled her car towards him, saving him the walk. She pulled alongside the curb and rolled her window down.

"I thought you had changed your mind."

"Apparently not. Just had a little trouble focusing, I guess." He removed his sunglasses, exposing one of his visual prizes from the night before.

"It appears so," she said, seeing the damage and looking him over for more. "It also appears that Annie was right: you need tending to."

He limped around the car to the passenger side. He heard the *ka-pock* of a tennis ball being struck on the court beside the parking lot, and somehow the sound seemed to resonate in his bad eye every time the racket struck the ball. He got in the car, doing his best not to slam the door. He heard more of the *ka-pock* sounds, not sure if they were real or in his head.

They talked little at the beginning as Isobelle drove him back to her place. He was not sure if the silence was making him feel better or not. He didn't know what to say; the drive seemed suspended in time. After a few miles, Isobelle broke the silence.

"How is it that you left the group last night?"

"I had my reasons, I guess. I probably would have felt better if I hadn't," Grant said

"There was no reason for you to leave."

"Seemed to me like maybe there was one guy too many."

"This other man, he did not stay long. After Kat struck him in the face, he left."

"That's what I hear."

"This was quite out of character for Kat, I think."

"I would think. Somehow, though, I can see maybe there is some pent up stuff there. I did hear her say some pretty funny stuff, that you wouldn't, you know, expect."

"I do not believe she has ever hit anyone until now. This man, he was very rude."

"Like Rex?"

"Rex is just having fun, and is very glad to be with his friends again. That is much different that this man, who was very rude, and his heart is not in the right place. Rex, his heart is big."

"That's surprising."

"What is surprising?" Isobelle asked.

"That you thought this guy was worse than Rex."

"This man wanted to force himself on the group, force himself on Annie.

Rex seems to be someone who does what he does. If people wish to come along, that is all right with him. If they do not, that is all right as well. This other man has a darkness surrounding him. Annie has a light surrounding her. They will not spend time together after this.

"This would confound me even if my head was clear, so I'm not sure what to say."

Neither one was looking at the other. Isobelle was paying attention to her driving and Grant was looking out the window.

"Grant, I am glad to have you come to my home. Annie said it was very important that someone keep an eye on you."

"I think I needed that a long time ago."

"Well, I was not around then, and that is your fault, but I don't want to get into your history, I am just giving help where it is needed. Annie believes you have a concussion and that someone needs to watch you. Your light has dimmed. It is much different than the light I saw when I first met you."

Grant said nothing, but stared out the window.

"I will make arrangements so that you do not get charged for extra days at the hotel," Isobelle said.

"You can do that?"

"Only in special cases."

"Special nut cases?"

"Something like that, though you might be my actual first."

"Great to be at the front of the line," Grant said.

"Of course you may have to show them a note from your doctor."

"I don't have a doctor."

"That is where you are wrong."

Isobelle drove thoughtfully, no sharp turns, no bumps. Grant was having a difficult time determining the route to her house, but he realized it wasn't important anyway. It was another beautiful day, and the deep blue ceiling of the desert sky looked like the deep blue blanket of the ocean where he lived. He had few other thoughts, only that he hoped they would make it to Isobelle's place soon, as he was having difficulty holding his head upright.

"Not much longer," she said, seeing he was riding uneasily.

"OK."

The next thing he knew, he was resting on the couch in Isobelle's house, without much of an idea how he had gotten there. He was as comfortable as he could have been, given his concussion and the many aches and pains. He noticed the items around the inside of her house. There were a great many crystals and rocks, a number of Kachina dolls, and Native American rugs.

"I think I might sleep a little, if that's all right."

"That is fine, but Annie said I need to wake you periodically. I am going to be here if you need anything. She said one is not supposed to let people with head injuries sleep too long without checking on them."

"What if they had their heads injured a long time ago?"

"Well, the damage might already be done then, and there is nothing I can do about that. If you die, I will get some of my friends to help get you back to the hotel and leave you there. It would be easier if I did not have to deal with it. The hotel is better equipped for that sort of thing. It happens, though not often."

"Yeah, I think I saw somebody in a bad way there last night. Don't think he died.You didn't have anything to do with that, did you?" Grant scratched his head.

"People die in hotels. Thankfully, no one has died in my home. I plan to keep it that way."

"Your friends, they would help you? They wouldn't say anything?"

"That is right, they would just help me and that would be that."

"Pretty reliable friends."

"That is the only kind I have, or ever will have; I do not have time for nonsensical things."

"And yet you made time for me."

"I liked your light from the first time I saw you," Isobelle said.

"Hmmm …."

"That is enough thinking for you. Get some rest, I will check on you in an hour or two." She leaned over, as if she were going to kiss him, then stopped short, and paused, as if catching herself. She tapped his leg, and pointed to his boot. He lifted his leg and she turned around, straddling it, her back to him. She lifted the heel, pulling up slowly until the boot came off. She repeated the process on the other leg and boot.

"You've done this before," Grant said, settling back on the couch.

"It is best that you give me at least one break. I could kill you in your sleep, you know."

"You wouldn't have to work very hard to do it," he said, closing his eyes.

Grant had strange dreams. He saw Annie, though he couldn't make out what she was doing. She was talking, but it was very low, and he couldn't hear her. He saw Rex; in the dream, he was eating something, which was nothing new. He saw Isobelle, though maybe that wasn't a dream. He might have opened his good eye a time or two, to see her standing over him, her hands over, but not touching his body. The dreams were strange, if they were really dreams. He awoke and Isobelle was looking at him.

"I was just getting ready to wake you, to check on you."

"How long was I out?

"A couple of hours, not long. Did you dream?"

"Yes. Strange dreams. I'm not sure I'm man enough to live out here in the desert."

"Why would you say that?"

"I managed to pass a mirror when I was still at the hotel, and it's pretty clear that my body can't take this for too much longer."

"You may not feel much better for several days. Your dreams may also be unsettling for a while."

"That's what I'm afraid of."

CHAPTER 40

Grant and Isobelle talked for a long time. He spoke to her unguardedly, perhaps because of his injuries, he wasn't sure. He generally opened up to nobody, but he was greatly fatigued and not at all sure why he was talking. Isobelle spoke the most, which he preferred. She told him she had been married once, though not for very long. She said it had just happened when she was too young and there was so much more she should have known before taking that step. She was hurt by the marriage, and the fact that it hadn't worked out, though she was no longer emotional about it, not openly, anyway. Grant agreed that it was a big thing, and asked how could someone ever be certain of their degree of readiness? Isobelle said that a person could be sure only of their love for someone, not whether they were prepared for what would come with the formal pairing.

"How could you know? You only know what is in your heart, you don't know how the other person is going to be a year from now, ten years from now, more. That is not only true for someone you love, or a lover, it can be that way just with people you know, friends, and such. You don't know how they are going to be. You know how you want them to be, or think you know, but you do not really know how anyone is going to be. You just hope. At least this is how we are when we are young," she said.

"You just hope they don't turn out to be crazy," Grant added.

"That is right; you just hope they do not turn out to be crazy. You love them, and you show them you love them, but you cannot keep them from going crazy. I am not like that anymore. Now I know."

"I suppose."

"You never talk much, do you?" Isobelle asked.

"Oh, I don't know."

"You do not, that is all right. Were you always that way, or did something happen to make you that way?"

"Always been that way."

"I thought so."

"That's all right. That way the other person doesn't have to try to talk over me."

"That would not happen. And what about you, were you ever married?" Isobelle asked.

"Came close once."

"And?"

"And, I messed it up."

"Maybe it was not you."

"Maybe it was completely me," Grant said.

"Most people can only know that they love someone, not what is or what is not going to happen. Did we not just talk about that?"

"Yes, except for you, who seems to know about things before they happen, as well as about things that have already happened, without having heard about them. But, that's just my observation. Anyway, it was my fault. I was just too … too reckless."

"I think that the things you did then were just a part of who you were then. I do not believe you are that same person now."

"I just made too many mistakes, and she got tired of me making them, and that was that."

"I know that you are not one who would be unfaithful. As for making the same mistakes, you would not do that." Isobelle said.

"No, I wasn't unfaithful. I just did stupid things. It had nothing to do with, you know. This would be more like … I could have been in the middle of something important and would end up going off to New Orleans, or something." Grant said.

"Distractions take many forms. Sometimes they are not distractions at all, but lessons."

"I don't mean like that. I mean like there was always that, I don't know, that boondoggle factor, but not with other women. Someone, usually Rex, would suggest something that might be funny, and I would go chasing after it. It had nothing to do with other women. There were none, only the one I wanted to be with. I just screwed up."

"Annie has not left. She still cares for you very much."

"Hmm."

"Let go of the past. We all make mistakes."

"I was stupid; I still am, based on my current physical condition."

"You were younger," Isobelle said.

"Is that an excuse?"

"It is an explanation."

"Maybe," Grant said.

"Have you told her how you feel about her?"

"I tried."

"Are you still in love with her?"

"How long have I known you?"

"A couple of days."

"Maybe I know you a few more days before I talk about this kind of thing."

"Maybe, but maybe you are dying and you wouldn't want to pass on without telling someone how you really felt," she said smiling. "That is how you should live every day, like there might not be another. I see things in her for you, and I see things in you for her."

Isobelle had a way of being very direct, yet she seemed to be very good at getting heavy things back to becoming light things. It undoubtedly had something to do with her years as a bartender, but probably came more from the special ability she seemed to possess. Things could get weighty in a hurry ,sometimes due to the person on the other side of the bar losing his inhibitions. The bartender needed to keep it fun. Nobody wants things to get heavy there. Grant had been in that profession and possessed that same quality himself, which was probably why he recognized it in her. The difference was that he had no intention of revealing much about himself, not on either side of the bar, and he would have had to know someone a while before he would go into much detail. It was not that he would never talk about personal things with her—just not right away. He did know he did not have the special power she possessed that seemed to guide her so well.

"Ok, do me this favor. Tell me about what kind of person she was then, if that is not too personal. If it is too personal, we can talk about, about cowboy boots, or something."

Grant paused, looking into Isobelle's eyes, but she only gave him an innocent smile. She had been in the business, she had the persona. She would be there, she wasn't going anywhere. He could choose to open up a little, or he could just sit there. It was his choice. It could be dull, or it could be a lot of things. He opted to open up to her, just a little.

"She was always the same. Calm, tempered with enthusiasm. She always got everything you said, she just took a little while to process it."

"No revisionist history?"

"No. I'm not giving her enough credit, rather than giving her too much."

"OK, just checking."

"No, she was, and still is amazing. She is the most generous and compassionate person I have ever met."

"I see that as well, but I wanted to know if she was always like that, or if something had happened to change her."

Grant said nothing, but looked down at his feet and then out the window.

"I have seen her too, I know she is beautiful. And I feel she has been this way her whole life," Isobelle said.

Grant again said nothing.

"It is a good idea to engage the person with the head injury in conversation."

"All right," he settled back, trying to get his body more comfortable on the couch, as his mind was not necessarily comfortable with the conversation.

"So she was, and is pretty, brilliant, and compassionate. You could be talking about me," Isobelle laughed

"Yes I could be. She is blonde."

"Sorry. I am just trying to make you laugh."

"No need to be sorry. You're both about the same distance from the floor to the top of your head, though."

Isobelle laughed at his reference to her size.

"You look great all the time, and are quite compassionate yourself," Grant said. "Taking in strays, and such."

"That's very sweet of you to say."

"Well, I'm all kinds of sweet."

"Not really," Isobelle smiled.

"Not really."

"So, are you are going to tell her how you feel?"

"Who said I was?"

"I do not believe in waiting to express feelings that are already obvious."

"Not sure I follow you."

"Being a bartender, you get to be the one who hears people's stories all the time. The funny thing is, they tell me, but they seldom tell the people that they should be telling the story to," Isobelle said, looking out the window.

"Hmm."

"I mean, you know, sometimes it is just good to talk to someone that is not involved with what you are saying, to get a different point of view. Or maybe not so much to get a different point of view, but just to say it. This is a lot for a man with a head injury."

"Not your fault. You have no way of knowing how crazy someone is going to get."

Isobelle smiled. "I should like to see you again. I like you very much, and I do not think that would be such a bad thing for you to be around right now. You must tell Annie what you feel, but you and I, we will see each other again. As I told you, you must not wait to let someone know how you feel about them. And no, all of the good times of your life have not come and gone. There will be many more. You should always remember to pay attention when they come, and enjoy them. Your life is a magnificent journey, not to be wasted." She leaned over and kissed him.

CHAPTER 41

Isobelle took Grant back to the hotel. He was feeling much better than when he had woken that morning. He had the feeling that talking to either Annie or Isobelle would have made him feel better even if there was nothing wrong with him. Parts of the night were coming back in pieces. The hostess, Savannah, popped into his mind. He had forgotten about her, though not because she was not memorable. She had very much wanted to get together with him. He wondered if she had actually gone to the club later that evening to meet him. He found that there was something innocent about her. She was simple, but very real, very tangible. She was quite a contrast to the complexity of Isobelle. His cloudy head wasn't helping him think things through. He already had trouble thinking about one woman; thinking about three would require fewer bumps on his head.

"You will take care of yourself, and you will remember what we talked about?" Isobelle asked.

"That's a pretty tall order."

"You are up to it, even in your current state."

"Hope you're right."

Isobelle leaned over and kissed him again. "This is to remind you."

Grant made it back through the hotel, a little uncertain of the conversation he had just had and where he had recently been. He arrived at his room to hear the phone ringing inside. He fumbled for the key and entered in time to answer, hoping it was Annie.

"Took you long enough," Rex said from the other end of the line.

"If I had known it was you, I would have taken longer."

"You say that, but you don't mean that."

"Wanna bet?"

"You probably spent all your money last night on women."

"That's pretty big, coming from you," Grant said, rubbing his sore head.

"Where the hell did you go last night? You missed all the excitement," Rex said.

"I didn't miss all of it."

"Well, you missed Kat knocking that douche bag on his ass. I woulda paid money to see that one, and I saw it for free. Well, not really for free, but I didn't have to pay extra to see it."

"I heard about it."

"Who told you about it?"

"Isobelle told me."

"You spend the night with her, did you?"

"No. What are you up to?"

"I'm heading for New Orleans, which is really funny," Rex said.

"You can't tell me you fell for those two and are taking them to New Orleans. That's stupid, even by your standards."

"Who said I have standards?"

"Good point. Remind me to remind you of that."

"I won't forget."

"You forget everything," Grant said.

"What were we talking about?"

Grant let out a breath, which pained his aching ribs. "You are not the biggest dipshit in the whole world, but you are in the top two."

"Always striving to pass you by."

"I'm not in your league."

"I always say that."

"So you are going to New Orleans with those two brainiacs?"

"No credit, ever."

"Show me something creditworthy, we'll talk."

"All right. I'm going to New Orleans … with Dawn."

"You're kidding."

"Nope. Take it back, you like me now."

"What happened to the twins?"

"I think they are still sleeping. That's OK. They were funny, but Dawn is more … more—more everything."

"So you are going to New Orleans with a real person … a real woman?"

"That's what these airline tickets say, and based on the fact that we are standing at the airport, I would say it is a pretty safe bet," Rex mumbled something away from the phone.

"Nothing is a safe bet with you."

"True, but I don't want to flush this much money down the toilet."

"You have before."

"Old me."

"He still shows up sometimes."

"What about you?"

"I don't know where to start."

"You end up with a woman last night?"

"It was complicated," Grant said.

"It always is with you, chief. You may learn to just go with things, but I'm thinking that won't happen in my lifetime."

"Well, maybe that would be the old me."

"I always knew there was another guy locked up in there. Several guys, maybe. This new guy, maybe I get to meet him sometime, take him on an adventure."

"He's too smart for that."

"If he came from you, he ain't. You tell Annie and Kat I'm glad that they got to see me," Rex said.

"They'll be crushed that you took off. Not sure how to console them."

"You'll think of something. Tell 'em they can come and stay at my place anytime."

"They'll cry tears of joy at that one. Who wouldn't?"

"One more thing."

"There always is with you."

"I'm still not convinced that the guy and lady with the sunglasses weren't there watching me."

"What are you talking about?"

"Do you remember when we were first in the bar, and a guy and a lady came in dressed funny, wearing sunglasses? I thought maybe they might have been watching me," Rex said.

"We were at a resort in Palm Springs. Everyone there dresses funny, wears sunglasses. I suppose that might be a description of you."

"Look, lots of weird stuff has been going on with this work shit."

"There's always weird stuff going on when you're involved."

"They might have been spying on me. For the government, maybe for the other side," Rex said, saying the last part very low.

"Has that happened before?"

"How would I know?"

"You wouldn't, just like you don't know now, so try to make this easy on yourself. And for shit's sake, make it a little easier on us. Trying to keep you from being you is really wearing me out, so just try to maybe dial it back a notch."

"But I—"

"What?"

"Nothing. Never mind. Just thinking. Take care of yourself, chief. Try not to drop off the face of the earth. You know, you have a lot to be thankful for, and you really should start by thanking me."

"For what?" Grant asked.

"In spite of your objections, you really made some headway this weekend, so keep that in mind. You saw the woman of your dreams and you met a woman who seems to be dreaming about you, so you really did gain some serious ground. So, like I said, don't go into hiding," Rex said, as if proud of his assessment.

"This coming from you. You're the one who didn't return my calls for years, fuck nuts, did you forget that? Did someone tell you to say that?"

"Nobody tells me to say anything. Hey, when I get back, I'm going to come to your place, so get the cockroaches out, and fire up that weird looking thing in the closet. You might not remember, but it's called a vacuum cleaner. Wash the goddamn sheets, too."

"Who said I was letting you in?"

"You will."

"We'll see. And you'll try to relax about all the shit at work?"

"I guess. They're going to do what they're going to do. I didn't do anything wrong, but sometimes that doesn't matter. What matters is that I not sit around and piss and moan and wait for whatever to happen. I'm going to go, or I'm going to go down, but I'm going to live, and have fun. Starting my own gig will be good too. You taking notes here, chief? Tell Señor Grant good-bye," Rex said, his voice fading from the phone.

"Good-bye Señor Grant!" Dawn shouted.

"Be careful with him," Grant said.

"He's harmless. Plus, I told him if he got out of line, I would have Kat kick his ass."

"I like that."

"Gotta go! Bye, Señor Grant!" Dawn said, and hung up.

Grant sat down on the bed, putting his hand up to where Annie had stitched him up, putting his other hand on his knee, which was now bandaged. His ribs hurt when he breathed.

"And he's leaving with the girl…."

There was a knock at the door.

"Probably wanting to throw me out of the room," Grant said, grimacing as he got up off the bed.

He opened the door and his spirits rose immediately.

"How's the patient holding up?" Annie asked.

"Much better now," Grant said, looking into her eyes.

"No, really."

Grant looked around the hallway behind her.

"You expecting someone?" Annie asked, looking around behind herself in the hallway.

"Not usually."

"We can stand here in the hallway and talk, if you are."

"Nope, come in."

"Thanks."

They entered the room, Grant gently closing the door behind her.

"So let's have a look at you." Annie said.

"No bleeding, so not sure you need to, but you're the doc."

"That's right, wait 'til you get the bill."

"I figured the injuries were payback for past sins, but I think I'm squared up now."

"Hush," Annie said, leaning up to kissing him on the cheek.

"You kiss all your patients?"

"Absolutely, every one of them."

"You spend the night with all of them, too?"

"Oh gosh, yes. I don't actually have a place to live; I just stay at wherever my current patient lives. It saves a lot on expenses," Annie smiled.

Grant smiled, put his arms around Annie and kissed her. Annie looked thrilled. She kept her eyes closed for several seconds, and then opened them slowly and looked at Grant. Her hands moved gently through his hair; her gaze, deep into his eyes.

"I'll bet it does," Grant said.

Annie laughed, and hugged Grant, mindful of his ribs.

"You remembered the ribs."

"I try to remember the patient's symptoms."

"Before you kiss them?"

"Well, sometimes I'm in such a hurry to kiss them that I forget, but not this time."

"I suppose that could be problematic."

"Sometimes. How did you do today?"

"You mean with all this?" Grant said, waving his hand from his head, down to his knee.

"With Isobelle, and with all of this."

"OK, I guess. I probably wasn't very good company. What was she watching for?"

"Erratic behavior."

"Just today? Or since I got here?"

"Well, I asked her only about today. She undoubtedly had been watching you since you got here," Annie said.

"How would she be able to discern, you know, normal from otherwise?"

"Well, I don't know. Have you been exhibiting erratic behavior?"

"Just today? Or since I got here?"

"Well, you just said that, so repeating yourself could be viewed as erratic behavior," Annie said.

"How about the difference between erratic behavior and stupid behavior?" Grant asked.

Annie smiled, and grabbed his hand. "Let's just focus on how you are behaving today—that would be a good place to start."

"And you can tell the difference? Between stupid and erratic, I mean."

"In you or in me?" Annie asked.

"I personally don't think you're capable of either."

"Well, I appreciate the vote of confidence, but I assure you I can do a pretty good job of either. I already told you, I'm tired of trying to be perfect. I just want to have fun. Perfect is too hard."

"Do you always lie to your patients?"

"Never."

"Even when the diagnosis is grim?" Grant asked.

"Not even then, but your diagnosis is far from grim," Annie said.

"Don't you have to leave?"

"No," Annie said.

"You planning on staying here to watch me?"

"Yes. Is there a problem with that?"

"You're the doctor."

"Did you eat today?"

"I don't remember."

"That's not good."

"Which? The not eating, or not remembering?"

"Both. How do you suppose the room service is here?"

CHAPTER 42

Monday Morning

Grant's memory was still not in top form, but he was certain that even if he had total recall, he would not have been able to remember a better morning, and that was all that he needed to know right now. He was still in a great deal of pain, but Annie was lying next to him and fingers of the bright, sun coming through the window was gently warming the two of them. There was no noise, no ringing. The only sounds he could hear were their breaths rising gently with the sun. He knew he couldn't stay here forever, but he wanted to draw it out as long as he could. He knew Annie was awake, but she said nothing. He felt her soft breathing and he held her hand as they lay there.

"I have a lot of things to do. Back home, I mean," Annie said.

"I know. I'm probably keeping you here too long."

"I didn't mean it that way, and I wasn't finished."

"Sorry."

"I have a lot of things to do back home, so I don't want you to be worried if we don't get a chance to talk for a week or two. We will talk; I am just going to be really busy, OK?"

"OK, which part?"

"The part about us talking again in a couple of weeks."

"That will be fine. Given the choice between that and not at all, I'll take the first option," Grant said.

"We did the 'not at all' one already, let's try the 'talk again soon' one this time, OK?"

"That'd be good."

"I would like it better," Annie said. "And when we get together after that, maybe you could refrain from disappearing off into the night?"

"Old habits die hard."

"You just might die hard if you keep that habit up, so don't do it, all right?" Annie said, squeezing his hand.

"You're the doctor."

"Is that what this has become, a doctor-patient thing?"

"Well, you said you kiss all your patients, and that you spend the night with them, so I think this is a vast improvement over how, you know."

"So you think you are going to take advantage of how I treat my patients? What if I change my approach, and only talk to you?"

"Still a vast improvement, for me, I mean."

Annie smiled, touching him ever so slightly on his face, moving her hand up to where his stitches were.

"Yes, it would be a vast improvement, wouldn't it." Annie said. It wasn't a question.

"I think so, but I've had a head injury."

"How about this? You promise not to get reckless for a few weeks, and I'll come to see you and check out your injuries. That work for you?

"Now it sounds like maybe you do have a head injury, but I won't argue with your prescription. How long do I have to not be reckless for again?" Grant asked.

"Let's start with, say a couple of weeks, and build from there."

"Can you narrow it down a might?"

"I have lots going on," Annie said, not taking her hand off of his face, "so I'm not exactly sure. But I will come check on you in a couple of weeks, when my stuff calms down."

"A house call. You're going to make a house call?"

"Yep. Although, I really wasn't looking at it that way."

"A house call would be good. You can call it what you like, I don't mind," Grant nodded.

"I promise I'll get there as soon as I can."

"That's still a pretty good offer."

"Good. Now let's check out the room service again, I'm starving."

"One last meal?"

"Hardly. When I come see you, you're going to cook for me. You know, at your house."

"All your patients cook for you at their houses?" Grant asked.

"Oh, yes, all the time."

Annie and Kat stood outside the hotel. They were happy to have no one asking them if they needed anything, or if they could get something for them. As nice as the hotel was, the change to just being two friends together was refreshing. They were both enjoying the quiet, both were tired but happy. They stood for several minutes, saying nothing.

"So you're going to India," Annie said.

"Yes, I was going to tell you. There was just so much going on," Kat explained.

"Well, it's what you've wanted to do, right?" Annie asked.

"Yes. What I would really like to do is to find someone to share my experiences with, but I guess all things in time," Kat said, looking towards the mountains.

"All things in time," Annie agreed.

"This weekend, it was sort of funny, don't you think?" Kat asked.

"Well—"

"No, really. I mean, you and Grant got to spend some time together, and that's definitely good. He adores you and doesn't embarrass you, at least not like—"

"Let's not talk about Clement."

"Good. I don't think you spending some more time with Grant would be a bad thing. He may not be the one either, but I think you could be happy."

"I think so."

"And that knucklehead friend of his had flowers delivered to my room today."

"He had flowers delivered to my room, too."

"Can you believe it?"

"I think after this weekend, I can believe anything," Annie smiled.

"Isobelle is pretty amazing, don't you think?"

"Yes, I do."

"You'd better watch out though."

"Why is that?"

"Because if you don't think you and Grant are going to be able to spend time together, she will be able to sense that."

"And …?"

"And she will gladly take over that time with him," Kat said, squeezing Annie's shoulder.

"I sort of thought so, too. I just wanted to hear it from someone else. I thought maybe I was just being, I don't know, jealous, or something, which is stupid."

"Annie, you still have feelings for him, so that's not stupid. How is he doing, by the way?"

"He's pretty beat up."

"I'm sure he's in good hands."

Annie smiled.

"Listen, I'll see you when you get back to town," Kat said, taking Annie's hands.

"When do you leave for India?"

"Oh, not for a while yet, so we'll have lots of time before then."

"Good, I would love that. You are a great friend," Annie said, hugging Kat.

"So are you. Love you," Kat said, hugging her back.

"Love you too. Drive carefully."

"I will. Tell Grant good bye for me. I'll be seeing him—and you—again soon?"

"I will tell him. And yes, you will," Annie said.

They hugged for a long time. They broke from their embrace and looked at each other, both smiling. Kat left the hotel, and Annie returned to see how Grant was doing. Instead of finding him in his room, he was waiting inside the lobby.

"Let's go for a walk," he suggested.

"Are you up for a walk?"

"I'm up for a walk with you." He took her hand and hobbled outside toward a path around the hotel grounds. They were quiet for a while and then Grant asked, "So are you sure you can come down?"

"We've been through this," Annie said.

"I have a head injury, remember?"

"I'm starting to think you had one before you met me."

"That's what I've been telling you."

"If you can remember telling me that, you can remember us talking about me coming to see you in a few weeks, so nice try."

"It comes and goes," Grant said.

"Right. I don't know where all of this is going, but it hasn't gotten there yet, so yes, I would like to come and see you. Isobelle said some things that seemed to really hit home. I am not sure I understand all of this, but I do understand the parts that feel good. Got it?" Annie said, squinting and wrinkling up her nose.

"Got it, yes."

"Good. Now, are you sure you're OK to drive?"

"Have to ask the doctor."

"Well, she thinks you are."

"Then I am."

They continued their walk, holding hands, staying very close to each other, looking at the beauty of the flowers in front of them, the valley below them. They stopped and gazed up at the deep blue sky, and the light breeze danced with Annie's hair. They turned and faced each other, and Grant leaned in to kiss her. They stood there, holding each other in the sun, the light wind continuing to embrace them. Neither one was in any hurry to let go.

Grant walked by the front desk of the hotel, his gait slow and deliberate as he favored his bad knee. He noticed the man and the woman with the sunglasses, the ones Rex had been stressing about. Rex's paranoia always made Grant laugh. He wanted to stop and tell the people that they had given him some comic relief, but he decided against it and just kept heading for the front door. He overheard a bit of their conversation as he passed.

"No, I'm sorry, Mr. Schmidt has already checked out of the hotel," the man behind the desk told the couple in sunglasses.

"Shit!" Grant said as he stopped. He hoped the man and the woman had not heard him. A doorman started walking in his direction.

"Is everything all right, sir?"

"What? No, I mean, yes, everything is fine, just fine," Grant stuttered.

"Would you like some help, sir?" the bellman asked.

"No, I just need to go home."

Even with his battered parts, Grant's drive back from Palm Springs was better than the drive out, aside from the hassle of driving a rental car. He was still hoping to get all of his memory back from Saturday night, but parts of it would probably just remain a dust storm. He thought maybe he just wasn't supposed to remember those parts. Maybe there was a reason that segment was wiped from his mind. There was no frenzy this time, no anxiety, no fear of rejection or of failure. There was only calm as he drove, thinking about the things he did remember, the things he wanted to remember.

He wasn't sure how long he had been driving, but his knee told him he needed to stop. He just needed some fresh air for a few minutes, needed to get his bad leg in a different position that did not involve driving. He found a place to pull off the road, admiring the way the dust swirled around the car as he came to a stop. He sat there waiting for all the dust to settle, looking up into the clear sky overhead. He opened the door of the rental car and got out.

"So far, so good," he mumbled.

He brushed himself off, moved away from the vehicle and the road, and made his way up towards some very large boulders. He was breathing heavily, but not because he was short of breath. Rather, he wanted to take in the sweet dry air, to absorb the memory of the desert through his breathing and preserve it like an insect caught in amber. He could hear the small rocks and dirt crunching beneath his boots as he took small strides, one leg dragging. He stopped for a moment to determine the best route up through the rocks, which were larger than his vehicle. He maneuvered as best he could, trying to forget about the injuries. He eventually found himself atop a very large, flat-topped rock, and the view of the territory towards the west was quite impressive. He stood there for a few moments, trying to catch his breath and get his bearings, and then suddenly the pain from his wounds washed over him.

"Shit."

He folded down on the rock, grabbing his knee and cursing. His head was pounding, and his eye wasn't much better. He took several deep breaths in an attempt to push the pain to some unknown region of his brain and clear his head. Despite his best efforts, he couldn't completely release the pain. He was pretty sure this was as good as it was going to get for a while. He sat on the rock for a very long time, contemplating. He looked towards the west, trying to think of nothing as best he could. His mind was clearer than it had been for at least a day or so, and any improvement was welcome. A red-tailed hawk began to circle overhead, and he could see smoke from a small fire off in the distance, chipmunks chattering nearby as they scurried across the rocky terrain. There was a light breeze, cooler than the one on the desert floor, now brushing past. Grant could feel the wind move his hair and his shirt. He sat there, unmoving, doing what he could to take in the events of the weekend and integrate them into what he was seeing and feeling now. Though he felt it strange to think it, he thought this might be what Isobelle would do. He moved his scuffed hand over his swollen eye, down to his unshaven chin, to his lap, where he locked it between the fingers of his other hand. He lay back slowly and felt the warmth of the sun on his face and the warmth of the rock on his back. It had been forever ago that he had been out in country like this. His run-ins with other vehicles over the past couple of days made him want to just stay out in the sun on that warm rock. He looked into the deepening blue receding into the black of infinity. The shape of a cloud that managed to sneak overhead reminded him of a dog he once had. The dog had followed him home one day, and just stayed and stayed. God, he'd loved that dog.

There were a great number of things from his past that came to visit him there on that rock: Some sort of reckoning with Annie; the conversations with people from other places; the conversations with Isobelle; and now he had finally reached his point of reckoning. Isobelle would say all was related. He kept his eyes open as long as he could before he drifted off to sleep, lulled by the warmth of the sun on the rock and the soft sound of the occasional breeze through the trees.

When he awoke, the sun was almost gone for the day. He sat up slowly, looking around, trying to figure out where he was, which had been a common question of his the past couple of days. The fire in the distance was almost out and the surroundings had become even quieter than when he had first arrived. The hawk was gone, and he found the view of the setting sun nearly as calming as lying in bed with Annie. He quickly glanced down to check his departure route, as he remembered nothing of how he got up there, and he was sure he didn't want to spend the night on that rock, though he had done stranger things. He worked out how he would make the descent, and then turned back towards the dropping sun, enjoying the way the remaining rays touched his face.

The sun began its final departure slowly at first, then quickly, disappearing with one last burst of light, letting loose a blast of orange, pink and bright blue ripples through the sky. Grant labored to rise and then to hobble down the rocks, limping back to the rental car, moving much slower than he had on the ascent. Part of him wanted to stay, and he thought that part of him probably did stay.

The drive back was quiet and he thought mostly of Annie. He wasn't sure how he could feel so drained and so full, all at the same time. The headlights of the oncoming traffic seemed to shine right through him as if he was an apparition, but he drove on, ignoring the piercing beams and concentrating only on getting home safely and finally sleeping in a familiar place.

CHAPTER 43

Six weeks later

Injuries aside, Grant experienced a feeling of renewal after he returned from the desert. He was trying to decide if it was the result of any one thing, or more just the cumulative effect of everything that had happened. Whatever the answer, he got a dog, and named her Julia. Having someone in his daily life was something he hadn't had since he and Annie were together. Julia was a Chesapeake Bay Retriever. She loved to go for walks, and she usually evoked some response from the people they encountered, especially women. The women sometimes commented, "How cute," or, "How adorable" she was, and how great they were together. After several of these exchanges, Grant was quick to respond that it was because he was the tender, understanding one, and Julia was the tough, smart one.

Annie had called him the week before, and they had a great conversation. They had spent hours on the phone, which was quite a change for Grant. Her work had delayed her, so it would be a couple more weeks before she could make it to Encinitas. Still, Grant felt good about the exchange, and very excited about her commitment to coming to visit. She could have changed her mind, but she did not. She didn't have to take time out of her busy schedule to spend hours on the phone with him, but she did. He thought it would be great to see her again; that she had been busy did not bother him. They were talking, and that was what mattered.

He had also spoken to Isobelle several times on the phone, and she came to visit him. She clearly wanted a bit more than he was willing to give right now, but he was learning a great deal from her, and he enjoyed when they talked, enjoyed when she came to see him, and he found himself unable to hide from her. She was helping him answer or eliminate questions he had always had. Most of them just faded away. Sometimes the answers were not always that important, he just needed to ask the questions. He took comfort in the feeling that he had at least gotten rid of, if not answered, many of his old questions and problems. Isobelle's efforts to help him were not wasted.

His eye was better, but was still not back to normal, and he knew he would carry a scar to remind him of that weekend. His knee was improving, but slowly. Instead of avoiding his usual walks, however, he went out more, always enjoying it in spite of the pain. He found that walking helped with more than just his leg, and Julia always eager to assist with his rehabilitation.

Grant was less absorbed in his own thoughts now. Seeing Isobelle helped with that, as well. She taught him to take his mind off of the things that were bothering him, and to live more in the present moment. She talked occasionally about moving away from the desert, saying that San Diego might be a great change. He did not try to dissuade her.

Rex stayed in touch this time, and he continued to see Dawn after they returned from New Orleans. Rex normally never saw any girls again, so this was a rather large step for him. He had decided to move to the San Diego area, with hopes of him and Grant working together. Grant told him he wasn't sure about the "working together" part, but Rex was unmoved, saying: "I don't give a shit what you think, I'm moving there anyway. Nothing holding me here. Plus, you need a goddamned keeper."

Rex's problems with the law, just like Grant's demons, seemed to evaporate. He was keeping in touch, so that meant something. Grant told him about the man and the woman with the sunglasses asking about him at the hotel, which obviously troubled him, but he didn't know what to do about it.

"They're either going to pop me, or they aren't. They want to mess with you, they mess with you. If it's the other side, well, they'll just kill me, or something. Fuck 'em," Rex said.

Having Julia helped Grant focus on something different, something outside himself. He was all right with seeing to her needs, which in a strange way helped with his own. She liked the beach, and living as close as he did, they spent more time there together than he ever did by himself. If she liked it, he liked it, and this move to a more simple approach to life seemed to heal some parts of himself that Grant did not know were injured. His life hadn't been all that complicated before, but he had taken steps to rid himself of the few demons that had made it seem so. He found, much to his amazement, that he was at peace. He and Julia would sit on the front porch together and watch what went by.

When they were not outside exploring, Grant and Julia spent time reading at the house and enjoying the tranquility. Julia went outside and brought back the newspaper every morning, and every morning they would walk. They made friends with people and dogs quickly, and Grant wondered why he had not noticed the abundance around him before. On this day, they took a particularly long walk and eventually ended up along Highway 101. Grant was neither sure of the time nor how long they had been walking. Based on the number of people at the outdoor tables of the restaurants there, it was lunchtime. They stopped at the 101 Diner, and sat at one of the outside tables so that Julia could sit beside him on the sidewalk. He watched the traffic and the people passing by. It was a beautiful day, certainly a good one to be outdoors. Julia was enjoying watching the people and the occasional dog nearby or across the street, which drew a glare and a muffled sound from her but she made no effort to advance. Grant stopped people-watching only when Julia started making noises.

"Think you're going over there, do you?"

Julia just huffed a little more, looking first at Grant, and then across the street, then back at him for approval.

"They probably won't serve us if you knock stuff over."

Julia stopped making the noise.

"You get us kicked out of here and I'm not going to be happy," he said, looking sternly at the dog.

Julia's ears lowered and she lay down on the sidewalk with a somewhat sad look on her face, sighing deeply as she did.

"That's more like it."

Grant took over the people-watching duties from Julia and his mind began to drift. He remembered sitting on the Mall in Boulder, Colorado years ago, by himself, before Rex had pushed the two of them into Annie's life. That day in Boulder, the sky had been an amazing blue, with the rock formations there, the Flatirons, reaching slowly and forcefully towards it, the air cool and crisp, chilling his face. He remembered thinking that day of where the path might lead and the number of miles that would go along with it. He had not yet seen Annie's face or heard the lilt in her voice. But maybe the beauty of the sky and the grandeur of the Flatirons that day foretold what was to come.

The sky today was a similar blue, and though there were no Flatirons, there was an ocean nearby. There was no cool air coming off of the front range of the Rockies, no turning leaves, no snow-covered mountains. There was just turquoise water, wave on wave, now and then touching somewhere in the distance, onto the shore.

"Usually we make people wait for these seats," came the voice of the waitress, taking Grant away from his visions.

"What?" he turned.

"Usually we—oh hey, Grant! I've been looking for you. I didn't really know where to look, there was no Señor Grant in the phonebook. I really shouldn't wait on you, because you never called me. But hey, I got a job here. I told you I was thinking about moving here."

"What?"

"You never called me. I was hoping you would, and you didn't," the waitress said, now noticing Julia. "Well, this explains it. Another woman, and she is beautiful!" she said as she bent down to pet Julia. Julia's large tail sprang to life, and she enthusiastically greeted the oncoming server with kisses and tail wags.

"Savannah?"

"Yes, you are a beautiful girl, aren't you," Savannah said, rubbing Julia's belly as the dog had rolled over for just such an exchange. Her hair was blonde this time.

"I'll be—"

"This is why you didn't call me. I understand now. You can still call me, but I have a new number, and some other things have changed for me since I moved from Palm Springs. I guess I'll wait on you, in light of this recent development," she said as she looked back down at Julia. "Let me bring you a menu, and a new phone number," she whispered the last part. "It's impressive that you remembered my name, we only met once."

"How did you remember mine?"

"I wrote it down, remember?"

He looked at her walking away and shook his head. He then looked down at Julia, who was also watching Savannah. Julia then looked up at Grant and started thumping her tail against his chair.

"Oh, you think so, do you?" he said, which elicited a prompt response. Her tail started moving about twice the speed it had been.

Savannah returned with a menu, a glass, and a bowl of water. She placed the bowl of water on the sidewalk in front of Julia.

"I'll give you two a few minutes to look at the menu," she said, placing the menu, the glass of water, and a card with her phone number in front of Grant.

Grant picked up the card, moving it back and forth, looking around at his surroundings, back down at Julia, and back up at Savannah. Julia repeated the same movements as before, watching Savannah, then up at Grant.

"You deciding this stuff now, are you?" Grant said, looking back down at Julia, then back at Savannah.

"Maybe I gave the menu and the phone number to the wrong one," Savannah said.

"That could be. She seems to be the decision maker now."

"She wasn't with you when we met, or I would have given the number to her."

"You're right, she wasn't with me then. We're living together now."

"Living together, sounds serious," Savannah said with a laugh.

"We have been making a point to not get serious, and it seems to be working out. As long as I keep the food around, keep up the walking schedule and good supply of tennis balls and dog biscuits, things seem to be OK." Grant replied.

"Does she get jealous when other girls give you their phone numbers?"

"She doesn't appear to."

"Does that mean she would be all right if you called me?"

"You would have to ask her."

"I would, if I knew her name."

"Julia."

"That's nice, Julia," Savannah said, patting the dog on her head. "Where did you get the name?"

"Some movie star."

"What, not the great chef? Julia, would it be all right if Grant called me?"

Julia was clearly enjoying all the attention.

"Seems all right with her," Savannah said, smiling. "How about you, is it all right with you?"

Grant looked back down at Julia, who was still enjoying the attention that Savannah was lavishing upon her.

"Yes, I think that would be all right. I still have a phone," Grant said.

"Great, it would be fun. We need to get to know some more folks around here. You can even bring Julia, if that would make you more comfortable."

"I might at that."

"Good. So what will you two have today?" Savannah asked.

"Coffee, with cream, and the special."

"I didn't tell you what the special is."

"Whatever it is, I'm sure it will be great. Just one rule: no haggis."

"No haggis, got it. We can do that, what will the lady have?"

"Bacon."

"She's OK with that?"

"Sure, she lives with me."

"OK, great. I'll be right back. And it is nice to see you again."

"Likewise."

Savannah walked back inside, and returned in no time at all with the coffee.

"Here you are! The food should be right out," she turned to walk back in.

"Wait a minute," Grant said.

"Everything OK?"

"Yes, sure. Did you—do you live here now?"

"Yes, I do live here now. I got tired of what I was doing and I moved here. Do you live close by?" Savannah asked.

"Yes, very close by. Walking distance."

"Do you come to this place much?"

"Not really, but she does."

"Well, maybe next time she'll bring you back with her, and I'll get to see you two again. I have a boyfriend now, so it will just have to be friends type of stuff."

"Friends would be fine, I would like that. Maybe she'll bring me back here, she never says. It's always a surprise." Grant said. "I seem to recall when I met you, you said something about not thinking too much."

"Well, I don't really remember saying that, but it sounds like something I would say," Savannah said, smiling.

"That really stuck in my head, at that particular time."

"Well, it only works if you don't think about it," she said, with a grin.

"Yes?"

"Yes. I will be right back. Don't leave before I get back. And, like I told you when I met you, don't think. I believe you'll find that it's much better that way, with the 'don't think' part. It's sort of difficult at first, but you'll get the hang of it," Savannah said, walking back inside.

"Friends, and don't leave and don't think. I can handle that."

Grant clicked his tongue and drummed his fingers on the table, looking around again. Normally this type of exchange with Savannah might have left him a little perplexed, but not this time. He was following her advice about not thinking, and Isobelle's advice about paying attention. Although it seemed to be illogical—not thinking while at the same time paying atention—it was, surprisingly, coming naturally to him. Since he got back from the desert, he had been doing a good job of keeping his past from haunting him. If he were ever going to get to that state that Isobelle had been telling him about, this could be the time. He suddenly felt that now it was within reach. The others were right; he was had gotten somewhere. In a very short time, Annie, Isobelle, Kat, Savannah, and now Julia, had all made an impact on him, and he was never going back, metaphorically speaking, to that bus stop in Palm Springs. The top of that boulder he had napped and meditated on, however, would be fine. Now that Rex was staying in touch and acting more like a regular person, or as regular as he could be, maybe that would be fine also.

He sat at the cafe and sipped his coffee, relaxing in his chair for quite a while. There was no more, no less. It was simple. The sun was shining in a marvelous blue sky over the ocean. Seeing Savannah reminded him how funny she thought it was that he had called it "the big lake." Julia was now sleeping, her head resting on his foot. She had no idea she had bacon coming. It would be a good day, nothing introspective. He took a couple of deep breaths, cleared his mind. Savannah would be returning shortly, and he wanted to make a good impression on his new friend that he was not thinking when she did return. He thought it strange that what began with a car plowing into the side of him in Palm Springs had brought him here, to a much better place, just a few blocks from his house.

CHAPTER 44

One week later

The phone in Grant's living room rang. It did that more often now. He had turned the ringer volume down, but he hadn't taken the phone out to the garbage just quite yet.

"Hello?"

"Hi Grant, how are you?" It was Annie.

"I'm good, how are you?"

"It is good to hear your voice again. Gosh, it's still just been crazy at work."

"Crazy good, or crazy bad?"

"Crazy good, gosh—there has just been so much going on."

"All things you like?" Grant asked.

"Well, like I told you on the phone last time, I am sort of starting over with my practice, so crazy is good." She paused. "I still think, you know, seeing you really was … was really great."

"Though a bit painful, physically. I'm trying to avoid run-ins with moving vehicles these days."

"Are you doing all right, and are you feeling better?" Annie asked.

"Yes, much better, thanks. I had top notch medical care."

"Like I told you before, if you wouldn't run off in the night, you wouldn't need medical care."

"I'm changing my ways," Grant said, smiling to himself.

"Hmmm, well I'm a bit skeptical, but it is good to know you think so," Annie said. "How about your partner? I guess we forgot to talk about him last time."

"I thought the conversation was fine without him being a part of it. He went to New Orleans."

"Gosh, with those two…."

"Nope, with Dawn. Been seeing her ever since."

"You're kidding!"

"Nope. The world as we know it has changed."

"My gosh, you are so right! Well, that is really something," Annie said.

"So, you still coming to visit?" Grant asked.

"Yes I am, if that's still OK. I need a break. I can't really take on anything else right now, but I think seeing you again would—would be just what I need. I'm already past when I said I would be there, and I'm sorry. Seeing you would be really—"

"We're talking about me, right?" Grant asked.

"We are talking about you and me seeing each other, yes, and I can get down there fairly soon. I hope that works for you. I mean, I hope you still want to—you are supposed to cook for me, remember?" Annie said.

"Again, we are talking about me, right?

"We are talking about you! And about you cooking for me. You're not trying to get out of it, are you?" Annie said, laughing.

"Nope."

"Well?"

"Well, let me think about it." Grant paused. "Yes, I think the schedule is flexible, and I don't have to cook, we could go somewhere."

"How did that work out last time, when we went somewhere to eat?"

"What if I promised no large crowds and no diving into the rocks to avoid midnight drivers who can't stay on the road?"

"How about we just stay in, at your house, for a few days? You have an ocean nearby, we could walk on the beach, you know, if you promise not to try to swim to the store, or to Catalina, or anything like that," Annie said.

"Suppose we could do that."

"You're sure?"

"Yep. I've had some time to think—"

"Uh, oh! You know what happens when you think."

"You're not the first person that's told me that recently," Grant said.

"Well, just so you know, I've had some time to think also. You know, I've spent a lot of time, a lot of my life trying to be perfect," Annie said.

"Sounds possible, but I think you're past the trying part, and have actually hit the mark."

"Hardly. So, I decided I can't be doing that anymore, and I'm going to have fun. It's too hard trying to be perfect."

"Have you bumped your head lately?" Grant asked.

"No, but I hear it happens to people. Just some of the things that happened, things that were said."

"Now let's get back to the having fun part? And you are actually coming here? You're actually going to walk through my front door?"

"The fun starts now. And I am still coming there."

"Then I can't see how it wasn't, you know, all worth it—for me anyway."

"All the injuries?"

"Well, maybe not *all* the injuries, but there were a lot of other things, things harder to explain," Grant said. "But you know what I think?"

"What do you think?

"I think … I think you already fixed the things that I really needed to have fixed."

"I think you did that for me, too."

"Fun will do that sometimes."

"Can you do something for me?"

"Sure, what?"

"Open your front door."

Grant's heart pounded as he got up from his chair. He stepped over Julia, who was asleep on the floor beneath his legs, and walked to the door. He opened it, and there she was, her brilliant smile and beautiful eyes lighting up his front porch. She stepped into his arms and pressed her lips to his. In the distance, the ocean was calm. The good things had come back around.

ACKNOWLEDGEMENTS

A large number of people were contributory to the completion of this book, some intentional, some otherwise. Both categories are appreciated beyond the normal available means of gratitude expression.

Tremendous vision and instruction from a wonderful person, editor, and friend Paul McCarthy. Not only did he provide a new dimension to approach writing, he also made it more fun.

People that answered so many questions and gave, and continue to give truckloads of self assurance. I am speechless in my gratitude to them, Benjo Masilungan, and Barbra Dillenger. Gratefulness here will carry over several lifetimes.

Norman Bukofzer seems to have been watching over me, even before all of this began. If you ever met someone and felt like you knew them from somewhere previous, this is how it is with Norman.

Margaret Brown, of Shelf Media, had no idea how much I would pester her for information when she extended her hand. I have to live to be 150 to reciprocate her kindness.

Kristina Blank Makansi and staff for their exceptional insight, skill and sense of humor (Hey, I want to be like that!).

The fabulous folks at Warwick's in La Jolla. Always willing to help, always encouraging me.

Sandra Poirier-Diaz, and Dina Barsky, Smith Publicity (How many questions can they answer from one person?).

Paul Burlingame, of Paul Burlingame Photo. An outstanding artist, photographer, web designer, and terrific friend. We fled corporate bondage the same week.

The truly fine artistry of Rachel Walling.

Angie Swartz for her friendship and guidance on social media.

The great guys at Postal Corner, who undoubtedly wondered how many revisions I was going to print.

Arlene Harris, for always helping, even when she doesn't know she is.

Gary Pisoni, for his friendship and support, and for being an example of the fabulous things that can happen when someone has a passion for what they do.

John Chanfreau for helping me take out my writing frustration, while not showing his own at having to listen to me week after week.

Lester Hayashi. I could not have made it this far without his guidance, and quiet confidence. I miss him more than anyone can possibly imagine.

All of these folks renew, and rejuvenate so much faith in the human spirit. Isobelle would love them all.

ABOUT THE AUTHOR

Edward Cozza is a Colorado native now living in Southern California. His first novel was written during travel around the United States and the world.

He has traveled five continents, the favorite being North America, and is eight states shy of tramping in all fifty states. This travel allowed for experiencing the different topography, cultures, and particularly for enjoying the diversity of language and conversation.

A student of the finer things of life, he now writes at home, with his two dogs and a bourbon nearby.

Nowhere Yet is book one of a trilogy.

CPSIA information can be obtained at www.ICGtesting.com
Printed in the USA
LVOW081624251112

308656LV00005B/554/P